PRESUMED DEAD

A NOVEL

Nancy Veldm

Nancy Veldman

To Heather and Rachael, my daughters, who continually shine a light into my life that helps me walk the path that will carry me home.

PROLOGUE

If in this journey we are
taking together
the love that is shared
between us
is not the same...

If in our time together
as little as it may be,
the giving is done in a
lesser way by one...

If our hearts are knit together
yet one of us
is afraid to feel
the pain of being so close
and far away,

let the more loving one be me.

Love, Smith

CHAPTER 1

A loud knock on the door echoed throughout the house. A roast in the oven was causing an aroma to find its way into every room of the house, and fresh vegetables were cooking slowly on the stove. On the counter near the window was a three- tier birthday cake with flowers all around the bottom edge. Grace was celebrating her fortieth birthday with some friends who were due to arrive in two hours, so the knock on the door was unexpected. She was standing in the hallway with her new jeans on and a fresh white blouse, holding a towel in her hand. She was not only a stunning woman; she was unforgettable. Her blue eyes looked right through you, her face had a porcelain finish, and her kindness was beyond words. But as the years passed, uneasiness had crept into her life.

There was no evident reason for her to be afraid, but as she stood there listening to the knocks on the front door her blood ran cold in her veins. "It's too early for my friends," she whispered into the air. She couldn't move. Her legs had become wooden blocks and there was a wisp of panic rising up in her body. She turned slowly to see out the front window, hoping perhaps to catch a glimpse of a car she recognized. Confirming her deepest fears that she'd been so successful at tucking away, she saw the rear end of a black government car parked at the curb in front of her house.

❧

Smith and Grace dated for three years and married in their home town of Paynesville, Georgia, madly in love and ready to share a life together. They bought a lovely home in a neighborhood filled with young couples and children, and Grace accepted the position of principal at Ross High after teaching five years at Brenton High down the street from their house.

Smith was tall, dark, breathtakingly handsome, and his intelligence was in between nerd and Einstein. He had the extraordinary ability to win you over so subtly that even if you lost at poker with him you'd walk away feeling like a champ. Grace had graduated magna cum laude from the University of Georgia and was fluent in three languages. She knew on the front end that Smith had taken a job with the CIA and she would never know where he was sent or the purpose of any covert operation he was involved in. This didn't seem like too much of a sacrifice at the time, for youth had placed a veil on the wisdom that would have protected her heart.

Smith was called out on the night of their honeymoon with no explanation of where he was going or when he would return. From that point on, as she sat on the bed in that lonely hotel room, Grace became rudely aware of what life would be like married to the CIA. In the beginning she tried to pry more details out of him about his work, but spite of the fact that there was a possibility that she wouldn't be able to withstand the secrecy, he never gave in. Smith built a relationship with the CIA over the years and proved himself to be the ideal candidate for the most dangerous of covert operations. He was told that if he got caught or died during one of these operations, it would be as though he never existed. No one would ever know he was gone, nor would his body ever be found or returned. This was critical to the safety of other members of the operation and was understood on the front end. He tried to prepare Grace for this event, should it ever happen, but the words always seemed lifeless and far away.

She lost herself in the day to day running one of the largest high schools in the area. She kept herself busy when Smith was away and made lots of friends. But always in the back of her mind sat a doubt that she would never see him again. It took her breath away to even allow those thoughts in; she almost felt like if she dwelled on them too much, they might cause something to happen. A ball would roll that couldn't be stopped. Her parents had been killed in a car accident when she was in college, so they never got to meet Smith. And she was an only child.

These facts made her more dependent on Smith, for he was her only family.

Smith promised her that if anything happened to him and he didn't come back, she would get a package in the mail. He never told her what would be in the package and she was afraid to even ask. After work she would come home, change clothes, go for a long walk, and then come in and prepare dinner. At some point she would walk down to the end of the long winding driveway. There, sitting at the end near the road was the mailbox, surrounded by brick and covered in ivy. Instead of looking forward to getting mail, she dreaded opening the lid and reaching inside. Her greatest fear was always that she would receive a package in the mail addressed to her with no return address. Most women would kill to hear from their husbands. She hoped she never got one single piece of mail from him. For that would mean he was gone.

On the days and weeks Smith was home, their lives were normal and they did everything together. One of the projects they were working on at the moment was helping rebuild Wilton Children's Home, which was old and deteriorating fast. She wanted to take a few of the smaller children home with her but Smith warned her that she would be raising them mostly alone. He couldn't promise how much time he could spend with her taking care of any children, including their own, if they ever had any. Smith was so tall and strong that the children loved jumping in his arms and wrestling with him. He led the construction and also helped with the fundraising. It was a powerful thing to do for the community and it tied them even closer together. He had a wonderful habit of leaving her notes in the house in the most unexpected places. She often found them when he was away on a trip and they helped her make it through the time they were apart. His words remained with her even now. The last note she had found haunted her as she heard the knock at the door . . . "*Let the more loving one be me.*"

This latest trip seemed to have increased the tension in the house and Grace had felt even more uneasy than usual when Smith climbed into the black sedan that picked him up. The men that met him at the front door were dressed in black and only nodded to Grace as they greeted Smith with a quick handshake. They were off and running before Grace could even grab another quick kiss from Smith.

༄

Grace finally got her feet to move and slowly walked to the front door. She took her time turning the knob but when she cracked the door open she could see someone dressed in black standing there motionless with no expression on his face whatsoever.

"Good evening, ma'am. My name is Agent Benjamin Parker. Do you have anyone here with you?"

"No, why do you need to know that?"

"I'm sorry to disturb you but I wanted to personally hand you this letter from the president of the United States and also inform you that your husband has been killed in the line of duty. I am certain that your husband has previously shared this information with you, but because of the nature of his death, his body will not be returning home nor will there be a formal service for him. As you know, due to the line of work your husband was involved in with the government, there will be no publicity concerning his death."

He paused for a minute to catch his breath and looked into her eyes. She thought she saw something flash across his face. "You will receive compensation monthly wired directly into your bank account until the time of your death. Do you have any questions, Mrs. Sanderson?"

Grace took the letter from his hand, shocked at his stilted words that were blaringly empty of compassion. She was speechless and had an irresistible desire to run. To get as far away from their house as she could. *He has no idea at all who Smith was outside of the CIA and probably doesn't care.* "I appreciate your coming by to tell me the news, Agent Parker. I suppose I'll never find out how he really died, right? You don't believe I have that right as his wife, do you?" Tears were streaming down her face. She was trembling.

"It has nothing to do with your rights, Mrs. Sanderson. It is the unquestionable policy of the CIA not to reveal any facts concerning the location of his death or the cause. As difficult as this may be for you, it is true that you were made aware of the dangers of his job, am I right, Mrs. Sanderson?"

"Oh, I knew as much as Smith could share with me. But nothing prepares you for this leveling shock. I've lost my soul mate, my best friend. My husband. He's merely a number to you. Now if you'll excuse me, I'll say good night." Grace was about to lose total control and didn't want to do it in front of this starched-shirt stranger at her door.

"My sincere condolences for your loss, Mrs. Sanderson. If you have any questions, any at all, call the number at the bottom of the letter." He turned on a dime and walked back to the black car, but just before he opened the door to get in, he shook his head and headed back to the house. He knocked on the door again, and Grace answered with tears running down her face.

"Yes, Agent Parker? What else could you possibly have to tell me?"

Ben Parker stared right into her eyes and whispered, "Just wanted you to know that Smith was my best friend." He reached out and hugged her and for a moment they were both lost in the embrace.

"Look at me, Grace. If you ever need anything, anything at all, please call me. Here's all my numbers. Smith took care of me many times, so I am going to be sure you are taken care of."

He hugged her one more time and turned and headed back to the car. Grace stood there watching him leave, and her heart felt like it was going to burst. He knew her name. This meant Smith had spoken to him about her before. *Smith's best friend had to tell me about his death.* She felt like a jerk for treating him so badly. She closed the door and walked over to the sofa and sat down. Now the house seemed unnaturally quiet and empty. Nothing but the clock ticking in the hallway. Grace sat in a stupor, her body in shock from the news of Smith's death. She felt like her heart had turned to stone and that her whole world had dropped from underneath her. "*If one of us is afraid to feel the pain of being so close and far away, let the more loving one be me . . .*"

CHAPTER 2

The smell of something burning was the only thing that caused Grace to get off the sofa, wipe her eyes, and walk into the kitchen. It was her roast burning. She jerked the pot holder off its hook, opened the oven door, and pulled the pan out of the oven and placed it on top of the stove. She had totally forgotten about her friends coming and it was about time for them to show up. It felt like everything was moving in slow motion. She turned and looked at her birthday cake sitting near the window. Tears streamed down her face and her chin was trembling. *Smith. You're gone. How in the world am I going to make it without you for the rest of my life? I just can't believe you aren't coming back! Dear God! Not now . . .*

She splashed cold water on her face and stood there looking at nothing, trembling. Her numbness was shaken by a knock on the front door. She realized in her grief that her friends had arrived.

The shock on their faces when they saw her made her realize that her appearance must be pretty pitiful. Her mascara had run down her face and her hair was a mess by now. She stood there looking at them with tears streaming down her face and they rushed to her and held her in their arms.

"Poor Grace. Please, let's sit down on the sofa and talk. What in the world happened? Is something wrong with Smith?" It was Martha playing mother hen. She put her arm around Grace and walked her to the sofa.

"Yes, it's Smith! I just received news that really caught me blindsided. I knew there was a possibility of something happening every single time he left the house, because of his line of work with the government. But I never dreamed it would be this time." She put her head in her hands and cried again. "They didn't give me any information at all about how he died. Or what he was doing at the time. I don't suppose I'll ever find that out. All I got was a black sedan pulling up into the driveway and some strange man dressed in black coming to my door with a letter from the president. He told me sternly that Smith had died in the line of duty. I was so shocked at his cold manner that I wanted to slam the door behind him. But right when he was about to leave he turned and told me that he was Smith's best friend. He said that he would see that I was taken care of . . . there were tears running down his face."

Celeste ran and got some Kleenex and wiped her face and Maryann brought a cold rag from the kitchen and placed it on her head.

"Lie back, Grace. You're white as a sheet." Martha sat down beside her and touched her hand, which was freezing.

"Smith told me it would be this way. He tried his best to prepare me in case this happened. I just never dreamed it would. You know? It's just such a shock!" She took a deep breath. "I'll be okay. I feel shaky inside and a bit overwhelmed." She smiled weakly at her friends and then sat up slowly. I don't know what to do next. He isn't ever coming back." She cried again and stood up. They walked her into her bedroom, pulled the covers back, and helped her into bed. They all sat on her bed, chatting, trying to soothe her with their words.

"What do they expect you to do, Grace? Plan a funeral? It's like he disappeared into thin air." Maryann brushed some strands of hair away from her face.

"I can't even think of a funeral. There is no body! How do I have a funeral without a body? Anyone have any ideas?" She was sounding hysterical.

"Grace, take it easy. You have plenty of time to do that. I guess you have to contact his parents first. This is going to be a shock to them big time. I know you're dreading that conversation."

"No kidding. They're getting older and not in the best of health. But they knew as well as I did that there was always a possibility of this happening." Grace sighed and lay back on a pillow. She closed her eyes for a moment and let her mind rest.

The three girls walked out of the room for a second and headed towards the kitchen to clean things up.

"What in the world happened to Smith? How can they not tell her where he is, or at least bring his body home? I couldn't have lived this way; she never knew when she wouldn't see him again. And now it's happened. I just don't know how she's gonna take it." Celeste rubbed her eyes and shook her head.

"All we can do is be here for her. She has no family. It's gonna to take a long time for her to deal with this. Let's clean up the kitchen and put away all this food." Martha looked around the kitchen and shook her head when she saw the birthday cake. "I'll stay here with her. She's gonna need someone when she gets up. It's her birthday, for cryin' out loud."

At the same time that Agent Parker was telling Grace that she had just become a widow, on the other side of the globe Smith was unconscious, clinging to life by a thread, in a tiny Pakistani village, being treated by a local doctor who was sympathetic to America's war on terrorism. He had no identification and the country he fought so hard for would not acknowledge they even knew him. When he'd been shot down, his fellow agents had left him for dead, pulling out to save their own lives. There had been no time to go back to see how bad he was wounded, nor would there be anyone looking for his body. Smith Sanderson was invisible to the United States and remained unconscious while strangers tried to save his life.

CHAPTER 3

The day of the funeral was one of the longest days Grace could remember, even though the service barely lasted twenty minutes. Only a few friends attended, along with Smith's parents, who were getting along in years. Grace had purchased a plot at Woodlawn Cemetery and placed a headstone there with Smith's name the date of his birth and death on it. After the service they all went to the cemetery and stood, weeping over the end of such a powerful life, a giving husband, and the love of her life. The limbs of a massive tree hovered over his tombstone perhaps they were God's way of showing her that Smith was going to be fine. It was all she could do to look at the tombstone, which she already knew would become a very familiar place to her in the near future. She didn't have the ability or the desire to let Smith go, so she made up her mind as the minister spoke a prayer over Smith's soul that she would come every single day and talk to him, even though his body was somewhere unknown to her and the rest of the world.

Grace could almost feel him beside her, his breath on her neck, as her head was bowed toward the ground. For so many years he'd been a vital part of her life, and their hopes and dreams would now have to be carried out by her. It killed her to know she would never feel his arms around her again or his lips against hers. His brown eyes had always pierced right through her, and that look had held her up until he came home from his trips to unknown places. She trusted him totally, but now she felt so empty. Her life had such a strong direction as long as they were a pair. *What was she to do now?*

Except for her three best friends who waited patiently in the car parked on the road, , everyone else had gone. Grace sat down for a moment to try to get a handle on her emotions and think about what Smith would have her to do. He wouldn't want her to remain sad and unmoving. But she knew in her heart that it was going to take months and months to adjust to his absence in her life.

From the car, Martha stared through the car window at her friend. Tears were pouring down her face as she looked at Grace, a lone dark figure, sitting on the bench. "How in the world do you let go of your best friend? I don't know how she is even able to be here. Did you see her face today when the minister was speaking about Smith? I thought I would die lookin' at her eyes."

"I can't look at her, Martha. We've known them too long, and it's un-bearable to think about what she's feeling . . . what she's thinking. And the saddest thing is that none of us can make it better." Celeste wiped her eyes and stared out the front of the car. The day was windy and gray, and the sky looked like the bottom was going to drop out.

"We better try to get her in the car. It's going to pour any minute. And I know she would stay here all day if we let her." Maryann opened the car door and stepped out on the brown grass. She walked slowly up to Grace and pulled her up and they walked quietly back to the car. It was a quiet trip back to Grace's house, for no one knew what in the world to say.

Out of the silence Grace spoke. "Smith's parents wanted me to come back with them to Martha's Vineyard. It would be nice any other time, but I really just want to be alone for a while. Does that sound terribly rude? I know they are hurtin' too, but I just don't feel like being around anyone right now." Her voice was a whisper.

"Of course it isn't rude. Good gosh, Grace! You need to do whatever it takes to help you get through this right now. We're here for you, but I totally understand if you want to be alone. Just don't hole up in your house too long. I think it might be better to get back into your routine at the school as soon as possible." Martha put her hand on Grace's folded hands in her lap.

Grace nodded her head and slowly turned to look out of the car win-dow. Everything outside was going by so fast as they headed to her house. But she felt like the world had suddenly stopped.

CHAPTER 4

For two weeks Grace stayed alone in her house, seeing no one and eating very little. Her bedroom was a mess with clothes dropped everywhere, glasses on the nightstand, the bed unmade. The house had a stale smell and she was slowly running out of things to eat. In her desperation to figure out a way to live without Smith, she had let go of the normal routine of life and slipped into a daze where nothing mattered but getting through the day. She would stand in his closet and just inhale the remaining smell he had left on his clothes. His cologne. She slept in his shirts and wrapped up in his sweaters, trying to feel him close to her one more time.

This particular morning her hunger woke her so she got up, stretched, and went to the kitchen to dig something out of the pantry to eat. She decided that she couldn't eat one more peanut butter and jelly sandwich, so she showered, put a dab of makeup on, and headed out the door. The fresh air hit her right in the face and she stopped and took a deep breath, pushing her hair off her face. It actually felt good to be outside again, feeling the blinding sun on her face. Fortunately, she had picked a beautiful day to break her mourning, even though it was spur of the moment.

Just as she was coming down her front steps a little dog walked by and stopped directly in front of her house. He looked up at her and sat down, wagging his tail. "Hey, buddy! What are you doin' out all by yourself?" Grace looked around to see if she could see anyone looking for him. He seemed to be all alone. She bent down and patted his head and he jumped up and licked her face.

"Aw, sweet puppy. Are you thirsty? Wait here and I'll get you some water." She ran up the steps and into the kitchen and grabbed a small bowl and filled it with fresh water. Outside, she bent down and sat the bowl in front of the puppy. He lapped up all the water and sat there looking at her, with water dripping from his tiny whiskers.

"Now what do I do with you? I need to run to the store. You better go back home! I'm sure your owner is looking for you!" She got into her car and pulled out of the driveway. The little dog just sat there watching her go. It felt so good to be out driving around. and she found herself feeling a little lighter than she'd been since Smith died. In the store she ran into Brittany, one of her students who worked in the school office during her free period. She walked up to her and gave her a hug. "Mrs. Sanderson, I'm sorry to hear about your husband. I hope you get back to school soon! We all miss you in the office."

"Oh, child, I miss you all, too. I'll be back soon. I'm feelin' better and I think I'm about ready to get back to a normal routine again. Good to see you, Brittany."

Grace hurried through the store, feeling a lump in her throat. She would have to get used to people bringing Smith's death up. Right now it felt like a burning in her throat. She almost wanted to avoid people for a while, but she knew it was inevitable that she would have to face the questions and condolences. *I need to come up with a reasonable answer when people ask how he died. I can say with honesty that he died serving his country. Most people would accept that without any further questions. The less I have to say, the better. Soon it all will be forgotten; old news.*

Filling her basket with vegetables and healthy foods, Grace headed to the checkout. As she passed the service counter she noticed a bulletin board on the wall where you could post notes of things for sale, or lost and found items. She decided to put up a note about the little puppy that had come up to her doorstep. She put her phone number on the note and described the dog, thinking someone just might have lost him somewhere close by. On the drive home, she rolled down her window and let the wind blow her hair. It felt good to be alive, even though she was overcome with a feeling of deep sadness. But it was not her nature to stay down. Two weeks at home crying and sleeping was about her limit; of course, this was the worst nightmare she'd ever lived through and it wasn't over yet. It was going to take a while.

As she pulled into her driveway and parked the car, she thought she saw something at the front door. She grabbed a few sacks and walked up the steps, and there sitting on the doormat was the little puppy, wagging his tail. She opened the door and walked the groceries into the kitchen as the puppy followed her, staying right by her heels. She almost tripped on him trying to put the groceries up.

"Come here, little guy. What in the world am I gonna to do with you? Do you have a tag on you? Where did you come from?"

She searched for a collar but found nothing. *Maybe he's a stray, but he looks so healthy.* She picked him up and kissed his face. *Such a cute little man. I guess it won't hurt to keep him for the night.* "Okay, sweetie, you're stayin' with me tonight. I could use the company and I bet you could use some food!"

She fixed supper and fed him from her plate, realizing that might be a mistake. Tomorrow, if no one claimed him, she would buy some puppy food. She had never had a desire to have a pet, mainly because she was working so hard and the dog would be left alone a lot. Now, if she kept this dog, she had no idea what she would do with it during the day. But right now she was just going to enjoy having him around. After doing some work on the computer and making a few phone calls to friends she felt like talking to, she showered and climbed into bed, pulling the puppy into the bed with her. She decided to call him Sully, after a dog she'd had as a child. He snuggled right up to her like he'd always belonged and they both fell fast asleep.

CHAPTER 5

She'd set her alarm to go off at 6:00 so that she'd have plenty of time to get ready to go to work. It was time for her to face her job at the school, and in a way she was ready to be busy again. She felt weak inside and shaky, but being around her coworkers would keep her mind off things for a while. After fixing her breakfast, she fed the dog some chicken she had baked the night before and decided to take him to work with her for one day. It would be tough being her first day back on the job, but what else was she going to do?

Hurrying out the door, she grabbed a small water bowl and set Sully on the front seat. He was calm and sat up looking out the window with his little tail wagging. She was beginning to enjoy having him around and hoped that no one would call about a lost dog. When she got to Ross High everyone was having a fit over Sully and greeting her with condolences. It was a bit overwhelming, and she had to wipe her tears several times, but she made it through the morning in better shape than she had imagined she would. People seemed to avoid asking her too many questions, which turned out to be a relief to her. Mainly because she had no answers.

"Why, Grace! What a great surprise to see you back at your desk this morning. I didn't expect you back so quickly. What in the world is that with you? A puppy?"

Grace sucked in some air and managed a smile. Mrs. Meriwether was what you might call "a difficult person," to say the least. As office manager she liked to know every single thing that went on, and acted like Grace had to answer to her. It took all Grace had to answer back politely. "Good morning, Mrs. Meriwether. I suppose you've already turned in the roll this morning. I need some time to play catch up in my office, so I'll talk to you in an hour or so." Grace got up and closed the door to her office and sat down with a sigh. It was going to take some getting used to, not having Smith in her life anymore. She suddenly felt all alone in dealing with work, and everything else in her life. Her desk was covered with mail that had been neatly put in a folder and slit open by her office aide so that she could get to it easily. Brittany was always a step ahead of her, and worked at making her job easier. The stress of being principal in such a large high school took a toll on Grace, but Smith had always been there to smooth her out when she came home. Now she'd be on her own. Except for Sully. She reached down and patted him, and tackled the stack of papers on her desk. Her eyes were watering.

"Excuse me, Mrs. Sanderson." It was Brittany with a cup of coffee in her hand. "I brought you some fresh coffee; just made a new pot a few minutes ago. I'm so glad you are back! You look wonderful."

"Why thank you, Brit. Come on in and let me give you a hug! It's so good to be back. How have things been around here?" Grace rolled her eyes in the direction of Mrs. Meriwether.

"Oh, we made it all right. Just a few glitches here and there. I tried to keep myself busy and out of her sight. But she made sure to come in here once a day and check out the papers on your desk. I didn't think she was supposed to be in here, Mrs. Sanderson. But there was nothin' I could do."

"I'll take care of it, Brit. Don't you worry one minute. I'm back now and feeling some better. It'll take me a while to get back to my old self, but at least you won't have to deal with her on your own. Any issues come up while I was gone?"

"Not really. Just Samuel Billings. As usual, he's comin' in late a lot and not doin' his homework. He keeps bein' sent in to the office because he isn't turnin' in his homework. Something's goin' on at home, Mrs. Sanderson. I just know it is."

"Remind me to talk to Samuel. I'm snowed under today but don't let me forget. Now, you go eat lunch, and we'll chat later. So good to see your smilin' face again!"

Mrs. Meriwether wanted her job. And she found every opportunity to point out Grace's mistakes and worked on making her look bad in all situations. She was an old battle- axe who couldn't get along with anybody. She was no threat to Grace's position in reality, but she made everyone's life miserable just the same. The students had given her a nickname of "Battle-Axe" and try as she might, Grace couldn't get that name out of her mind. When she heard students mumble that name under their breath, it was all she could do to keep from smiling. But her position required the utmost professionalism and there was no room for siding with the students in name calling. So Grace worked hard to develop an atmosphere of creativity and positive energy for the students and let the rest go.

The end of the day came fast, with the bell ringing loudly in the hallways and students clamoring down the main hallway by the office on their way out the door. Grace waited until her office was empty and the school was quiet except for Joe, the maintenance man, who was mopping the lunchroom floor. She stood in the main hallway with Sully at her feet and just looked around. This was her life now. There was nothing for her at home anymore. It felt strange to think that, because they'd been married for so long and their relationship was so rich. He was her life, her reason to go through the day. God had given her a perfect match and she had never taken it for granted. But she knew when she married Smith that he was a very independent man. A man's man. He felt drawn to the CIA and excelled at what he did. That's what put him in extreme danger, his excellence. And that is what she loved about him. What he did, he did to the absolute best of his ability. There was no room for error in his job, but that skill seeped into his whole life. He incorporated what he learned on the job into his daily life, which included their marriage. He remembered every single date that was special to her, every song she loved, her favorite colors, her favorite restaurants and food. It was incredible how all that was stored somewhere in that brain of his and he could recall it when he needed it. He could pull any information up that he had learned. Some things he knew, he could not tell you how he knew. It just came in by osmosis. But it kept Grace on her toes, for she struggled to remember all the special things about him that he could remember about her. He was a man that other husbands could resent because he made them look bad. However, his personality was so engaging they couldn't help but like him.

The one thing that set him apart from the other agents who worked with him on covert operations was the single fact that he could recall to the nth degree the structure of a building, the location, every single important fact about the building that his team needed to know—where the doorways were, the alarm systems, vents, electrical wiring, windows. A photographic memory. Something you read about that sounds amazing, but when you actually see it in action in real life, you never forget it. It changes how you think about the human brain.

As she stood there thinking about Smith, tears were streaming down her face. She did not see Joe watching her from the lunchroom. In his gentle way, he was keeping an eye on her. She had been nothing but nice to him since she came on board at Ross High, and he aimed to do what he could for her. He shook his head and watched her head towards her office. Grace turned and picked up Sully, attached his leash, grabbed her purse, turned out the light, and walked to her car. Joe watched from a window in the lunchroom, wiping his brow with his huge callused hand. He knew exactly where she was going after work.

CHAPTER 6

Walking in the door, Grace spotted the answering machine light blinking. Her stomach sank. *Could it be someone calling about Sully?* She put Sully down beside her and pressed "play." Her worst fears came into reality as she heard the recorded message of a young girl. "Mrs. Sanderson. This is Janie Littleton. I live two streets over from you on Mimosa Avenue. We lost our little puppy the other night when we opened the door to let him out. He took off like a bullet and we never found him. I was so worried! Can I come over and see if you have my dog? His name is Brinkley. My number is 278-6798. Please call as soon as you can because we are so anxious to get him back home."

Grace sat down in the chair by her desk and wiped her eyes. Now she had to give Sully up and she was just getting attached to him. It kind of felt good to have another living thing in the house with her. She took a deep breath and dialed the number. "Hello, Janie? This is Grace Sanderson. I think I do have your puppy. Do you want to run over right now and see if this is your dog?"

"Oh, my gosh! Yes! I'm so excited. What's your house number?"

"My house number is 4578 Waynoka Drive. I'll have the garage open so come in the back door, okay, Molly?"

"Sure. Be right there."

Grace bent down and picked up Sully and snuggled close to him. "I thought I'd found me a puppy, Sully. I wanted you to be mine, but it looks like you belong to Janie." She kissed his face and let him lick her for a moment. Then she put him down and gathered his bowl and leash to give to Janie. There was a knock on her door and she ran to open the door and let Molly in.

"Hi, Janie! Is this your dog?

"Oh yes! Brinkley! Come here, Brinkley!" The puppy ran up to her and licked her face and wagged his tail. It was obvious to Grace that he knew Janie very well.

"Well, Janie! It looks like you have your dog back! I know you're so relieved. Please take this leash if you need it, and my water bowl."

"Thank you, Mrs. Sanderson. But we already have a leash for Brinkley. And now we'll be using it a lot more so he won't run off again."

Grace put the leash down on the counter and hugged Brinkley one more time. "Goodbye, Janie. Enjoy your puppy."

"'Bye, Mrs. Sanderson. Thank you for calling me back. And for taking such good care of Brinkley for me."

"No problem. Have a good night."

Grace sat down at her kitchen table and rubbed her eyes. Maybe it was better not to get attached to anything right now. She was just too fragile. She had one more thing to do before she started dinner. She grabbed her purse and headed out the door.

The winding road to the cemetery was lined with tall oaks whose boughs were full of leaves. A light wind was blowing and it caused shadows to dance across the headstones that lined the ground. Grace felt uneasy as she parked the car and walked up to Smith's headstone. She felt odd visiting it because she knew his body wasn't there. But she still wanted to come and sit and talk to him for a while. It made her feel close to him even if he wasn't there. It was all she had.

She sat down on a bench that was placed close to Smith's grave and looked around. She didn't see anyone else on the grounds and she lifted her head to feel the breeze. She let her thoughts go, thinking of the last time she and Smith were together. She could almost smell him. She got up and knelt down on the grave and brushed off the dirt.

"Smith, I've had quite a day today. It was very difficult for me to go back to work knowing you wouldn't be home tonight when I returned home. I miss you so badly, Smith. You have no idea what this has done to my life. I know how dedicated you were to your work, but our love was so strong. So special. I know you felt it. You shared with me so many times how special our love was. Well, that love is going to have to carry me through. I'm aching inside, Smith. I ache for you. I'd give anything in this world to have you hold me again. To kiss me. To sleep beside me. I don't know how I'll go on without you. And somehow I can't shake this feeling that you're still alive. . ."

Grace stopped and wiped her eyes. It felt so good to talk out loud to him.

"I found a puppy yesterday and kept him overnight. Took him to work with me. But as it turns out, he belonged to a little girl on Mimosa Avenue. She came this afternoon and picked him up. I had just gotten attached to him, and now he's gone. I've decided that maybe it isn't a good thing for me to get attached to anything right now. It hurts too bad and I don't think I could take any more hurt, Smith. I miss you. God, how I miss you."

She pulled herself up and stood over the grave, crying. She felt like she was going to die inside, so she decided to go back to the car.

"I'll be back, Smith. Tomorrow. I'm trusting God and this great oak tree to watch over you tonight, wherever you are. I wish I was with you. You are my forever love."

The drive back home was painful, but the next time she went to the cemetery maybe it wouldn't be so hard. She looked in the rear view mirror and noticed how worn out she looked. Stress. She decided to call Martha and see if she wanted to run out and get a bite to eat. She could use her best friend now. A good chat and some laughter. This was going to be her life from now on. And she was going to have to live it one day at a time. Alone.

CHAPTER 7

Ben Parker was ready to walk away from his position with the CIA. He had worked in total blackout for the last ten years in Special Operations Group, an element of SAD (Special Activities Division), which was responsible for the paramilitary operations. After experiencing the death of his best friend, Smith Sanderson, Ben couldn't do it anymore. He had lost his focus; his faith in what he was doing. He was dangerous to himself and the other men on his team. However, the CIA was like a brotherhood. The Mafia. They didn't give you up easily.

"So I hear you wanna leave us, Agent Parker?" Director Pauley raised an eyebrow.

"Yes, sir. I'm done. I just can't do this anymore. I know what you're gonna say, sir. But this time, I'm out."

"We trained you with kid gloves, Parker. You know things no one knows. I don't have to explain what this means to the United States, much less to the other men on your team. I don't wanna lose you. What will it take to make this go away?"

Ben shifted his feet. He knew this was coming. "There's nothin' you can do to change my mind this time. I wanted to leave five years ago, but you put me with Agent Sanderson so I'd stay. We all wanted to be with him; you knew that. So yeah, it worked for a while. But now he's gone. I have no desire left to remain in the CIA. Can you understand that, sir?"

Pauley slammed his fist on the desk. "No! I can't! How can you walk away after the time we've put into you? We made you what you are. There are men who'd give their right arm to do what you do. Hell, I know it's tough. I've been where you are. I still have to hide what I do, and it gets old. Real old. My wife nearly left me several times over it. But she knew when she married me that this was the deal. It hasn't been easy but I have grown to love what I do. Don't tell me you hate it! You couldn't have pulled off the operations we sent you on if you didn't love what you do. Why, you've been places on this worm-eaten earth that most people don't even know exist! And I don't even know how you survived that last operation."

A smile was tugging at the corners of Ben's mouth. *Oh, he was good. Really good.* "You aren't tellin' me anything I don't know, sir. I was in those shoes that walked next to people who would've blown my head off if they'd known I was there. I smelled the breath of the enemy. I ate their food. I drank their wine. I know all about it, believe me. But I can't do it another day of my life. We respected Agent Sanderson; we hung on every word he spoke. He was like a god to us. I learned so much workin' with him and we became like brothers to each other. We were trained to work as a team, as one. And we were all over that. But for some reason, I need some fresh air. This last operation in Pakistan nearly took us all out. And to think we had to leave Smith's body over there was too much for me. I can walk away from situations that would ruin most human beings. But losing Smith has done somethin' to me."

"I don't want to interrupt you, Parker, but you've got to get over that. I'm tellin' you, it gets easier as time goes on. I've been doin' this for twenty years now. Never dreamed I would last this long. But now I wouldn't think of gettin' out. It's my life . . ."

"Well, I don't wanna be so damn hardened that when my best friend gets killed I can just walk away and never look back. We all nearly got killed tryin' to get outta there. And what's worse, I had to tell his wife he wasn't comin' home. It was my first time to have to look into someone's eyes and tell them that the one person they loved in all the world was not ever comin' back home. No funeral. No body. Nothin'. It really opened my eyes to the fact that this job never really ends. You finish one operation and it moves right into another life-threatening situation. You're totally on your own out there; no one's gonna back you up. I took that responsibility for years, representing a government that pretended I didn't exist. But I can't do it anymore, I tell you. I can't."

Pauley paced back and forth in front of the window that faced the courthouse. "Look, I've been out in the field. I know exactly what it's like. As you know, we're trained to do a job, not to think about our own personal position. We have skills that the normal human being cannot fathom, and that's what allows us to survive in what would normally be a death trap. These operations are illegal in the target state and in violation of the laws of the sponsoring country. In both covert and clandestine operations, our lives are put at risk while our very existence is denied." He turned and looked square at Parker. "I don't blame you one bit for wanting a life. But I fear you'll find that when you leave, this is all you know, and it will be increasingly difficult for you to merge yourself into a normal way of living. Do you understand that, Parker?"

"Sir, not to sound trite, but I've watched several officers leave the CIA and develop very successful lives outside in the normal world. I'm not so naïve as to believe I won't face problems out there. But they certainly couldn't be as insurmountable as what I've already lived through. I could work for the local police department as an undercover agent. I know there's plenty out there for me to do, and still use my skills."

"What I'm tryin' to say, Parker, and you're just not hearin' me, is that you've been trained at such a high level of skill that the ordinary life will not be enough for you. You'll get bored. And that often leads to gettin' into trouble. I want you to stay; we all want you to stay. You're one of our best men. Have you spoken with your family about this?"

Parker shook his head. "You've not looked in my file in a while, sir. My parents are both dead. But I know without sayin' that they both would want me to do what I feel is right for me. Now, what do I need to do to get out of here?"

"Your cover will not be lifted, Parker. No one can ever know what you've done, or where you've been. You know the drill."

Ben walked up to the director and stuck out his hand. "It's been a pleasure and an honor to serve my country under you, Pauley. I couldn't have picked a better man to work under. I'll leave my I.D. and weapon at the desk with Mrs. Wilson. Thank you, sir. It's been a ride." Just as he turned and reached out for the door, Pauley spoke in a quiet, direct tone.

"The next operation is in Afghanistan. Sure you don't wanna stay?"

Parker shook his head and smiled. "And it still bothers me that no one ever found Smith's body." The door closed quietly behind him and Pauley stood there for a few minutes rubbing his chin. Ben's last comment stuck in his throat, but he wouldn't allow himself to think about it. He had just lost one of his best men. And that left him with one of the worst headaches he'd ever had. He now had to build a new team for this operation in Afghanistan.

CHAPTER 8

The alarm went off at 6:30 a.m. and Ben rolled over and shut it off. For a second he forgot that he no longer had to jump out of bed for work. He lay back on his pillow and yawned, thinking about what he wanted to do today. His first thought was to get dressed, grab a bite of breakfast, and head out to look for a house to buy. His apartment was fine when he was in the CIA, but now, a free man, he wanted something that felt more like a home. Paynesville was the perfect place to settle down, and he would be near Grace Sanderson, which was part of his plan. He'd promised Smith that he would look out for her, and that was exactly what he planned to do. She would never know he was around, but it would make him feel better to check in on her from time to time.

He showered and ate a quick breakfast, put food out for the stray cat outside, and headed out the door. It was a sunny summer day and the air was already warm. There was a smell of freshly cut grass in the air, and birds were everywhere. He went to the east side of town where some of his friends lived, and turned down Shady Grove. He'd always loved this area of town because there were hundreds of old oak trees and the houses sat on larger lots. He couldn't stand to be closed in on all sides; he needed some space to breathe. He saw an open house sign at the end of a cul-de-sac so he turned in the driveway, parked and walked up to the door and knocked.

"Good morning, sir. My name is James Dolton, with Worthington Realty. Come on in."

"I was drivin' around and saw the open house sign. Could you show me around? I'm lookin' for somethin' in this area."

"Great neighborhood. The homes on this street rarely come up for sale. You'd be lucky to get into this place, you know?"

"Sure do, buddy. Now let's see the house."

They walked through the house and Ben noticed all the wood, arched doorways, heavy stained oak doors, hardwood floors, and wide molding. He fell in love with the house in ten minutes but made himself finish walking through the rooms. The back yard was fenced in and there was a large deck on the back with a pool. The front had a deep porch with rockers on either side of the front door. He was pretty much sold on it, but decided to look at a few other homes in the area before making an offer.

"What's the price for this house, James?"

"Their asking $247,000, but make me an offer, Ben. I'm sure we can make this work for you."

"I'll check back with you after I look at few more houses. Do you have a card?"

"Sure do. Just give me a call and we'll go from there."

"Thanks, James. Talk to you soon,"

Two hours later, Ben had placed an offer for $250,000.00 on the house, and the offer was taken. No point in delaying the inevitable. The closing date was three weeks away. Just enough time for him to get his affairs in order with his landlord at the apartment complex. He climbed into his car and sped off down the street, screeching his tires as he turned the corner sharply. He had a feeling things were going up from here. It was about time he had a life of his own.

෴

Sitting at his desk, Jim Pauley noticed a news feed coming across his computer:

The Taliban has bombed the bridge and the Khyber Pass region in Pakistan, cutting off the supply lines to NATO forces in neighboring Afghanistan. The attack is a reminder that the supply line through Pakistan is extremely vulnerable. The administration might consider alternative routes through Russia, but that isn't the best alternative at this time. Needed in Afghanistan are intelligence and special operations forces and air power that could take advantage of that intelligence.

Fighting terrorists will require identifying and destroying small dispersed targets which will lessen the need for supplies and the number of troops deployed.

The phone rang on Jim Pauley's desk and he grabbed it, already anticipating the call. "Yes, sir. I understand."

"Are you aware of the situation, Pauley? There is no room for error. I want your best team on this immediately. And make sure Ben Parker is on that team. After we lost Sanderson, Parker is the next best man. He'll pull that team together and get the job done. I don't want to lose another man, Pauley. Is that clear?"

"Yes, sir. However, Parker left the job today, sir. He's no longer with us."

"I'm going to pretend you didn't say that, Pauley. I won't take no for an answer. Now you get that man back on the job, and do it now! We can't risk putting men out there that are green. Do you get my message?"

"Loud and clear."

"Good. Now let me know when Parker is in, and I'll set up a meeting. "

"Good day, sir."

Jim sat at his desk rubbing his eyes. He had a pile of papers on his desk, information was streaming on his desktop, and he had another headache coming on. He picked up his phone and dialed Ben Parker's cell. This wasn't going to be a good conversation. He might have to make a trip over to Parker's apartment to speak with him in person. Somehow he had to convince Ben to come back for this operation. He had no choice but to get him to say yes. And he would do whatever it took to get that answer.

CHAPTER 9

It was a typical summer day in June when the sound of lawnmowers filled the air, flies were swarming, and the smell of steaks cooking on the grill found its way into every yard on the street. Grace was sitting out by the pool with Martha, discussing a possible cruise to the Bahamas, when she saw the mail truck pull up in front of the house.

"Martha, hold on a second. The mail's here. I'll be right back." Grace grabbed her robe and wrapped it around her and walked through the gate to the driveway. She got to the mailbox and pulled the lid down and reached her hand into the box. It immediately rested on a large fat envelope which she pulled out, closing the door behind her. The envelope was addressed to her but she didn't recognize the return address. There was no name, just an address. Her hand started to shake and she pulled the envelope into her chest and ran into the backyard.

"Grace? What's wrong? What came in the mail?"

"I think my package came in the mail. From Smith. The one he promised would come if he died."

"Oh, my gosh. Sit down, Grace. Here, sit in this chair by the table and let's see what's in the envelope. You've been wonderin' what Smith was gonna send you. Now you'll finally know."

Grace sat down slowly and laid the envelope on the table. It felt like she was moving through quicksand. She grabbed her iced tea and took a long drink. Her mouth was as dry as cotton and her heart was racing. She actually dreaded this day coming but at the same time she was curious about what would be in the envelope. Smith had only mentioned it once, but he was very serious when he talked about it.

She pulled the tab across the top and pulled the slit open, reaching inside to pull the contents out. On top of the pile was an envelope with her name on it. Underneath was his wedding ring in a clear pouch and a cross he'd been given on their wedding day, and two of her favorite shirts. Tears were streaming down her face as she held the cross and ring in her hand. *Smith.* She picked up the shirts and smelled them. It was him.

"You okay, honey?"

Grace took a deep breath and turned to look at Martha. "I have no idea how I feel right now, Martha. I feel sick and I feel warm inside to have this ring in my hand. I want to read the letter, but it's gonna be hard." She took a deep breath and opened the envelope and pulled out the letter. When she saw Smith's handwriting she burst out crying. "I can't do it, Martha. I can't read it."

Martha reached over and hugged her. "I know it's hard, honey. Just relax and take your time. This is an important moment for you and you don't want to miss it. The last words you'll ever hear from Smith."

Grace unfolded the letter and sat back in the chair looking at the handwriting. Her heart was bursting in her chest and she could hardly see for the tears. She took a deep breath.

> Gracie,
>
> If you're reading this letter, then you already know I won't be coming home. I can't tell you how difficult it is to write this note to you because I wanted to spend the rest of my life with you. Grace, we started something wonderful rebuilding Wilton Children's Home, and I loved watching you around the children. Because of me you weren't able to experience being a mother and that's one of the things I regret about my career. I wish now that I'd allowed you to have a baby so that you would have that child to carry you through this traumatic time.
>
> What I hate is that I can't share where I was when my death happened, or how I died. It isn't fair to you, baby, but we talked about all of this long before my death. I want to thank you for tolerating all the secrets about my job, and all the nights we spent

apart. You're the most wonderful woman I could've ever hoped to have as my wife. And I cherished every single moment with you. Please know without a doubt that I loved you with all my heart, and at the time of my death I was thinking of you.

Promise me that you will not spend your days mourning my death. I want you to find a new life and live it to the fullest. That would make me happy, Grace, to know you're happy. Let's be thankful for the love we had that most people never get to experience. And I promise you one thing; I will have taken a part of you with me to heaven. And when I face God, I will share with Him that the light within you showed me the way to Him. And you and I know that's the greatest gift anyone can give another human being.

We have a forever kind of love. And I will love you into eternity. And Gracie, I'll be waiting for you on the other side of the moon. And I'll save a dance for you, angel. Bye, honey. I love you.

Smith

Grace carefully folded the letter and put it back into the envelope. She felt like she couldn't get a breath. Martha grabbed the envelope and Grace's arm and pulled her up.

"Let's get inside, Gracie. Come on. I'll get you something to drink and we'll work through this together."

Grace was shaking all the way into the house, in shock from finally getting the letter she'd been dreading. Her mind was racing as she sat down on the sofa, the cross digging into the palm of her hand. *Smith. You seem so far away from me. Reading your words has ripped my heart out. How can I do this without you?*

Martha shook her and spoke loudly. "Grace! Listen to me! Things are going to be okay. You just have to let all this sink in. Give yourself time and know that it's okay for you to feel overwhelmed. Especially now after receiving this letter. God only knows how difficult it was for Smith to write such a thing."

Grace was staring into space. She heard Martha but she had no answer. She felt herself sinking and tried to shake it off. "Martha, get me a glass of wine, hurry! It's in the refrigerator."

"I'll get it now. You just sit still and don't try to get up yet. You're white as a ghost, girl." Martha poured the glass of wine and handed it to Grace, watching her sip it slowly. It burned going down, a slow, deep burn that hit the bottom of her stomach and made her feel warm all over.

Grace laid her head back on the sofa and stared at the ceiling. She turned slowly and looked at her friend sitting beside her. "You know, Martha, we just never know how life is going to be. Somethin' can come so quickly that literally removes the bottom out of your world. I feel I'm hanging on by one single thread that could snap in a second. I was ready to get back to a normal life and now I feel like I've heard his voice again. It sort of pulled me back into that dark place of mourning him again. Seeing his handwriting makes it feel like he's still around. But I know he's gone. They said he was gone."

"You poor baby. Grace, why don't you come home with me tonight? Don't you think that would be best right now? Ken wouldn't care one bit if you stayed with us for a while. What do you say?"

"Not now, Martha. I know you are tryin' to help me recover, but only time will do that. I've been back to work and enjoying the students again. I'll just have to bury myself in my work and keep on putting one foot in front of the other. One day I'll see the sun shining again in my world, but right now it looks pretty dim."

"I know what you're saying is true. It does take time. But I can't stand seein' you like this. The offer stands. Just say the word and we'll be there for you. Grace, you would do it for me, right? I know you would. What about a cruise, like we were talkin' about before the mail came? Is that a possibility now?"

"Let me have a few days to think about it. I'll let you know. Now, you go and be with your husband. You guys have a good night, and I'll talk to you tomorrow. I promise you I'll be fine tonight. It just hit me pretty hard seeing that letter. And his wedding ring. I'll be fine. Really."

Looking a little skeptical, Martha stood up and grabbed her purse off the bar stool in the kitchen. "Okay, lady. But if you aren't feelin' better tomorrow, I'll insist you come home with me, you got that?"

Grace cracked a smile and nodded. "Okay, 'Mother'! Now go before Ken wonders where you are."

CHAPTER 10

In the middle of the night a black Pave Hawk hovered close to the ground while a team of eight Special OPs members grabbed their gear and dropped to the ground running. Their mission was to locate and destroy a terrorist cell that intelligence had shown possessed a stolen Russian nuclear device. The cell's intention was to deliver this device to Iran, which would cause Iran to become a greater threat to the United States, the Middle East, and especially Israel. The team had four hours to complete their mission, at which time the Pave Hawk would return at the designated location to extract them.

Focused on the mission, Ben led the team into the Toba Kakar Range on the Afghanistan side of the Durand Line. After setting up a base camp in the dust and heat, they did a recon to establish the exact location of the cave and the conditions of the surrounding area as well as other possible entrances to the cave. Based on that information, Ben activated the mission and divided his team into three groups: one to cover the rear entrance to the cave, one for the initial attack, and a backup team. Ben and two other agents were the lead assault team.

As they entered the cave in dead silence and darkness, using their night vision goggles, they came to an opening with a doorway to the right. In the haze of darkness they saw a crate with a Russian symbol on it and a radioactive label, and they knew they had found their target. Ben's heart was racing as he turned and nodded to the men. At the same moment that they identified the object, they heard voices and somebody screaming in Urdu, "Enemy, enemy!"

Ben heard rapid gunfire deep inside the cave. He nodded to the men to grab the device and they began their exit. As Ben was retreating he opened fire into the cave with his UZI and took a bullet to the leg. Wincing, he ran as hard as he could, heading towards the backup team, one of whom was ready to throw a flash grenade into the cave.

Binding his leg to stop the flow of blood, Ben sent two of the backup team to retrieve the two men covering the rear entrance of the cave. Sadly, the backup men discovered that their intelligence was flawed and what they thought was the rear entrance was actually the main entrance, heavily guarded. Both men were killed instantly. The shots Ben heard deep inside the cave were the shots that killed his men.

There was no time to mourn the death of their teammates. Time was running out for them to escape. Ben radioed the helicopter team and coordinated a rendezvous time. The men were extracted without incident and the mission was accomplished. The Pave Hawk ascended into the air, leaving no trace of the mission except for the two bodies of the special OPs team who would never make it home. The mission was finished but not without loss of life. And Ben Parker regretted again accepting the mission; he'd seen enough death for one lifetime. And he was playing Russian roulette with his own.

∽

When Ben and the team dropped into base camp, he was taken immediately to a field hospital, where his leg wound was treated. Luckily, the bullet had come clean through the muscle, barely grazing the bone.

"Hey, dude. What happened to your leg? That could've turned out to be a one-legger, ya know?" The male nurse stepped back from dressing the wound.

"Man, tell me about it! Close call. But I'm done now. Headed home."

"Don't blame you. I've seen enough blood to fill a stadium back home. I'm outta here real soon, myself."

"I'm not one to talk about pushing the limits, but don't wait too long. You do this too many times you never go back home." Ben raised his eyebrows and then gave a wink. This guy was young. He'd already seen too much. Ben shook his head and lay back down on the cot. Another day and he'd be headed home for good. His thoughts wandered off to his friend Smith, and he felt depression creeping into the corner of his mind. *Smith.*

CHAPTER 11

The hot humid breeze reminded Grace that summer was around the corner. Everything was in full bloom and the smell of freshly cut grass was in the air. She was walking down the steps toward her car when someone called out her name.

"Grace! Oh Grace! How in the world are you?" It was Margaret Wade, waving frantically at the fence.

"Maggie! You're finally home! I'm so glad to see you." Grace ran over to the fence and wrapped her arms around Margaret. Tears were finding their way down her face, ruining her makeup. "I've missed you so much, Maggie."

"Well, honey, I've missed you too. We have a lot to talk about, I imagine. I'll be home tonight if you want to come over and talk. I'll fix supper, so just come over after you get home from school. You look tired, Grace."

"I am tired. I'm at a place I don't want to be, Maggie. But we'll talk tonight. I'll be home around 4:00, if that is okay with you."

"I'll be waiting, angel. Don't you worry about anything, I'm home now."

Grace smiled as she got into her car and drove to the school, mindlessly touching the cross around her neck that had belonged to Smith. A sadness hung over her that she just couldn't shake. Sometimes in the night she still woke up feeling like she couldn't breathe. Martha was on her all the time about going to the cemetery every single day. She knew it probably wasn't healthy, but for some reason it gave her some peace at the end of her day. She felt closer to Smith there and the quiet of the cemetery was soothing in an odd way.

Brittany met her in the parking lot. "Mrs. Sanderson! I'm so glad you're here. Samuel Billings is really in trouble this time. Mr. Joe found him in the kitchen stealing food before his first class. It's not the first time. I don't know what's going on with him, but he's sitting in the office waiting on you."

"I'll take care of it, Brit. You go on to class and I'll catch up with you later today." Grace shook her head. *I'm going to have to get to the bottom of this once and for all. Something's going on in that kid's life that is causing such erratic behavior.* Grace walked into her office and saw Samuel sitting there with his head down. Her heart jumped but she kept a stern face when she spoke to him.

"Samuel, come on into my office and take a seat. Let's see what's going on with you."

Samuel walked into her office and plopped down in the first chair. His clothes were torn and ragged, but they were clean. Grace took a minute to think before she spoke. She took a long drink of coffee and looked straight at Samuel. "Okay, buddy. Let's talk real. I want to know what in the world is going on in your life that you have to take food out of the cafeteria before class. Now talk to me."

Samuel squirmed in his chair. "Um . . . well . . . it's hard to talk about, Mrs. Sanderson. Um . . . we don't have any food at home. We haven't had a good meal in so long that I can't remember. My mom is sick. Real sick. My father is gone. Been gone for years. I don't know what else to do."

Grace had to hold back a tear. "Sam look at me. You know you can come in here at any time and talk to me about anything. This is serious, Samuel. Do I need to see about getting help for your mother? Has she been to a doctor?"

"Well, she got the flu bug and she just ain't never got any better. She's coughin' at night and sounds pretty bad. I don't have any money to get medicine for her. What am I supposed to do? I was starvin' and didn't think the school would miss what I took. My mom needs food so I put some of the rolls in my pocket to take home for her."

Grace put her face in her hands for a second and thought about what she could do. "Sam, let me make some phone calls and see what can be done. For now, I want you to go into the lunchroom and eat a big breakfast. I'll tell your English teacher what's going on. Just get some food in your stomach and then head on to class, okay? I'll track you down later on today with some answers about your mom. Something's got to change or you won't graduate next year, Sam. Let's see what happens today. Now go! And don't worry."

Samuel got up, smiling at Grace. "Mrs. Sanderson, I 'preciate what yur doin', and I don't know how I'll ever pay ya back."

"You don't worry about paying me back. I just want you to graduate and go to college. That would make my life, Samuel."

He shook his head and walked out of the office and into the lunchroom. This would be the first day in six months that Samuel had a good meal. Grace picked up the phone and called Mrs. Meriwether. "Anne, I want you to find me a doctor who will treat Samuel Billings' mother today. And don't take no for an answer. She's very sick and needs medical attention immediately. The United Methodist Church has a food bank; please contact them and let them know this family needs food. We'll address the clothing issues later. Any questions?"

Anne Meriwether knew better than to question Grace Sanderson. "I'm on it, Mrs. Sanderson. I'll let you know as soon as I get a response."

"Oh, by the way, Anne. At my next meeting with the teachers make sure that this issue is on the agenda. We need to find a way to be aware of the children who are falling through the cracks right in front of our eyes. This just isn't acceptable."

Grace sat back and smiled. She loved doing this. How many people would love to have her job and get to experience the reward of helping kids have better lives? She made a note to remind herself that next week was tryouts for singing at graduation. There were fifty kids that had signed up to perform, so it would be an interesting project. She picked up the list that Brittany had dropped off and studied it to see if she recognized all the names. Suddenly she saw a name at the bottom of the list that she recognized—*Samuel Billings*. She let the list fall to the floor as she leaned back in her chair.

I didn't know he could sing. What have we done to this boy? Has he been hidden all these years in this school, underneath ragged clothes and hunger? How many more children are like Samuel, unable to be who they were meant to be because of the poverty that covers their lives? If I'm honest, I saw his despair and I did nothing. I didn't take the time to find out more about him. Now I'll know the whole story if it's the last thing I do, because I'm not gonna let him stay in the shadows anymore.

41

A wall walker. The halls are full of them; students who walk next to the walls so that they are invisible. I can't stand it anymore.

The light lit up on her phone and she picked up. It was Anne. "Mrs. Sanderson, I have a Dr. Field who has agreed to see Mrs. Billings. We need to bring her in now to see him. And I contacted the United Methodist Church and they will be delivering food to Samuel's house this afternoon after he gets home from school. So one of us needs to pick up Mrs. Billings and take her to the doctor. Do you have any idea who that person would be, Mrs. Sanderson?"

Grace smiled. "Yes, Anne. That person is you. Find out what class Samuel's in, and pull him out of that class to go with you. Let's see if we can't get his mother back on her feet." The ball was rolling, and now things were finally going to get done.

CHAPTER 12

Margaret Wade was a delightful lady with an accent that was point-edly southern. At seventy-five years old she still could keep up with the best of them and she loved to cook. Her once brown hair was a beautiful shade of gray and she had deep dimples on either side of her mouth. She wore lots of jewelry and makeup and had an array of hats that she pulled out every Sunday morning to wear to church. She drove a white 1966 Cadillac DeVille with whitewall tires and had it washed every Saturday morning. No matter what day you came to visit Margaret, her house would be filled with an aroma that made your mouth water.

It had been a busy day at work and Grace was really too tired men-tally to be around anyone. But she'd promised Margaret that she would have dinner with her, so there was no way out of it. As she walked up to the door, Lola, Margaret's miniature poodle, was barking through the window. She was sitting on top of the sofa looking outside, wagging her tail and barking at the same time. Grace loved the dog and opened the door and bent down and picked Lola up. "Hey, darlin'. I've missed see-ing you so much."

Margaret peeked her head around the corner of the kitchen and smiled, showing her white teeth. "Hey, honey. You just make yourself at home! I'm so glad to see you again, and cannot wait for us to sit down and talk. Dinner's almost ready."

"No hurry, Maggie. I'm gonna sit right here on the sofa and love on Lola for a few minutes."

"She sure loves to see you, Grace. I think she knew you were comin', because she's been lookin' out that window all afternoon, like she was waitin' for you."

Grace looked around the living room and studied all the family photos. Margaret had five children and they were all married and had grown children. Some of the grandchildren had married and there were great grandchildren in the photos. In the middle of the wall near the door was an old spinet piano that Margaret loved to play. It had a white doily across the back of it and an old Baptist Hymnal was propped up, opened to "The Old Rugged Cross." Above the piano were three diplomas from Emery University and a photograph of her with Dean Whitaker. She had been an esteemed English professor at Emory for years with a master's in educational studies, and probably would still be teaching if her health had allowed it. Her weight had slowly worn out her hips and she now walked with a slight limp and a cane. But the fire was still there, and she had a mind like a steel trap.

"Come on, Grace. While it's hot! We've got so much to talk about, and I don't want to waste one minute of our time. You sit here at the end of the table and fill that plate up with some of this good food. Girl, I can tell you haven't been eating right! Look at you!" Maggie looked Grace up and down and shook her head.

"Oh, Maggie, stop fussin' over me! You know how hard this time has been for me, losin' Smith. For a while I didn't think I could make it without him. It was the weirdest feeling to know he wasn't ever comin' back. I still have trouble with that one."

"Oh I know, honey. I've been down that road. Walter died when I was in my forties and I never did remarry. I dated a few, don't you know. But nobody could replace my Walter."

"I couldn't think of dating right now, Maggie. I'm just puttin' one foot in front of the other and focusing on my work at the school. I haven't been to the orphanage in so long I bet they think I've forgotten them. I need to get on top of things and stop sittin' so much in my house, thinking."

"Don't be so hard on yourself, Gracie. It's gonna take some time for you to adjust. There's no hurrying it."

Grace took another bite of the roast and sat back in her chair, enjoying the flavors mixing in her mouth. "You're right about one thing, Maggie. I haven't eaten this well in a long time. I need to come over more often to experience your cooking. You need to write a cookbook!"

"Don't think I haven't thought about doing just that, girl! Too many women don't know the first thing about cookin' and this is just down home southern cookin'."

They ate in silence for a few minutes, and then Margaret spoke up.. "Grace, tell me what you know about how Smith died. I don't even know what he did for a living.

"All I know is that he worked for the government so it had to be something pretty classified. I will never know how he died, or where, Maggie. It's so frustrating to find out he's dead and no other information. It's near impossible to have closure without knowing more information. I keep feeling like he's gonna show up somewhere and things will go back to normal. It feels like a nightmare, Maggie."

"Just take it one day at a time, honey. No one said this life would be easy, and God only knows we all have something to deal with most of the time in our lives. I've stayed pretty busy in the last twenty years, but that doesn't stop me from thinking about Walter. I loved that man and still do."

"When did you buy this house, Maggie?"

"I moved here from Druid Hills after I retired from Emory. Paynesville was just small enough to make me feel like I was away from the hustle and bustle of Atlanta. I was ready to slow down and this neighborhood spoke to me. I was a widow, alone, and everyone here seemed so friendly. I was thrilled when you and Smith bought that house next door; just knew you would be good neighbors."

Margaret cleaned off the table and brought in fresh apple pie and ice cream. "I know we shouldn't eat like this, but tonight I wanted you to have something special. How are things at the school, Grace?"

"Going great. I just had an epiphany today. I realized how many of the students were falling through the cracks, walking the walls of the school but going unnoticed. One in particular, a Samuel Billings, really opened my eyes to how students can be going through something pretty traumatic and the teachers and myself just don't see it. Or we're not looking close enough."

"What happened with Samuel?"

"He stole some food today and the maintenance man turned him in. But I found out that his mother was very ill and they had not had food for weeks in that house. He was stealing rolls to take home to his mother. I let him go to the cafeteria and fill his stomach up and then go on to his first class. But we also contacted a doctor who agreed to treat her free and my office manager and Samuel took her to his office. I also got a food bank to bring food to their home. So for now Samuel and his mother are taken care of, but how many more students are there who don't have enough food or are in an abusive situation? It's a tough world out there, Maggie. And I know I'm not telling you anything you don't know."

"Girl, I hear you. I've seen things I never thought I'd see, working with students. It's amazing how people can survive on so little. I don't know what the answer is, but we have to do what we can where we are. I'm sure Samuel appreciated your help."

"He certainly was shocked at what we did today for him. And to top it off, I noticed that he's trying out to sing at graduation. His name was the last name on the list. I didn't even know he could sing."

Margaret sat up in her chair and looked at Grace. "One more thing, honey. I hear you've been visiting the cemetery nearly every day after you get home from school. Do you think that's healthy, Grace? I'm a little worried about you."

Grace looked down and quickly wiped a tear from her eye. She forced a smile and looked back at Margaret. "No, I love going there. It's peaceful and helps me wind down after a busy day. I talk to Smith and just sit there for a few minutes and think. Then I'm able to go home and finish out my day without feeling depressed or lonely. I know it may seem weird but I really feel close to him sitting out there."

"Well, just know that I'm here if you ever need some company. You're good for me, too! We'll have to do this more often now that I'm back home."

Lola was standing by the back door so Margaret let her out in the back yard. "I'm heading home, Maggie. I think I'll take a hot bath and stretch out on the sofa with a good book. I can't tell you how I've enjoyed this meal with you. You're just what the doctor ordered!"

"Honey, I'm going to be here for you, and we're gonna get through this time together. Now you go take care of yourself and if you need anything at all, you just call me, all right?"

"Yes, Maggie. I love you. Thanks so much for the good food."

∽

Margaret watched Grace walk next door, shaking her head. She could tell that Grace was depressed and had noticed how hard she tried to put her best face on. But Margaret could see through the smile, the bags underneath her eyes, and the tired look on her face when she was looking the other way. Smith's death had really taken a toll on Grace and she planned to watch her closely.

I don't understand why the government withholds so much information about the death of an agent. He probably worked for the CIA as a special agent and I know there's a lot of secrecy in that area of government. But the spouse should be able to know. It seems so unfair. It's been months now and she's still going to the cemetery every day. She's so young to have to go through this. . .

CHAPTER 13

Ben sat at the rear of the crowded plane in a window seat, watching the darkness below. How he'd allowed Pauley to talk him into that last mission was beyond comprehension. He was seriously done with the CIA and all of its glory. His father was dead and he hadn't seen his brothers in years. His parents had divorced and his mother had not been close to him for a long time. Now he had a new house that had a lot of work to be done. He was more than ready to settle down and have a new life. Free of secrets. It was going to be a challenge to acclimate back into civilian life, but he was going to give it all he had. He'd heard some nightmare stories of agents who tried to get jobs and just couldn't make it. They felt frustrated, traumatized, misunderstood, and bored with the eight-to-five job. He almost felt like a soldier who'd been to war and was coming home to find his place in the world. The things he'd seen and done would haunt him for a long time, and it was made worse by the fact that he was not allowed to share any of his secrets with another soul. The secrecy got old after a while.

It was nighttime as they were flying over the Atlantic Ocean headed to the States, and most of the passengers were sleeping, so it was quiet. Ben laid his head back against the seat and let his mind wander back to the last operation with Smith.

It all happened so fast. The recon took months of them carefully working the area, developing relationships with certain people, and winning their trust, all to attempt penetration of the Taliban. Everything was going so smoothly. Way too smoothly. Unbeknownst to them, during the mission, the Taliban was doing a counter-infiltration of their operation and contacts. Both Smith and Ben missed an elementary omen of covert operations: When things are going smoothly and as planned, something probably is terribly wrong.

It was. One of their most trusted contacts betrayed them, and they were ambushed at what they considered a safe house. In a split second, their entire mission was compromised and they were hit with a hail of gunfire.

The one thing I can't get out of my mind is my having to leave Smith on the ground in my attempt to save my own life and the other men on the team. I didn't have time to look back. I'll regret that for the rest of my life.

∽

The auditions for singing at graduation were at 4:00. Grace looked at her watch and looked at the students filing in, excited about the chance to sing in front of their peers. There was a piano on stage and someone was setting up the mike, trying to get the sound right. The auditorium had great acoustics and it was a perfect place for the tryouts. Grace got lost in her own thoughts, remembering how much Smith loved the kids at the orphanage. *He would've loved to have sat in on this tryout . . .*

"Mrs. Sanderson! Are you ready to call the first student up to the stage? Mrs. Sanderson!"

It was Mrs. Meriwether. Her voice was shrill and she was very tense. She hated having to stay after school for any event, but especially this one. Music was not her thing.

"Michael Hodges! Michael, are you here?"

Michael stood up sheepishly. "Yes, Mrs. Sanderson. I'm here."

"Well come on up to the microphone and let's hear what you can do."

Michael waited for the pianist to play an intro and he started singing. It was like scraping your fingers on a blackboard; he was so off key that kids were covering their ears. Laughter skipped across the room and Grace stood up and stopped the singing. "Michael, thank you very much. Can you sit down now?"

Michael ducked his head and sat down in the front row next to his friends. He didn't look too happy.

"Peter Schultz. You're next. Peter?"

Peter ran up to the stage, jumped the three steps in one leap, and stood at the microphone, pushing his hair back off his face. People were clapping and hollering out. "Okay, kids. Settle down, now. We have fifty students to listen to this afternoon and we need to keep this moving. Go ahead, Peter."

Peter waited for the intro and started singing and it was pretty good. At least he could carry a tune.

"Okay, Peter. You can sit down. Anna, you're next."

Anna walked slowly up to the microphone and waited for her cue. When she started to sing, she sounded like an angel. All the kids started clapping and she stopped and looked at me. Her face was a bright red.

"That was lovely, Anna. Now take your seat."

Forty-five students filed up to the microphone one at a time and sang, hoping to make the cut. Some were impressive, and some were tone deaf. Grace had begun separating the good singers from the bad; good on the right, bad on the left. There was an unequal amount on both sides at this point in the tryouts and Mrs. Meriwether was shaking her head. Five more students left to sing, and Grace was getting worried. She needed at least twenty to make the cut, and right now the good side was a little weak.

"Okay, Brad. Let's hear what you can do. And take the gum out of your mouth."

Everyone fell out laughing and Brad began to sing. He had a great tenor voice and everybody clapped. He ran down the steps and plopped down on the right side, grinning. Three more people went up on stage and made the cut.

The last student was Samuel Billings. He was sitting way back at the end of the auditorium and Grace could barely see his face.

"Samuel! Are you singing today or not?"

He got up slowly and walked to the stage and climbed the steps. He seemed unusually quiet and yet there was something else different about him. He seemed to be moving in slow motion. Grace knew he was thankful that his mother had been to see a doctor. She hoped it gave him confidence.

"Okay, Sam. Let's hear what you got. You might want to raise the microphone; it looks a little low for you."

The students were whispering as the intro began, and Grace was expecting the worst for Samuel, watching him stand there motionless, taking a deep breath to relax. He opened up his mouth and began to sing, and suddenly it was dead quiet in the auditorium. All the kids were watching, stunned. Grace covered her mouth and felt goose bumps go all over her body. Samuel could sing. His voice was rich and strong and he leaned his head back, closed his eyes, and let the music come from within. Mixed within the words he sang were all the problems he wrestled with in his life. You could feel the pain, the loneliness, the sorrow, and resignation. He suddenly let go and hit a high note and the whole auditorium stood up and roared. Samuel opened his eyes and saw all his peers clapping and yelling him on and he got a big smile on his face. Samuel had found himself at the end of the tryouts in front of those peers he'd been afraid of. Rejected by. Grace walked over to him and gave him a big hug. She raised her hand to the crowd and everyone sat back down and waited to hear what she was going to say.

"This is an extraordinary time for us here at Ross High. We are about to face graduation for the seniors here and we want to have a powerful group to sing. We are going to be working four afternoons a week for the next two weeks, preparing for graduation ceremonies. If you can commit to this, and you are in the group on the right side, then come up here on stage and give me your phone numbers. I have a slip of paper for you to give to your parents to sign, giving you permission to remain after school and practice. If I don't get this paper back, you can't sing in the group, is that clear?"

Everyone nodded as they were walking up on the stage. "The rest of you students who did not make the cut can leave. I appreciate your efforts."

Grace was thrilled as she drove home. Samuel was going to make this thing magical. She couldn't believe his voice. Not in a million years would she have guessed he would have had a voice like that. He was so still up on the stage, closing his eyes and letting his voice cover the auditorium. It was amazing, but he seemed to have no fear while he was singing.

You can't look at the outside of a person and decide who they really are. For they may be hiding a gift that could change the world. She couldn't wait to tell Martha and Maryann. They had planned a dinner for Saturday night and she was looking forward to relaxing with her friends. She smiled as she turned the corner and headed to her house. She still halfway expected to see Smith standing in the driveway talking to Maggie. He did get such a kick out of her.

CHAPTER 14

The sun was beaming down in Zhob, Pakistan, and people were standing in the shade, fanning themselves from the heat. Dr. Irfan Sheikhani was sitting by the bedside of an American soldier, checking his vitals, and cleaning his wounds. He was conscious but totally unaware of his surroundings. His injuries were not life-threatening but he appeared to have amnesia and could not answer any questions he was asked about why he was in Pakistan. He didn't know his name, nor did he remember the explosion or gunfire that caused his injuries. Dr. Sheikhani tried one more time to get information from the soldier.

"I know you're in pain, but please try relaxing and thinking about question. Do you know why you're in Pakistan?"

Smith looked at the doctor with a blank stare. "No, I have no memory of why I'm here. I need to know who you are, and where you found me. Who was I with?"

"You were alone when civilians discover you. They brought you here because they knew I was understanding to what United States was doing against terrorism. They knew you needed medical attention; there was blood. I don't want you be afraid. I have told you before I am Dr. Irfan Sheikhani."

Smith shook his head. He felt lost listening to this doctor who spoke with broken English. His mind was so foggy and he had absolutely no memory. He didn't even know his own name, where he was from, or why he was in Pakistan. It was frightening, and he was sweating, straining to remember.

"Sir, I want you eat this food my wife has fixed for you. It will give you strength and help you heal. If you can relax in your mind and concentrate for getting stronger, then there's a possibility that memory will come back for you."

Smith felt an overwhelming sadness come over him. *Why can't I remember what happened to me? My name? Why I am here? This is driving me crazy.* He took the meal and began eating. He felt very weak and his whole body ached. The wounds to his legs and chest were deep but had not required anything but a few stitches. Dr. Sheikhani had bound his chest and left leg with white bandages and he changed them often. Whoever this man was, he certainly had taken good care of him. He hoped the doctor was correct in his thinking that his memory would return if he gave it time. It was a disconcerting feeling not to know who he was and why he was in Pakistan. He was determined to find out somehow.

Dr. Sheikhani watched as the soldier ate. He was assuming the man was a soldier but there was a chance he was simply a civilian in Pakistan. He seemed to be in excellent condition and this would help in his recovery. He decided to keep a journal on the soldier just in case something was said that would trigger a memory in him. He was taking a huge risk hiding the American in his home. Even though Americans lived in Pakistan, it had become increasingly dangerous as terrorist groups were targeting locations where Americans visited or dwelled. He was willing to take the risk because he felt it would be for a short period of time. He would make the decision of asking the soldier to leave if he felt the risk heightened to a dangerous level.

Smith ate until he was full and thanked the doctor and his wife for their hospitality. He walked slowly around the exterior of the house, which had a tall fence around it. It felt good to have the warm sun on his face, but he got weak after a short time and went back into the house to lie down to rest. He fell asleep immediately and dreamed of a different place he didn't recognize. In the far distance of the dream was a woman and she had a cross around her neck, but he couldn't see her face. She faded into darkness as he fell deeper into sleep.

∽

The doctor called to his wife and they sat down at the kitchen table to discuss the soldier.

"I'm uncomfortable having this American here in our home, Irfan. Are you not afraid for us?

"I am aware of risk, Mahsa. But I feel the need as a physician to take care of him for a short time. I am hoping memory will not escape him much longer. I don't know why he came to Pakistan, but for reasons unknown I do not feel he will harm us."

"I am not willing to lose my life to save him, Irfan. Please watch carefully our home and listen to the people out on the street. We need people listening for us, so that we can be aware of what is going on around us. I am certain this soldier would not want us harmed while he is recovering from bad wounds."

"We will be fine, Mahsa. Don't overreact. I will take care of it, I assure you. Now let's allow him rest and see how it is with him in the evening. It may take some time, but he will start to remember things soon."

☙

There was word on the street that an American soldier had been found. There were whispers of his being hidden. But no one knew who he was or why he was there. And for a time this lone American was lost in the dust of his rescue and stayed hidden in a safe house searching for memories of a life that eluded him. The mind is a peculiar thing. It remembers things we want to forget, and lets go of things we want so badly to remember . . .

CHAPTER 15

Bentley's was a fine dining restaurant with starched white tablecloths, lots of dark wood, rich green plants, and trees scattered through the dining room, and all male waiters with white shirts and black ties. There was soft music playing in the background while a band got their instruments out for a set. Grace was seated in the back at a table near the window, and she was just enjoying the dimly lit atmosphere when Maryann walked in. Grace waved to her and waited for her to join her at the table.

"Hey, girlfriend! You picked a wonderful place for us to catch up with each other. I haven't eaten here since my Smith's birthday. I remember how wonderful the food was. So how are you?"

"I'm fine. Bob's been driving me nuts to learn how to play golf, but I've avoided it this long so I'm gonna keep on making excuses. You look wonderful, Grace! How are things?"

"Oh, I have my days even now, Maryann. Sometimes it feels like yesterday when he was here, and other times I can't remember his face to save my life." Grace touched the corner of her eye but forced a smile.

"I don't know how you've coped so well. I've thought of you so much, Grace, wondering how you've handled the nights. Is that a tough time for you now?"

"Yes. I absolutely hate the nights. But I've developed my own routine and I try to stick to it. I stay busy until it is time to turn out the lights, so I don't have much opportunity to just sit and think. I know you don't want to hear it but I've been visiting the cemetery a lot lately. It is my one place where I can talk to Smith and feel some peace."

"Don't worry about what I think, or anyone else. You do what you have to do to make it through this time. None of us knows what we would do if we lost someone we love. I'm just glad you are back to work. How are the kids?"

"Oh, they are my heart, as always. Some days they drive me up a wall and other days I wish I could take them all home."

Maryann looked towards the door and saw Martha coming their way. She waved and looked at Grace. "I hope Celeste comes. I called her but had to leave a message on her machine."

"Hey, girls! So glad we can get together tonight to catch up with each other. How you been, Gracie?"

"I'm good. Gosh, it's good to be with you two again. Why do we wait so long?"

They all smiled and sat down to look at the menu. They decided to get an appetizer and give Celeste a little more time to show up before they ordered their meals. "I'm starving for some reason! Maryann, how's Bob?" Martha opened up her menu and scanned it quickly.

"He's good. Working too hard, drinking too much, and playing way too much golf!"

"You say that every time we ask! I know your life can't be that bad." Martha laughed.

"Grace, you look fab. How are things at the school?" Martha was not wasting any time.

"It's going pretty good. I was about to tell Maryann that I've really had a great week. We are practicing for graduation and I've discovered some very talented students. I'm really excited about it."

"Are we invited?" Maryann smiled.

Grace laughed. "Did you forget? I mentioned it at the last dinner we had together! I'd be angry if you didn't show up."

They were halfway into their meal when the cruise idea raised its ugly head. "Grace, you given any thought to that cruise we spoke about months ago?" Martha smiled through the forkful of salad she was about to plunge into her mouth.

"Frankly, no. A cruise was not on my list of things to think about! Why? Are you guys still wanting to take a cruise? And where to, might I ask?"

"Well, we could go to the Bahamas. Not far away. And we don't have to go for long, either. A four day cruise would be perfect, don't you think?"

Maryann was sitting there shaking her head yes, poking Martha under the table. Grace knew she didn't have a chance. "Well, I guess it would do me good to get away, but I don't feel ready. Maybe I'll never feel ready. Still a little shaky from time to time. It doesn't feel good living alone when I thought my marriage would last forever, ya know?"

They nodded in silence. What could they say?

"I won't ruin our meal tonight by getting us all sad. I'll give it some thought. And when did you want this to happen, my dear?" Grace looked at Martha and raised her eyebrow.

"Pretty quick here, girlfriend. Like three weeks from now. Summer is right on top of us and you'll be done with graduation. Let's book our trip and take off. If we put it off too far in the future, one of us will chicken out and then it's over. I've already passed it by Ken and he's all for it. "

Grace knew she was right, but why did she feel so uneasy about going? It wasn't like Smith was going to show up at the house while she was gone. No one would even know she was gone except Margaret and that was because she lived next door. "I'll let you know next week. Let's meet again for dinner and discuss our plans. Is that a good idea?"

They all stood up and hugged. "Sounds perfect, Gracie. Call if you need anything, and I'm really looking forward to this short trip with you." Maryann headed out the door dialing her cell. Bob wanted her to pick up something on her way home. He had texted her three times during dinner but she'd ignored it. Now she had no excuse.

Martha hugged Grace again and pushed her away for a minute. "Let me look at you. You really doin' okay, Grace? You're not just sayin' that, are you?"

"No. I can't fool you, Martha. Really, things are fine. Nothing I can't handle. Just the usual restlessness at night and occasional fears that creep in. But I'm adjusting as well as anyone would who has lost their soul mate. So don't worry. I'll call you tomorrow! Thanks for the lovely dinner. I'm stuffed!"

Grace walked to her car, tossing around the idea of a cruise. It would be fun to spend time with her friends and she needed something to look forward to. *Why couldn't she snap out of it?* She reached inside the neck of her blouse and touched the cross that lay against her skin. And a single tear found its way down the side of her face and landed on her arm. She didn't feel it because she was transported to a memory of when she and Smith got married and went on their honeymoon. There was a breeze blowing against her skin and she would swear later that she could smell Smith's cologne for a moment. But when she told Martha about it later, her friend argued that it must've been the jasmine blooming on the fence behind the restaurant. Whatever it was, Grace had moments when she felt so close to Smith. It made it even tougher to let him go. To start her life over.

She drove home with her thoughts a thousand miles away, and when she walked into the house there was a message blinking on her answering machine. She pushed the button and when she heard a male voice, for a moment her heart skipped a beat. It was Ben Parker, the agent who had informed her of Smith's death. *Wonder what he wants?* He left his phone number and asked her to call him back as soon as she could. She decided to wait until morning. She put on her tennis shoes and jeans and hopped back in the car to drive out to the cemetery. It was going to be another hour or so before the sun set, so she had plenty of time for a short visit.

❧

The winding drive that led into the cemetery was lined with flowers and tall shrubs. There were quite a few cars parked in the lot when Grace pulled up. She got out and walked the short distance uphill to Smith's gravesite. Just as she walked up, Ben Parker was about to walk away. Grace saw him first and her first instinct was to try to hide but there was really no place to go. Ben had his head down like he was thinking; he was standing at the grave wiping his eyes. She watched him for a moment, thinking how tall he was, just like Smith. His hair was light brown and he had broad strong shoulders. He could have been Smith's brother from the back. But when he turned around, his eyes gave him away. His eyes were brown and very gentle but they spoke of things he'd seen and done that could never be said aloud to anyone.

"I'm sorry, Ben. Didn't mean to walk up on you. I just never dreamed anyone else came here."

Ben looked startled. "I had no idea you were standing there, Grace. How are you?" He came towards her and put out his hand.

Grace felt the strong grip of his handshake and smiled shyly. "I'm doing as well as can be expected. Lost my parents early in my life. Smith was my only family left. And now he's gone. It's been tougher than I would have ever imagined finding my way back to some sort of life."

"I can't imagine, Grace. He was my best friend and it's been very difficult for me. How often do you come here, if you don't mind my asking?"

Grace paused for a minute. "I come every day unless something keeps me from it."

Ben was impressed. But that meant she really was having a tough time. "How do you feel, Grace, being here? Is it a comfort, or is it upsetting to you?"

"At first it nearly killed me. Because his body isn't here, I really didn't feel I had closure. But now I've learned to just sit here and talk to Smith and let that be enough. There's no point in wishing anything was different because nothing's going to change."

"No, I can see that. Acceptance is best under these circumstances."

"Did I see you limping? How did you injure your leg?"

"Oh, just a work related injury. Nothing serious. Well, I guess I need to let you have your time here; sorry if it was upsetting for you to find me here. I've come a few times; it's a miracle we haven't run into each other before."

"It sure is, since I come nearly every day. Well, take care of yourself Ben. I know you must've cared a lot for Smith to call him your best friend."

"I learned so much from that man. He was highly respected. Say, I left you a message on your answering machine. Did you get it?"

"As a matter of fact, I did. Was going to call you tomorrow. What's up?"

Ben swallowed hard and brushed some dirt off his jeans. "I was wondering if you wanted to have dinner some night. Not a date or anything, just dinner with a friend."

Grace was taken aback by his invitation. It felt odd to be asked out to dinner and she wasn't really ready to date. He was probably trying to be nice and she appreciated it, but . . .

"I can tell you are hesitating and that's okay. I just thought it might feel good to get out and have dinner and talk. If you ever need anything, Grace, please let me know. I'll try again soon. Who knows? You may just change your mind."

Grace appreciated his letting her off the hook. She really didn't want to hurt his feelings because she could sense he missed Smith, too. But she just wasn't ready to sit at a table with another man just yet. She smiled and watched him walk away, limping. He was a nice man and must have been good company to Smith. She sat down on the bench next to the grave and relaxed, thinking about her day and finding Ben here when she walked up. *Odd how things happen in life.* The very person who had brought her the news of Smith's death was asking her out to dinner, standing at her husband's headstone. It was a little eerie but at the same time seemed almost apropos. She remembered that Ben had told her he'd promised Smith he'd watch out for her. Take care of her. So perhaps he would be around in her life from time to time, and that was a comforting thought sitting in the cemetery alone.

You know, Smith. Now the words of that poem are being reversed. Now I'm having to be the more loving one. It's almost like you knew this was going to happen when you wrote that poem. I not only married you, but I married your job. The CIA. They basically made you play Russian roulette with your life.

Grace got up and walked away from the grave feeling a little depressed. Frustrated. What she would give for one more conversation with Smith. Just one.

Ben had not planned on running into Grace at the cemetery. He was certain that it ruined his chances of taking her to dinner for the time being. Now all he could do was wait. That last mission had opened his eyes to how short life really was, and how serious this promise was that he made to Smith. It was a stupid thing for him to do in a way, but Smith would have done the same thing for him under the circumstances. He headed home with emptiness in his heart, missing the camaraderie he'd shared with Smith. He needed to get on with his life and find something to do. As he walked back to his car he turned and looked back at the gravesite where Grace was sitting. The sight of her sitting there grabbed at his gut and an anger rose up that surprised him. *The fragility of the mission, the fact that one thing missed could bring death to whole team, made all covert operations insane. The longer an agent was involved in covert, the blinder he became to the fact that death was imminent. I lost sight of the fact that at any moment any of us could have been killed and left behind. I sure never thought it would be Smith. I thought he was invincible. But I was wrong.*

CHAPTER 16

There was a warm, humid breeze blowing as Grace got out of her car to head in to Summer House. Martha, Celeste, and Maryann were waiting for her at a table near the windows. The restaurant was a refreshing sight with its travertine floors, spacious rooms, drapes that rose high to the ceilings and gathered in puddles on the tiles, music drifting in and out of the rooms, and lovely trees that brought warmth to the whole atmosphere. All the tables were filled and conversation was floating in the air as Grace found her way to the table.

"Hey, beautiful lady! It's so good to see you again." Martha stood and hugged her and whispered into her ear. "I hope you're feeling better. I've missed you!"

"Hey, girls! I'm doing fine and stayin' very busy. It's so good to see you guys again."

"We could do it every week if we could afford it!" Maryann laughed and took a sip of her wine.

The waiter walked up and asked if they were ready to order now that Grace had arrived. They all placed their order and when the waiter left Celeste grabbed Grace's hand. "So what's going on at the school? I know graduation is around the corner now."

"Yes, it's always hard this time of year to pull things together with the students. All they have on their mind is that school is about to end and they have three months of freedom! And the seniors are nowhere. Their concentration is zilch towards the end of school." Grace laughed and took a sip of her wine, pinching off a piece of bread, dipping it in the olive oil, and popping it into her mouth with a smile.

"I can remember how I felt when I was a senior. All we thought about was getting out of school; we had no clue about what was ahead of us with college and finding a direction in our lives," Martha said, raising an eyebrow.

"There's no good way to prepare students for what they're about to face. We do the best we can to help them find direction, but most of them don't have any idea what they want to do with their lives until they have nearly completed their four years of college," Grace remarked.

"Maryann, don't you agree that life is so different than what you imagined it to be when you were eighteen?" Celeste asked.

"Are you kiddin'? I was so naïve it was pathetic! I wish I'd known what I know now. My decisions would have been so different."

"No joke. But the irony of the thing is that we wouldn't have listened had someone tried to tell us what life was all about. Youth has deaf ears to wisdom. When we were young we believed all things, hoped all things, and dared to do things that our parents would have warned us would fail. But sometimes our parents were wrong and we succeeded. So there is a line we have to draw with the youth, because a lot of our warnings to them stem from our own failures and fears. We don't want to kill their enthusiasm for life, and also their dreams," Grace said with gravity.

Everyone was silent for a moment and then they all laughed. "Doesn't take us too long to get into something serious! We always did cut to the chase, didn't we?" Martha laughed and wiped the sauce off her mouth.

"Seriously," Grace said. "You guys are coming to graduation, aren't you? I could use the support. At least stay through the singing, because you are gonna have the surprise of your life."

"Oh, we'll be there, girl. We've been revisiting graduation ever since you took the job at Ross High! It's like ground hog day for us. We keep on graduating!" Maryann laughed.

"Come on, Grace. What's up with the surprise? Tell us what's goin' on!" Celeste finished her bite and sipped the last drop of wine from her glass.

"Well, I'll tell you this much. I've been helping a student who's a junior; Samuel Billings. He's a black student who has really been struggling with his home life and he's been so worried about his mother, who has been very ill. We had no idea the gravity of his situation until recently. I had to get medical help for his mother and they had no way to buy food, so we contacted a local food bank. Everyone has stepped up to the plate and really helped this family get back on their feet. It opened my eyes to other students who might be having issues in their lives that we are oblivious to. All of that affects their grades and their ability to focus and learn. We are meeting with the school board to see what can be done. Free lunches are already being offered, but a lot of these kids have no breakfast before school. Their home lives are less than satisfactory; I know there are limits to what we can do, but we have to try work with these families and help them get stable so that these kids can be free to be kids. Instead they are spending a lot of their time at home worrying about how the family is going to make it."

"Grace, what an amazing thing you are doing! I bet Samuel is so relieved now that it's out in the open. I know he had to be struggling inside, being the man of the family. He felt all the weight of the situation on his shoulders. How's his mother now?"

"Celeste, you would be shocked at the difference it made just getting her medical care. She's a new woman now. We've made sure they have plenty of food and she knows that Samuel isn't so worried about her health. I think she smiled for the first time in a long, long time when she heard he tried out for the choral group that's singing at graduation! And that's all I'm going to tell you! I've already said too much."

They all laughed and raised their glasses to a toast. Martha spoke first. "Here's to a new beginning for Samuel Billings and also for Ross High in changing the lives of their students in a new way."

Celeste spoke next. "Here's to Grace, probably one of the most effective principals in the school system!"

Maryann grabbed her chance. "Here's to a new beginning for Grace. A chance to start over with her life and find her way again."

Everyone drank to the toast and they hugged each other. "Guys, this was great. Only I haven't heard one thing about what you've been doing. What are your plans for the summer?" Grace looked at Celeste and raised her eyebrow in question.

"Steve and I are planning a trip out West this summer. He's always wanted to see the Grand Canyon. It sounds boring to me, but I'm puttin' on a smile for him," Celeste replied.

"Do you really think anything is going on new in my life?" Maryann laughed. "Why, Bob just wants to play golf all the time. That's it. That's all you ever hear me say. Every weekend is spent on that golf course. I'm a golf widow!"

Martha spoke last. "Well, nothin' is new at my house, either. Between hunting and golf, Ken spends lot of time doing what he wants to do. I can't complain, though. He's a good husband and we do take trips from time to time. But I wanted us to get away for a few days, girls. What about our trip to the Bahamas? Anyone interested?"

"Oh, my gosh! I totally forgot we were supposed to nail down this trip tonight!" Grace picked up her purse and pulled out her calendar. "June is open for me. I feel guilty because I haven't been back to the orphanage since Smith died. But I can jump into that in July; maybe I'll feel better about it then. So what do you guys think? Is June good for you?"

They all agreed that June was perfect and Martha decided that they would set the date for the second weekend in June. "I'll make the reservations. I'll need money from all of you to pay for this cruise, so I'll check on prices and departure times and get back with you. How does that sound?"

Everyone stood up and hugged each other. "What a nice evening. Now we have something fun to look forward to. No backing out, now. You hear, Gracie?" Martha looked at Grace and raised her eyebrow again.

"I hear you, Martha."

On her way to the car, Celeste caught up with Grace and tugged at her arm. "Gracie, are you really doing okay? Do you still feel overwhelmed with it all?"

Grace stopped at her car and turned to face Celeste. "I never dreamed it would be this difficult to live without Smith. But it's taking everything I have to make it through each day. I know it has to get easier, but right now life sucks." Grace wiped a tear out of her eye and looked away. "I don't mean to complain, Celeste. But I hope you never have to go through this. I love you guys and I appreciate all you're doing to help me through this. But the void is huge and sometimes it feels like it's going to swallow me up."

Celeste grabbed her and put her arms around her. "Grace, you never complain. We're amazed at how well you've done. But you have to have someone to let it all out with, and we're your friends. We're here for the long haul; the good and the bad. Hey! Don't think for a moment that there won't come a time when I need you this bad. Life happens to all of us, you know?"

Grace nodded and smiled. "Yes it does! I'll be fine. I know I will. Thanks for being here for me. It means the world to me, Celeste. I'll call soon and we'll have lunch or dinner just you and me."

∽

There was a message on her answering machine when she got home. "Hey, Grace! I know you just turned me down for dinner. But I really want to have a talk with you. Would you consider a Saturday lunch? Or we could just go get some coffee somewhere? You could even meet me at Starbucks; what do ya think?"

Grace sat down at her desk and smiled. *This guy just is not going to give it up. And maybe, just maybe, I need to allow myself time to talk to this man who Smith deemed his best friend.* She dialed his number and the phone rang.

"Hello, Grace? Is that you? Wow! Didn't think you'd call me back!"

"Yeah, well. I figured you were just going to keep on trying, so here I am. I love the idea of coffee, but let's meet at the park in town. It's so pretty outside now with all the trees blooming. Is that okay with you?"

"That's perfect. Saturday at 2:00. See you there!"

Grace hung up and walked into the living room and sat down. The house felt so empty all the time. She was tired of having to busy herself or have the television on just to feel normal. Something needed to change in her life, but she wasn't sure what just yet. Oddly, she didn't feel single yet. She looked down at the ring on her finger and grinned. She loved being married to Smith and she wasn't ready to take the ring off yet. She went into the bathroom and looked in the mirror. Her hair had been short for a long time because it was easiest for her. *Maybe I should grow it long again? I need a change big time . . .* She noticed her nails looked bad and she needed a new look everywhere. Maybe this was a good time to change some things in her life.

She grabbed a few magazines and found a few hairstyles she liked. She made a decision to grow her hair longer, buy some new clothes, and get a manicure. She walked around the house and looked for simple things she could change without spending too much money. Something to help her focus on going forward instead of hanging on to what had been.

She filled the tub with hot water and bubbles and climbed in for a long soak. She had lit some candles in the bathroom so there were shadows dancing on the walls. Thirty minutes later, she was relaxed and ready for bed. She clicked on the television to catch a late night show and snuggled down in the covers. Somehow she had to make this work.

She glanced over at the other side of the bed and thought about Smith for a moment. It just didn't seem real that he was gone, but she had to retrain her mind to not think that way. He wasn't coming back home again and somehow she had to accept that. But one more time she allowed herself to think of his face, his lips, how good it felt to be in his arms. He was the strongest man she'd ever known and she thanked God for the years she had with him. She hung on to every memory of Smith, going over the sweet moments between them, until she was so worn out she fell asleep with the television on.

Across the ocean on the other side of the world there was a man who had no name, no home, and no memory of his life. But he hung on to a thread of hope that one morning he would wake up and it all would come back to him. What he wanted to know more than anything was who the woman was in his dreams.

CHAPTER 17

The heat was almost unbearable in Zhob as Smith bent over to put his shoes on. He was helping Dr. Irfan everyday in the clinic, partially as payment for all the care the doctor had given him, but more for allowing him a safe place to stay until his memory returned. It was getting more and more frustrating for him not to be able to remember where he was from and what he was doing in Pakistan. Nothing made sense to him. He was just walking through the clinic door when he heard the doctor call for him.

"Bita! Can you help me with this woman?" The doctor had begun to call him *Bita*—"son" in Urdu— because he couldn't remember his name. "Sure. I'm coming, Dr. Irfan."

"Help me pick her up and put her on the table. She's lost her leg from an explosion. This is going on in the outskirts of the city. People are scared to be out on the streets anymore after 10:00 at night."

"What can we do for her, Doc?"

"We stop the bleeding and I will sew her leg up. She will need to stay here overnight and then we can send her home to heal. Get the bandages for me, and we will wrap the remaining part of her leg. I know it will be hard for you to do, but it is our only way of helping her now."

Smith winced when Dr. Irfan unwrapped the blanket from the woman's leg. She was crying and grabbing at her leg. The doctor cleaned the stump and gave the woman pain shots. She calmed down and moaned, crying out for her husband.

"Now we have calmed her down, we can work on her leg so that it won't get infection. I am glad you are here to help me, Bita. You will get used to watching people suffer. Hand me the myrrh. I'm going to place it in the wound to prevent infection."

Smith nodded and handed him the sterile herb. But he doubted he would ever get used to this. He couldn't understand why there was so much fighting going on but he listened closely to what Dr. Irfan said. He was picking up their language bit by bit and asked so many questions that sometimes it flustered the doctor.

The next few patients were poor and could not afford medical help. They had been led to Dr. Irfan's clinic as a last resort. He was patient with them and taught Smith a lot about diagnosing and treating even the most fragile. Smith learned fast and found that he really enjoyed working around the doctor. He was grateful for his help, but inside he was tormented about his loss of memory. Somewhere he had had a life. He just didn't know what that life was.

His injuries were healing and Dr. Irfan kept reassuring him that at some point things would start to come up to the front of his mind. No one could tell when this would happen, or what would trigger it. Smith had no choice but to wait, so he threw himself into any work that Dr. Irfan gave him, surprising the doctor with his strength and intelligence. His mind was almost photogenic and the doctor took note of his incredible ability to remember the smallest of details.

After putting in a long day at the clinic, Dr. Irfan and Smith headed back to the house, where Mahsa was cooking dinner. "Let's sit down at table and talk, Bita, while we are waiting for dinner. I want to talk to you about things in America."

In a way, Smith hated these conversations because he felt so frustrated. "Okay, Dr. Irfan. But we never get anywhere. I don't know why you keep talking to me about it when nothing ever triggers a memory."

"We have to try, Bita. We do not want years to pass without you remembering anything. So the more we talk about America, and anything I can think of to ask you, the better chance of your memory coming back. I have seen this before and I know. It can work, Bita. Patience is key."

"Well, what are we going to talk about tonight?"

"I want you to sit here and close your eyes. I am going to bring up things about America and I want you picture them in your mind."

"Okay. Go."

"I want you to think about the Statue of Liberty. A grand lady holding a torch standing tall in the harbor of New York. Do you see anything in your mind?"

"Not a thing. Just a blank."

"What about baseball? Did you ever enjoy going to baseball games? Football? Can you remember playing football or coaching a team?"

"I don't remember ever playing football or baseball. Hey! Dr. Irfan. What if I went to America? What if I was able to walk around and see things? That might trigger my memory faster than just us talking about it."

"That is true, Bita. But I have not found safe way to get you home yet. And we don't know anyone to contact in America for you to stay with. We have no connections yet. Besides, what if you were living here? We just don't have enough information to work with yet."

Smith rubbed his face and let his head rest on his arms on the table. He felt so discouraged. *How am I ever going to remember anything?* He got up and reached for a book they had found in Dr. Irfan's clinic that had some photos of America. He sat down and turned the pages slowly, listening to Dr. Irfan describing what he saw. It was like he was looking at pictures of any other country. It didn't feel like home. It was a weird sensation to realize he was totally alone on the earth with no memory of friends or family. He felt so displaced and lonely.

"I can see you are getting depressed, Bita. Don't kill your hopes with your discouragement."

"I'm certainly trying to keep focused on the work at hand, but my mind wants to wander. So I let it sometimes, hoping to remember something, anything that would help bring back who I am."

"We keep on until you have back your life. I can assure you it will return to you."

"I wish I had your certainty. But I sound ungrateful, Dr. Irfan. Forgive me. I will try to have more patience; you've given me a place to stay and food. How will I ever be able to repay you?"

"Food is ready, Irfan. You and Bita wash and come back to table." Mahsa was tired and ready to eat and get dinner over with. She'd been helping at the clinic too, alongside Smith.

"Come, Bita. Let's clean our hands, and eat. It has been long day."

The food sat well in Smith's stomach, but the ache in his heart would not leave. He was learning to love being with Dr. Irfan, as he wasn't a difficult man to be around. But somehow he had to learn to cope better with his emotions and anger at not remembering his past. He had absolutely nothing. A blank slate. It was frightening.

CHAPTER 18

After sending out resumes for months, Ben ended up taking a job at the local police department in the search and rescue division. He had plenty of money saved for retirement but was in no way ready to just retire and sit on his front porch. He was only forty-five years old and had a lot of working years left in him, so he tried to get excited about taking this new position. James Winters was Chief of Police and he really enjoyed meeting him. He was heading in to get assigned to his search and rescue dog and meet his partner Keith Mitchell.

"Mornin', Ben. Please have a seat and we'll let you meet your dog in just a few moments. There are a few things you need to know before you meet Houston, a German shepherd mix. He'll be your right arm and I want you to get to know him from the ground up! He'll eat with you, sleep with you, and learn to trust your every word. If you've never been around a search and rescue dog, this will be a real treat for you. We are excited about your being here with us and hope this turns out to be a good match for you."

Ben stood up and shook the chief's hand and sat back down, eager to meet his dog. Keith Mitchell came into the room and shook his hand and sat down beside him. "Ben, it's great to meet you. We are going to have a great time working together. I hear you used to work for the CIA so I know you are well prepared for this job. I can't wait for you to get to know Houston. He's terrific!" Keith laughed and slapped Ben's back.

"I look forward to working with you, too, Keith! Now let's see this dog you guys keep talking about."

James let the dog in from the back room and Houston came walking in on a leash. James brought him up to Ben and allowed the dog to smell him. Ben took his time before he reached out to pet the dog, stroking his head slowly and talking low to him as he was directed to do. Houston immediately showed an attraction to Ben; he could tell right off that Ben was at ease and soon he was licking his hand and wagging his tail.

James stepped up to Ben and spoke. "Ben, after you feel comfortable with Houston, I want you to take him home with you and spend some time together. We will put you through some classes with Houston that he's already familiar with. Then you will be ready to go out in the field with him on a search and rescue mission. The more you bond with the dog, the better job you both will do. Got it, Ben?"

"I think I understand the situation here. Houston and I are a team and we work as one. I'm familiar with working with a team so this will be an easy transition for me. I love animals; especially dogs, so I look forward to getting to know Houston. He's a beautiful dog."

Keith walked Ben to his car, talking about the dogs and how much they really help in rescue. "You'll love this job, Ben. I know it won't be the same intensity as you are used to, but it is rewarding to find a lost child or adult who's been missing for a few days."

"If you check out Special Ops on the Internet, you'll see the level of training I've had for the last fifteen years. I think this will be an easy transition for me, Keith. I'm so glad we are partners and I can't wait to get started on a rescue. How long will it take before they let us go out?"

Keith laughed. "That all depends on how you and Houston bond. And how quickly you pick up the commands that are needed for this job."

"I get it. Well, I'm headed home now with Houston and we'll see how we do tonight. It'll be nice to have another breathing body in the house besides my own!"

"Have a great time with him, and let me know if you have any problems. Here's all my numbers. I'm available to you 24/7, Ben. Seriously."

"Thanks, Keith. Hopefully I won't need you, but it's nice to have those numbers just in case. Thanks and I'll see you on Monday. I'll have all weekend to get used to Houston, so this should be fun."

Ben put Houston in the car and laid the leash on the seat. Houston sat up tall and strong, looking out of the passenger window. It felt strange to have a dog in the car, but it was something he was going to have to get used to. Houston was pretty much going to be with him until he left the job at the police department, so he had to grasp the fact that he was a proud owner of a rescue dog. He turned to look at Houston and smiled. What a great dog he was! His coloring was beautiful, gray with patches of black on his neck and back. This was going to be a good weekend, and Ben was already anxious to get back to the department and work on those obedience classes. He actually felt excited about his life again, and that was a new feeling after that last covert. Life was looking up.

～

Grace planned to meet Ben at Central Park in the center of town. It was almost 2:00 and the sun was bearing down on her as she sat on the park bench in a pretty light pink floral sundress waiting for him to arrive. The trees were swaying in the breeze and the air smelled of freshly mowed grass. Some kids were playing in the distance and she got caught up in watching them and didn't see Ben walking up the hill with Houston on a leash. She turned her head just as he was approaching the bench and stood up to greet him.

"Hey, Ben! What a great dog you've got there! Who's this?"

Ben hugged her briefly and laughed. "This is Houston. I wanted you to meet him, Grace. He's a search and rescue dog and we're partners now!"

Grace bent down and patted Houston. His tail was wagging and he licked her in the face a few times. She stood up and laughed, wiping her face. "What a beautiful dog. So is this what you wanted to talk about? You've joined up with the local police in search and rescue?"

"Yeah, I was so ready to find something I could sink my teeth into, and that was a tough thing to do after working with the CIA. Everything else seemed to fall short when I compared it to the type of job I had before. But this should be fascinating and also very rewarding. I really look forward to going on a rescue mission with my partner."

They sat down and Houston lay down beside Ben's feet. "What a great day to be outside. It feels good to be out in the fresh air, doesn't it?" He was dressed in khaki shorts and a light blue polo shirt and loafers. He had a baseball cap on with the brim pulled down over his eyes.

"Yes, it does. I forget how pretty this park is. I'm glad we decided to meet here! I need to take the time to come here and just watch the kids play. It's refreshing. I bet Houston would love to run around with them! Would he run off, Ben?"

"No way. He minds better than most kids do. I'm new with this, but they'll put me through some training with him so that I know how to handle situations that we'll come across. Houston here is a pro at it; I'm the new kid on the block."

"Let's walk across the street and get an ice cream cone and sit here and watch the kids." Grace got up and headed across the street to the vendor parked by the curb, with Houston and Ben at her heels.

After they got settled again on the bench, Ben opened up to her about why he wanted to see her today.

"Grace, I really just wanted to spend some time with you away from everything and everyone. Get us both out in the fresh air so that we could talk and be relaxed. I've been goin' through my share of grieving and visiting the cemetery. We were trained to deal with this sort of thing but when it hits home all those classes fade into the background and the pain is the reality. I'm pretty tough and I think you are, too, but this knocked us both down a bit."

Grace was staring off in the distance and didn't answer. But she'd heard every word Ben said. "I just want you to know I'm here for you. Not right up under your feet, but a phone call away. I've taken on this job to keep myself busy and to try to enjoy life again. I always feel better when I'm bein' productive and this job has its own set of challenges. But you are fixin' to be out for the summer and you'll have extra time on your hands to think. I just hope you can find some new way to enjoy your summer and have some fun, too."

"I appreciate your thoughts, Ben. It's gonna be tough for awhile and I'm already thinkin' about what I want to do with my time while I'm off. I've got some ideas that I might share with you at some point but I'm sure I'll find somethin' to do. My three girlfriends will keep me busy and believe me, they won't let me stay down for long!"

Ben stood up and got a ball out of his pocket and unhooked Houston's chain. He threw the ball and Houston went running after it. Grace laughed and grabbed the ball, and threw it out farther into the park. They spent the next thirty minutes walking around the park, playing with Houston and watching the kids playing. Finally Grace looked at her watch. "I guess I'd better go, Ben. This was so nice and I really appreciate your talking to me. I know you're gonna love working with this dog; he's such a gentle soul but I bet he could rise up to the occasion if he had too."

"I have a lot to learn about workin' a rescue dog, but if you want to know the truth, I'm chomping at the bit to do some rescuing. I have him for the whole weekend and then we go to school next week. He'll live, eat, and sleep with me 24/7, Grace."

"Let me know how it goes, Ben. I have graduation on Friday next week. So I'm gonna be quite busy gettin' ready for that with the choir and makin' sure the seniors are ready. Talk about excited! They're unmanageable right now. Might as well be out of school!"

"I'll keep in touch. I enjoyed sittin' here with you and am so glad you got to meet Houston! By the way, you look pretty today!" He smiled at her and winked. "You have a nice evening and call if you need anything."

Grace walked to her car, turning back to see Houston jump into Ben's SUV. What a nice afternoon. Ben is a sweet guy and I can see why Smith liked him. I wish I didn't feel so misplaced all the time; I don't feel single and I don't feel married. It's an odd place to be and I don't like it at all. I guess time will take care of it, but right now my life feels like it's hanging in limbo. I can't plan for the future because I am still living with one foot in the past.

Driving home she thought about Sully and smiled. Maybe one day she'd have a dog around the house. Hopefully it'd be as good a dog as Houston.

CHAPTER 19

Ross High graduation was at 8:00 and Grace was really looking forward to this year's ceremony. Perhaps because of the deep loss she had incurred, this year more than any year she had poured herself into the kids at school, allowing herself to get closer to them, where before she'd held herself back. Pulling the chorus together had been something she could sink her teeth into, and it had turned out better than she'd expected. There was real talent in this group of kids and she could not wait for them to sing.

The auditorium was filling up with parents and friends of the seniors, and there was excitement in the air. Behind the curtain, the choir was getting into position, as they would sing at the beginning of the program. Grace knew that the audience would not be expecting anything special, just the usual graduation songs chosen by the seniors. But this year, Grace had chosen a medley of songs that showcased one student doing a powerful solo. And it was going to bring the house down.

She walked back stage and whispered to the kids. "Guys! Quiet! Now I want you to be crisp and on your best behavior here. The whole town is out there to hear you sing! I know you're excited, and this is a special night for you. But remember how we practiced this medley. Pronounce your words and keep a smile on your face. This is going to be a night you will remember forever."

Brad Henson walked up to Grace and patted her on the shoulder. "Mrs. Sanderson, where do I stand when I sing my partial solo?"

"Remember, Brad—stand to the right of the center mark on the stage. After you are finished, turn and get back in the row you were in. Don't worry if you forget when the time comes for you to sing. No one will know where you're supposed to stand!" She smiled at Brad and turned to face Samuel.

"Sam, I know this is big for you. But don't think for a moment that all the people who are here aren't at a place in their lives where they need to hear what you are singing. They need to hear your voice and your soul. Because that is how you sing, from a place inside yourself where all the things you've been through in your life come through to a single pure note. It's obvious you were born to sing, and your voice will lighten up some hearts here tonight. Music is life changing, and we are about to change some lives tonight."

Samuel hugged Grace and walked back to his place in the chorus. He was sweaty and nervous, but more excited than he'd ever been in his life. Ever since he'd opened up to Grace his life had taken a turn for the better. And he could actually see light ahead. That was new for him. Real new. And he kind of liked the change from darkness to light. It had a nice ring to it. A single pure note he could hear in his sleep and in his waking. And that note was what he was going to sing tonight.

The hands of the clock went straight up 8:00 and the curtain opened up slowly to a quieting audience. You could hear a few people talking low but then it went silent as Grace walked up to the stage. She turned to the audience and smiled, slowly turning around to her kids who were standing with their heads down. The music started and they began to sing "Amazing Grace" in a low hum. It built and built until Brad walked out and started singing his solo. The audience did not move a muscle as the song moved from "Amazing Grace" to "God Bless America." Anna took over and sang a short solo as the music moved into a lovely version of "Somewhere Over The Rainbow." One of the students had a guitar and they moved to the front of the stage and played while Courtney sang in a lilting voice and James moved in and sang harmony. Everyone clapped hard and then quieted back down, waiting for the finish.

Samuel moved to the front and took the microphone while all the rest of the kids moved in closer to him, and he began singing in his powerful voice, letting the words roll out of his lungs in a way Grace had never heard before:

"When I am down and oh, my soul so weary, when troubles come, and my heart burdened be; then I am still and wait here in the silence, until you come and sit a while with me."

There wasn't a dry eye in the room as Samuel let the words become life. His voice was so warm and so rich that it brought people to their feet. No one expected this magnificent voice to come out of a young man who'd struggled so hard to stay in school. His teachers were astounded by his presence on stage and nodded to each other, knowing now that there was more to Samuel than they'd thought.

Grace's knees were weak as she looked out over the auditorium, spotting Martha, Maryanne, and Celeste in the back row. She was thankful they'd come to support her, but mostly, she was glad they would hear what these kids were capable of.

Samuel sang that last line of the song: "You raise me up to more than I can be."

The room exploded with applause and whistles. Samuel was overcome by the response to his singing and bowed his head, tears streaming down his face. The whole chorus clapped, hugging each other and patting Samuel on the back. Grace walked up to the microphone, clearing her throat. She was so full of emotion that she could barely get any words out. But graduation had just begun and she had the rest of the ceremony to get through.

"I know you all stand with me in awe of what these kids were able to do in two weeks of hard practice. I've never seen such talent in all my years of teaching and I think this performance was a wonderful way of ushering the seniors into a new segment of their lives. If you'll take your seats, we'll begin the graduation ceremonies as the students come up to receive their diplomas. Beth Simpson is the valedictorian of the senior class. Please come up, Beth, and share your thoughts with your classmates."

༄

Graduation ended on a grand note with all the seniors throwing their caps up in the air and shouting. For the seniors, their time at Ross High was over a week ago, and the ceremony was merely something they had to get through before they could celebrate. But they would talk about the music for years to come, and one particular student who rocked their world for one night, Samuel Billings. A young man who was basically unknown until he stood up and held a microphone in front of his peers.

Unknown to Grace, Ben Parker was sitting on the last row of the auditorium with one of his fellow officers in search and rescue, Matthew Henson, Brad's father. He had asked Ben to come and hear his son sing. When Samuel Billings opened up his mouth and sang, Ben nearly came out of his seat. He'd never heard a voice like that. When all the kids had received their diplomas and Grace was headed out the door, Ben pushed through the crowd to find her.

"Grace! Grace! I just wanted to congratulate you on the singing tonight! It was magnificent!" He was smiling so big Grace had to laugh.

"Oh thank you, Ben! What brought you here tonight?" Grace was surprised to see his face in the crowd.

"Brad's father is a new friend of mine at the police department. and he asked me to come tonight to hear his son sing. I'm so glad I decided to go. I really enjoyed that performance by Samuel. He's something else. I know you're proud of him."

"'Proud' does not begin to cover how I feel about Sam. But I do appreciate your comments. . I'm looking forward to this new position on the force and hope I can do a good job for the chief. So, we gonna have dinner sometime soon? I really want to see you again, Grace. What do you say?"

Grace was surprised at his invitation riding on the tail of his praise for Samuel. "Well, you've caught me off guard, Ben! I guess we can plan dinner soon. When were you thinking about?"

Ben laughed and gave her a warm hug. "Guess it wasn't quite fair of me to ask you right now, with your emotions all high from this celebration. But a man has to grab any chance he can! Why not tomorrow night? If we put if off too long it'll never happen."

Grace thought a moment and shook her head. "Okay, I give. Let's eat somewhere casual where we can talk. You have my number. Give me a call and let me know when and where. And thanks again for your comments about tonight. That means a lot coming from you. I know you're aware of how much I miss Smith these days. He would've loved to have been here tonight."

Ben looked down. *Smith. You'll never know how heartbroken Grace is over your death.* "I do understand, Grace. You've been extremely brave through this time. I'll give you a call tomorrow morning. By the way, you look lovely tonight. I'm proud of you, Grace."

Grace blushed and turned to go. When she looked back, Ben was lost in the crowd of people trying to find their cars in the parking lot. *What a wonderful night it's been.* Just as she was about to head to her car, Samuel Billings grabbed her arm. "Mrs. Sanderson. Just wanted to say 'thank you' for bein' so good to me these days. I hope I did you proud tonight."

"You couldn't have sung it any better, Sam. I'm so proud of you I could burst!"

"Aw, shoot. I tried. That's all I can say. I tried. But it's the best night of my life, Mrs. Sanderson. The best night."

Grace reached out and grabbed Samuel and hugged him. She pulled away and looked him straight in the eyes. "Samuel, I want you to listen to me. If you were my son, I couldn't be more proud of you than I am right now. You amazed me. You amazed the whole room full of people. And we will never forget this night as long as we live. I have high expectations of you now, Sam. So look out. Things are going to change for you, and it will be tough sometimes. But you'll have this night to look back on to steady your course. Remember that, will you? This is the beginning of your journey upward. And I'm grateful to have been here at the beginning; I only hope I'll be around to see where you end up!"

Samuel had a big grin on his face when he looked back at her. But in the darkness of the parking lot she didn't miss the lone tear that found its way down his black shiny face. She reached up and wiped it off and turned and headed to her car. If he'd been younger she would have been tempted to take him home and raise him. But he had a mother waiting for him at home, and that mother needed him so much more than she did. He was a good son and he had the makings of something rare these days. A hero. Yes, he had a hero's heart.

CHAPTER 20

There was something about a dealership that turned a woman off. As soon as Grace got out of her car and started down one row of cars, four salesmen came out of the front door and walked towards her. One of the men made it to her first, introducing himself as Frank Jones and asked if she needed help. He had his toothpaste smile on and a clean crisp shirt tucked in too tight. His hair was slicked back and he smelled like he'd bathed in his cologne. Grace stifled a laugh and introduced herself.

"Good morning Frank, I'm Grace Sanderson. I'm looking for a new car this morning and I would love to just look around for a few minutes."

Frank was a car salesman to the bone. "I'd be more than happy to show you around, Grace. We just got a new shipment in; what kind of car are you looking for?"

Grace spotted a white Z4 BMW hardtop convertible and a grin crossed her face briefly. "Uh, how much is that white car across the lot there?"

Frank turned to look in the direction she was pointing and ran his hand over his greasy hair. "We just got that car in. It's a newly designed BMW Z4 hardtop. Let's go take a look at it." He took her arm and guided her over to the car. "So you're looking for a sports car, are you?"

"Actually, I wanted something sporty, but didn't know exactly what was available. This was a spur of the moment idea to go car shopping this morning. I really haven't given it much thought, to tell you the truth."

"Sometimes that's the best way to shop for a car. You'll know it when you see it."

Grace looked at the car and asked if she could sit in the driver's seat. He opened the door and let her squeeze into the front seat. The smell of a new car weakened her. This would be the first new car she'd ever bought by herself, and she wanted to make the right decision. "Can I take it for a quick spin, Frank?"

He smiled and ran to get a dealer tag and told her to take her time. "Drive it around the block a time or two and see what you think. It drives like a dream."

Grace didn't need any encouragement on how this car drove. She eyed this car in commercials and now that she was sitting in one, she really loved it. It fit her like a glove. For a few minutes she actually felt happy; she was still aware of the sadness hanging in the back of her mind. *Smith would have died to see me in this car.* She rolled the window down and let the wind blow her blonde hair, taking a deep breath of the fresh air. The car drove like a dream, just like Frank said. She pulled onto the freeway and floored the car; it flew like a bird and was so easy to drive. She took the next exit off and pulled back into the dealership. Frank was waiting by the front door, watching her in the car. He could tell she was loving the ride.

"Hey, Grace. How'd it ride?"

"You don't even have to ask that. You said it when I pulled off. It drives like a dream. Fast. Good gosh, it's fast. I don't really need a fast car, but it's definitely a woman's car. Don't you agree?"

Frank laughed. He didn't tell her he owned one himself. "You look lovely in this car, for sure. So what do you want to do, Grace? Need to look some more or is this the one for you?"

"I think this is it. When I spotted it across the lot I knew it was the one. So let's go talk numbers. That will be the clincher." They walked into the dealership and Frank led her into his office.

"Now Frank, I don't want play any games here. I've done my homework and I know what my car's worth. With my trade-in, give me the bottom line."

Frank grinned and shook his head. This woman looked frail but that was deceiving. She was tough as nails. He did some figuring and passed her a paper with a figure on it and looked her square in the eyes.

Grace looked at the figure and shook her head. "You've got to do better than that, Frank. I know you can."

Frank smiled but sweat was forming on his brow. He needed this sale. He left and headed to his manager's office for another figure. Grace sat and waited patiently, hoping the next figure would meet her budget.

Frank walked in and slowly laid another figure down in front of her. She looked at it and smiled. Frank thought he had her, but she stood up and grabbed her purse. "Frank, you're not serious enough yet. You have my number. Call me when you are ready to sell me that car."

Frank hesitated for a moment and then said, "Hold on, Grace. Let me see what I can do. There's no point in you leaving and having to come back."

Frank was gone for fifteen minutes. When he came back, he sat down in his chair and looked at Grace with a solemn face. "This is the lowest number I can give you. All kidding aside. I hope it's something that you are comfortable with, because that car is definitely you."

Grace looked at the amount he had written on a piece of paper and sat back in her chair. "Now we have a deal." Frank blew out a sigh of relief and handed her a stack of papers. She signed over the title of her car, signed all the other paperwork, accepted the extended warranty, wrote out a check for the balance, and walked outside and climbed into her new car. It was one of the most exciting days of her life and went a long way in helping her start a new life. As she drove out of the dealership in her new white Z4, she looked back at her old Tahoe and remembered the years she and Smith had spent hauling kids around from the orphanage. It was time to move forward and she'd made huge steps today. But it still hurt deep inside. God only knew how she didn't want to let go.

CHAPTER 21

In the dead of night Dr. Irfan was awakened by shots being fired right outside his window. Without hesitation, he jumped out of bed, grabbed his gun, yelled to Mahsa to take cover, and headed to Smith's room. He knew without a doubt that the terrorists were after the American. Smith was in a deep sleep but roused when he felt the doctor shaking him. "Bita! Bita! You must wake. We have to hide you in the floor of our house. Remember the place I showed you?"

Yawning, Smith grabbed his pants and shirt and stumbled towards a door in the floor in the living room. It was a cellar that they stored their vegetables in, along with some medications that needed to stay in a dark cool place. Mahsa handed him some water and fruit and closed the door quickly. They covered the door with a rug and put a table on top of the rug. They headed back to their room and lay down in the bed shivering, even though it was one of the hottest nights they'd ever had.

Smith could hear Irfan talking to Mahsa through the floor above, and he heard her answer in Urdu, though he only knew a few words of the language. "Irfan, I told you this was dangerous for us. Our family is at risk for this stranger you have taken in. Do you see that now?"

"How can you sound so cold, Mahsa? He is helping us in the clinic now. He is healing fast. One day soon he will come back to his memory and we will have to let him go his own way. You have to trust me, Mahsa. I know it is frightening for you, but we will be safe. You will see. If he is from America, we must believe someone might try to find him. If he was living here, then he will have to find his way."

Shots rang out in the night but it sounded like they were moving away from the house. "Remember when we hid the children from that orphanage here several nights? The terrorists were targeting the orphanage because they thought Americans were hiding there. The children were so frightened underneath our floor in the dark."

As Smith listened to their conversation something was coming back to him in the dark of the cellar. Something about an orphanage, but he couldn't quite bring back the memory. A picture of an orphanage came into his mind for a split second and left. *What did that mean? Is it from my past?* He tried hard to piece something together; to put meaning into what he saw in his mind. But it left as quickly as it came, and he was left with a strange feeling.

The shooting faded away and Irfan moved the table and rug away. He opened the door and motioned Smith to come out. He was sweating and tired, but he was also shaken inside from the short vision of that orphanage. "Dr. Irfan. You spoke of an orphanage. The children you hid here not too long ago. I had a flashback, I think. I'm not certain, but I think a memory was there of an orphanage in my past. How can I be sure it was real?"

"Don't struggle with it, Bita. Just let it come when it chooses. The more you try to chase it, the farther away it will go. So relax and sleep. We are safe for a time. I am certain they will return to see if you are here. Rumors are running through the village and even if they are not sure it is true, they will turn every stone to find you."

Smith lay down on his bed, sweating and worn out with trying to remember. He was more afraid of not having his memory return than he was the terrorists. He closed his eyes and drifted off into a fitful sleep.

It was not long before he was seeing the orphanage in his dreams, and he was building something. He just couldn't see what. In his dream he was struggling to see, but he was blinded by the fog. He woke up with the covers wrapped around his legs and he got up to get a drink of water. When he lay down, he felt lonely.

It was not the first time the realization hit him that he was in a foreign country with no idea how he had gotten there or who he was, but the training Smith had received all those years in the CIA had given him an incredible ability to endure. But one fact remained that had stood the test of time. Everyone has a breaking point. Even Smith.

CHAPTER 22

The moon was peeping through the clouds before the sun had rested its elbows on the horizon, and there was a nice breeze blowing as Grace pulled up to The Sierra Club to meet Ben for dinner. Her hair was growing slowly and she had been able to pull it up off her neck in a clasp for the evening. She wore a pretty soft floral dress that came to her ankles and new sandals that were covered in crystals. Her nails were painted and she actually felt pretty for the first time in a long time. All the stress that she'd been under had taken a toll on her appearance, but over time the worry lines had softened and she was feeling stronger inside. She was nervous about dinner with Ben because for the first time since they'd met, which wasn't under the best circumstances, she could feel a little stronger interest coming from him. She saw him as her body-guard in a way, someone she could always call if anything went wrong. Her mind was nowhere near ready to wrap around the idea of dating, so she was rationalizing this night as a chance to get together and just catch up on things.

Her life was full and she was happy about the way things were pro-gressing at Ross. Her next move would be to tackle working in the orphanage again without Smith being around. That was going to be a tough one, but it still had to be done. She'd spent years with the direc-tor of the orphanage, Ted Mullin, and that was where her heart was. It would be difficult at best to face the kids and or even walk on the grounds because Smith had played a huge role in the fund raising and construction of new dorms for the kids. She'd made up her mind that when she returned from the cruise with her friends, she'd make a call and set up a meeting with Ted to see how things were going.

As she walked into the restaurant she immediately spotted Ben at a table on the side of the room near the windows. It was a lovely place with huge plate glass windows looking out over a large lake. There were lights around the lake and a walking path with seats. A long pier stretched out into the water where people could fish for free, and there were always a number of men and children with fishing poles laughing and having fun. Ben stood up as soon as he saw her and escorted her to her seat. She reached for her chair but he pulled it out for her and made sure she was seated before he sat down.

"Don't you look lovely tonight! It's good to see you, Grace."

Grace blushed but managed to sit down gracefully. "Thanks, Ben. Just wanted to dress up for some reason. I don't get out much and it felt good to be going somewhere nice."

"Well, I have to say how grateful I am that you would even consider having dinner with me with the schedule you've been keeping at school. I thought it would give us a chance to talk without being interrupted; I really want to get to know you better."

"I'm happy to get to know you, Ben, because I know Smith must have considered you a wonderful friend. You knew Smith in a different way than I did, so it'll be interesting to hear some of your stories. I realize because of your job that you're limited in what you can share." She paused and looked around the room. "What a lovely place to have dinner. I don't think I've ever been here before."

"It looked like a quiet place to eat, and I love this window that looks out on the lake. Did you see the geese lined up on the edge of the water?"

"Yeah, I did. Adorable. I . . ."

The waiter came up to the table and interrupted their conversation, asking them for their drink orders. He handed them a menu and left quietly, and Grace spent the next few minutes checking out the entrees. Her heart was beating faster than usual and she could feel Ben staring at her. She raised her eyes once to see if it was true, but he had his head down reading the menu. She laughed at herself and tried to decide what she wanted to eat. The waiter returned and they both ordered, and Grace took a long sip of red wine and watched the children on the pier.

"Ben, could you believe how fantastic Samuel Billings sang last night? I'm still not over the emotion of the whole evening."

"It was awesome, Grace. You did a terrific job with those kids. There's a lot of talent in that school; too bad they can't sing more often for the public."

"Next year I want to have a chorus at Ross. That way the kids could perform on a regular basis and it would give them something to do in the afternoons instead of getting into trouble. Music is big for kids, as you probably know."

"It was for me as a young man, but I think it's almost an obsession for kids now. With YouTube and iPods, and ITunes, I think music has taken the forefront in technology, vying for their time over reading or homework. I'm not sure it's good because it can consume too much of their time, but what does a parent do to control it?"

Grace laughed. "A lot of parents are having that same issue in their own lives! It's hard to put a limit on the amount of time one spends on the computer, iPod, iPhone, iPad, whatever. Nothing replaces getting outside and experiencing activities with your children. But a lot of families don't spend much time together anymore."

Ben nodded as the waiter brought their food to the table. They both ate quietly for a few minutes before Ben spoke.

"Grace, I want to apologize for the way I had to tell you about Smith. The look on your face that day still haunts me now, and even though it was the policy of the CIA for me to handle it in that manner, I wish I could've done it in a gentler way. I guess there's no good way to tell someone their husband isn't alive, but it came as such a shock to you."

"No words can explain the feelings I had when you were standing there talking. I was angry at you, very angry. But inside, I did know that this might happen. So even though I thought I was prepared, I really couldn't have been ready to hear what you had to tell me." Grace reached out and touched his arm. "Ben, don't let that eat at you! I don't blame you anymore."

"I felt your anger and extreme sorrow and that's why I risked my position to walk back to your door and hug you and let you know I loved Smith, too."

"I know you only saw Smith during covert operations, but how close were you with him?"

"We were as close as team members can get under those circumstances. We learned out of necessity to trust each other explicitly and to almost know what the other one was thinking way before words were spoken. The intensity of the work and the high risk involved causes a team to become tight and that's the only way it can work. There can be no loose ends. Obviously, accidents happen, but when they do, usually a life is lost. There are no small errors during covert operations. I still can't believe Smith is gone and there isn't a day go by that I don't think of him. I want you to know that."

"Because he was gone a lot, I did adjust to living without him for a time. But nothing could get me ready for life without Smith permanently. His spirit's gone from the house and that's huge for me. I have no other family so he was my family. He was my everything." Grace caught a tear before it dripped down her face.

"You're a very strong, brave woman, Grace. And I know if Smith were alive today he would be so proud of you and how you've handled all of this." He looked at Grace and their eyes locked for a second.

"On a lighter note, I bought a car this morning!" Grace smiled slyly.

"You what? Awesome! What kind of car did you get?"

"A BMW Z4 white convertible."

"Well, that's a great car. How does it drive?"

"You know without asking that it's a smooth ride. Fast. But I needed a change, and I'm trying to let go of some things that might keep me in the past, ya know? It's completely out of character for me to buy a convertible, but you know what? It feels great!"

"You'll have to take me for a ride soon and we'll go get some ice cream! I want to feel how it drives on the highway."

"I'd love to. I'll have to let you drive it, because it's got a lot of power. You'll enjoy the ride."

౿

They kept the conversation light for the rest of the meal and when they were walking to the car Ben suggested that they walk out on the pier for a second to see the moon on the water. Grace agreed and followed Ben to the pier. Most of the people had left so there were only a few couples standing on the pier looking at the water. Ben took her arm and led her to the end of the pier and they rested their arms on the railing and just inhaled the warm breeze.

Ben turned to her and smiled. He brushed some hair away from her face and reached out to hug her. She stepped back instinctively but he moved forward and took her in his arms. She gave in for a minute and just allowed herself to be held. He didn't force anything, but he wanted her to know he cared.

"All of us need a hug from time to time, Grace. And I've wanted to hug you again so badly. Please forgive me if this caught you off guard. But you're a very special person and I feel sort of close to you in an odd way. Like there's a connection between us because we both loved Smith."

Grace stepped away from Ben and turned to look at the moon. Her heart was racing and she felt so nervous inside. "Ben, you know I'm not ready to move into a relationship with anyone yet. But I do treasure your friendship and want us to be close. Just give me time, will you? It feels good to be close to you but I'm mixed up inside. I do appreciate your caring about my feelings, but I think I need more time."

Ben nodded and stepped back a little. "I understand, Grace. I wouldn't push you for anything in the world."

"I'm planning to go on a short cruise in June with my three girl-friends. When I get back, I'll give you a call and we'll take the car out for a spin. How does that sound?"

"I love it. You'll have a great time on the cruise and I'll be looking forward to hearing all about it. Maybe sometime I can meet your girl-friends; I don't know that many people around here. We'll talk about it more after you get back. Thanks for a lovely evening, Grace. I hope you enjoyed it, too."

"I have, Ben. It's been nice to get out and relax and have good conversation with someone. You've been so kind to me. Understand that my hesitation in developing a deeper relationship with you just yet has nothing to do with my feelings for you. I'm just not ready. I do enjoy talking to you and you make me laugh. So thank you so much or this wonderful evening!"

Ben walked her to her car and said goodnight, hoping he hadn't made a mistake by hugging her. This was really the first time he realized he might be attracted to Grace on a different level than just protecting her. He decided to guard his emotions for now and not push things. He had a new job to put himself into and that was going to take up a lot of his time. But it sure was nice to spend an evening with a pretty woman like Grace, as it'd been a long time since he'd done that. She was so warm and the perfume she wore smelled heavenly. He walked back to his car whistling, knowing that if Smith were watching he would be smiling. He would remain a gentleman when it came to Grace; no matter how much he might want to get closer to her, he couldn't let that get in the way of his promise to Smith. If she weren't so beautiful it would be a lot easier.

❧

Grace climbed into bed and turned out the light, but sleep seemed elusive to her. She clicked the light on, went into the kitchen and made some decaf coffee, and headed back to the bedroom. She clicked on the television and sat up in bed, sipping her coffee and reminiscing about her evening with Ben. Subconsciously rubbing on the wedding ring on her finger, she smiled ,remembering how she had stared at Ben for a few minutes, studying his face. He was handsome and strong, but he also had a kindness in his eyes. It was that kindness that Grace really admired and appreciated and she wondered if Smith had seen it. Men see different things in people and she knew they were under extreme conditions during an operation.

Once she had also caught herself looking at his hands; they were wide and strong and clean. She had a hard time imagining herself with another man, but if she were honest, Ben was growing on her. He had been persistent at a distance, always there, always smiling. It had to have been tough duty to walk up to her door and tell her about his best friend. He had done a pretty darn good job of keeping a straight face, absolutely no emotion showing at all. She had been so angry at him for sounding so cold. So direct. But when he had walked back up to the door and hugged her and she heard a slight crack in his voice, she knew then that there was more to the story than she'd heard.

She sat the cup down and turned off the television, lying down on her side. Her hand instinctively pressed across Smith's pillow. It was so cool and empty. He was gone forever, and all she was left with were memories of a once-in-a-lifetime love and his best friend, Ben Parker, to watch over her. As she lay there with a slight smile on her face, thinking of Smith, it occurred to her that Smith might have handpicked Ben to be around her after his death. Maybe he knew Ben would love her one day. Or that she might even fall in love with Ben herself. That was an interesting thought as she drifted off to sleep, wanting to meet Smith in her dreams so that she could ask him a million questions. In her dreams, when she did see Smith, it seemed he was trying to tell her something, but she never could figure out exactly what that was.

❧

Across town, Ben Parker was struggling to fall asleep. His mind was running at the speed of light, remembering every covert operation he'd been on with Smith. The laughter, the sweat, the smell of fear, and the sound of gunfire pounding in his head. But he also recalled the day when the discussion of mailing the package came up. He'd told Smith it wasn't a good idea, because if he did die, Grace's emotions would skyrocket. A package coming in the mail would be too raw. Like he was talking to her from the grave. But Smith insisted; said he'd already told her all about it. She was expecting it if he didn't come home. So Ben did as he was told and mailed the package to Grace. But it ripped his guts out the day he had to drive up her driveway and tell her Smith was gone. Her face had contorted into a cry for a nanosecond but there was no sound. She had been deep in shock and all alone. He went against policy to walk back up to her door and show the emotion he showed her, but he couldn't have lived another day without telling her he had loved Smith, too. She was so fragile and so beautiful. Yet he was amazed at how strong she was. Tonight he had touched her hand accidently and it was so soft it was like touching a feather. He dared not allow his mind to wander down that road of falling in love at first sight. But every fiber in him was screaming for just one chance to get to know Grace. He would hold back. He was incredibly disciplined in his life. He had to be. He was trained to not listen to any desires in his body or mind. But when he was alone and could not sleep, like tonight, he allowed his mind to think what if.

Smith knew him like the back of his own hand. He knew how he was made and every desire he'd ever had. He knew his humor, his likes, and dislikes. To the bone. So that meant Smith knew he would probably fall in love with Grace. Maybe that was why he asked him to watch over her. *Pretty sly, Smith. But you failed to realize how strong her love was for you. That she just might hold out until she died, before she would allow herself to love another man.*

Ben yawned, turned over, and finally gave up the fight, not knowing that his light went out at the same exact second as Grace's.

CHAPTER 23

The cruise ship was docked in Miami, and passengers were boarding, excited about the trip to the Bahamas. It was a sunny, cloudless day, with the sky a pastel blue. Grace had packed nearly everything she owned because she couldn't decide what she would need. She wore a white sundress with a large-brimmed sunhat on and white sandals. Her hair was blowing in the wind and curling up in the humidity. She squinted through her sunglasses and saw Martha coming up the ramp. She waved and caught Martha's eye.

"Hey, lady! Aren't you lovely! It's so good to see you! Aren't you excited? We're finally getting away, Grace."

Grace hugged Martha and threw her head back and laughed. "Oh, my gosh. I didn't realize how badly I needed this. You have no idea how good it feels to just get away from it all."

Martha nodded her head in total agreement. "I'm so with you on that, girl. Ken and I needed a break from each other. Could it be a prettier day? I'm in heaven!"

Celeste ran up the plank and spotted her two friends talking non-stop. "Hey, guys. You seen Maryann yet? This is a great ship! It's so huge when you actually get aboard."

Martha smiled. "Told you this was the best one around! Maryann's always late. But this time she better get here, 'cause they're not gonna wait on her for long."

They all laughed and looked out past the ramp, trying to spot their friend. Celeste saw Maryann in the distance running, pulling her luggage and holding on to her hat. A light wind had kicked up and was about to blow her hat off. She hurried up the ramp and stopped, breathing hard, when she reached her friends. "Good heavens! I nearly didn't make it! My car had a flat tire this morning, of all things. Can you believe that? I asked Bob to check my car out last week, and he totally forgot, because his head is stuck down in his golf bag most of the time!"

The girls left their luggage to be loaded and headed to the main deck. It was an unspoken agreement that they would not discuss work or anything that caused them stress. This was their time together to just relax and have fun. That is, if they could remember how. They plopped down in luxurious lounge chairs and got ready for departure. Grace was nervous as this was her first cruise, but Martha quickly stepped in to calm her down. She was the pro.

"Now, Grace, don't start getting nervous now! This is a trip we'll remember for the rest of our lives. Just sit here and relax, feel the sun on your face, and enjoy being with your friends. You're safe and sound in the cabin. Okay?"

"I know, I know. I have to admit it does feel nice being aboard such a large ship. Can we order something to eat and drink?"

As though he had heard them, a handsome waiter walked up and asked for their order. The girls were delighted and sipped on strawberry daiquiris and nibbled on snacks that were served. Suddenly they felt spoiled.

The ship pulled away from the dock and they settled in for a week of relaxation and some of the best conversation they'd had in years. Uninterrupted by phone calls and husbands. A slumber party that would last four days. The food would be gourmet and unending. The restaurants were open 24/7 to the guests, so Maryann and Celeste would make sure there was something to eat all day long. The sun was warm and they talked nonstop, eating, laughing, and enjoying the view. Five hours later they pulled in to port in the Bahamas. Their reservations were at Old Bahama Bay Resort, and they had reserved a two-bedroom suite facing the ocean, which was quite expensive except for the fact that Martha found a deal they couldn't refuse.

They walked into the hotel, checked in, and headed to their room. Inside the suite, the rooms were spacious with marble bathrooms, Jacuzzi tubs, granite sinks, and thick towels. The balcony was panoramic and the view was breathtaking. Grace was overwhelmed at how lovely everything was.

"Man, I feel like I'm at the Taj Mahal! Could those towels be any thicker? And what a view! Good thing you caught that four-day cruise special, Martha! No telling what this would've cost us if we hadn't gotten that special deal!"

"Don't worry about the money now, Grace. It's worth every penny just to have this view. Let's get our swimming suits on and sit outside for a bit, and have a drink of wine. Does that sound good to everyone?" Martha opened up the French sliding doors and took in the fresh breeze blowing off the water.

Celeste was already in her suit and headed out to grab a lounge chair. It had a thick cushioned seat that she sank deep into. She stretched hard and yawned. "I don't know about you guys, but I could sleep out here. This is wonderful!"

Maryann followed suit and plopped down in a chair. "If only Bob could see me now!"

Grace was just getting settled in her chair, balancing a glass of wine and trying to grab a few grapes. The refrigerator was fully stocked with foods that Martha had requested for them; mostly light snacks that were fairly healthy. That was only to make up for all the wine or desserts they ate while they were there.

"Okay, Gracie-girl. Let's hear about the date with Mr. Ben Parker. You're being way too quiet about this guy. Tell us the scoop." Celeste raised her eyebrow and smiled slyly.

"There's really nothing to tell, really." Grace smiled and took a long sip of wine. "We went out to dinner and talked about absolutely nothing, and then I went home. It was a nice, quiet evening and nothing more. You already know I'm not ready to get interested in anyone yet, so don't give me that eyebrow look, Celeste."

"Well, we just want to keep up with things, ya know. Do you think he's cute, Grace?"

Maryann joined in. "Yeah, Grace. Is he good lookin'?"

"He's handsome enough, but I really don't think of him in that way. He promised Smith to look after me and I don't believe he sees me as girlfriend material!"

"Oh, Grace, you are so naïve. What man in his right mind wouldn't see you as girlfriend material? Huh?" Martha said, smiling.

"Hey, he knows more than anyone how hard this has been on me. I'm grateful he's not trying to take advantage of the situation. He has called a few times trying to get together with me, but when we finally made a dinner date, he was a perfect gentleman." She paused and looked at them staring at her, waiting for more. "Now, I'm not saying I don't think he's nice. Or cute. But I'm not sitting around wanting him to call, ya know? I enjoyed the time we shared but I'm okay right now being alone. I need this time to heal."

"Well, the glimpse I had of him on graduation night looked pretty good to me!" Celeste laughed and poked her elbow at Grace.

"How did you know that was him?"

"I saw you guys talking in the parking lot, so I figured it was him. He's pretty darn good lookin' if you ask me."

Martha laughed and ate some crackers and cheese. "I don't know about you guys, but I'm ready to hit the hay. How about you, Maryann? You tired?"

"Yep. We've eaten so much all day long that I'm not really hungry for a heavy supper."

They all went inside except Grace, who wanted to sit a while longer on the terrace. It felt so good to feel the breeze off the water, and her mind was floating back to Smith now that the girls had gone inside.

He would have loved to have been here with me, she thought, sipping her wine and feeling sleep creeping up on her. I'd give anything to have one more night with him but it's a waste of mental energy thinking like this. I need to just enjoy the time with the girls and let my memories rest for a while.

Grace got up and walked inside, pulling the doors closed and throwing the lock. She could hear Celeste and Maryann talking in the other bedroom. She brushed her teeth and walked carefully into the master bedroom and climbed in bed next to Martha, who was already fast asleep. In the darkness of the night Grace tried one more time to see Smith's face, but it was futile. She touched the cross around her neck to her lips and laid her head down on the pillow, falling fast asleep in spite of the snores coming from the other side of the bed.

෧෧

On the other side of the world a man was waking up, wondering again for the millionth time who he was, and why he was in Pakistan.

Smith sat on the edge of his bed rubbing his face, trying hard not to get discouraged about his memory returning. He knew what Dr. Irfan had said but it seemed to be taking too long. He was healing nicely and felt sharp in his mind. But when he tried to think back to something in the past, there was nothing. Just blank spots. He did have that one jog in his memory about an orphanage, but at this point he had no idea why. It had given him such hope, yet nothing else came of it. A glimpse. He wanted to scream but he kept his screams inside where no one could hear them. And he prayed to God for his life back, before it was too late. He was grateful to Dr. Irfan and owed him his life. But he would give anything to have his life back. Whatever that entailed. And at this point, only God knew what that was . . .

CHAPTER 24

The phone rang at 6:30 in the morning, echoing throughout the house. Ben was dead to the world. He'd gone to bed late and had had a difficult time going to sleep. When he finally did, he crashed. He jumped when the phone rang and sat up groggily, wiping his eyes and trying to get his bearings. He'd been lost in a dream and it was hard to push that drugged, sleep-induced fogginess away. It felt like he was climbing out of quicksand when he picked up the phone.

"Hello?"

"Ben? Keith here. We've got a case. They're ready for us to head out on a search. You need to come on in with Houston. We'll be leaving in about thirty minutes."

Houston was already up and wagging his tail as if he knew what the phone call was about. Ben climbed out of bed, tripping on his shoes, and stumbled into the shower. He grabbed a protein bar and bottled water, put a leash on Houston, and jumped into the car. His adrenalin was pumping as he headed in to the station. This was his first rodeo and he wanted to do a good job with Houston. He had a lot to learn, but Keith would be around to show him what to do.

Keith walked out of the station just as Ben pulled up. "Hey, buddy. Glad to see you! Just go ahead and put Houston in my car with Charlie. They get along famously, and I bet they can feel our energy this morning. They know somethin's up!"

"No kiddin'! Houston practically pulled my arm off tryin' to get into the car. I think he knows exactly what's up."

"Well, he's done this before, Ben. You're the new kid on the block in this group, but believe me, you'll pick it up pretty quick. There's really nothing to do but follow the dog. Once he has a scent he's gone. We are searching this morning for a little boy who got away from his family on a camping trip in the Ridgeland Campground. There are a lot of lakes in that campground and they are worried that the little guy might be tempted to get in the water. He's seven years old and a Cub Scout. The parents think he wandered off looking for a type of tree leaf for his second badge. This happens with kids. They have no concept of where they are or where they're goin'."

Ben shook his head in disbelief. "I know those parents are frantic. How long has he been missin'?"

"Two days. But that's a long time for a little boy to be alone. So let's get there and see what we can turn up. We've got some of his clothing that will give the dogs a scent. You'll enjoy this, Ben, especially if it turns out that we find him today. Let's hope nothing has happened to him. His name is Billy West. We can call out to him, but the dogs should be able to pick up a scent if he's been where we are going to start looking."

They pulled up to the campground and Ben got Houston out of the SUV. He was pulling on the leash and Ben spoke sternly and got him to heel. He was a great dog and responded immediately, but was caught up in the energy he was feeling from Ben and from Charlie. They both were German shepherd mixes so they almost looked like twins.

"I'm going to let Houston and Charlie smell the shirts and socks that belong to Billy, and let them get familiar with his scent. Then we'll walk out on the grounds and see what happens. You remember to be fragrance free, Ben?"

"Yep. Don't ever wear anything with fragrance. That's from years with the CIA. So I'm clean. Don't have to worry about that."

The dogs took off on a trail and the men followed close behind. It was a beautiful summer day and the air was clear. Not a cloud in the sky. Which meant it could be hotter by noon, and Billy was out there with no water or food that the parents knew of. There was a tension in the air and the dogs picked it up; they were scurrying around, having a hard time picking up a direct scent. They walked for about a mile and suddenly one of the dogs froze at a spot near a fallen tree. He'd picked up a scent and was going crazy around the tree. Keith pulled Charlie away and kept him moving and he picked up the scent again down the trail near a lake. Houston had his nose to the ground and was moving right in front of Charlie. The scent was sporadic but Billy had definitely been around the lake area.

One of the dogs stopped and smelled in a bush and pulled out a child's tennis shoe. Keith called out to Ben towards him so he could show Houston the shoe. The lake water was still and they both looked closely at the edge of the water to see if they saw a body floating anywhere. This particular lake was clean but there were several more scattered around the campground. The dogs took off again running and Ben and his partner had a difficult time keeping up with them. They went through a small grouping of trees and suddenly one of the dogs started barking. He seemed focused on a tree and he was jumping up and barking frantically.

Ben looked up and saw a little boy sitting on a limb, crying. He pulled Houston down and let Keith hold the dog while he grabbed Billy and sat him on the ground.

"Hey, little fella. Don't be afraid. We're here to get you back to your parents. Are you okay? You hurt anywhere?"

"I . . . want my daddy," he whispered.

"We're gonna take you to your parents. I'm so glad we found you." Ben picked the boy up after checking to see if he was hurt. He had a few scratches but no other injuries were apparent.

"Did you wander away, Billy?" Keith asked gently.

"Uh, yeah—sort of. I was tryin' to find a tree leaf for a badge in my Cub Scout pack. But I guess I got off on a path and got lost. Where are we?"

"You're still in the campground but it got dark and your parents couldn't find you, so they called us. Our dogs found you pretty fast! Isn't that cool, Billy?"

Billy was drinking from a bottle of water Ben had given him, and smiled, wiping his mouth on his sleeve. "Yeah, that was cool. I got pretty thirsty up there."

"Were you scared up in that tree? Did you get hungry? " Keith asked.

"I had a part of a candy bar I ate yesterday and some gum I had in my pocket. But I got real thirsty today. It got real hot out here."

Keith phoned the office on the grounds and spoke to the office manager. He put the parents on the phone and Keith told them the good news. "Mr. West! We've found Billy! Yes, we've found him!"

Screams on the other end of the phone. "What? You're sure? You found him? Where in the world was he?"

"Mr. West, calm down. He's fine. A little hungry and thirsty but no injuries that we can find. We're headed your way in the car."

Keith hung up the phone and smiled at Billy. "Your parents are waiting for you at the office. They are going to be so happy you're safe."

"I'll never do this again, ya know? I thought I knew where I was goin'."

"It's easy to get lost," Ben remarked, turning into the parking lot at the office. "Anyone can get lost out here with all the woods. Especially at dusk. Now run inside and hug your Dad and Mom. They've been going nuts trying to find you!"

Keith wrote up a police report and phoned into the station to report what they'd found. "The chief will be pleased that this case turned out so well. It always helps when we find the missing person alive," he said to Ben.

Ben walked up to the parents and shook their hands. "I know you're happy to have your son back. I'd let a doctor check him over to make sure he's not too dehydrated or anything. You're one lucky set of parents! I know you must've been sick with worry."

"You have no idea, Mr. Parker. We owe you our lives for finding our son! Thank you so much."

Ben walked outside and got into the car where Keith was finishing up the paperwork. They both smiled as Keith headed back to the station.

"So, what do ya think now, Mr. Ben? How was your first rescue mission?"

"I think it turned out pretty darn good, Mr. Mitchell! I tell you one thing though; I would not have wanted to be those parents searching for their son. That had to be gut-wrenching!"

"You'll see worse than this if you stay around long enough. Behind the storefronts and nice looking houses in this town, there are a lot of sick things going on. Let's go get something to eat. That sound good to you?"

"I'm starving! I'd eat anything right now."

༄

The two men entered a small café near the police station and took a booth near the back. The place was filling up so they grabbed a waitress and ordered quickly. "Say, you married, Ben? I haven't heard you talk about a wife!"

"Nah. Not married yet. Just haven't found the right woman. Well, that's not totally true right now. . . . I've found someone but she's not really available. My luck, of course."

"That doesn't sound too cool, Ben. She's not married, is she?"

"No. No way. I don't date married women. That's a dead-end street. No, she just recently lost her husband so she's not interested in getting into a relationship right now."

"How did you meet her, man?"

Ben hesitated. He didn't know how much he should say about his past. "Well, that's sort of tough to explain. You know I worked for the CIA, right?"

Keith looked at him with a puzzled expression on his face. "Yeah, I got that part. So what has that got to do with this woman?"

"Well, for one thing, I can't talk about it, and secondly, you know her." Ben looked at him and grinned, but his lips were sealed.

"Is she hot?"

"What? Oh, my gosh. What a question! I'm not answering that. But she's pretty!" Ben doubled over with laughter.

The waitress brought their food and Keith took a huge bite out of his cheeseburger. He waited a minute, chewing fast, and gulped down a sip of Diet Coke. "So I know her and she's pretty. Let's see. You and I just met so how could I know a woman that you know? That's ridiculous."

Ben shrugged his shoulders and took another bite out of his club sandwich. He wiped his mouth and just sat there looking at Bob. He wasn't giving him anything else.

"Come on, Ben. Help me out here. How do I know her? Give me something, will ya?"

"I can't. I'm sworn to secrecy, as you can imagine. But it's right in front of your face. That's all I'm sayin'."

Keith thought for a moment and then a light bulb lit up in his head. "Oh, my gosh! It has to be Grace Sanderson, the principal at Ross High. How in the world do you know her?"

"I didn't say I did."

"You know I'm right. Now come on, Ben."

"I can't say a word. You have to respect that."

"Damn. How in the world did you meet her? You haven't been in this town that long. And all those years you worked for the CIA you were travelling a lot, I know that's right."

"I certainly did my share of travelling." Ben tried to act cool about it all. But inside he was getting nervous. He'd not told anyone about Grace. At least how he met her. He wasn't about to let the cat out of the bag now, with Keith.

"I know it's her. She's beautiful, all right. I do remember something about her losing her husband. Am I digging too deep here?"

Ben nodded and finished off his sandwich and drank a long drink of tea. "I wish I could talk about this, but I'm in a compromising situation. There are certain things I just can't talk about with you."

Keith put his hands up and grinned. "Okay, buddy. Sorry. You just piqued my interest, is all. I know I was pushing you and I'm sorry. But hey, Grace is one lovely woman. If you get a chance to date her, go for it, man."

"I've taken her out once and we had a wonderful time. But she let me know in a kind way that she's not ready yet to have a romantic relationship. It hurt but I knew it was coming. So here I am with you, Keith! You're my replacement!"

Keith fell out laughing and picked up the ticket for their lunch and waved down the waitress. She came up to the table and he handed her a credit card. "Well, you won't be bored in this relationship, big guy. Because I have a feeling that this is just the beginning of our busy season. For some reason we get called out a lot during the summer season. I guess lots of families are out on vacation and kids get lost at camp. Let's hope all of them end like this one did! You did great today, by the way."

Ben blushed and shook his hand. "I have a great teacher. See you soon, Keith. Thanks for the lunch."

On the way home from the café, Ben could think of nothing else but Grace. He wondered what she was doing, and then remembered she'd mentioned that she was going on a four day cruise to the Bahamas. He smiled, knowing she would have a ball. But he couldn't help but wish he was there with her. He turned to look at Houston and their eyes met for a moment. A wonderful bond was forming between them that was unspoken. A man and his dog . . . how apropos.

110

CHAPTER 25

Dr. Irfan was using Smith more and more in his work. He made some house calls in neighborhoods that he felt were safe for them and dressed Smith in the traditional *salwar kameez*. It would call too much attention if Smith wore his fatigues. His beard had grown out and was full; he'd dyed his hair dark along with his beard for protection. So for the most part, he blended in with the people on the street except for his American accent. He was working on the language but could understand it better than he could speak it. They visited homes where the sick were unable to get out, and helped many people. Dr. Irfan had hired a nurse who could speak both English and Urdu, so Smith could converse with her, also. Mishael was beautiful and very intelligent, but her shyness made it difficult for Smith to get to know her. She was patient with his language difficulties and helped him when working on a patient. He found himself staring at her, lost in his own thoughts.

After one of their visits to a house that was broken down, unclean, and full of sick children, Smith and Mishael were sitting at a table at Dr. Irfan's home talking about all the sick people who couldn't get needed medical attention. Smith knew that Dr. Irfan could not keep treating people who were unable pay him some money. But he had a difficult time turning the sick away. Mishael explained that Dr. Irfan felt he had to do it to please God, so that made it even more important to him. She had worked for many doctors in Pakistan and Dr. Irfan was the best. Smith had great respect for the man and owed him so much.

"Mishael, he saved my life. I owe him my life, can you understand that?" He felt lonely and it was so good to be able to talk to someone about what he'd been through.

"I understand, Bita. I do not know whole circumstance but I can see your admiration for the doctor."

"He explained to me that people found me lying in blood near a cave. There had been an explosion and gunfire, only I don't remember any of it. They took me here to Dr. Irfan, and he nursed me back to health. I cannot remember anything about my past, Mishael. I know nothing about my life."

Mishael bowed her head and wiped tears from her eyes. Bita was a good man and it upset her to hear how close he had come to death. "It must be devastating not to remember your life before."

Smith was touched by her emotion and leaned over and hugged her. She pulled away but smiled.

After Mishael left, Dr. Irfan came into Smith's bedroom and sat on his bed. "Bita, be careful what you speak about yourself to others. I know you feel safe with Mishael, but the more who know about you, the more danger you put yourself in. It is risky for you to be here, and I try hard to keep you safe. You also need to know custom of women and men here. Custom here is you do not hug woman unless she is close relative. So that is why Mishael back away from hug. More time must pass for her to know you. Be patient, my friend. You are healing quickly but do not let your loneliness move you too fast toward Mishael. Respect is critical here for woman."

Smith bowed his head and put his hands over his eyes. He was so tired of not knowing about himself, his past; anything at all that would give him a clue as to what in the world he was doing here. Mishael was easy to be around and so beautiful. He wanted to hug her but somehow it had not felt quite right. "I will be respectful, Dr. Irfan. You have been too good to me, and I would never do anything to shame you."

"Bita, you are good man. Now sleep. We have much work to do tomorrow."

Smith lay back on his pillow and closed his eyes. He soon was lost in a dream, walking down a street that was familiar but he wasn't sure why. He fell into a deep sleep and didn't move until morning.

∽

The clinic was full when Smith walked in. Babies were crying, and there was a man lying on the floor, bleeding. He rushed to get clean rags to stop the bleeding and antiseptic to put on the wound until Dr. Irfan could see the wounded man. Mishael came and knelt beside him and helped clean the wound, and they carried the man back to a room where he could lay on a bed. Dr. Irfan was moving from room to room calling out to Bita for supplies and medicine. It was an exhausting morning, and the heat was unbearable outside. There were fans in the clinic but they did nothing but blow the hot air around. Finally the rooms cleared out and Mahsa had lunch prepared.

"Come, Bita. We eat now and get ready for the afternoon. I fear we are going to run out of supplies if this keeps up. I can get more, but it will take a day to arrive."

"I don't know how you keep up this pace, Dr. Irfan. It is grueling. And you are not getting any younger." He smiled at Dr. Irfan and pushed away from the table. The heat had taken his appetite away.

"I don't like to see you not eating. I work hard to get you back to where you are now, and I don't want you to slip in your health. You are still fragile inside, Bita. It will take a while for you to gain total strength."

"I can tell I'm still weak, but you cannot do this alone, Dr. Irfan. It's too much for one doctor. Can you bring another doctor into the clinic? Is that possible?"

The doctor stood up and walked to the door. He turned to look back at Smith with a worried look on his face. "Yes, it is true that I need help here. But I cannot risk someone finding out about you. Remember, Bita, the more who know about your existence, the more risk of your being killed. I have grown fond of you, Bita. It is my hope that you find your life back and I will do all I can to keep you alive until your memory comes to you." He turned and walked through the door and headed back to the clinic.

Smith sat at the table feeling helpless. But he was more determined than ever to assist Dr. Irfan now that he understood the grave danger he was in by being in his home. He and Mahsa were risking their lives to save him. He had to honor that by staying safe. He was so tired of trying to dig into his mind to pull up some shred of memory about his past. It was making him crazy inside knowing there was a life he had lived, a family perhaps waiting for him, and he could not remember anything about them.

He got up from the table and peeked into the kitchen to thank Mahsa for lunch. She was already walking to the clinic so Smith headed in that direction. As he was about to leave the house, Mishael came through the front door looking for Mahsa.

"Have you seen Mahsa, Bita? Dr. Irfan is looking for her!"

"No, I was looking for her here, but it looks like she's already gone to the clinic."

Mishael looked worried. "She is not there. I am worried, Bita. Some men were standing at the corner when I passed by. I think they were Taliban. They laughed when I passed them. I fear something is wrong."

Smith grabbed Mishael and they headed out the door. When they approached the corner where Mishael had seen the men, no one was there. In fact, the whole neighborhood was quiet, which was unusual for this time of day. The streets were cleared. Smith instinctively knew that something had happened and hurried with Mishael to the clinic. Dr. Irfan was working on a woman who was about to give birth and looked up when Smith walked into the small room.

"Bita! Help quickly. This woman is having a baby now. She is in great pain. We must get baby out quickly so she will not lose her life."

Wanting to ask about Mahsa but seeing the urgency in Dr. Irfan's face, Smith put on the rubber gloves and assisted Dr. Irfan in getting the baby out. The woman was screaming and pushing hard, straining to get the head out. Smith couldn't understand what she was saying, but he knew by the look on Dr. Irfan's face that they were in a critical situation. He rubbed her arm and talked soothingly to her, trying to relax her muscles. The more she screamed and fought, the more difficult it was for the baby to be born. Smith started humming a lullaby that popped into his head, and Dr. Irfan looked at him with a raised eyebrow.

"What is that song, Bita? Where did that come from?"

"I don't really know! It just came to me and I was thinking it might calm her down."

Dr. Irfan smiled, knowing that this might be the beginning of his memory returning. The girl did get calmer and as soon as she relaxed, the baby was born. He handed the baby to Mishael and Smith saw that it was slightly blue, which he knew meant that the baby wasn't getting enough oxygen.

Mishael worked with the baby, clearing out its nose and breathing passages. Suddenly there was a loud cry and Dr. Irfan smiled. The mother was crying and wanting to see her child, so Smith ran to get the infant. He walked into the room where Mishael was and suddenly was overcome with her beauty again. She was sweating, bending over the baby, and when she looked up she saw Smith staring at her.

"You must hurry and get this baby to the mother, Bita. It is still very fragile."

"You look beautiful, Mishael. I'm sorry. But I can't refrain any longer from telling you how lovely you are." He reached for her and hugged her, kissing her forehead. "Please forgive me."

He grabbed the baby and left the room, shaking inside. He was falling in love with Mishael and he knew that it was something he wasn't going to be able to share with anyone.

When he returned to the room where Dr. Irfan was, the mother had calmed down and was smiling, waiting for her baby. He handed the baby to her and motioned to Dr. Irfan to come outside the room.

"Where is Mahsa? Has she made it to the clinic? I have not seen her since lunch."

"I was hoping she was still at the house, Bita. Did you not see her on your way in?"

"No. Mishael returned to the house to look for her. She said there were men standing on the corner near the grocery store, and they were staring at her and laughing. The streets were cleared out and she felt the danger. I'm worried, Dr. Irfan. What if something has happened to Mahsa?"

Dr. Irfan rushed out of the clinic and looked up and down the street. There were a few people milling around but not the usual crowds. He called the house and the phone rang and rang.

"It's not like Mahsa to disappear like this. Something is wrong."

"Can we contact the police? Will they help you?"

Dr. Irfan shook his head. "You don't understand, Bita. They may have found out about you living with me and have taken Mahsa so that they can get to you. They may be punishing me for harboring you in my home."

Smith sat down in a chair shaking his head in disbelief. "They must have heard the talk on the street about an American being hidden. But why would they take Mahsa? Why not just kidnap me?"

"When your mind is disloyal to God, there is no reason in what you do. We must close the clinic today and go home. I have to think about what to do."

Smith and Mishael hurriedly sent the other patients home, reassuring them that they could return tomorrow for help. Dr. Irfan suggested they leave from the back door and walk through an alley that led down some side streets. He moved quickly, looking from side to side, worried that the terrorists were watching them. They got to the house with no incident but noticed how quiet the streets remained.

Just as they were about to sit down in the living room, someone knocked on the door quietly. Dr. Irfan rushed to the door and opened it. A short man came in, breathing hard. "Dr. Irfan, I come to tell you about Mahsa. I have seen her. The men that were in town today have taken her to a cave on the outskirts of town. I was watching from my house and saw her when they passed by. Her hands were bound but she seemed all right otherwise. What can we do?"

"Thank you for coming by, Saba. Keep your eyes open and stay safe. We will have to wait and decide what to do." Dr. Irfan was shaking but his voice was calm and firm.

Saba left hurriedly, going out the back and heading down an alley road. Dr. Irfan turned and looked at Smith.

"I fear we need to hide you in a special place for a while, Bita. They are wanting you, and took Mahsa to get me to tell them where you are."

"I can leave, Dr. Irfan. You have done enough for me. I can move into one of those caves for a while if I take food with me and water."

"I do not want you wandering about, Bita. They will find you. I was thinking of a home two miles away that is a friend of mine. They would not connect you to this home. You would be safe there until things calm down. I can talk to them and find Mahsa, if I allow them to come to my home and look."

"I'll get my things now and head to this house you spoke of. Will you call the people to let them know I am coming? Will they object?"

"No they will accept responsibility as they trust me. I have done much for this family. They will now give back to me by harboring you. But please don't walk about at night or go far from this home. I will contact you as soon as you can return to us."

Smith went directly to his room and gathered all of his possessions, which were few. He had a small bag to put his clothes and journals in. He felt sad leaving this house—it had come to feel like home. And his thoughts were of Mishael when he hugged Dr. Irfan and headed out the back door. It was getting dark and that would help to cover him while he ran to the new location. He cut through yards and took back streets so that he would get there quickly. Even though he was moving very quickly, no one seemed to notice him moving in the streets. When he finally arrived at the house that Dr. Irfan directed him to, he knocked on the door and someone answered and pulled him inside.

"You are Bita, sent by Dr. Irfan Sheikhani. Come in, please. My name is Khan Saleem and I welcome you to my home. Please come. I have place for you to hide."

Smith looked around the sparsely furnished room and followed Khan to a room up in the attic. It was hidden well but was a very small space. There was a tiny window that looked out on the street but it was high so he would need a chair to stand in to look out. A single bed with a mattress, pillow and blanket was in the corner, along with a small table, lamp and some books. He sat his personal things on the bed and looked around. He didn't want to appear ungrateful.

"Thank you so much for your help. I am sorry to put you at risk for having me in your home. I will stay out of sight so that you are not in danger. Maybe I will not have to be here long."

"Do not worry, Bita. They will not connect you to me. You will be safe here for a short time. I will bring you water jug and food for tonight. In morning we will talk more." He hurried out of the room and climbed down the tiny stairs and closed a door. Smith sat down on the bed feeling frustrated and very alone. *How can I live like this, hiding and putting other's lives in danger? And what has happened to Mahsa? Hopefully they have not harmed her. I was just getting settled in with Dr. Irfan and now I am in a stranger's house alone.*

Smith closed his eyes and lay back on the bed. It was quiet in the house and the room was cool. He closed his eyes and dozed off for a few minutes; he was awakened by a gentle knock on the door. He rose and opened the door and Khan handed him a large water jug and some food.

"Thank you so much for your kindness, Khan. I appreciate this so much."

"No worry, Bita. Rest well tonight and we talk in morning. I live alone, to let you know. We are only ones in this house."

Smith nodded and closed the door. He suddenly was starving and sat down on his bed and ate the meal Khan had left for him. It was hot and fairly tasty so he ate until he couldn't eat another bite and laid the tray on the floor by the door. He stood on a small chair and looked out of the window. The streets were busy with people and cars. It was dark and he had nothing to do but go to sleep. But when he lay down on the bed his eyes would not stay closed. His mind was running a mile a minute, thinking about Mahsa and Dr. Irfan. He finally fell into a restless sleep worrying about his new family.

◡

The night passed without incident at the home of Khan Saleem. But Dr. Irfan was up all night making a plan to get his wife back from the men who took her. He was afraid for her, but felt pretty confident that if he showed that he had no American in his home, they might let her go free. If they found any trace of the American in his home, it would be fatal for him and his wife. There were times when Americans could come and go in Pakistan, but now it was different. There were a few terrorist groups who were targeting the Americans regularly, and these men must have come from this aggressive group.

Morning came and Irfan headed towards the clinic, hoping to see the men waiting outside on the street. He opened the door to his clinic and suddenly three men jumped him and slammed the door shut.

"We know you have American in your home. You must take us to him if you want your wife to live. Do not lie to us, or we will kill you now."

"I will gladly take you to my home. But you will find there that we have no trace of an American in our home. You will be pleased to see the home is empty of company."

"Go immediately and we will follow. If you are lying we will kill your wife in front of you."

Irfan walked quickly to his home and opened the door. The house was quiet and the men rummaged through the rooms looking for any sign of the American. They opened drawers, looked in closets, ran up the stairs to the attic and looked in the basement. When they made it to the back room where Smith had slept, they found nothing but a bed covered with stacks of folded laundry and towels. The windows had been cleaned and were open, and the closet had their winter clothes and shoes inside. The men looked puzzled as they finished their search of Irfan's home.

"We cannot see where you had the American. But rumors were on the street that he was working for you. Do you have a man working for you now?"

"Yes, I did. But he left days ago to go back to his family in Iran. Now I only have Mishael, and she is a nurse. You can see tomorrow at the clinic that I do not have any other workers there with me."

"We will be in here watching you. If we see anyone come in here that is suspicious, we will blow this clinic wide open and you and your wife will die. Is that clear, doctor?"

"Very clear. Please, I do not want my wife to die needlessly. We are not harboring an American, as you can see. Please bring her home safely."

"Your wife is safe now, but she will not return until tomorrow after we have seen the clinic when it is open."

Irfan shook his head and locked the door to the clinic. When he turned around to speak to the men they were gone. He had a chill come over his body and he hurried home. He had no appetite and lay in bed worrying about his Mahsa. He was also worried about Bita and what they would do with him after this nightmare was over. He might not be able to remain in Pakistan. There was just too much unrest right now.

CHAPTER 26

Staying in the Bahamas turned out to be one of the greatest decisions Grace could have made. The weather was perfect and the food was delicious. Dinner that evening was at the Grand Hotel and the girls could not wait to dress up for a change. They'd lain around for two days doing absolutely nothing, eating and talking and having a few glasses of wine. "Few" being the key word.

"What dress are you wearin', Gracie? I want to borrow that red dress you brought." Maryann was licking her fingers after eating a cat's claw that was left over from breakfast.

"I thought I'd wear the light blue dress. It goes well with my eyes and besides, it's strapless and I'm feelin' daring tonight!"

"Well, girls, I'm wearin' my white sundress and heels. I'm ready for some fine dining!" Martha was painting her toenails and nails a bright red and already had her hair in rollers. She looked like something out of the 1970s with the rollers going on.

"We have reservations at 7:00 and it's 5:45 now. Pace yourselves so we won't be late!" Celeste was already dressed and sitting outside on the terrace.

On the way to dinner the girls were laughing and reminiscing about old times, which sometimes brought Smith into the conversation, and then Grace would get quiet. She had to get used to talking about him in past tense and that was going to be a challenge. "I still feel like he might show up at any moment. I wonder when that feeling will pass?"

"Who knows, Grace? You guys were so close and had such an unusual relationship, with Smith travelling all the time. You are making new memories right now, my sweet friend. That's what's gonna help you get past losing Smith. Making new memories," Maryann remarked, holding her dress down in the gusty wind.

"I know what you're sayin' is true, but I really don't want to let go of all my memories of Smith. He was so wonderful." She paused as they walked into the restaurant and were seated at a round table near the center of the room. "Can you see all the palms in here? Good heavens. It's so tropical!"

"I told you, Grace, that we would have the time of our lives on this trip. Let's check out the menu and order and then we can talk. We never seem to run out of words, do we?" Martha passed the menus around and listened as the waiter recited his spiel on the new chef entrees.

After they had ordered, a band began to play and people got up and danced. A man who was standing near the doorway of the restaurant watching the women at the round table walked over and asked Grace to dance.

"Madam, may I have this dance with you?"

Grace was polite but firm. "Oh no, thank you. I'll sit this one out."

He wouldn't take no for an answer. "Come on, Miss, I just want one dance with you! Enjoy yourself tonight!"

The girls urged her to do it, so Grace got up slowly and took his hand, and as she turned to look back at her friends she stuck her tongue out. They fell out laughing and clapped for her. The man was a fabulous dancer and soon had Grace swirling all over the dance floor. After the song was over, Grace returned to the table breathless, laughing.

"Now it's your turn, guys. That's it for me! Although I have to admit it was fun to dance with someone who is such a great dancer!"

"You looked pretty darn good out there, Gracie. I didn't know you could dance like that." Celeste took a bite of bread and slathered butter on it.

"I don't dance. But he pulled me along and I sort of caught on to the rhythm and could move with him. It really makes a difference when the man can dance better than you!"

The waiter brought their meals and Grace breathed a sigh of relief. At least she had a reprieve from being asked to dance again. It was nice but she felt odd dancing with another man. The food was out of this world and they all chose different entrées. But each entrée was covered in a sauce that was rich and flavorful. It was a three course meal and dessert was crème brulee.

Grace looked around and noticed the open windows that looked out on the water. The drapes fell to the floor in soft puddles, and the lighting was dim. This was almost like a dream when she thought about her life at home. She missed her kids at school and was ready to visit the orphanage when she got back home. As she ate, she listened to the conversation at the table, lost in thought. She wanted to sink her teeth into something when she got home, but she wasn't sure what yet. In the back of her mind she was toying with the idea of adopting a child from the orphanage. It had been against Smith's better judgment for her to do that, but now that he was gone, it would give her great comfort to have a child around. She wanted to mention it to her friends but was afraid of their response. Martha saw her drifting off in her own world and snatched her back with her usual wit.

"Hey, girlfriend! Can you let us in on that trip you are taking? I can see that you haven't been listening to what we're saying!"

"I'm fine, 'Mother Hen'! But I was thinking something and now may be the perfect time for me to put this out in the open for you guys to think about." She paused and wiped her mouth with her napkin. "For quite some time I've wanted to adopt a child. I know you are aware of that already, but when Smith was alive he was against it because he was gone so much and didn't want me to have the total responsibility of raising a child. Now that he's gone, I think it would be wonderful for me to have a child around the house. They bring such life to a home and I need that right now. So let's talk about it! What do you think?"

She looked at the women and all their mouths were open, and Martha was speechless for one of the few times in her life. Finally, Celeste spoke up. "I hear what you are saying, Grace. I can see why you would want a child now that you are alone. But do you realize all of what that entails? The fact that you would be tied down 24/7 to raising that child? You would not have anyone but us to give you a break. It would change your life big time. Are you ready for that?"

Martha finally un-muted herself and spoke up. "Grace, now listen to me. I know you're lonely and I can so see why you want a child now. I almost wish you'd had a baby with Smith because then you'd feel like you had a part of him around you. But you are a principal of a huge school with tons of responsibility and little spare time. Would that be fair to a child? Could you give them the time they'd require without letting something else go?"

Maryann jumped in before Martha could continue. "I think it's a grand idea! Why are you guys so against it? Grace, you've been so active in that orphanage all along and you've loved being around those kids. It seems a natural transition to me for you to adopt a child from that orphanage now that Smith is gone. I'm behind you one hundred percent! In fact I'm ashamed of the other two girls for being so negative about it."

Grace looked at all three of the women and laughed. "My goodness, I didn't know we'd all be so opinionated on this subject! I just wanted to throw it out to you tonight and see what you thought. I really am missing the kids at the orphanage and am going to get involved again as soon as we return from this trip. I do realize how busy I am and maybe that wouldn't be the perfect thing for me to do. But there is no perfect situation for parents. Nowadays most parents work, and leave their kids in a daycare center. Right? I won't be the first single parent who tried to raise a child alone, and I don't plan on being single forever. One day I'll meet someone who I could love, and maybe marry. So how am I so different from any of the millions of women who have children and have divorced their husbands? And why would my home environment and the love I could give a child be worse than how they are living in that orphanage, without a mother or father to give love to them?"

You could hear a pin drop at the table. Martha had no words to say, but knew she had spoken without thinking. They all smiled at Grace and nodded, agreeing she was right. Maryann finally spoke up and said, "Grace, you do what you feel is right for you. We aren't in your situation, and we don't know exactly how you feel. I don't blame you for wanting children now that Smith is gone. You have so much to offer that child, and besides, they would never have to fear being sent to the principal!"

Everyone laughed. They dug into the crème brulee and drank that last bit of wine. The music was playing softly in the background and they all finished the night off by talking about where they'd want to retire one day. When they headed back to the room they decided to stop and shop at some of the local shops along the way. By the time they arrived back at the hotel, their arms were laden with bags full of clothes, shoes and jewelry from local artists. They changed into comfortable clothing and sat out on the terrace to relax. The sound of their laughter went on for hours and was whisked away in the breeze that was blowing, and the bright light of the moon left a shimmering trail across the water and cast shadows against the wall.

❦

Smith gazed out the lone window in the small room that had become his home. He was lonely and confused about what his life would be like as long as the terrorists were hunting for him. His hope was that they would get focused on something else and he would be able to return to Dr Irfan and Mahsa. He stared at the moon wondering about America not knowing that his wife was looking at the moon thousands of miles across the ocean.

And he had no way of knowing that her last thought before going to bed was about a poem they'd read somewhere: "*. . . and when I go I'll be on the other side of the moon waiting for you.*"

CHAPTER 27

A pattern was beginning to form in Ben's life. His phone rang again at 5:30 in the morning and it was his buddy, Keith. "Good morning, beautiful! We've got another job to do. And don't tell me I woke you up!"

"No way. I was sitting here waiting on you to call. What's the deal this time?" Ben covered the mouthpiece and yawned loudly. *Can't a guy get some sleep around here?*

"All kidding aside, this is a serious situation, Ben. A young woman, Laura Yarbrough, is missing, has been for two weeks. Someone found a shoe on a dead end road. We're working with cadaver dogs today, so that means they don't expect her to be alive. Meet me at the office in about twenty minutes. Can that be done?"

"I'm out the door now." Ben slammed the phone down, wondering for a split second if he'd made a mistake taking this job. He ran into the bathroom and splashed cold water on his face, brushed his teeth, and put a cap on his head to cover his unruly hair. Forget shaving. No one would notice. Houston was already aware of what was about to happen, but this time he was staying home. That would be tough because he was used to heading out the door with his master.

Ben let Houston outside to do his job, grabbed two breakfast bars, patted Houston on the head, and jumped into the SUV and took off. He pulled up at the station in exactly fifteen minutes and beat Keith there. He got out of his truck, leaned up against it, ate the last bar, and swallowed the last of his coffee as his partner was pulling up into the lot.

"Dude, you gonna sleep all day?" Ben loved this part.

"You're ridiculous! What did you do, sleep in your clothes?"

Ben laughed and gave him a high-five. They both headed inside to get the cadaver dogs and turned to leave when the chief called out to them. "Hey guys, pop in here a sec, will ya?"

"Sure. You got any info on this case, sir?" Ben asked, stifling a yawn.

"I sure do. Her husband, Charles, is under suspicion for murder. Seems there was some domestic violence and we're not sure if the wife was seein' someone else on the side or not. There are three children involved and the story is that the husband and kids were home and the wife left to run errands and never came home. Neighbors aren't talkin', and no one's seen anything. So when a shoe turned up on this dead end road over by the mill, the husband identified it as his wife's shoe. We don't know what to expect here but I wanted you two to be on it early; hopefully the dogs will turn up somethin'."

"We'll get on it right away, Chief. Our radios are on and we'll keep you posted." Keith headed out the door and Ben turned to look at the chief.

"How often do you have cases where there is a death involved?"

"Ben, it happens more than you care to know. The other day when you found that young boy, that was a miracle. I didn't make too much out of it, but I was proud of you guys for finding that kid. He could have easily drowned or died of dehydration. He was small and his body couldn't take that much trauma. You did a great job. I only hope this one isn't a bagger. Those three children need their mom."

Ben nodded and walked out of the office. Keith was already in the SUV and the dogs were in the back.

"Ben, these dogs' names are Joe and Whitey. They been around a long time and they'll do all the work. All we have to do is keep up with 'em."

"What's the first thing we do when we get there? Give 'em the shoe to smell?"

"Yep. And any other clothing or articles that have her smell on them. And then we wait to see what the dogs will turn up. Just get ready for what we might find. I know you're used to death but it's never pleasant, and this isn't war like you're used to. Much more personal. This is a woman who has three kids. It can get to you real fast."

"I know. I can tell already that it feels different from anything I've experienced. And I've seen some pretty rough stuff, Keith. I'm here to tell you, I've seen it all. But this is bad, real bad."

They drove towards the outskirts of the city and headed down a gravel road. Keith told Ben to turn left at the last road near the woods. Peyton Road. Potholes were everywhere and felled trees from the last storm. They came up on a police car that was pulled over on the right side of the road. Office Simpson got out and they all shook hands.

"Here's the deal, men. I have a shoe here that we'll let the dogs smell. And some clothes that were recently worn by the woman involved. Her name is Laura Yarbrough. I'll show you where we found the shoe; it's marked off over there on the edge of the road."

Ben and his partner walked over to the side of the road and studied the area. They bent down and let the dogs smell the shoe and also the blouses that belonged to Laura. The dogs were ready to go, so Keith waved to the officer and they took off down the road. At first the dogs stayed along the roadside, but soon they headed off into the woods. Their noses were flat on the ground and they didn't waiver one second; it was as though they were driven to finding her.

"Keith, is this how it usually is with the dogs? I mean, they're unstoppable. It's difficult for us to keep up with 'em."

"Yeah, this is how they behave on a hunt. Somehow they seem to sense what's goin' on, but they're trained for this extensively. You never know what you're gonna find. She could be alive even though it's been days since she left her home. So I never get in my mind ahead of time that I'm gonna run up on a dead person. In our world we call it 'a bagger.' I know it sounds cold- hearted but somebody started it and it sort of caught on."

Ben shook his head and ran after Whitey. The search lasted about two hours, with the dogs going deeper and deeper into the woods. Finally, they came up on a wooden shack that was barely standing, and the dogs went crazy barking at the door. Vines were growing all over the shack, making it difficult to see from a distance. The door was practically hanging off its hinges and the windows were all broken. Keith pulled his gun out and motioned for Ben to do the same. He stood on the left side of the door and pointed for Ben to get behind him with his gun aimed at the door.

Keith whispered in Ben's ear, "I don't know what we're gonna find when I open this door, but don't shoot unless you have to."

Ben nodded and Keith opened the door and the dogs rushed in barking loudly. It was dark inside and their eyes didn't have time to adjust. Ben pulled out a flashlight he had in his back pocket and whipped it around to scan the place out. All of his years of training in the CIA kicked in full force. His senses were electrified as he checked out every square inch of the dark room. Nothing was in the center of the room but as he put the light towards the left corner, he spotted a blanket stretched over something. The dogs were growling and tugging on the blanket fiercely. Keith pulled them off and slowly pulled the blanket away. Ben shone the light on the body of a woman. He reached down with gloves on and touched her leg and she screamed. It was a weak scream but it was loud enough to make the hair stand up on his arms.

"Damn! She's alive! Ma'am, can you hear me? We're police officers and we're here to help you."

Dead silence. Ben reached down and touched her arm. No movement. He got on his knees and pulled her out of the corner and laid her on the floor where they could look at her. She had a bad wound on her head and her hands were bound together with a thick rope. They had cut into her skin and there was dried blood on the rope. Her hair was bloody in places and her eyes were swollen shut. It was obvious she'd been beaten badly and that she was now unconscious. The smell of body fluid was strong.

Keith called for an ambulance and phoned the chief to let him know what they'd found. They hadn't identified the woman yet and they wanted the EMTs to arrive as quickly as possible. It was very warm in the shack and Ben knew she had to be severely dehydrated.

Ten minutes later the ambulance had arrived to take care of the woman they believed to be Laura. She fit the description, but because she had no identification on her and she was unconscious, they had no way of confirming who she was. Keith headed to the SUV with the dogs. Ben hopped into the back of the ambulance and rode to the hospital with the woman so that he could talk to the doctor in charge in the emergency room. Laura's husband was notified and told to go directly to the ER at Mercy Hospital to help them identify the woman.

If this, in fact, was Laura they'd found tied up in a shack in the woods, this information would hit the 5:00 news and it would be all over town. They arrived at Mercy Hospital in minutes and the EMTs carried the woman on a stretcher into the ER. She was taken immediately into a room where the attending physician and nurses went to work. One of the staff members took information from Ben and as he finished up with the nurse, Charles Yarbrough walked through the double doors, yelling for help. He was loud and unruly, but Ben gave him some slack considering the circumstances. He walked up to Charles and shook his hand.

"You must be Charles Yarbrough. I'm Ben Parker, with the police department. We just brought in a woman we need you to identify. Can you do that for us, Charles?"

"Get out of my way, officer! I need to see if this is my wife! Damn woman, she's always goin' off and gettin' herself into trouble." He pushed Ben aside and tried to walk past him through the double doors that led into the ER room.

Ben grabbed his arm and swung him around. "Now look here, Charles, you're gonna' have to settle down a bit. We don't know at this time that this is your wife. But whether it is or not, you need to calm down. I don't know what you're so angry about here, but if this is your wife, she nearly got killed. She's in rough shape; we don't even know right now all the injuries incurred. So take it easy. You're not goin' back there with that attitude."

Charles took a deep breath and stepped away from Ben. He turned his back on the officer and broke down crying. Ben went up to him and put his hand on his shoulder. "It's okay, Charles. I know you've got to be at the end of your rope. Anyone would be. It's not easy comin' in here to identify your wife, but maybe there's nothing seriously wrong except some minor injuries. I just need you to be strong right now and help her through this." Ben pulled Charles around and looked into his eyes. "Think of Laura right now, Charles. Think of what she's been through. She needs you to be loving and gentle. Do you see that? You're the one who can affect her healing the most."

Charles nodded and wiped his eyes. "Sorry, Officer. My nerves are shot, like you said. My kids are asking for their mother and I don't know what to tell them. You can imagine the looks in their eyes. I can't even look at them anymore."

"Let's go back into her room and talk with the doctor working on her. When you see her face you'll know immediately if it's Laura. Then we can go from there. Can you handle that, Charles?"

"Yeah. I think so."

The two men walked back into the ER and turned into the second room on the left where Paul Anderson, the attending physician, was working on the woman. "Excuse me, Doctor. I'm Officer Ben Parker and this is Charles Yarbrough. He's here to see if this woman is in fact his wife, who's been missing for days."

Dr. Anderson stepped away from the woman and nodded. "Go ahead, Mr. Yarbrough. Look at her face and tell us if this is your wife."

Pale and visibly shaken, Charles walked slowly up the bedside and looked at the face of the woman lying on the bed. For a moment his face froze and then he broke down crying. " Laura! Laura! My God, don't die, Laura." He put his hands on her shoulders and shook her.

The doctor came over and grabbed his hands and pulled him off his wife. "You can't do that, Mr. Yarbrough. We're trying to treat her wounds and find out the extent of her injuries, and we just need you to say that this is your wife. You can't just shake her awake. She may have a concussion; we just don't know yet."

Charles put his hands by his side in defeat and sank into a chair by the bed. He put his head in his hands and cried. Ben walked over and put his hand on his shoulder to console the man, knowing this all had to be a shock to him.

"Officer, it appears this is Laura Yarbrough. When will you know the extent of her injuries? Have you taken x-rays yet?"

"We've cleaned her wounds and taken x-rays, but we may have to do an MRI or CAT scan to see what's going on in her body and head. She has had some trauma to her head and we need to find out what's going on. It might be best if Mr. Yarbrough waited out in the lobby until we get more information on his wife. We're working as quickly as we can to stabilize her and we'll let him know as soon as we find out any other information."

Charles got up and Ben walked him out to the waiting room. "I'll get you a nice cold drink and you just sit here and settle down a minute. I know this is hard for you, Charles, but at least we found her alive. You can be thankful for that."

Charles looked up slowly at Ben and cracked a slight smile. "Oh, I'm thankful all right, Officer Parker. You have no idea how happy I am that you found my wife. I just hope she lives, is all I got to say. My kids will go nuts if their mother doesn't make it. And I'd have to raise 'em alone. I have to work, Officer. I can't be home takin' care of kids, ya know? She's got to make it. She's just got to."

"I'll be right back with your drink. Just relax, Charles. They'll tell us something pretty soon here and then you'll feel better about this whole thing."

Ben got a Coke out of the vending machine near the cafeteria and walked back and handed it to Charles. Then he stepped outside and phoned the chief. "Hey, Chief! Got some good news. Charles Yarbrough is here at the hospital and he identified the woman we found as his wife, Laura."

"You're sayin' that Laura is alive?"

"Well, at this point we don't know how bad her injuries are. She's unconscious and they've done x-rays and may do more soon to find out what's goin' on. I just wanted you to know we did find her and it is Laura Yarbrough. I'll keep you posted on any further information we get."

"Great work, Ben. I knew you and Bob would locate that woman, if she was to be found at all. Keep me posted and watch out for the reporters. If they get wind of this they'll be up at the hospital taking photos and buggin' the heck out of you."

"I'll avoid them at all costs, I assure you. Talk to you soon, Chief."

❧

When Laura came to she was being prepared for surgery. She had a broken hip and several cracked ribs. She had a cracked humerus on her right arm and several fingers broken on her left hand. Her head had contusions and needed stitches but there were no life-threatening injuries to her body.

Her mind, however, was another issue. She could barely remember anything about the kidnapper, and the police were hoping her memory would get clearer as time went on. She'd been through a lot of trauma and it wasn't unusual not to be able to remember details.

Ben stayed with Charles Yarbrough until the surgery was over and they took Laura into recovery.

"Charles, I'm headin' home. If you need anything, here's my number. The doctors here will take good care of your wife, so don't you worry about a thing. Make sure you eat and get some rest, because she's gonna need you when she comes out of this."

"Thanks for all you done, Officer Parker. I know you didn't have to stay here this long and I really appreciate it. Her parents have the kids and I know they are sittin' on pins and needles wantin' to know how Laura is doin'."

"Is there anyone else who can sit with the children so they can come to the hospital and sit with you?"

"I guess I could call my parents to see if they'd help out. Don't you worry any. I'll get it worked out. I just want to thank you for all you done. You found my wife and I'll owe ya the rest of my life."

"I was just doin' my job, Charles. But I'm happy that she is in good hands now, and if there's anything we can do for you just let us know." Ben turned to go and thought of something else. "Hey, Charles, you might be careful about the press. I'm surprised they haven't already been here askin' questions. Head then off if you can, and don't tell them anything you don't want in print. They have a right to print anything you say."

Charles nodded and Ben headed out the door. It had been a long emotional day and he was worn out. Besides, Houston was going to need to get outside pretty soon. He called Keith and told him the news on his way home.

"Keith, she was identified as Laura. Did the chief tell ya?"

"Yep. We kinda knew that, anyway, right?"

"Yeah. Good work, buddy. I'll talk to you soon. And I hope it's not tonight. I could use a good night's sleep."

"Well, don't get to lovin' that sleep too much, my friend. Thanks for the call."

Ben pulled up at his house and walked in to find Houston zoned out on the sofa. He'd chewed up one of Ben's favorite pair of house shoes and it was obvious he was getting revenge for being left alone all day. Ben took him outside and ran him in the field next door and then fed him a good dinner. He grabbed a large TV dinner and wolfed it down. Then he showered, climbed into bed with Houston, and fell into a deep sleep. Even Houston's occasional snore didn't wake him up.

CHAPTER 28

After the terrorists checked out the clinic and determined that no American worked there, Mahsa was left on a side road with her hands tied and her mouth bound, beaten pretty badly. It was a warning from the faction; but they nearly killed her to make their point. A man was walking down the street looking for his dog who'd run away that morning, and he spotted Mahsa lying on the side of the road. She was whimpering but alive. He called home and told his wife to bring the car so they could take Mahsa to their house. She had no identification on her so he figured he'd just take her to his house and clean her up and try to find out who she was.

An hour later, after she'd been given warm tea and soup, Mahsa was sitting up with a swollen face, trying to talk to the strangers who had saved her life. Her lips were swollen and bleeding, her nose was broken and she could only see out of one eye. She hurt everywhere on her body. She told them to call her husband—that he was a doctor in town. When they dialed the number and told Dr. Irfan they'd found his wife, he wrote down the address and hung up, falling to the floor and sobbing. His poor Mahsa had been assaulted, the very thing she had feared when they took the American into their home. Irfan took the entire blame for the whole situation, for allowing Smith into his clinic where others could see him. Even though he had darkened his hair and beard, his speech was weak. People talked and word got out. At least enough to make the terrorist group question things. Irfan had learned his lesson the hard way.

The trip to get Mahsa seemed to take forever. When he arrived, Malik answered the door, allowing Irfan to come in. Mahsa was lying back on the sofa with a cold cloth on her face. Irfan walked up to her and knelt down beside her. She started to cry but stopped because her face hurt too much when she cried. Irfan hugged her and gently looked at her injuries. He had his black bag with him and some antiseptic that he put on her wounds. He then wrapped her wrists where they had been bound, and told her he wanted to take her home. She was afraid to go but she knew Irfan would take care of her.

Irfan and Malik carried her to the car and put her on the front seat. Irfan shook hands with Malik, telling him to bring his wife in any time to the clinic if she was ill. He was very thankful for the kindness that Malik had shown his wife.

"Mahsa, I cannot say enough how sorry I am that you have suffered this way. Bita would be so upset if he knew how you were treated. I will send word to him at Khan's house so he knows you are with me again. I should never have allowed Bita to be in the clinic so much. People talked too much, and that put us in more danger. Please forgive me, Mahsa."

"I was worried all along, Irfan, about risking our lives for the American. I like Bita, too, but am worried now if we should bring him back into our house. What is your plan, Irfan?"

"I have no plan as of now, but Bita cannot remain with Khan forever. I know his memory will return soon and then he can decide what he wants to do. But I think we will have to bring him home for a while. He will not be able to help at the clinic or be seen on the street. It will be difficult for Bita until his memory returns."

"Why won't you take him to the nearest American outpost in Afghanistan, Irfan? Would that be an impossible task?"

"Right now I want to let things settle down, Mahsa. I know you are anxious for him to go, but we have to wait for the right time. Otherwise, he will be caught and surely die. And all my work to help him heal would be in vain."

Mahsa sat quiet the rest of the way home. She was so tired and every bone in her body hurt. When they got to the house, Irfan helped her in, bathed her with warm water, and put her on the sofa. He brought pillows and a clean warm blanket and helped her get comfortable. He made her some supper and asked her to drink plenty of liquids. He was going to have to take her to the clinic tomorrow and set her nose if he could. He would take an x-ray and see how badly it was broken; it might possibly be fractured and they could let it heal on its own. It felt good to have her back home, but he knew the strain between them would not clear up until Bita was gone for good.

※

The clinic was buzzing the next morning with people asking many questions about Mahsa. Word on the street was that she had been killed by the Taliban or one of the terrorist groups. Dr. Irfan reassured everyone that she was alive and well. He decided after hearing so much talk about Mahsa that he would bring her to the clinic at night to x-ray her and take care of her wounds. Luckily she was mainly bruised and sore but he still had to find out if any bones were broken.

One of the patients had known Irfan for years and was a good friend he could trust. Irfan decided to confide in him about Smith. "Ahsan, I need your help. Can I trust you to take a message to someone?"

"Of course, Irfan. You have known me for a long time. We are trusted friends. I will do anything for you. What do you need me to do?"

"There is no risk in this for you. I need a message taken to Khan to let Bita know that Mahsa is at home now. She is injured but not seriously. Tell him that we are trying to figure a way to bring him back to the house and I plan that to happen near end of week."

"I will take that message to Khan for you, Irfan. Do not worry. I will let you know if a message is sent back to you."

"Be careful, Ahsan. Do not tell anyone why you are going. Take a gift with you so that if someone should ask, you can tell them you are bringing a present to Khan."

※

Irfan worked into the night nursing Mahsa and making sure he had a handle on all of the areas of her body that had been beaten. Just being home with her husband caused Mahsa to rally and have new energy. But there was an unspoken wall between them concerning Smith and his return to their home. Mahsa had certainly paid a huge price for allowing Smith refuge, and Irfan did not want her to suffer anymore. On the other hand, Smith was so close to recovering that he wanted to give him that time in a safe place. At some point his memory would kick in and they would know if he was living in Pakistan or here for military purposes.

Nothing would give Irfan more joy than to hear Smith talk about his past; this was the day he was longing for, as he had his own opinions of what Smith's life was like before the amnesia. Irfan had noticed what good shape he was in, and his ability to remember small details was uncanny. In the clinic Bita's mind was always racing ahead to the next situation, and he had a unique ability to read people.

But in all of this, he could not allow his marriage to fall apart in order to save Smith. He stayed by Mahsa's side all night, lying down briefly, giving up to the sleep that was pulling his body down. In the early morning when Irfan was asleep at last, Mahsa rolled over carefully and placed her hand on his chest. She loved her husband more than life and could not remain separate from him for long. She had grown to love Smith, also, but did not want their lives at risk. If there was no other way for Irfan to deal with this situation, then she would have to again put her trust in her husband, even though doing that might cause her death. There was such unrest in Pakistan with the Taliban's agenda that harboring an American in their home was almost a death sentence.

CHAPTER 29

With summer settling in full force with a familiar cloak of humidity, Grace and her three friends returned home from their adventurous trip to the Bahamas. When Grace woke up feeling refreshed from a good night's sleep in her own bed, she felt a longing to visit the cemetery and talk with Smith. For a few days her mind had been able to let go of the sorrow and enjoy the laughter and camaraderie of her three best friends, but now in the familiar surroundings of her home where there were so many memories, she found again the deep longing for Smith. She wondered if there would ever be a time that she didn't miss his love, his laughter, and the feel of his arms around her.

After a light breakfast she headed out the door, picking up some flowers on the way at a delightful florist not too far from the cemetery. When she arrived she pulled up in the parking lot and got out, looking around to see all the tombstones. The trees were in full bloom and weighted down with rich green leaves. It was a lovely place of rest and she was so glad that she didn't dread coming. However, in spite of how well-kept the lawns were and how breathtaking the landscaping was, there was still a feeling of loneliness there that she couldn't shake. She wondered if others felt the same way when they came to visit the graves of their loved ones. It was quite eerie to look down and see the name of the person you loved on a plaque or tombstone. Nothing made that easier, but there was something drawing her here that she couldn't explain to her friends. Margaret understood, but she was older and had lost her husband. However, she did remark one evening over dinner that over the years she found herself going less and less to the cemetery. Until one day she stopped altogether. Grace couldn't imagine not coming to talk to Smith but she had found that life had a way to taking us down paths we never dreamed we would walk.

The sun was warm on her face as she sat on a bench beside the grave. She breathed in the fresh morning air and closed her eyes, trying to picture Smith's face again. She spoke out loud in a low voice. "Oh Smith, wherever you are, I want you to know I love you so much. I did enjoy myself on this trip to the Bahamas, but inside I feel so lonely. I don't feel quite as heavy inside, but there are times when I want to join you in the grave. Don't worry, honey. I won't ever do anything stupid; I'm just sayin' that thought makes an appearance in my mind from time to time. I think it's normal but I just wanted you to know.

I have something I want to talk to you about this mornin'. I'm plannin' on visiting the orphanage tomorrow. I haven't been since you died and it's time for me to make an appearance there and let them know I haven't forgotten them. I am toyin' around with the idea of adopting a child. Now I know you are raisin' your eyebrow at me, and that makes me smile! But Smith, I need a child to put myself into. It would be good for me at this time in my life and I think I have a lot to offer a child who has had no parents' love or attention. I wish I could this with you. You would've made a fantastic father."

Grace stood up and wiped her eyes. She had sworn she wouldn't cry this time, but her heart had failed her. "Please know that I'll choose wisely on which child I'll take home. I've already decided that I would do it on a trial basis first before I talk to them about adoption. I think they'd prefer that, anyway. I still can't bear to think of living the rest of my life without you, Smith, even though if I allow myself to really hear that statement, I know how self-destructive it is. I'll pull through this, and part of what will help me do it will be having a child. Rest well, sweetheart. I'll be back soon for a visit with you."

Grace got up and walked down the path to the car. She felt good about talking to Smith but in a way it made her miss him more. Maybe that's what Margaret meant by her not going as often, and then quitting altogether. Perhaps it becomes fruitless after a time.

CHAPTER 30

The Wilton Children's Home was off the road on a hill, surrounded by massive trees and landscaping. It wasn't just the average orphanage, as the land had been donated by an anonymous donor many years ago. The grounds were kept up immaculately and because of the renovations that Smith and Grace and others had engineered, the rooms the children lived in had been updated and refurbished. The long driveway heading up to the main building was lined with tall poplars that bowed and swayed in the summer breeze. The buildings were red brick with black shutters and the grounds were richly landscaped. The main building where the office was located had high ceilings and a lovely grand entrance. When you walked through the door the view was amazing; there was a massive lake behind the buildings, and you looked right out on the water from the front door. So the whole wall was solid glass. It really brought the outside into the room and the children loved it. There was a big lounge area with several televisions and computers that sat in little cubby holes so that the child using the computer had some privacy.

Smith had seen to it that the home was fully staffed and there was one adult for every ten children living at the orphanage. At this point in time, there were one hundred children living full time in the dorms and they paired them off two by two. The rooms were decorated according to the age of the children with wall murals painted by local artists. The bedding was always fresh and clean and the whole orphanage lacked the usual odors that go along with bedwetting issues. During the daytime hours volunteers were around to help assist the workers with the children's activities or homework.

There was a child psychologist on board and she had her own office. Mary Ingram had been at Wilton for twenty years and would probably retire there. She was delightful and the children loved her. Her hair was long and shiny brown, and her eyes were equally as dark. She smiled easily, which put the children at ease when they had to come in for counseling. In her office were Normal Rockwell paintings lining the walls and she had toys in a basket in one corner. Two tall ficus trees were standing by the window and there was green ivy growing at the base of each tree, finding its way to the floor and curling back up again, reaching for the sun. On the far wall were bookcases reaching to the ceiling full of reference books, books Mary loved, and children's books she'd share from time to time with the children. She lived alone and had never married, so she became attached quickly to all of the kids at Wilton. And they adored her.

Eight years ago, a little girl named Molly Ann Johnson was left at the front door of Wilton Children's Home. She was only two years old and was sitting on the steps with a coat wrapped around her and a knit cap on, shivering in the winter wind. Her mother rang the doorbell and ran off, getting into her car and leaving the little girl alone on the steps. It was after visiting hours and the director, Sharon Edwards, had already left for the day. Mary had stayed late to finish some paperwork on a new child who had been accepted into Wilton when she heard the doorbell ring. It took her a few moments to get to the door, but when she pulled the heavy door open, she saw a little girl sitting on the steps, cold and nearly hysterical. Mary took her inside and picked her up, holding her close and trying to get some sense of what had happened out of the child. There was a note tucked into the pocket of the little girl that the mother had written stating that she no longer could take care of Molly and needed the orphanage to raise her. She left no phone numbers and no address where Mary could reach her. She did leave some information about Molly: her birthday was May 15, and she had no sisters or brothers. Molly had with her a pink blanket that was torn on one end and a doll whose hair was a mess. But she clung to those two items like they were her lifeline. Mary took her to the dorm but couldn't put her down. Molly clung to her and screamed when Mary tried to sit her on a bed. The other children came around her but she was petrified and kept asking for her mother.

Mary decided to stay the night with her and see if she could get her adjusted to being at the orphanage. It had to have been such a traumatic experience being left on a porch in the cold of winter and watching her mother drive away. That feeling of being left could remain with her for a lifetime, affecting many areas of her life. Molly had blond hair and was very tiny. She didn't even weigh twenty-five pounds when she arrived at Wilton. She was quiet and didn't say anything for months. It took a lot of time working with her, playing and laughing, and taking her outside with the children before she began to open up and talk. Eight years later she was a bright little ten-year-old who had many friends who loved her. She loved computers and animals, watched Disney shows on television, and adored American Girl dolls. Her hair had grown long and healthy, she had beautiful teeth, and her grades were excellent. But she still struggled with rejection and lack of attention from her parents. She had no memory of her mother or father and yearned to know who they were and why they had left her at Wilton. When people came to Wilton to visit or to pick out a child that they wanted to adopt, Molly Ann hung back and sat near the wall, convinced that the couple would not want to choose her. Even though she one of the most beautiful children in the home, she felt ugly and unwanted. No words could change that feeling she carried inside. No person could reach her. . . .That is, except for Grace Sanderson.

CHAPTER 31

For the first time in months, Grace drove to Wilton Children's Home. She had mixed emotions. The last time she had walked through the double doors of the home she had had Smith with her. All the kids loved Smith and she was dreading them asking where he was or what happened to him. When she pulled up to the home she noticed how rich everything looked, how clean and professional it was. Smith would be proud. She opened the front door and walked into the office. The first person she saw was Sharon.

"Well, look who's comin' into my office! What a breath of fresh air you are, lady! How in the world are you?"

Grace let a smile slip across her face and hugged Sharon, checking out the new paintings on the wall as she pulled a chair over to Sharon's desk and plopped down, hanging her purse on the back corner of the chair. "I'm doing as well as can be expected, Sharon. It sure is good to see you again! Walking through those doors was a little tough, I might add?"

"I can only imagine, Grace. We've been thinkin' of you for months now, hoping your life had settled down a bit."

"I really have no choice, do I now?"

"No. Not really. So what brings you here today? Want to check out the dorms and see how they turned out after all the hard work you and Smith did?"

Grace stood up and bowed to Sharon. "I'll follow you, lady. I'd love to see how things have turned out. It feels like years since I've seen the place. When I walked in it felt new like it was the first time I was seeing it. I already see new art in your office and that chandelier in the foyer is a killer."

"I thought you'd like that. Let's head to the dorms. The kids are in classes now so it's the perfect time for us to check out their rooms. Come on, let's go."

Grace followed behind Sharon, looking into every room she passed along the hall. The ceilings were high so it gave a feeling of spaciousness when actually the hallway was not that wide. There were framed photographs of all the children living at Wilton in the hallway, and one section of the hallway was dedicated to artwork done by some of the students. Grace was amazed at how talented they were.

"Have you ever thought about selling some of this art at a public auction? I'd buy them in a New York minute!"

"Yeah, we have talked about that in our board meetings. It would be a great way to raise money for the Home. And for school supplies. You may already be aware of how many pencils, notebooks, and backpacks we go through in a year. It's mind boggling."

They turned a corner and went through some massive polished walnut doors. When they closed, the hallway leading to the dorms was silent. All the children were in class so the dorms were empty. Grace poked her head into the first set of rooms, which were for the youngest of the children at Wilton. The walls had fairytale murals in pastel colors and the bedding was playful yet practical. Everything could be thrown into the washing machine, so keeping the dorm fresh and clean was easy. The children made their spaces personal by putting up some photographs of friends, and each had their own favorite toys or dolls around them.

As Sharon led them down the hallways, Grace was amazed at how creatively the dorms were designed. The older girls had iron beds with the latest bedding. They had cell phones in their rooms but were not allowed to take the phones into their classrooms. The school had been built years after the orphanage, and it handled grades one through twelve. Teachers vied for positions at Wilton's school because the pay was excellent and the classes were small. It was a perfect learning environment. Smith and the Foundation had seen that the school had the most updated technology, and the teachers were handpicked by the Board. Once you got the position at Wilton you never quit. So the children got to know the teachers and grew very close to them. It was like one big happy family.

∽

It was a bit overwhelming to realize what it took to house one hundred children under one roof. The staff had to be incredibly organized and on top of things 24/7 because there was little room for error. There were meetings twice a week to discuss issues with the children and then separate meetings for the older children. Their needs were different and their progress was tracked more closely than the younger children's. It was critical that the juniors and seniors be prepared for college, for that was one of the requirements at Wilton. All the students had to enter college and graduate, fully prepared to support themselves and live on their own. It took precision and a lot of assistance from volunteers to keep the older children focused and tutored. There was a lot of pressure from the outside on the school at Wilton, and this made the teachers work even harder to push the students to learn and achieve more than they would normally learn in a public school. Some of the seniors were through the first-year college curriculum when they graduated their senior year at Wilton.

Sharon was proud to show Grace the improvements that had taken place since she'd been away. Some of the construction took place when Smith was still home, but the completion had been done in the last six months.

"I am so proud of you, Sharon. This looks fabulous. I know it has taken a lot of time and effort on your part to see this thing through. I'm sorry I wasn't around to help."

"You did your part on the front end, Grace. You and Smith started something that was so powerful for the community and Wilton. Now we have a solid foundation to build on. We've only begun here at Wilton changing the lives of many children. I can't wait for you to see some of the kids. I know they'll want to see you!"

"Well, I don't know if I have the strength yet to see them. I know it will be tough on me, as Smith was such a huge part of this endeavor. This was our love, Sharon. Our passion together."

Suddenly the bell rang and the kids came running out of class, talking and laughing. Grace could hear them coming and almost panicked. "I had no idea what time it was, Sharon. I guess they're out now!"

"Yeah, here they come. They always come to their rooms to put up their books and papers. Then they head to the lunchroom to get snacks before doing their homework. We do that because the volunteers leave at about 5:00 every day. We need them to help with homework issues; if they were not here, we'd never get it all done."

Grace looked up and saw the seniors coming down the hallway. She ran to meet them and they all screamed out her name and ran to her. Tears were streaming down her face as she hugged them and called out their names. There were about thirty juniors and seniors, and the rest of the children were in middle school. Grace walked into one of the rooms and about fifteen of the kids came in behind her. She sat on the edge of one of the beds and they climbed in and sat beside her on the bed and all around the floor. She listened as they shared how their year was going, what they were taking, and what their dreams were. They seemed like such happy children and she tried to hug them all. It still haunted her that they had no parents to be around, no one from their family to care about what they were doing. As warm as the orphanage was, it still seemed cold compared to a family and a home. But this was all a lot of the older kids knew. They had no comparison so they were happy with what they had.

Word was spreading around the school and dorms that Grace was in the building, so the younger kids were fussing because they wanted to see her, too. Sharon pulled her away from the older children, promising that she would return soon. Grace then headed to the other dorms where the younger children lived. She walked into a large room where another television was and a lot of chairs and sofas. The kids came rushing in, yelling and pushing each other. They all wanted to see her first.

"Hey! You guys give her a second to sit down! James! No pushing!"

"Oh, it's all right, Sharon. I've missed them, too!" Grace grabbed a few of the kids and hugged then, noticing that they snuggled into her, smelling her perfume. She kissed on them and laughed, pulling new toothbrushes out of her purse for them. She had a lot of things in her car that she wanted to share with them but decided to allow Sharon to pass them out after she left. After she'd seen all the kids and they'd settled down a little, she asked Sharon about Molly Ann.

"I haven't seen Molly Ann, Sharon. Is she okay? Is she sick?"

Sharon shook her head and frowned. "No, Grace. This is normal for her. She hides in her room when anyone comes because she feels like no one wants her. She is really struggling with insecurity. Her counseling is ongoing and she's made progress, but when she heard you were here she immediately went to her room. I know for a fact that she wants to see you. But she just can't bring herself to come in here. It's the saddest thing, for she's brilliant and an absolutely lovely child."

Grace got up and walked down the hall, with little Andy showing her the way. "You're such a great help to me, Andy. You know where Molly Anne is, don't you? You're gettin' so big, Andy. Thanks for your help!"

Andy smiled from ear to ear and grabbed Grace's hand. He pulled her down two hallways and they turned left and then right. Andy stopped at the first room, dropped her hand and smiled a toothless smile.

"Okay, Miss Grace. She's in there, ya know. You can go in now."

"Thank you, little man. I do appreciate it!"

Grace walked in and Molly was sitting by a window with headphones on, listening to her favorite music. She didn't even hear Grace come in. Just when Grace was going to walk up to her, Sharon came in and said she had something for her to see. Grace turned and walked out and Molly never looked up. As they walked down the hallway, Sharon took her hand and pulled her into a large new auditorium that was built for performances, graduation, and any other events that would require a lot of seating. At the front of the auditorium was a huge plaque on the wall that took Grace's breath away.

We at Wilton Children's Home dedicate this auditorium to Smith Sanderson for his efforts to improve the lives of the many children who call this place HOME. We honor him and his dedication to making our world a safer place to live with the ultimate sacrifice of his life.

Grace was shocked and overwhelmed at the love and appreciation and thanked Sharon for this wonderful honor. "I know Smith would be proud of what he accomplished and also what the children have done to make this a better place. It really feels powerful when you walk in here and I know that has to have a monumental effect on the children. It was both our desires to make Wilton not only a safe place but an environment that evokes in the children a desire to learn and rise above whatever happened to them to become productive, happy adults. What we didn't want was for them to bring into their own lives the brokenness of their past."

"I so agree, Grace. That's why we were so thankful for what you and Smith did with getting so many involved. I was amazed at how much support you got from a community who had at one time turned its head away from all the orphans in Paynesville. I think you both made everyone more aware of the good this orphanage was doing, and also, the possibilities of what we could do to help change these children's lives. Sometimes people just need to be educated about something and then they are more than willing to help. I think orphanages as a whole can make people uncomfortable because they can bring feelings of sorrow that are overwhelming. No one wants to see a child grow up without their parents. You've done so much to make Wilton a happy home for these kids. Yes, they still are sad and want their mothers, but we can go a long way in making their lives feel more normal."

Grace swallowed a lump in her throat and grabbed Sharon's arm. "If I'm honest, I have a difficult time every single time I walk through those big doors. I can't help but think of all the kids here who have no home or family. But this has become a big family for them and they really don't seem as sad and broken anymore."

"The changes made here, the colors of their rooms and new bedding, the clothes they received, and the opportunities you afforded them have dramatically changed their attitudes about being here. They now are provided all the learning tools that other children have. They have the same clothes, the same books, the same dreams that they now feel are reachable. That's powerful, Grace."

"I know it has to be, Sharon. I'm thankful to be a small part of making Wilton work for these kids."

"Well, I know you can't stay all day but I really am glad you finally came back to see us. I was worried about you, girl."

"I just had to wait until I could take comin' through those doors without Smith."

They headed back towards the main building and Grace again remarked about how amazed she was at the students' art work. She reminded Sharon about offering the art for sale to the public and Sharon made a note on her desk to work on that. They hugged each other and promised to make a time for lunch with the children.

Grace turned to look back and saw Molly Ann standing against a column near the televisions. She almost called out to her but decided to make that another time. Her heart couldn't stand much more. She ran out of the door feeling like she needed to feel the wind on her face, wondering again for the millionth time how she would make it through her life without Smith. He was all over the orphanage. Everywhere she turned there was evidence of Smith.

She headed home feeling mixed emotions of joy for Wilton and the kids and a deep ache in her gut for the love of her life. Her throat was burning as she turned into her driveway, and she was just about to lose it when she heard Margaret call out her name.

CHAPTER 32

"Girl, I've been wantin' to talk to you! How in the world have you been? It's been so long since we had dinner. Grace? Grace!"

Grace heard Margaret but couldn't talk to her. She turned her face away from her neighbor and hid her tears. Maybe it'd been too soon to see the kids and what had been accomplished at the orphanage. Margaret walked carefully up to the car and put her hand on Grace's shoulder. That was all it took. The tears came tumbling out and Grace completely lost it.

"Oh, angel. I've said the wrong thing. Hold on while I open the door."

"I. . . .It was too much, Maggie. I . . ." I think you use too many . . ."

"Don't try to talk. It doesn't matter. Come on. Let's go inside and get you somethin' to drink. Somethin' stronger than a Coke this time."

Grace stumbled into Margaret's house and slumped down on the sofa, grabbing a Kleenex from the end table and blowing her nose. "I thought I was ready. . . .The kids. . . .They were so sweet . . ."

"Now, now, Grace. Take it easy. You shouldn't have gone alone. I know you're strong, but maybe it was tougher than you thought it would be." Margaret gave her a sip of wine and smiled. "Now honey, sit back and sip on this glass of my best wine. I'd rather you drink it than anyone else. Let's see if you settle down in a moment."

Lola came running in and jumped up on Grace's lap. She was getting hard of hearing and didn't hear Grace come in. She put her paws

153

up on Grace's shoulders and licked her tears, whimpering as though she knew Grace was upset.

"Oh, you sweet puppy. You're just what I needed tonight. I've missed seein' you!" Grace hugged the dog and put her down on the sofa so she could talk to Margaret. "Maggie, you have no idea how much I needed you tonight. That was a tough one! I had no idea I'd break down like that after leavin' Wilton. I had a lovely time and Sharon couldn't have been any nicer to me. She took me on a tour of the whole place, and, oh! Maggie! It looked fabulous. There was so much new energy in that place. And the art that the students had done was magnificent. You must see it!"

Grace was talking ninety miles an hour. "Hold on, angel. You're going so fast now that I can't catch up with you. I'd heard that the renovation went well, but I haven't taken the time to stop by and see how things were goin'. Lord knows I should have. So did you see the kids?"

"They were in school when I arrived but the bell rang just as I was leavin'. I wanted to see one girl in particular but she was alone in her room. Just when I was about to talk to her all the kids came barreling down the hallway. Maybe it's just as well because I would've fallen apart in her arms had she said anything to me at all."

They laughed and then Margaret shared about her visit to Texas with an old friend. She was amazing, traveling around at her age. Grace shifted her position on the sofa, sipped her wine, and shared about going on the cruise with her friends.

"So you finally took a cruise and got away from everything! That's wonderful, honey. I know you had a great time with your friends. It's like havin' a slumber party for four days. The food on a cruise is deadly, if I remember correctly." She leaned her head back a laughed, shaking all over. "You been home long?"

"No. We just got back. I visited the cemetery and then decided to go see the orphanage. I really did enjoy myself and am glad I went, but I just didn't realize I'd be so emotional upon leaving. I'm really thankful the children didn't see all the tears. They've had enough sadness in their lives."

"Well, I'm sure you'll be going back for a visit soon. You feelin' better honey?"

"Yes, I think I can go home now. Thanks so much for the wine, Maggie. I need to get some dinner and read up on some things about adoption. I'm toying with the idea of adopting a child from Wilton; have I ever mentioned that to you before?"

Maggie's jaw had dropped to the floor. "Heavens, no! I know I'd remember that conversation! You been thinkin' about this for long, darlin'?"

"Just in the last few months. I'm lonely, Maggie. And I have a lot of love to give a child. I'd wanted to do it before Smith died, but he was against it. Now I have every reason to do it, and I'm getting excited. I do have my work at the school, but when I go home, I'm all alone. A child would bring life back into the house, don't you agree?"

"I certainly do. That's just what you need! And I'll help all I can. I'll want to be a grandmother to the child, of course! I can watch her after school if you have meetings. Oh, won't this be fun, Grace?"

"Now, Maggie. I don't want you to be thinkin' you have to help me out. Of course I want you in her life, but you have a life of your own."

"Nonsense! Now I have dinner already made so I'll send some home with you. There's no point in you havin' to cook tonight." She got up and walked into the kitchen to get the food and brought back a covered dish and handed it to Grace. "If I'm remembering it right, this is your favorite meal in all the world. Chicken pot pie!"

Grace smiled and felt her mouth watering. "Oh Maggie! You're too much. Thanks for the food and the talk. I'm much better now. I'll stay in touch and let you know how the adoption goes. I may have to be a foster parent first; I'll find out the protocol this week."

Grace headed home with supper under her arm and warmth in her stomach from the wine. She would have to pace herself about going to Wilton if she wanted to hold it together. She started thinking about Ben and realized she hadn't heard from him since she got back from the cruise. The thought occurred to call him but she forgot after she got home and ate her dinner. She took a hot bath and piled up in her bed to read before going to sleep. Just as she was about to doze off, her phone rang.

CHAPTER 33

Ben was hesitant to call Grace so soon after she returned from her cruise. But truth be known, he'd really missed seeing her. It was dangerous ground but he couldn't keep her off his mind. While she was away he kept thinking about her, coming up with reasons to call her cell. But now that she was home it was absolutely necessary that he take her to dinner and hear all about her cruise if he was going to be a gentleman.

"Hello, Grace! How was the cruise?"

Surprised to hear from him, Grace sounded a bit reserved. "Oh, it was fine, Ben. Thanks for asking."

"I want to hear all about it. Can we have dinner tomorrow night and you can tell me how the Bahamas were?"

Grace paused, taken back by the butterflies in her stomach. "Well, I suppose we could go out. Dinner? Where did you have in mind, Ben?"

She sounded so formal. "I was thinking of the Red Moon Chinese Restaurant. Does that suit you?"

"That would be wonderful. I look forward to it."

"Great. I'll pick you up at 6:30. I promise not to keep you out too late."

Grace smiled and hung up the phone. What was with the butterflies? She pulled the covers up and turned out the light and lay in the dark thinking of Ben. He was cute, but she hadn't allowed herself to really notice him. At least not that kind of noticing. *Oh, one more dinner with him couldn't hurt a thing. I'm making too much out of it. I have enough drama in my life without creating more.*

She turned over and yawned, stretching hard. It had been an exhausting day.

⁓

Ben was so nervous he could hardly get dressed. For some reason he'd been consumed with thinking about Grace, knowing the chances of their really getting together were slim and none. He'd not had a good solid relationship with a woman for at least ten years, after Jennifer Mason broke his heart. Right at the very moment he was about to ask her to marry him, and after they'd worked through all the issues of his working for the CIA and travelling alone to places she would never know, she dropped the bomb that she'd been secretly seeing another man. It took a lot for Ben to give his heart to a woman; he'd been raised by parents that fought all the time and he'd sworn as a young child that he'd never marry. But Jennifer had been different than most girls he'd dated. She was raw and exciting, always changing with the wind. She was vibrant, throwing her head back and laughing at all his jokes, ready to do anything at the spur of the moment. What he failed to see was that she had commitment issues that kept her from fully falling in love with him. She did not think single-mindedly, and unbeknownst to him, she'd always had several men on the side. He couldn't believe he'd been so blind to her, always believing her excuses about why she couldn't see him on certain nights. She worked at one of the largest architect firms in Weston, and was active on many boards and attended all political rallies. She loved to be wined and dined, and he was captivated by her beauty. She was stunning. Long legs, long hair, and eyes that looked right through you. What he didn't know was the simple fact that she did look right through you, never seeing you. She allowed no one in.

Now Grace was another picture altogether. She couldn't be farther from Jennifer if she tried. Her mind was on a purpose and she was sincere in every area of her life. Commitment was no issue with her. She was loyal to the bone. Oh, she was beautiful all right. Enough to take his breath away. Average height, perfect figure from what he could tell, and eyes that had soul. She could see into your heart and it sometimes made Ben uncomfortable because he was afraid she could tell what he was thinking. She made him want to be a better man.

So tonight was important to Ben. He somehow wanted to move their relationship to another level without seeming pushy. Grace would not do pushy. She was still in love with Smith and might always be. He had to find a way to show her there was room for someone else even though Smith would always be her first love. That just might be the toughest mission he'd ever attempted in his life. Because nobody would come between Grace and her feelings for Smith.

And Ben had his own feelings about Smith to deal with. He still wasn't sure that Smith didn't know all of this might happen if he asked Ben to watch over her. That he would trust him with his wife was amazing. There wasn't a man alive that wouldn't want her. So as he dressed for this date, he prayed he'd find a way to win her heart. He was a little early when he pulled up in her driveway. He sat there for a moment looking at the house, thinking how big a presence Smith was when he was alive. How much he could affect the atmosphere in a room by just walking through the door. What a waste his death was, and how it flat had turned Grace's life upset down.

He saw her look out the front window and got out of his car and walked to the door. He couldn't help but recall the first time he'd walked up those steps.

"Hey, Ben! Come on in. I was wondering who that was out in my driveway."

He avoided the urge to run up and hug her. "Oh, I was just sitting there thinking. I was a little early . . ."

"Well, I'm ready to go, are you?"

Ben looked around the living room and spotted some photos on the mantel. "Is that a photo of you and Smith?"

Grace walked over to Ben and smiled. "Yes, that's us. We were in Colorado skiing, and someone snapped this photo for us. That was a great trip and Smith was amazing on those slopes."

"I can only imagine. Where was this one taken?" He pointed to another photo of her dressed in a long dress, so pretty and graceful.

Grace laughed. "Oh, I was dressed to go to the opera. We were in New York that weekend; he'd promised me a short trip to New York before he left on one of his trips. We had a ball and it was refreshing to dress up like that and be exposed to some culture."

Ben laughed and scratched his head. "Speaking of culture, let's go get some Chinese food!"

They headed out the door and drove the few miles to the restaurant talking about how the neighborhoods had grown and how many new schools had been built in the last couple of years. Ben really liked

Paynesville because it was growing by leaps and bounds and industry had moved into the town. They pulled into the parking lot of the Red Moon Restaurant and Ben opened the door to help her out of the car. He leaned over to take her hand and got a whiff of her perfume. For a moment he was overtaken by her beauty but caught himself before she saw the dazed look on his face.

"This'll be fun, Ben. I've not eaten here for years. What made you choose the Red Moon for tonight?"

"I don't really know, Grace. It just seemed like a perfect place for us to enjoy a meal and talk." He sounded stupid to himself.

"Are you hungry?" Grace smiled at him.

"I'm starving!" He actually had no idea how he would eat at all because he was so nervous. *What is going on with me tonight? I'm as nervous as a teenager!*

The Maitre d' asked Ben's name and checked the reservation list. "Come this way, sir." He bowed and led them to their table on the side of the room. Tall green plants were everywhere, scattered between the tables so it gave a feeling of privacy. Grace sat down and looked around; noticing a fountain in the center of the restaurant that was pouring water down three levels. It was a very relaxing sound, along with the soft music in the background. People were piling into the restaurant, which made Grace think the food must be delicious. She noticed Ben acting a little strange but shrugged it off as her imagination.

"What are you ordering, Grace?" He was deep in the menu trying to find something that sounded good.

"Lettuce wraps! They sound tasty to me."

"Okay, well, I think I'm having sweet and sour chicken with sticky rice and vegetables."

The waiter took their orders and left the table, and Ben dove in with both feet. "So how was the cruise? Did you enjoy being away from here for a while?"

"Oh, my gosh, yes! Ben, it was lovely there. So relaxing. I don't know why I fought them for so long to take that cruise. It was the best thing that could've happened to me. Perfect timing."

"Well, how was the food there? I'm sure you girls took advantage of all the great restaurants."

"We ate the whole time we were gone. I gained five pounds over that four day period! Can you imagine?" She laughed and buttered a piece of bread.

"I thought about you while you were gone. Wondered how things were goin'." He decided to step into the water a little and see how she responded.

"That's sweet, Ben. I really needed to get away. Things were gettin' a little heavy here. But I do have somethin' to talk to you about. When I came home I went to visit Wilton. The orphanage, you know?"

"I think I've heard of it, yes."

"Well, Smith and I spent a lot of time raising money to refurbish and expand the orphanage. It was such a rewarding visit! The dorms look inviting and the children seem to have really taken to the new colors. I am so proud of them; they've done some lovely art work that's hangin' in the main hallway and really, Ben. They are very talented." She paused to take a bite of bread and a sip of wine.

"Were they expecting you at Wilton or was it a surprise visit?"

"It was a total surprise for Sharon, the director. We had a great visit and then she showed me around each building. The last thing we saw was the auditorium and I really was touched when I saw a plaque dedicating the auditorium to Smith. Pretty emotional moment."

"That's pretty cool. I know he would have loved to have seen the improvements completed. I know you were proud of him, Grace."

"You have no idea. Or maybe you do. So what have you been doing, Ben? Did you start your new job?"

Ben swallowed a big bit of bread and butter and wiped his mustache. "Oh, I started my job, all right. We've already had two search and rescue jobs and I've had my eyes opened, I'm tellin' you right now. My partner called me both times at around 4:30 in the morning tellin' me to get out of bed and meet him at the station. I jumped out of bed and got Houston, my rescue dog, and hurried to get there. It was pretty intense, Grace. Luckily, both of these rescues turned out well. I've heard it doesn't always turn out like that."

"I know that has to be tough. But it was exciting to be working again, wasn't it?"

"You're right about that. I've seen a lot, Grace. Way more than most. But this is closer to home. Real people in trouble. I didn't realize how difficult it would be emotionally. As it turned out, my training in the CIA has been a real plus for me. For just when my emotions want to kick in, the training takes over and I can do the job without allowing my emotions to ruin my judgment. That's the danger of any job when you're using a weapon or in any type of danger. Your mind has to stay clear and your reactions have to be on target."

Grace smiled. He reminded her of Smith. "I know you will do a great job, Ben. It's right up your alley."

The waiter brought their food so they spent the next few minutes eating, listening to the music and enjoying the atmosphere. Grace finally broke the silence by asking Ben a question. "You ever think about having children, Ben?"

That was about the last question he would have ever expected her to ask. "Me? Kids? Well, I've not given it too much thought lately, Grace. In my line of work it was out of the question. And besides, I had no wife!"

Grace smiled and nodded. "I know. I just wondered if you wanted children. I've been thinking that it might be good for me to have a child around. You have any opinions on that?"

"Well, I know you must be lonely. Did you and Smith ever talk about having kids?"

"Yeah, we did. But like you said, it was out of the question in Smith's mind. Because he was going to be gone so much he felt like it would've been too much for me alone. But now it's different. I really want to foster a child and see if it feels right."

"I think that would be a wise thing to do first, Grace. That way you would know if you could handle having a child and working full-time like you do. At least you are home in the afternoons and off in the summer. Were you thinking of a child from Wilton?"

"Exactly. I even have one I am thinking about. Her name is Molly Anne. She's about ten years old and has no clue that I would want her to come live with me. She's shy and has had a rough background. She's been at the orphanage for years; I believe her mother dropped her off when she was two. A sad story. But a lovely girl."

"Whoa, Grace. That's bitin' off a lot, ya know. I'm not sayin' I know anything at all about raising a child. But takin' one on that has had a rough background; you could be asking for problems. Could you talk to this Sharon lady about it?"

Grace paused. She'd just had an idea. "Ben . . . Would you consider going to the orphanage with me? I'd love to show you around and then you could meet Molly Anne. I know Smith would have loved for you to see the place and see what he'd been workin' on for years. He really put a lot into makin' this a better place for the children. It has energy now. It's exciting to see how different the kids are. Would you go with me once?"

Ben looked at Grace for a moment, straight into her eyes. Gosh, she was beautiful. He'd just about go anywhere with her—but he never imagined it would be to an orphanage. "Grace, if you need me to go with you I'll be more than happy to go. When were you thinkin' about? Soon?"

"I was thinking I need to do this before the school year begins. So I can get her used to being at my house; we could do things together and get to know each other before she would start into public school. That would all be new to her and I want to give her time to adjust."

"Well, you pick the day and give me a heads-up so I can see what my schedule is like. Of course I could get called out at a moment's notice for a rescue, you know. But let's give it a shot."

Grace was surprised at herself for asking him, but it would feel better having him around. This was a big step for her to take on a foster child. Besides, she was excited about showing Ben what Smith had accomplished. He would be impressed at the auditorium and the dorms. They finished their meals and nibbled on key lime pie for dessert.

"You love your dog, Ben? Are you used to havin' a rescue dog around?"

"Are you kiddin'? We're like brothers. He sleeps, eats, and drinks with me. But I did have to get used to his snoring." He threw his head back and laughed and Grace caught herself watching him. His laugh was so deep.

"I guess that would be difficult to get used to! What kind of dog is he?"

"German shepherd mix. But a beautiful dog. Eats like a horse, though. I'm serious."

It was her turn to laugh. She hadn't been this relaxed since she was on the cruise and it felt so good. So normal. "Ben, this has been such a lovely night. To be honest, I was sort of dreadin' it because I was afraid we'd end up talkin' about Smith all night. But it hasn't been like that at all. I want to thank you for a wonderful evening and meal!"

Ben took her arm and walked her to the car. The night was warm and humid but there was a nice breeze blowing. "Say, Grace, you want to drive by Southern Thunder Cycles? I was wantin' to check out one of those new Can-Am Spyders."

Grace looked puzzled. "What in the world is that, Ben?"

He laughed. "It's a motorcycle that's called 'a three wheeled roadster.' You'll love it, Grace. Come on, let's go check it out."

She nodded and climbed into her side of the car. They took off down the road and Ben grabbed her hand. "You're gonna love this, lady. I'm nuts over this thing and want to take one for a drive so bad. I'd have to get a motorcycle license first. It even comes with GPS navigation."

They spent the next two hours walking through the massive dealership, checking out all the bikes lined up. Grace had never been that interested in motorcycles, but Ben's enthusiasm was contagious. She found herself wanting to sit on a bike to see what it felt like. So Ben motioned over to her and got her to sit on a huge Yamaha. Then they found the Spyders and Ben was speechless. He'd never seen one up close before and it just made him want it even more. The salesman came over and smiled at the two of them, shaking Ben's hand.

"It's a pretty mean piece of machinery, isn't it, sir?"

"No kiddin'. I've been wantin' to sit on one since they first came out. I've read up on it and I keep seein' commercials. These things are ridiculous. How much does one of these things go for?"

"They run from seventeen to twenty-two thousand. Not too bad for what you're gettin'."

"That isn't bad at all. Thought it would be worse. Grace? Don't' you love it?"

Grace laughed and shook her head. "Now, don't pull me into your addiction. I'll have to admit, though, that it's good lookin' and I can only imagine what it'd be like ridin' this thing."

"Well, one day we may just find out. Thanks for lettin' us look around. It just whetted my appetite even more. We'll be back, I'm sure."

They headed back to the car laughing at how quickly they had gotten pulled in. "Those things are sick. The price isn't bad and I noticed they didn't have very many of 'em. I just may get my motorcycle license in case I decide I can't live without one of those roadsters. You'd ride with me, wouldn't you, Grace?"

"I never thought I would, but after seein' them I probably would."

"That's my kind of woman. Well, guess I best be takin' you back home. If we stay out much longer I know I'll get us in trouble."

∽

Walking Grace to her door was tough. He wanted to kiss her so bad but didn't want to ruin the night. He turned and faced her, hugging her for a moment. "Grace, thanks so much for going to dinner with me. I really enjoyed being with you. Now you call me when you're ready to go to Wilton. I'll be glad to take you, and if that gives you the strength you need, then so be it. Just be sure you think this thing through, okay? It's a commitment and it's involving another person. You sure don't want to hurt her if it doesn't work out for you, and she thinks she gonna live with you, ya know?"

Grace looked at Ben and swallowed. "I know it's serious. And it's worse because it's a child who's already been rejected. So if I do this thing, it has to be for real. I know you're makin' me think hard about it, and I need that. It's just that I've wanted a child for so long and that desire hasn't gone away. I know I'm on my own now and it would be tough."

"You can count on me to help, either way. I'll be there for you and I can't wait to meet her. She sounds totally adorable. But just take your time in bringing her home. She just might fall in love with you like I have, and not want to leave!"

Grace blushed in spite of trying to hide her reaction to what just came out of his mouth. "Oh, you're being silly now!" She swallowed and took a deep breath. "I did have a fabulous time tonight. You sure know how to wine and dine a lady. And I don't take our friendship for granted, Ben. It's just hard for me, and I know by your sigh that you're gettin' tired of me sayin' that. Let's get together soon. I'll call you about visiting Wilton. I don't want to wait too long, so I hope your schedule isn't too full."

Ben took the chance to take her in his arms and hold her close. Surprisingly, Grace didn't pull away. He kissed her face and looked at her. It felt terribly close to Grace. "Ben, you've been extraordinarily good to me. I adore you. But I can't get my breath."

"Join the club, Grace."

"My heart is still hangin' back with Smith and I know that's okay with you. But it makes it hard for me to receive what you are tryin' so hard to give me. Does that make sense?"

He nodded slowly. "I'm blowin' it here, aren't I?"

"I see in your eyes that things have changed in your feelings towards me. I wasn't goin' to talk about this because I didn't want us to feel awkward. I do care about you and I have a ball with you when we're out. But remember how large Smith was in my life, and how incredibly difficult it is to just let all that go. It's waning on its own; I've had to clean out his closet and finally get rid of all the things that were his. So I am progressing. Just not as fast as you'd like, I suppose."

He hugged her again and laughed. "I'm only human, Grace. I find you irresistible and at the same time I feel a desire because of my relationship with Smith to protect you. It's an odd combination but I'm kinda likin' it. I just ask one thing. Let go a little. It doesn't hurt to enjoy yourself. Smith would want it for both of us. And I have a feelin' he knew I'd fall for you. That'd be just like him to set this up so that he'd know you'd be taken care of."

Grace was blown away by this revelation. She'd had a similar thought not too long ago. She looked at Ben and for once, she didn't know what to say. She leaned her head in on his chest and just stayed there a moment. His cologne drifted down to her and she felt a tear coming down her face. *It would be nice to have a man around again. It would be heaven to be loved. But is it too early? And can I really love Ben back?*

"I better go inside, Ben. But I do hear you, and you might just be right about Smith. He was very protective of me and would've certainly been up to creating a scenario that made him feel okay about leaving me." She raised up on her toes and kissed him lightly on the mouth. His heart nearly burst in his chest.

"Thanks for a totally awesome night. I'll call you soon and we'll visit Wilton. That would mean a lot to me for you to be there."

Ben whistled as he walked to the car and then realized how that sounded and laughed at himself. He was like a school boy who had gotten to take out the prettiest girl in the school. The cheerleader. The prom queen. His heart was racing as he headed home to Houston, remembering her words about Smith, and his realization that Smith had had a hand in this whole thing. *He was smarter than I thought. And I walked into this promise totally blind as to what would happen between Grace and I. Pretty cool actually. Very clever on Smith's part. But also very unselfish, which is par for the course for him. Not many men could provide for their wives another man, in case of their own death. However he had no assuredness that she would fall for me. And that remains to be seen.*

CHAPTER 34

The factions that were targeting Americans in Zhob had moved to Quetta, nearer the border of Afghanistan. Irfan found this out when he was talking to people in town, trying to figure out if it was safe to bring Smith home. Things had quieted down on the street and there weren't as many shootings around his clinic or neighborhood. It had been two months and nothing had happened so he spoke to Mahsa when he came home from work to see how her feelings were about Smith returning to their home.

"Mahsa, come sit with me a moment. I wish to speak with you about something very important."

Mahsa walked into the living room and Irfan was sitting on the sofa looking somber. "I am here, Irfan. What is it on your mind?"

"You are aware of how long it's been since Bita left our home. I am ready to bring him back so that I can monitor his recovery. At this point I have no way of knowing if his memory is returning or not. I have only spoken with Khan a few times during the months to be reassured that Bita is doing okay. I am concerned about depression, as that could hinder his healing."

"Go on, Irfan. What is it that you want to say?"

"I know for a fact that the level of risk has gone down in Zhob for us to have an American in our home. It seems that the terrorists groups have moved on to Quetta, leaving us in peace for a time. I want to bring Bita home for a while and see if we can get his memory to return. I know how you feel, Mahsa. I do not want to anger you. He will have to stay in our home and not come to the clinic for a while."

Mahsa rose and walked to the window. "I don't know how to respond to you, my husband. I was harmed and terribly afraid when they kidnapped me. But I know you are aware of the dangers. If you feel it is safe to bring him home I will not stand against your wishes. But please check out all areas before you make this decision. I again state that I do not want to die so that Bita can return to this house."

Irfan bowed his head, knowing he was asking a lot from his wife. "I do feel God wants me to finish with this man. Even though it is a risk, I feel it is smaller now. I would not do it if the risk were still high."

He walked over to Mahsa and held her in his arms. "My Mahsa, I love you. I will protect you as best I can in this situation. I do not want harm to come to us, my dear wife. But I feel God pressing on me about this man. He has been through tremendous trauma and needs to come to grips with his life. Somehow the memories must return so he can have his life back. Saying that, I know that I may lose him. And I have grown fond of him, Mahsa."

"That is obvious, Irfan."

He smiled. "Yes, I know. I only hope your trust in me has not failed."

Mahsa hugged him but her heart was heavy. She had been through so much, but she knew it was for a good cause. Still, she had mixed emotions about having Bita back in her home. He was a good man and it was not fair what life had done to him. A cruel joke. Perhaps there was hope, like Irfan said. That his memory would return so he could have his life back. But she had seen his face when he looked at Mishael. She wondered if he would get so rooted in his life in Pakistan that he wouldn't be able to let go when his memory came back. Once again she put on the cloak of trusting wife, but inside her heart remained unsure of the outcome for her family.

❧

Smith was beyond feeling caged in the room that Khan had provided. But they had become fast friends and occasionally Smith was allowed to come down and have supper with Khan at this table when Kahn thought it was safe. They had pleasant conversation and Smith learned much about Pakistan and the people there from Khan. There were many questions that remained unanswered about Smith and his life before. Khan asked many questions and Smith only shook his head. There were no memories yet.

Tonight was different. Khan was serious when he asked Smith to come down and eat. When Smith was seated at the table, after Khan blessed the food he looked at Smith very seriously. His eyes were like small black beads, and there was great emotion in them. "Bita, I have heard from Dr. Irfan."

Smith sat up straight and raised his eyebrows. "And what did he say, Khan? Can I return to his home yet?"

"That is what we were discussing. The danger seems to have lowered and he is anxious for you to return to his home. He has spoken with Mahsa and she has agreed that you can return even though there will always be some risk involved for them. I am impressed at how intent Irfan is on you getting your life back."

"I am equally anxious to find out who I am and where I was living. I have no memory of why I am here. It's very eerie, Khan. And frustrating."

"I know you can be good help to Irfan, but it will be a while before he allows you in the clinic again. He is planning on sending someone to get you on tomorrow. So you can get your things ready. I have enjoyed you being in my home. I wish you well, Bita."

They finished their meal in silence, as they had formed a wonderful bond between each other and Smith was very grateful for the safety of his home. There was no way he could repay this kindness, but he made sure Khan knew how he felt.

After supper they walked into the living room and Khan pulled out an Atlas. He sat with Smith on the sofa going over all the countries in world and then they looked at America. Khan asked him questions about the government in the United States and several of the cities they pointed to. But Smith was blank. No information came to him. He did feel an excitement when they talked about America, but nothing seemed to open up his memory. He wondered sadly if this was how his life would be. No past. No plans for the future. He thought many times about Mishael, knowing the restrictions on their relationship. It was discouraging to fall for a woman he could never have. And he saw in her eyes a struggle in her feelings for him. He didn't want to dishonor her in her own country.

Smith went up to his room and gathered the few things he had and put them in a duffel bag Irfan had given to him. He picked up his journal and made some notes before packing it away. It felt good to write down events and feelings so that he could look back and see if he'd progressed any. It was odd not having a memory of his past, his parents, and a home. He craved to know who he was.

〰

Morning came quickly and Smith was up early. Khan asked him to come down for breakfast, as this would be their last meal together. "Good morning, Bita. Hope you found sleep to come last night. I know you are anxious to see Dr. Irfan and he is looking forward to having you back home. Please take care of yourself and if I can ever be of help again, let me know. You are an easy man to have here and I've enjoyed your company."

"I, too, have enjoyed our conversations, Khan. You are a good man with a kind and generous heart. I will be forever grateful for what you've done and the risk you took for me."

There was a knock on the door and Khan answered it quickly. It was Dr. Irfan and he entered the house, looking around outside before he stepped through the door. "Bita! I have missed you terribly. How are you?"

Irfan walked over and hugged Smith and then stepped away. "You look wonderful. I can tell Khan has fed you well."

"Dr. Irfan. It is so good to see you again! I have missed you and Mahsa. How is she?"

"She has recovered nicely."

"I fear she may not want me back, Dr. Irfan. I would totally understand."

"We have spoken and she has agreed to it. So nothing more need to be said. But I warn you that there will always be a risk. We must work on your memory returning, Bita. That is my main goal here. To get you back to your life, whatever that is."

"I ache for that knowledge, Dr Irfan."

"Let's go before it gets late. I was going to send someone to get you, but decided to come myself; I was so anxious to see you. We will talk along the way."

Smith said goodbye to Khan and grabbed his things and headed out the door with Irfan. They were quiet for a block or two and then Irfan spoke quietly to him. "Bita, I have great feeling about you while you were away. I have feeling that you were doing something very important while you were here. You are so strong and agile and I have watched you long time now. Your mind is excellent; you can remember the tiniest details. In the clinic you seemed already to know about the human body; you were a natural cleaning wounds, helping the sick. I know something will come back to you. We have to only be patient and find that thing that triggers a memory. Once it begins, it will not stop."

Smith listened quietly to what Irfan was saying. He'd noticed himself how agile he was. He felt strong. He must have worked out in his past life because even during his recovery, his muscles were strong. "You feel it is safe for me to return to your home, Dr. Irfan?"

"As much as we know, the faction has moved away from us, but we are never totally safe. People tend to talk too much, but you've been here for a while now and perhaps the conversation is on something else."

"I don't want to put Mahsa in danger again, or you. Maybe I need to make plans in the near future to move to some other location. Even now it might be difficult to get me to an American base."

"We need to keep that in mind. I would prefer your memory return even before the Americans get their hands on you, but I have no control on how quickly this will happen. There is such unrest in this country that we are never safe. It will sadden me for you to leave, Bita. I have enjoyed having you here. I feel in my heart you are like a son."

When they arrived at the house Irfan entered and let Mahsa know they were home. She had prepared lunch for them and welcomed Smith. "It is good to see you again, Bita. I know you must be weary of moving around, feeling like you have no place to go. Our home is your home until you understand your past."

"That is more than gracious of you, Mahsa. I will try to stay out of sight so that I don't bring danger to your family again. I cannot say enough how sorry I am that you had to suffer because of giving me a safe place to live. That is the ultimate sacrifice and I am a stranger to you."

"You are fast becoming part of our family; Irfan is very fond of you. So I welcome you into our home for as long as it has to be."

Bita took his things back his bedroom and sat on the edge of the bed. It was a bitter sweet homecoming because he still felt so misplaced. He silently prayed that his memory would return as he felt anger rise up in him. He had no control over his life, he was totally dependent upon Irfan for his welfare, and he had no idea how long this would last. What kind of life was that? If this was how he had to live his life, then he knew he needed to find a better way to blend in and get involved. Most of the people around Dr. Irfan accepted him with no questions. It was only the terrorist groups that were an issue. Mishael crossed his mind and he smiled; she was a joy to be around. But even Mishael was untouchable; his feelings towards her could cause major problems in her life.

After lunch, Irfan and Smith walked into the backyard and sat down in chairs under a shade tree. Summer was passing quickly but it was still very warm. "What is our plan, Dr. Irfan? How can I remain here and have any kind of life?"

"I know you are worried, Bita, and frustrated to have no life. I will find a way for you to work and feel productive in your life while you are here. But we always have to be careful. The people who talk mean no harm. And most of those who know me and have seen you around are becoming accustomed to your presence. So the talk will cease and you will blend in better in society. There are Americans here and usually it is not much problem. It is only when the factions rise up that trouble comes."

"I understand the situation and will do everything I can to blend in. I need to work on the language more. Is there a way Mishael could help me with that? I do miss her."

"You must be very careful being alone with Mishael. Her family would not approve. She can see you and work with you, but you must respect her and understand the limitations of that relationship. Is that possible, Bita? I know you feel something toward her. It is quite obvious."

Smith couldn't help but laugh, but quickly agreed with Irfan. "I don't mean to make light of it all. I didn't know it was so obvious. She is a beautiful woman, I agree. I'll honor her and try hard not to cause any problems. She is pretty strong. I—"

Irfan interrupted. "She's a woman, Bita. And she has feelings, too, that wrestle with her. It will be up to you to be the strong one."

Smith looked at Irfan and knew he was right. "May I call you 'Irfan?'"

"Yes, of course, Bita."

"I know you are right." He got up and paced around the patio, rubbing his beard. "I'm lonely, Irfan. I'm sick of having no life. If I am to be here who knows how long, then I need a life. I need to be able to have friends. I cannot stay cooped up in that room and only see you and Mahsa. I love you both but that is no life for me."

"Bita, the more frustrated you are, the harder it will be for your memory to return. One day something will trigger a thought and then perhaps it will all come flooding back. We'll find a way for you to feel productive and I can have people over to the house who will accept your being in my home. Or better yet, we can go to their home and not worry Mahsa. Right now we need to be thankful you are safe, Bita. God has protected you."

Smith bowed his head and sat down. "I'm not ungrateful. There's no way I will be able to ever repay you and Mahsa for saving my life. And that continues even now." He stood up again, frustrated and full of emotion. "The worst part of all of this is that I know I had a life somewhere. I may even have a wife and family. I'm missing out on that life. So do I create a new life here and let go of wondering who I was? And how do I do that if there are so many limitations on my relationship with a Muslim woman?"

"All of these things are a problem, Bita. It hurts me to hear your frustration, and I knew this was coming. The healthier you become, the more frustrated you will be. All I know is that we have to put one foot in front of the other and walk each day out until you know who you are and come into a full understanding of what happened in your life to bring you here. There is wisdom in this, Bita. We have to have wisdom about your life and your desires and actions."

"I see that, Irfan. I respect what you're saying. But the challenge is this; how do I fit in here and have some semblance of a life without getting involved? I am a man and I have desires which I can contain for a while. But I'm human and I have needs as a human being. I do not fit in anywhere here. Can I meet other Americans here? Is that more dangerous now?"

"I don't have all the answers, Bita. But we can search this out and find the answers. In the meantime, we need to get you working and feeling productive. Your focus needs to be on helping others and finding your way here. And I'll do all I can to help you."

The two men stood up and embraced. "You've been good to me, Irfan. Like a father to me. And I do love you and thank you for what you've done. I don't mean to offend anyone or sound ungrateful but I think you're right. The healthier I become the more I want to be on my own and have a life. I've been studying the government situation here in Pakistan and also in the surrounding countries. I found a book at Khan's about America and I read the whole thing, swallowing the information I could find about that government and their relationship with the Middle East. I can't explain the hunger I have but I will also add that some of what I read did sound familiar. I don't know what to do with that information, but I do feel that the more I read and study, the quicker things may come back. If it is okay with you, I will be wanting more books to read and study. That can't bring harm to us, Irfan. And it makes me feel like I'm heading in the right direction."

"I agree with what you're saying and will help you find more history books to read."

"I know you have a gun in the house, Irfan. I want to learn to use it."

Irfan rubbed his face and looked over his glasses at Smith. "That may be a more difficult task, for I am not sure where you could practice shooting without attracting attention. Gunshots in this neighborhood would draw attention immediately."

"We'll find a wooded area somewhere that we can go. I feel the need to learn so I can help protect us if something should occur like last time."

"I'll see what we can accomplish, Bita. I feel your strength returning and I'm happy about that. One step at a time, Bita. One step."

Smith felt relieved after talking to Irfan and returned to his room for a short nap. When he awoke he heard voices in the living room and got up and washed his face and walked into the front of the house. Sitting on the sofa was Mishael, talking with Mahsa and Irfan. He felt something rise up in him when he looked at her. She was so beautiful and mysterious to him. As he stood in the doorway watching, Mishael glanced his direction and smiled. Their eyes connected for a moment and there was something that flashed across her face for a second and then disappeared. But Smith knew then what he had suspected. She loved him as he loved her. And this love had to remain unspoken between them.

CHAPTER 35

Maryann had arranged another girls' night out and everyone was meeting at Michelle's Steak House on Main Street. It was pouring down raining and the streets were like glass as Martha drove into the parking lot. The forecast was for severe thunderstorms until after midnight, but for now, it was just a bad downpour. Balancing an umbrella and her purse, Martha splashed through puddles to the front door and slipped in, barely getting her umbrella down before the door closed. She looked around the half empty restaurant and spotted the rest of the group at a large round table in the center of the room. There was a musty smell in the room and it felt quite humid, but nothing overshadowed the good food that was served. As she reached the table she landed in a chair close to Grace and placed her purse on the back of the chair.

"How's it goin' Grace? You recovered from our cruise yet?"

"Oh, yes. I'm right back in my old routine! How are you and Ken doin'?"

"He didn't even miss me. Played golf the whole time I was gone. Guess the honeymoon is over!"

"Oh he talks big, Martha. But he's pitiful when you're gone."

Martha smiled and nodded. "I know that. But I don't think it's reached that thick head of his yet."

Grace looked at Celeste and winked. "How was Steve when you got home? Taking care of the business and eating TV dinners?"

Celeste laughed out loud. "You've got him pegged, Grace. He's gained weight and the house was a mess when I got home. But it still felt great to get away. I needed a break."

They ordered their entrees and a bottle of Zinfandel. After the waiter poured the wine and left the table, Maryann asked Grace a question that had been on her mind since the cruise. "You mentioned to us, Grace, that you were toying around with the idea of adopting a child. Anymore thoughts on that?"

Grace didn't expect this to come up so soon and looked up to see all of her friends staring at her, waiting to hear her answer. "Well, since you asked, I've been thinking a lot about it. I went to visit the orphanage when we got back and really enjoyed seeing what Smith had accomplished. He even has an auditorium dedicated to him. It was really sweet."

"That's impressive. Did you see any children?" Celeste asked, sipping her wine.

"Just for a few minutes. It was pretty emotional for me going back there so I didn't want to add to that by getting involved with the kids. I'll see them soon; I have in mind one student in particular that I would like to have as a foster child for a while. Just to see if it would work. If I can manage my schedule and theirs."

"Sounds like you've really thought this thing out, Grace. Would this be long term or just for a weekend occasionally?" asked Martha.

"I would keep the child for a year if it felt right. You have to give it time for both parties to adjust or there's no point."

Maryann popped into the conversation with a mouth full of steak. "So you've already chosen a child that you'd like to try this with?"

"You guys are really worked up over this, aren't you?" Grace took a bite of her baked potato that was piled high with sour cream.

"Just curious, Grace," said Maryann.

"I have a girl in mind that's about eleven years old. I've known her for quite some time and we have a sort of connection. I haven't spoken with Sharon, the director, yet about her. But I have a feeling she'd agree that this young girl would be a good match for me."

"Not to change the subject or anything, but how's that good lookin' Ben doin'?" Martha asked, wiping the butter off her lips.

Everyone laughed and Grace finished her bite of salad before answering. She wasn't quite sure what to say to them because she hadn't figured out that relationship yet herself. "He's doing fine. Busy doing search and rescue with his dog. I've only seen him a couple of times since the cruise, and he seems to really be into his work."

Celeste looked at Grace with a raised eyebrow. "So how do you feel about him? Does he interest you at all, Grace?"

She blew out a sigh and rubbed her hand over her face. "Boy, you guys are really pushing me for an answer and I'm not sure what you want me to say!" She pushed back from the table and smiled at them, but there were tears in her eyes. "If you want to know the truth, I feel guilty goin' out with Ben and havin' a good time. He's so easy to be around and we click on a level that is refreshing. There is no strain between us. But having said that, we both loved Smith in our own way and that's always between us, it seems. So this relationship is a tough one in that neither of us wants to betray the man we loved." She got up and excused herself and headed to the restroom.

The table was quiet. Then Celeste spoke. "We didn't have to push her like that, guys. She's still fragile over losing Smith and we're acting like she's on a manhunt. We need to back off a little. Now we've upset her."

Martha got up and walked into the lady's room to check on Grace. She could hear her crying in the stall and she called out her name. "Grace? Are you okay? I'm sorry if we were being too nosey. We just care, is all. We weren't tryin' to upset you. Okay?"

Grace blew her nose and opened the door. "I know, Martha. But to be honest, I don't know how I feel about Ben. He's handsome, a wonderful man, but I'm holding back a little. I can tell he really likes being around me and that feels good. But I don't know where this is goin'. I'm not sure where I want it to go, ya know?"

Martha put her arms around Grace and hugged her tight. "Hey, I love you. I just want you to be happy. I think we're all so eager for you to have a good life and be happy that maybe we're being too aggressive with our questions. Now let's go finish our dinner. It's gonna be a bad night out and we don't wanna be out on the road in the middle of the worst storm."

Grace walked back to the table and shrugged her shoulders. Everyone laughed and finished eating. After dessert, Celeste put her hand on Grace's arm and whispered to her. "Gracie, I wouldn't upset you for the world. I just wanted to know if you were getting closer to Ben. Sorry for pushing too much. You mean the world to me."

"It's okay, Celeste. I don't need to be so sensitive about it. But maybe it's because I really don't know my own heart right now. It's still tough for me. I do like Ben, though, and will continue doing things with him. We have a wonderful time together and it's refreshing to laugh and enjoy myself again."

"Well, I pushed too hard and I'm sorry. Lesson learned. I hope you forgive us. You're like a sister to us, Grace. And we've been friends too long. "

"Enough said, Celeste. I'm just overloaded with thinking about adopting and allowing myself to feel again with Ben or anyone. I appreciate all of your concerns and don't think I haven't noticed that you guys are there for me at a moment's notice. I'll keep you all posted on the how this goes with Wilton. I'm excited at the prospects."

∾

Grace headed home with thoughts running rampant in her head. She was a student at heart but there was no book out to guide her through the next phase of her life. She was curious about what she was supposed to do with all those feelings she had stored away; her love for Smith, anger at how he died, fear for what the future held. Even though she knew all of that was perfectly normal, it was scary going through it alone. The girls were there for her, but nobody could really walk it with her. Life seemed to be like that in the best and worst of times. So she prayed one more time for strength and pulled into her driveway, suddenly noticing that one of her favorite songs was on the radio. She laid her head back on the seat and closed her eyes and just listened to the words . . . " . . . You better let somebody love you, before it's too late." One day at a time. One day.

CHAPTER 36

Keith was sitting at his desk at the station when a 911 call came in. Two Boy Scouts had gone to camp and had disappeared on a hike. They had been missing for three hours and the Scout leaders were panicked. The parents had been notified and were already at the campsite searching for the boys. The Boy Scout Camp was on 100 acres of land that included large lakes, wooded areas, and a large ditch that ran at the back side of the camp. There was a fence bordering the whole area off, and massive gates that were locked unless campers were going in and out with troop leaders. Abutting the camp was state preservation land that held thousands of acres of forest set aside for camping and hiking.

A hike had been arranged and the boys were given compasses and set off in groups of ten to follow a map and return at the starting point in an hour and a half. Everyone returned except two of the boys who had strayed from their group, and no one had seen them since. Several of the troop leaders took the path that was mapped out and searched those areas that were off the beaten path, but there was no trace of the boys anywhere. The boys didn't have cell phones on them because all the phones had been turned in at the beginning of camp. The Scout leaders were becoming increasingly worried as time went on, because even though the boys might find water, it might not be safe to drink, and the food they carried in their backpacks probably wouldn't last long. No one knew for certain what animals lived on the premises, either, so they were also concerned for their safety.

The police were called in to bring search and rescue dogs to the campsite in hopes of locating the boys before it was too late. At 2:00 Ben pulled up with Keith and the dogs, ready for the search. It was already getting hot and humid and the forecast predicted a slight chance of thunderstorms.

"Good afternoon, officers. I'm Mike Helms and this is John Stenson. We're the scout leaders here at the camp, along with ten other adults who've volunteered to help. As you may have been told, we gave the boys a compass and set them out in groups of ten with one adult, to follow a map. These two boys broke away from their group and wandered off." He showed Ben photos of the two boys.

"Their names are Michael Johnson and Bobby Simpson. They are fifteen years old and have been scouts for several years. Never given us any problems before. They do have food in their backpacks and water, but not enough for several days. They've been gone from the group now for three hours, and we've searched the surrounding area pretty well. This isn't the first time John and I've been here with the boys and we know this place pretty well. However, there's preservation land surrounding this campsite and we are not familiar with that area at all. I'm worried the boys got lost trying to take a shortcut back to camp. I sure hope you can find them with the dogs."

Ben and Keith shook hands with the two men and tried to reassure them. "We'll do everything we can to find these kids. Do you have some clothing with their scent on it? That would be a great help."

Mike pulled out two shirts for the officers to use. "The boys went north down the path you can see here, with the other eight scouts and Fred Jones, a parent volunteering at the camp. They walked for a couple of miles and took a break and sat down on some fallen trees. Fred was explaining how important it was to set markers on the trail so that they'd know that they'd been there before and could find their way back to the starting point. In these woods it's difficult to keep your bearings even with a compass. They all picked up their backpacks and started the hike again, and an hour later Fred noticed that two of the boys were gone. Apparently, nobody saw them leave. We think Michael and Bobby were going to try to find a shortcut back to the starting point and win the race. There were ten other groups doing this same hike and the boys can be quite competitive."

Keith pulled his dog off the shirts and Ben and Houston headed towards the path. They were carrying backpacks with supplies and both noticed the weather changing. Clouds were building up on the horizon, which could mean a storm was headed their way. They waited until they got deeper in the woods to take the leashes off the dogs, but it was difficult to hold them back. "Ben, this could take some time, so we need to pace the dogs. At the same time, we'll have to keep our eyes on the weather. If it gets bad, we'll have to pull back."

⟲

Hours into the search, dark clouds were building and the forecast had changed from light showers to severe thunderstorms. It was crucial that they find the boys but they couldn't remain in the woods during a thunderstorm.

The dogs were going northeast when they suddenly took a turn directly east and ran through the woods with their noses to the ground. Ben ran ahead and saw that the dogs had run up on a canteen that must have belonged to one of the boys. He took the canteen out of Houston's mouth and stuck it inside his backpack, and they headed east to see if there was any other sign that the boys had come through there.

It was getting increasingly dark and Keith was about to make a call that they head back when they noticed a fence that bordered the state preservation land. He ran up to it and saw that the fence had been pushed down enough to get across.

"This doesn't look good, Ben. The woods on the preserve are denser and more difficult to get through," Keith remarked. They decided to phone Mike to let him know what they'd found and discuss the impending weather.

"It looks like from here that the boys did enter state land, as a fence is down on the east side. I don't even know how they got the fence down unless it was already leaning. It looks very ominous from here, and we're thinking about heading back to the camp. We can't risk being out here in the woods in a lightning storm with the dogs."

"I agree. But I sure hate to have those boys out there alone if it's a bad storm."

Ben nudged Keith and whispered. "Hey, let's go for it. If we hurry we may run up on them soon and we all could head back together. A little rain won't hurt us."

"I know you want to find them, but the chief would frown on us being irresponsible. I think we need to head back."

"Keith, this is what I'm trained to do. Let me go forward with Houston and find the boys. If you need to head back, go ahead. I know I can find them. This is too serious to turn back because of a little rain. I'm aware of the risks involved, and if I lose my job, then so be it. But we came here to locate those boys and that's what I'm gonna do." Ben was not used to such restriction being placed on a search. In his line of work he along with the team leader made all the decisions and high risk was not a deterrent.

Ben put a leash on Houston and headed across the fence. Keith told Mike they were finishing the job they came there to do, hung up, and stood there for a moment wondering if he made the right decision. Then he realized he had no choice; his partner had already made the decision for him. He took off with his dog after Ben, knowing he'd have to trust him blindly because of his training with the CIA. And there was no talking him out of it. So they both headed east into the state land, tromping over fallen trees and heavy brush. The dogs seemed to have a scent and were heading farther east where, according to the map, was a huge deep ravine. Both men knew that the two young boys had no map and would have no way of knowing there was a ravine in front of them. It took a long time to get to the point where they could see the ravine because of the heavy brush, and a strong wind had kicked up, blowing the trees above them.

As they approached the deep ravine, there were large trees that had fallen and they blocked their path. They looked north and saw an opening, and plodded through the brush and fallen limbs to an area that was clearer. Both men were sweating profusely and the dogs were getting hot. The temperature had cooled down some because of the dark clouds and wind that had picked up. They could hear thunder rumbling and saw some lightning in the distance.

Ben knew that timing was going to be critical in finding the boys if they were going to beat this storm. He had no desire to be crouched down in the woods during one of the worst thunderstorms of the season, but at the same time, the decision to leave the boys out there was not a good choice, either. He made a plan in his mind and explained it to Keith, who was squatted down checking the front paw of his dog.

"Keith, you go north along the upper edge of the ravine and I'll move south. Look down into the ravine and also check for any signs of the boys, like a backpack, etc. It'll be difficult to see anything in this brush, so I'm hopin' the dogs will catch any clues even before we do.

Hopefully our phone signals will hold out. Ring me if you see anything. If it gets too bad out, we'll make a call on this search. But I'm not too keen on leavin' without findin' the boys."

"Okay, Ben. I'm lettin' you make the call; I agree we need to find the boys. I'll let you know what I see. The chief isn't gonna like it, but the longer the boys are out alone, the less chance we'll have of findin' them alive."

Ben hooked Houston up to his leash and walked through brush and uneven ground, following the edge of the ravine. He looked down in the ravine and on both sides, hoping to see some clue that the boys had been there. He must have walked for a mile, when suddenly Houston jerked the leash and stood at the edge of the ravine barking. Ben grabbed hold of the leash and pulled Houston away from the edge. Then he squatted down and spotted what looked like a backpack halfway down the side of the ravine. He called out the boys' names and his voice echoed through the woods. Houston started barking when Ben yelled, and he quieted him down. He wanted to be able to hear the slightest sound in case the boys were down deep into the ravine. He phoned Keith to tell him about what he'd seen.

"Keith! Just spotted a backpack halfway down the side of the ravine. I'm about a mile south from where we started. You might as well head my way. We may be onto somethin' and I'm gonna need you to help me down the side of that ravine. I've got a rope in my backpack. I'll wait here for you."

Keith turned around and headed south, holding his dog back, looking down the ravine for any clues. His heart was racing at the news that Ben had spotted a backpack. That was a good sign, but where were the boys? He hoped they had not fallen into the ravine; it would be difficult to get them out or even find them. Just as he was about to reach Ben, the rain started. Huge drops began to fall and thunder was all around them, rumbling in the sky. The wind was picking up and the bottom was about to fall out of the sky. Ben waved him down when he spotted him and they tied the dogs to a limb that was attached to one of the huge trees that had fallen.

"Keith, I'm tyin' this rope around my waist and hookin' it to a vest I'm wearing. I brought some equipment I used in my other job. My shoes have a slight cleat on them which will help me grip the side of the ravine better; things could get pretty slippery in this rain that's about to happen."

"I'll tie the end of the rope to this tree. You tell me what else I need to do . . ."

"Just hold the rope and slowly lower me down the ravine. I'm goin' to reach the backpack and see if I find anything else that the boys may have dropped. Let's hope the boys are not at the bottom of this friggin' ravine."

Ben started down the side and Houston began to pull on his leash, barking. His clothing was getting snagged on a lot of brush on the sides of the ravine and he was looking around quickly, hoping to spot any movement or signs of the boys. He hollered out and his voice sounded muffled as he got farther down in the ravine. The rain was coming down hard now and Ben noticed there was already water on the bottom from a previous rain.

He finally reached the backpack and slung it over one shoulder. He hung there suspended looking around, hoping to see anything that would give him a clue that the boys had fallen into the ravine. Lightning was everywhere now, and it was raining so hard it had become difficult for Ben to see anything past twenty feet on either side. He knew the longer he stayed in that position, the less chance he'd have of finding them, as the ravine would start to fill up with even more water. Looking up he could no longer see Keith through the sheeting of rain, and he knew he had to make a decision whether to drop down farther or head back. His gut feeling was that the weather was only going to get worse, but he chose to head to the bottom and he tugged on the rope and began to descend.

There were rocks on the bottom and along one side of the ravine. Ben's foot touched down on the rock and he was able to walk along the bottom edge. His rope was going to run out if he walked too far, but something was pulling him farther south.

He didn't go far before his instinct proved to be right. There was a huge tree that had fallen into the ravine and he saw through the rain what looked like a body lying over the tree. He walked through the water, sloshing over the rocks to the body of one of the boys. He slowly lifted the boy and turned him over so he could check his pulse and any injuries incurred. The boy was limp and appeared dead, but Ben immediately found a pulse and knew the boy was alive. It was obvious they'd fallen unaware into the ravine and this child had slid and landed on the fallen tree. He was unconscious but began to moan as Ben moved him around. He could tell some bones were broken in his arm and one of his legs. There were scratches on his face, but nothing serious. He called out to the boy to reassure him that he was going to be okay.

"Son, it's okay. I'm here to get you back to camp and you're gonna be okay. Can you open your eyes? Can you hear me?"

The boy's eyes suddenly opened. In the pouring rain Ben took off his hat and shielded the boy's face so he could see Ben standing over him. Ben smiled so he wouldn't be afraid. "Can you see me, son?"

The boy nodded and started crying. He began to shake and Ben picked him up and put him over his shoulder and carried him back to where Keith was standing at the top of the ravine.

"Keith! Can you hear me? Keith!"

"Yes! Did you find anything?"

"I'm tying a rope around one of the boys! Pull him up when I tug on the rope."

Ben struggled to tie the rope around the boy's waist and spoke to him above the pounding rain.

"Son, can you hold on the rope with your good arm? Is there any way you can hold on to the rope? I've to get you out of here and I can't take you up myself. You're gonna have to hold on like a brave Boy Scout. Can you do that?"

Michael nodded and a smile formed at the corner of his mouth. He was in shock but tried to hold on with his right hand, holding his left arm close to his side. One of his legs was dangling but he seemed to feel no pain. Keith slowly pulled against the fallen tree and raised up the boy slowly to the top edge of the ravine. He tied off the rope and ran to pull the boy the rest of the way up. He had to be careful not to hurt the broken arm and when he was reaching over the edge to grab Michael's shoulder, he nearly fell over the edge. He caught himself with his left hand, grabbing a limb that was protruding out of the side of the ravine. He finally got the boy over the side and laid him on the ground and untied the rope. He picked him up and took him underneath some trees and sat him down. Rain was pouring down and there was no dry spot, but it didn't seem to matter to Michael.

Ben walked further down a few feet and saw the other boy lying against the side of the ravine. He wasn't moving, but Ben had hopes that he was just unconscious. He bent down and picked up the boy and rolled him over.

He immediately saw the boy's neck was broken and that he was dead..Ben caught himself before he screamed out, and grabbed the boy and put him over his shoulder. He couldn't allow himself to show any emotion now, because he had to get back up the ravine with the body of Bobby Simpson. He approached the area where Keith was standing and grabbed the rope. He tied it around his waist and tugged on it.

"Keith! Can you hear me? I'm bringing up the body of Bobby Simpson. He's dead. You're gonna have to pull both of us up. I'll use my cleats on the side of the ravine, but it's gonna be tough to pull us both. Do you think you can do it?"

Keith thought a moment and looked around. He looped the rope around another tree and stood behind the tree. He began to pull and realized it was more weight than he was going to be able to lift. Ben could feel a slight slack on the rope and dug into the edge of the ravine with his cleats. He used his hands to help Keith and yelled, "Keep pulling!"

The rain was making the sides slippery and it was difficult for Ben to get a good grip on anything. They made some headway and then Keith's hands slipped on the rope and Ben went down a few feet. He got a better grip on the side by grabbing some brush that was still rooted into the ground. Keith pulled harder, the blood vessels popping out in his neck and his hands being ripped to shreds by the rope.

Finally Ben made if over the edge of the ravine and fell to the ground with the body. Both men were exhausted, yet they knew Michael was staring at the limp body of his friend. They looked up and Michael was crying and shaking.

"Bobby! Bobby! Wake up, Bobby! They're takin' us back to the camp. Bobby!"

Keith walked over to the boy and leaned over, blocking the rain from his face. "Son, your friend's dead. The fall was too much for him and he didn't make it. Now I need you to help us get you back to camp so we can get you to the hospital. You're lucky to be alive, son. I know it hurts, but we have to get out of here and I'm gonna need you to be brave one more time."

Ben came over and picked Michael up and held him in his arms, letting Keith get the dogs untied. Ben grabbed Houston's leash and started walking, while Keith put the body of the other boy on his shoulders and took his own dog and headed out. They started the long trek back across the state land, hoping to get to the area where the fence was down so that they could call for help. "There's a service road that runs along the edge of the camp and a vehicle should be able to get through to us," Keith said.

It took longer to get back to the fence in the driving rain, but as soon as they saw the fence Keith phoned the camp. Ben squatted down to rest his legs and arms, and Michael tucked his face into Ben's jacket. He was crying and shaking and Ben tried to calm him down. Keith put the body down on the ground and rested for a moment, out of breath.

"It won't be long now, buddy. And your parents are waiting back at the lodge for you. Be strong, Michael. I know this is tough."

Shortly a black Tahoe pulled up and two Scout leaders jumped out to help get Michael into the back of the vehicle. They had placed a pillow on the floor of the back and had blankets to wrap him in, as he was beginning to feel some pain and was moaning. They placed Bobby's body in the back seat and covered him in a blanket. Ben and Keith both jumped into the truck and headed quickly back to the camp lodge, where an ambulance had just arrived. Michael's parents came rushing out with Bobby's parents right behind them. Ben walked directly to Bobby's parents and pulled them away from the vehicle. The look on their faces said it all.

"Mr. and Mrs. Simpson, I'm sorry to tell you that your son was found on the bottom of a deep ravine and he apparently was killed from the fall. I'm so sorry. I know this is a tragic accident. The ambulance is loadin' his body now with Michael and headin' to the hospital. You need to . . ."

Fran and James pushed past Ben as though they hadn't heard a word he said. They rushed to the ambulance yelling and the EMT allowed them to see their son. Michael was crying and his parents were holding him, trying to comfort him. After a few minutes, the ambulance pulled away with both sets of parents following in their cars.

Ben and Keith walked over to Mike and John, who were talking to some other parents who had been helping at the camp. Everyone was visibly shaken and getting soaked standing out in the rain. They all walked back into the lodge office and Mike got coffee for both the officers.

"Mike, I know this is tough. It was a miracle that we found those boys at all. When I first spotted one of 'em, which turned out to be Michael, it looked like he was dead. Fortunately, he only had some broken bones, but when I saw Bobby, I knew he was gone. The ravine was so deep it was nearly impossible to pull 'em out, and the rain was makin' the ground so slick." Ben sat on the corner of a desk and sipped the hot coffee, feeling its warmth go down his throat. Even as experienced with death as he was, he felt shaken.

John spoke first. "I don t know how to thank both of you. You risked your lives to save these boys and we really appreciate it. I didn't think you should've stayed out there in the lightning, but now I'm glad you did. Michael may not have lasted through the night out there alone with his injuries. We had no idea that the ravine existed, but now that we do we'll make sure this never happens again. Those parents are devastated and we could be facing a lawsuit."

"I doubt they'll sue. It's a risk they take allowing their son to come to the camp. But no one suspected this to happen. And the weather just added to the danger. I can't tell you enough how thankful I am that you both came." Mike got up from his chair and walked over and shook their hands. The other men patted them on the back and asked if they needed anything to eat or a change of shirts. Keith and Ben said no and headed to their vehicle with the wet dogs. There were blankets and towels in the back so they scrubbed the dogs and made a bed for them to lie on before returning to the station

"Man, that sucks. I was hoping against hope that you'd find them both alive, Ben. This is the part of this job that I hate. And someone has to do it, I know. But doesn't get easier. You okay?"

Ben nodded and sipped on the rest of his coffee. "I've done a lot of things in my life that were difficult and high risk, but this one was one of the toughest to deal with emotionally. That young boy's life was cut short and Michael will have to live with this memory the rest of his life."

The rest of the way back to the station the men were quiet, thinking their own thoughts about the situation. When they got to the station, they went inside, wrote up the reports needed, and laid them on the chief's desk. Ben sat down in a chair near the door and rubbed his eyes. "How do parents deal with losing a child, Keith? How in the world do they ever move forward?"

"One day at a time. If you've ever lost someone you loved, you already know the answer, Ben."

Ben stared off in the distance and his eyes filled with tears. "One day at a time. I've heard that before, Keith. Sure have."

CHAPTER 37

It was dusk and the air was clear of humidity with a slight breeze blowing. Sitting in her jeans and t-shirt out on her porch sipping a fresh cup of coffee, Grace had an hour-long conversation with Sharon. They were in a long discussion about the best way to approach Molly Ann and introduce her to the idea of coming home with Grace. Traditionally, any parents who were interested in adoption would come for several visits at the orphanage and spend time with a child they were drawn to. But in this case, Grace already knew Molly Ann so there would be no point in that visitation procedure. Sharon was discussing some issues that they were dealing with at the school with Molly and how they might affect how she adjusted to living out in the real world with Grace. The children were pretty protected at the orphanage and none of them had ever been to public school. Molly was so young when she came that the orphanage was all she really remembered. She had no memory of her mother or father.

They decided that Grace would come in the afternoon on Sunday for a visit to Wilton and ask to take Molly out for dinner. "I'm pretty comfortable with Molly Ann, Sharon. But I know she gets moody from time to time, and I assure you that won't bother me one bit. I'm so excited and know in my heart this is a good fit for us both. She'll have her own room. Any girl would love that!"

"Grace, I warn you. She's eleven going on fifteen. And it will be new to her to enter the public school system. She makes friends fairly easily and I know this would give her opportunities that she wouldn't have if she remained at the orphanage. But it may not be as smooth a transition like you would want it to be."

"She'll be good for me and I think the timing is perfect. I am hearing you, Sharon, and am trying to be prepared for whatever comes up. I'm sure it might feel strange to be in a house with no other children. She's used to having another child in her room. We'll have to work through all of those things. But I'm more than ready to tackle this challenge. I would love to give her the opportunity to have a wonderful life and also know what it feels like to have a mother figure. Someone she can look up to. You know? She's never had that."

"You're absolutely right about that. But let's hope she allows you in. She's pretty private. I realize in saying this that she's taken to you more than anyone else who's been to Wilton. You have a chance, Grace. Let's give it a shot."

"I'm going to plan to be there on Sunday afternoon if that's good for you, Sharon. And I'll take her to dinner. I already have an idea tossing around in my head. If you're okay with that time, I'll see you then!"

༄

Grace dialed Ben's number and the phone rang and rang. She was just about to hang up when he grabbed the phone and answered. "Ben! I hope this isn't a bad time."

He laughed as he sat down in his favorite leather chair beside the fireplace. "Are you kiddin'? How are you?" *I'm lovin' this phone call.*

"I'm doin' fine. Remember the other night I spoke to you about goin' to Wilton with me?"

Ben scratched his beard and nodded. "Yeah, I recall you mentioning you wanted me to go with you sometime."

"Well, I want to go over somethin' with you. Is this a bad time?"

"No. Is it bad news? 'Cause if it is, I don't want to hear it today. I've had a rough week!"

"It's great news. I've been thinking about what you said, and I made a phone call to Sharon,, the administrator at Wilton. We think it might be a good time to try this thing with Molly. I want to adopt her, Ben."

Ben sat up in his chair, shocked. "Adopt? I thought you were going to try being a foster parent. Now it's progressed to adopting?"

"I've been thinkin' about it for a while now. I know it may sound sudden to you, but really, Ben, I've given it a lot of thought. And hey, I'm alone now. I would love to have some life in this house."

Ben was speechless. That was a big decision and it caught him off guard. He wondered quietly if it would deter their getting closer. "If you are sure you're ready for this, I'll go with you. When were you thinking about this taking place?"

"I want to go on Sunday afternoon, Ben. But I have a favor to ask. Could you bring Houston? I think he'd be a great ice breaker!"

He laughed. "That's perfect. A great idea! Am I meeting you there or picking you up?"

"Well, I wanted to take her for dinner. Let's make at 4:00 and I'd love for you to go with us to dinner, but what about Houston? Can he stay in the car that long?"

"Let me work all that out. I'll pick you up at 4:00. Do you know where you want to take her to dinner?"

"Any ideas?"

"I think The Steakhouse on Third Street would be perfect. It's casual, and there's a good menu for kids. She'll love it."

"Okay. I'll trust you. Thanks for going with me. She's gonna love Houston and it'll help her not feel so awkward. All of this will be so new to her, and I'm excited to be able to take her out for a while."

"Well, I can't think of a better person to do that for Molly. You're a principal of one of the largest schools in the area. She'll have it made at school." He laughed at his own joke.

"Oh, stop it. Anyway, I'll see you Sunday. Ben, thanks for always being there. 'Bye."

Ben sat in his chair motionless for ten minutes thinking about what just transpired. If he was honest, he had to admit to himself that he was more than a little interested in Grace. He'd toyed around with the idea of even marrying her. But he knew that was way off in the future, if at all. With this news, he didn't know if he had a chance. She just might want to raise this little girl by herself. Maybe there was not room for a man around.

He got up and walked outside, taking Houston with him. The fresh air felt good and cleared his head. He was tired and a little washed out over the emotional ups and downs of the last rescue. After he had worked on his car, mowed the yard, and cleaned up around the outside of the house, he came inside and took a long shower. He decided to grab a bite to eat at the corner deli and call it a night.

❧

Grace stripped her bed and washed the sheets, ironed a few pieces of clothing, and cleaned her bathroom and kitchen floors. The whole time she was cleaning, she was thinking of Molly and how it would feel to have her at her home. She walked into the second bedroom and thought about how she could change it to fit the young girl. She might even allow Molly to pick her own bedding. But she was jumping too far ahead. She didn't even know if Molly would want to come and live with her, even for a weekend. She made a few phone calls to her best friends, listened to their pros and cons of the situation, and hung up feeling frustrated because she wanted their support.

She opened up the refrigerator and nothing sounded good, so she headed out the door without changing clothes to the neighborhood deli for supper. When she pulled up in the parking lot she thought she saw Ben's SUV parked on the side of the building. She walked through the door and took a table near the windows. She ordered a ham and cheese sandwich and iced tea and heard her phone beep. She took it out of her purse and there was a text message that had just come in. It was from Ben.

"Hey, girl. You followin' me or what? If you are, then you can buy me dinner!"

Grace smiled and looked around, thinking, what in the world is going on? She suddenly saw Ben sitting in the very back in a booth against the wall. He had a hat on and was slumped down in his seat looking at a menu. She texted him back a short note; "Not in your dreams, buddy."

She watched his face when he got the text and saw a smile slip across his face. He looked up and saw her watching him and burst out laughing. He got out of his booth and walked up to her table.

"Can I sit here, madam?"

"Oh, sit down! Everyone is staring at us!!"

Ben laughed and sat down in the chair facing her. "What a nice surprise! What brought you here for dinner?"

Grace grinned shyly. "Well, I've cleaned all day and didn't see anything I wanted in my refrigerator, so this was my next option."

"That's exactly what I decided. I was too tired to cook. It has turned out to be one of my better decisions today."

Grace couldn't help but laugh. He was so amusing. "Did you have a nice day today?"

"Yeah. Needed a break from the rescue thing. It's been a great job for me, but the searches don't always turn out well. And when they don't, I have to come home and deal with it so that I can face the next rescue mission."

"You're pretty well prepared for that, Ben, after the work you did for the CIA."

"You'd think so. But this is different somehow. These are real people with families who are torn apart. I had no idea it would affect me like this, but I'm sure I'll adjust to it."

Grace had a worried look on her face. "Maybe this isn't the work for you now, Ben. You've done your share of risk taking and no telling what else. Maybe you need something a little easier, something you can just enjoy without it ripping your guts out."

Ben shook his head. "Grace, you haven't known me long, but in time you will find out that I need that challenge. I crave it. And I've been trained to do what I'm doing and I love it. But this hits home a little more and is much more personal. I'll get a handle on it, I promise you that. Don't worry."

Grace reached over and squeezed his hand. "I wouldn't want to lose you, Ben. I don't think I could take that right now. I'm growing to understand how powerful the promise you made to Smith is. And I appreciate having you around so much. Don't ever think I take it for granted."

"I don't even think in that direction, Grace. With you it's different. I won't go into it now, but it's different. That's all I'm sayin'."

They ate their sandwiches and talked for two hours, sitting in the near empty deli. It was the closest Ben had ever felt to Grace. Something special happened that night, in the dirty, dimly lit diner, that was unspoken between them but was just as real as the iced tea they were drinking. When they parted, Ben leaned over and kissed Grace lightly and walked to his car. But he'd given anything to have held her close . . . not just for the night. But forever.

CHAPTER 38

The house smelled of meat cooking and there was a cake on the counter to celebrate Irfan's birthday. Smith and Mishael were sitting at the table going over the Urdu language and talking about the news that had spread throughout Pakistan that Osama Bin Laden had been killed in a mansion in Abbottabad. It had created quite a stir in Zhob and people were out on the streets talking in groups. It was a joyous time in Pakistan and also a precarious time, for no one knew what the factions might do to retaliate.

"Mishael, I'm trying to learn this language but just can't get it. I am struggling, just like you are with your English. How do I get past this?"

"Time, Bita. And hearing language all day long. Soon your mind will hear in Urdu and you will not strain to speak the language."

"How do you feel about Bin Laden going down? I wish I could understand what was going on and remember why he was such a danger to the world."

"I rejoice as your country does, but I am not calm about what factions might do. They have no strong leader now, but one will surface soon. We have to be prepared for what comes now and not put guard down."

"Do you know how frustrated I am that I cannot even know about my own country? When will this end? I need to know about my life and why I was even here in the first place. It is driving me nuts."

Smith pushed his chair back and walked to the window, anger rising up in him. He had to learn to deal with the frustration without taking it out on other people. Mishael got up and walked over to him and tried to comfort him. He turned to look at her, their eyes locking for a moment. He smiled and apologized to her for getting so angry.

"I know you don't understand how angry I am for having no memory of my life. I can't even touch you, Mishael. I am lonely and I need to have a relationship with someone, and you are here and we can do nothing. I don't understand the restrictions here but I want to respect you. It's so hard to know what to do."

Mishael nodded and smiled. "I do understand what frustration is. Except I grew up here and these rules have been passed down from generations. It is all I know. But that does not mean I do not have feelings."

Smith looked at her and grabbed her arms. No one was in the room. No one would know. He pulled her close to him and kissed her quickly on the mouth. Mishael did not resist, but backed away quickly, moving back to the table where she gathered the papers in a pile and clipped them together. "Bita, we are through for the day with our studies and I need to head home. You are doing much better each day. I am proud of you."

Smith walked over to her and raised her head up where he could see her eyes. "I really care about you, Mishael," he whispered. "I am not dishonoring you. Do you believe me?"

"I do, Bita. I feel, too. But we must be careful. It will ruin my life. Not yours."

He reached up and touched her face and smiled. She was so lovely. "I will let you set the pace of our relationship. But remember I am a man and I have no family. You and Irfan and Mahsa are all I have right now."

"I see your life is small and I know that must be hard for you. I don't know what I can do to make things different for you. In this country, as a Muslim, I'm not allowed to be seen kissing you or holding your hand. So if I ever do touch you it will be in a place where I know it cannot be seen."

"I respect that, Mishael."

Mahsa came out of the kitchen and asked if Mishael would help her with the food. They walked back into the kitchen as Irfan came traipsing through the front door. He embraced Smith and walked into the kitchen to wash his hands. He saw a cake on the counter for his birthday and he grinned. "Mahsa, you have fixed my favorite meal and made a cake. That is so kind of you. I know you are tired and yet you still made this for me."

"You are my husband, Irfan. I love you."

"She has lived this long with me, Bita. And she still loves me. I have caused suffering in her life and the love does not change."

"I am watching, Irfan. That is how I will live my life." Smith smiled.

Mahsa asked Mishael to stay and have dinner with them, so she sat next to Smith at the table. The talk was about Pakistan and the passing of Osama Bin Laden and how his death would affect the country. The factions were dispersing for fear that more Seal teams would appear. This might mean that Smith would be able again to work in the clinic without worrying about being attacked, at least for a time.

"I would like you to come to the clinic tomorrow, Bita. I know you cannot hang around in the house much longer without getting depressed again. How do you feel about going back to the clinic? The patients are asking about you."

"I'm more than ready, as long as it doesn't threaten Mahsa's life again. I never want that to happen again because of me. I'm learning the language more and more, with the help of Mishael. It shouldn't be too long before I can speak as well as you!"

Irfan laughed. "You're doing fine, Bita. Do not worry. My main concern is that your memory return. That is what I'm praying for."

"I pray that every night, Irfan. I fear God does not hear me."

"It will happen, my son. But you must be ready to face what that memory is. Have you thought of that?"

"Of course I have. Many times. But since I have no way of knowing what my past is, I cannot prepare for what I will remember. I am at the mercy of time and hopefully will run up on something that will trigger something in my mind. That is what I live for, Irfan."

Mishael bowed her head and took a bite of the potatoes and meat on her plate. It troubled her to think that one day Smith might leave Pakistan and return to America. She would never see him again.

As though Smith knew what she was thinking, he reached over and touched her hand under the tablecloth. "Until I know what my life was before, I will make a life here as best I can. I am surrounded by people here who love me and you will be my family until I know differently."

Irfan nodded his head in agreement and ate his birthday meal in silence. He could feel the energy moving between Mishael and Smith but said nothing. He knew in his heart that Smith was an honorable man. He would ultimately do the right thing even if his heart got in the way momentarily. It was a difficult thing to watch day after day, a man who had nothing but a blank slate about his life. More than anything he didn't want depression to sink in, because he had no way of knowing how long it would be before Smith remembered his past. The best thing would be to keep him busy, and that was just what Irfan planned to do.

"Mishael, since I've asked Bita to come to the clinic tomorrow, I hope you will be there to help. I'd like Mahsa to stay home and rest. She's been pulling the weight of two people and I cannot ask her to do that anymore. And until we know that things have settled down, I'd like her to be here at home where I know she's safe."

Mishael nodded and agreed to come to the clinic. But inside she was afraid of where she was headed with Bita. Her heart was racing thinking about the kiss he gave her. It felt wonderful to be so close to him, but it went against all that she had been taught. She was fighting her heart and what she knew was right as a Muslim.

When it was time for Mishael to leave, she gathered her papers and put them in a folder. Smith walked her to the door and went outside with her to say goodbye. "It's dark, Mishael. Will you be safe walking home?"

"Yes, I know a back way and besides, things have calmed down now. We don't have to worry as much about the Taliban. They are not watching us right now; their minds are on the death of their leader. I will see you tomorrow, Bita."

Smith grabbed her and held her close and then turned and went inside. His heart was racing and he had to fight the impulse to go after her and kiss her again. Dr. Irfan was waiting in the living room when Smith walked back into the house. "Son, I know you are feeling strong towards Mishael. I cannot tell you what to do, but I have shared the dangers with you." Irfan put his arm around Smith. "I don't want harm to come to you, Bita. We have worked so hard to get you well and I don't want anything to set you back. Remember one day you will remember who you are, and you don't want to do anything here that you'll regret."

Smith walked back to his room and sat on his bed. The words that Irfan said echoed in his head, and he suddenly felt more alone than he'd felt since he arrived at the doctor's home. How could he live here and not make a life for himself? Was he supposed to live the rest of his life in limbo, waiting for his memory to return? What if it never came back?

The questions ran through his mind until he drifted off to sleep, and the answers were as elusive as a butterfly. Just as he thought he might be remembering something, it turned to dust in his hands. It was a long lonely road and Smith was almost at a breaking point. Something had to give.

CHAPTER 39

Margaret was planting flowers in front of the house with sweat pouring down her face. Her khaki crop pants had dirt all over the knees and her gloves had holes in the tips of the fingers. There were stacks of rich topsoil stacked near the beds and she was hard at work pulling out the weeds that had successfully taken over her garden. She spotted Grace coming across the lawn, and stood up, wiping her brow.

"Hey, lovely lady! Good to see you! What's goin' on, darlin'?"

"I'm so excited, Maggie! Remember I told you I might want to adopt a child from Wilton?"

"Oh, yes! I've got my grandmother shoes waiting in the closet!"

"Well, get them out, because today I go and talk to Molly Ann about coming to stay the weekend. If it all works out like I want it to, she'll be coming to live with me permanently. It may take several visits before we can make that big of a decision, but I'm so excited, Maggie!"

"I can tell! Are you leaving right now to go pick her up?"

"Ben is picking me up shortly with his dog Houston. We're heading to Wilton to see Molly and take her to dinner. I want to bring her home but we'll see how things go. I don't want to push her; it just depends on how she reacts to the whole idea. I'm nervous, Mag. I don't know if she'll come or not and I've gotten my hopes up too high, I think."

"Nothing wrong with thinking positive about it, my dear. Just be yourself and let God take care of the rest. If it's meant to be, then it'll happen. You need something wonderful to happen in your life; this just may be the ticket."

Grace was grinning from ear to ear. "Ben was so good to agree to come and bring his dog. I just thought it would be a good icebreaker and Molly will love that dog. I'll let you know how it goes, Maggie. Give me a hug."

"Land, you're gonna get dirt all over you! Have fun and try to relax. No point in both of you being nervous. She'll love you, Grace. And I'll have a little something for her when you bring her home."

"Oh, that'd be wonderful, Maggie! I'll call you as soon as I know." Grace brushed off the dirt from her shirt, laughing as she walked back to her house. Just as she stepped inside to touch up her makeup, Ben drove up with Houston in the back of his SUV. He got out and came up to her door and knocked and Grace came running to answer it.

"Hey! You're right on time. I was just touching up my makeup. Is Houston in the back?"

"Oh, yes. He's ready to meet little Molly. He's on his best behavior, I promise."

"Oh, you! Let me get my purse and I'm out the door." Grace hurried to the living room and grabbed her purse and a gift for Molly and headed back out the door. Ben helped her into the truck and jumped in and started the engine.

"Not like we're too excited or anything . . ."

Grace laughed nervously. "I've thought of nothing else all day. I don't want to second guess what'll happen but I sure want her to have a good time tonight. Houston will play a big role in that, I think."

Ben nodded in agreement. "She'll love him. Now what do you want me to do when we get there?"

"I was thinking I'd go in first, but in a way it'd be nice if we took Houston in. I'll ask Sharon if that's okay and we might be able to walk Houston through the halls into Molly's room. That would be so cool."

"Perfect. I'm so happy to be a part of this day. I have to admit I was blown over when you mentioned you were ready to adopt a child. It really caught me off guard, Grace. That's a bigger step than fostering a child. But I know when I meet her I will understand why. So here we go."

They pulled up into the parking lot and Houston seemed to know what was going on. He was wagging his tail and kept trying to jump up into the front seat. "Whoa, buddy. Hold on. We're not getting out yet!

Grace, you go in and just give us a signal if you want me to bring Houston in."

Grace was nervous and excited, but she knew she had to get her energy level down so that she didn't scare Molly. Sharon was in her office and got up to meet Grace.

"Hey, girl. So good to see you. I know you're here to take Molly this afternoon to eat dinner. I've told her you were coming. She's looking forward to seeing you." Sharon hugged Grace and looked at her with a finger pointed at her face. "Now don't hurry things, Grace. Take it slow. She's excited to see you but she has no idea that you're thinkin' about takin' her home. Even just for the weekend. So see how things go at dinner and feel her out. She'll let you know if she's comfortable and havin' a good time."

"I hear you. I'd planned to take it easy. If it doesn't work out tonight then that's fine. We can do it later. But I just wanted to get her used to me and I have a great friend outside with a dog that I wanted to bring in. Is that okay with you? Can I bring this dog in and walk into her room?"

"I think that's a terrific idea! Go for it."

Grace went to the door and waved at Ben. He took Houston out of the SUV and put him on a leash. He was all brushed and clean and his tail wagged with anticipation and excitement at getting out of the truck. Ben walked him to the door; they were quite a sight with Ben dressed in blue jeans, a baseball cap, and sporting a beard, and Houston black as night and raring to go.

"Sharon, this is Ben Parker and his dog Houston. Okay, we're ready to head back to her room. Wish us luck!"

Ben and Houston followed Grace down several halls to Molly's room. Grace stuck her head in the door and said hello. Molly was sitting on her bed putting things in her purse. "Molly! How are you?"

Grace walked in and sat on the bed with her, smiling, and gave her a big hug.

Molly blushed and closed the purse. "Hey, Miss Grace! Good to see you. Um, are we goin' out to dinner?"

"Yes, angel. Tell me how you are! We haven't talked in a long time."

"Oh, I'm cool. Just glad to be gettin' out tonight. We don't go anywhere much and it'll feel good to eat out in a nice restaurant."

"Well, I've got a nice surprise for you, Molly. I've brought a good friend who's gonna eat with us tonight. Ben! Come on in!"

Molly looked surprised and a little wary. Ben walked through the door with Houston and Molly screamed out. "Oh, my gosh! What a great dog! He's beautiful."

She ran over to Ben and squatted down to pet Houston. He acted like he loved her at first sight. He began to lick her face and nearly knocked her over trying to get to her.

Molly was laughing and petting Houston. Ben pulled him back a little and spoke to Molly in a kind and quiet voice. "Molly, this is Houston. He's a search and rescue dog. So he lives with me and we work together. Isn't that neat?"

"That's cool. So he finds people? Is that what you mean?"

"Yes. So he's a very smart dog."

"Is he gonna go eat with us?"

Ben laughed. "No! But we're gonna take you to the park first and Houston can play catch with you. How'd you like that?"

Molly squealed and ran over to Grace. "Oh, this is the best night ever! The kids won't believe what I'm getting to do tonight! Can we leave now? Before it starts gettin' dark?"

"We're heading out right now. Let's go have some fun, Molly!"

They headed out the door and jumped into the SUV. It was a lovely afternoon and the sun was still warm. The park was full of kids flying kites and playing in the water of the fountain. Houston was panting with excitement and he jumped out of the back of the truck, eager to see what was going on. Ben kept the leash on until they were settled under a huge oak tree. Ben took out the Frisbee and let Molly have it so she could play catch with Houston. She ran and threw it, and Houston caught it before it hit the ground, making her squeal in delight.

Grace and Ben found a spot under the tree and put a blanket down, watching Molly and Houston. There was a breeze blowing out of the west and it made the heat bearable. Grace filled him in a little about Molly's background and asked his opinion about how to ask Molly to stay for the weekend..

Ben was keeping his eye on Houston and also noticing the worry across Grace's face. "Relax, woman. She's fine. Just try to enjoy right now, Grace. She's so young and has been through so much. But she doesn't remember any of the bad, except the fact that she doesn't have parents. Not that that's not enough. But she's had a good life and the only life she really remembers at Wilton. Right?"

"You're so right, Ben. I'm glad you're here with me, because I'm puttin' too much emphasis on her coming to my house to spend the night. It may not be the right time now. And that's perfectly okay. Thanks for reminding me."

Ben squeezed her hand and smiled. "That's what I'm here for!" They both got up and ran to Molly and Houston and played fetch for about thirty minutes. Then Grace asked if Molly was ready to go eat supper.

"I'm havin' so much fun with Houston! I wish I had a dog like that!"

"Well, you'll be seein' a lot of him, girl. I can tell he likes you too!"

Grace smiled and hugged Molly. "Let's pack up and go eat a good supper. If there's still light out we'll play some more later."

Molly walked over to Ben and put her arms around his waist. "Thanks, Mr. Ben. I love your dog. Can he eat with us?"

"No, Molly. He has to stay in the truck. But he'll be fine; I'll leave the engine running so he'll have plenty of air."

Molly laughed and skipped beside Grace to the truck. The ride over was filled with laughter and conversation about Houston. He was the star of the show. Molly sat back and let Houston smell her hair; they were fast becoming best friends. Grace punched Ben in the arm and winked. Ben nodded. "Too bad we can't take him in the restaurant!"

❧

After the meal was ordered, Grace looked and Molly and smiled, watching her play with the crayons the waitress had left for her. "Molly, have you ever spent the night out away from Wilton?"

"No, ma'am. Sure haven't. Besides, I'd have no place to go!"

"Well, do you think you'd ever want to spend the night out? Just for one night?"

Molly sat still and thought a moment. "Never really thought about it. But maybe. I guess."

She was coloring and not looking at Grace. "I was just thinking that it might be fun if you went home with me tonight and spent the night. I have a bedroom you could sleep in, and the covers are soft and fluffy. We could watch a movie and fix popcorn! Wouldn't that be fun?"

Molly looked up and wrinkled her nose. "All alone? Would I go all alone?"

"Yes, just you and me."

"Um, could Houston go?"

Grace raised her eyebrow and looked at Ben. He shrugged and looked at Molly. They had gotten cornered by a dog.

"We could ask Mr. Ben if Houston could come over. But I thought it might be fun if you spent the night with me and kept me company. I live in that house all by myself."

"Well, I might go if Houston was there. We're best friends now! I wish I had a dog like Houston!"

Ben laughed. He suddenly had a great idea. "Hey, why don't I bring a big tent and we all three sleep outside under the stars and then Houston could go, too!"

Grace's mouth opened, but Molly beat her to it. "Oh, gosh! Could we really? I've never camped out in a tent!" She looked at Grace and smiled the biggest smile.

Ben started laughing when he looked at Grace's expression. She was speechless. A tent?

"Well, yes, that would be fun! I've never thought about sleeping in a tent, but I guess we could do that." She looked at Ben with a frown. "I didn't know you even had a tent, Mr. Ben."

He rolled his eyes and shrugged his shoulders. "Well, you never asked, did you?"

Grace laughed and Molly chimed in. "So are we gonna sleep outside? Does Miss Sharon know? I'd have to get my pajamas and stuff."

Grace grinned. "I've already taken care of that. In the car there's a little suitcase with all the things you'll need. Miss Sharon packed it for us just in case you agreed to spend the night with me! Isn't that wonderful?"

Molly giggled and jumped out of her seat. "Well, what are we waiting for? We better go get Houston and set up our tent!"

༄

After an exhausting night of Ben going to get the tent, setting it up, and playing every game there was to play, Grace spent a few minutes reading Molly a book and getting her to settle down so that she would sleep. Houston lay right beside her and she finally fell asleep at 11:00. Grace was certain that was the latest she'd ever stayed up in her young life. Ben brought two adult sleeping bags, a lantern, and a boom box to play music for Molly. He'd thought of everything.

He and Grace moved gently out of the tent and sat in lawn chairs on the patio, sipping a glass of wine and nibbling on some snacks left out for Molly when she was playing with Houston. "Ben, you're amazing. You have no children and look at you! This is exactly what Molly needed to feel safe and I can't tell you how grateful I am that you're here with me tonight."

"She's easy to fall in love with, Grace. I can see why you like her so much. What a delightful child and to think her mother had to give her away. It's heartbreaking."

"I can't even think about what that mother was going through the night she dropped Molly off at Wilton. I'm thankful, however, that the orphanage was there and that they were able to take her in. She's really turned out well and that's one of the reasons Smith and I put so much into helping Wilton grow. We saw the good work they were doing and wanted to further their endeavors so that the children would have the same opportunities as those children raised with two parents and going to public school."

"This is a big step, lady. Just being here tonight has opened my eyes even more to how big a step this is."

"I know. I'll have to take it slow. She's hesitant to stay away from Wilton and that's understandable. But somehow I'll win her over and if it's supposed to work, it will. She's always loved my coming to Wilton and often sat in my lap while I read to the kids. So she's used to me being around. I just stayed away this past year because of my grief. Way too difficult for me to go there and see what Smith had accomplished."

"I'll be around, you know. And Houston. Any time you need company to go to the movies or walk in the park, we're here. He grabbed her hand and squeezed it. "Shall we try to sleep now? I bet she's gonna wake up early and want to play again!"

Grace laughed. "She'll be up with the roosters, and so will Houston." She paused and touched his hand. "Ben, what would I do without you? I resisted you for a while but now I see that Smith chose you because you have such a big heart. I'm honored that you feel so dedicated to looking out for me. But it's more than that. You're not afraid to get involved, and that's what's so amazing to me. Most men would back away from all of this. It's a lot of drama at times. But you're not backing away at all. I mean, look at you, in a tent in my back yard!"

Ben laughed and then covered his mouth, not wanting to wake Molly. "I do it without thinking, Grace. Because I love being around you. I've grown very fond of you very quickly and fear that I may push too hard at times. Please forgive me if I do."

"Don't apologize, Ben. I pulled way back, and rightly so. My husband was killed and it knocked me off my feet for a while. But all that you've done for me, including today with Molly, has helped to pull me out and let me see I can enjoy life again and not betray Smith."

Ben felt a stab in his chest for a second and rubbed his beard slowly. "I must be honest, Grace. Many times I've felt that I might be betraying Smith because of my feelings for you. But after a time I've come to believe he knew this would happen. That is the one thing that has helped me sort out how I feel and what he wanted for your life."

"I don't know about all that; it's hard to believe he gave that much thought to taking care of me if something happened to him. But I cherish the relationship I had with Smith and hope one day to be able to love someone that much again. It's hard to believe I'm even saying that to you."

Ben nodded and got up and stood beside her chair. He reached down and pulled her up to her feet and wrapped his arms around her. It felt so good to hold her again. Grace struggled inside for a moment—*I've only been married to Smith, and I've only loved one man.* But after a moment she relaxed and just allowed the closeness of Ben to warm her heart. He somehow had the ability to make her feel like everything was going to be all right.

"Grace, I'm gonna be honest with you again. I'm feeling so strongly towards you that it's gettin' more difficult to hold back. I want you to be honest with me, Grace. If you want me to back off, say it now. Otherwise, I'm movin' forward with my feelings. I wouldn't hurt you for the world, nor do I want a relationship that's one-sided. So let me know how you feel about my being in your life as more than just a friend, will you?"

Grace turned away and dabbed her eyes. She wasn't ready for this talk, yet somehow she had known it was coming. It felt so right, but was it too soon? And how did Smith know she'd like Ben? How did he know that?

"I do love being with you, Ben. I never dreamed I would be saying this to you. But let's take things slow because I really want this to work with Molly. I feel stronger about it even after tonight. She's a lovely child and I would love to make a home for her and give her the solid foundation she needs to have a good life. She deserves it. So just for a short time I'll be putting a lot of energy into her adjusting to being with me, and also getting her ready to enter the public school system. A lot of changes for her and for me."

Grace pointed towards that tent and smiled. "You obviously have a way with women. She's happily asleep beside your dog and she just met you both today!"

She walked over to Ben and he kissed her softly. "Just how slow do we have to go, Grace?"

Grace laughed and raised an eyebrow. "I'm not sure you know what slow is!"

They both laughed and headed to the tent. Grace lay beside Molly and Houston and Ben lay at the other end of the tent. They turned out the lantern and fell asleep. The stars were out and it was a clear night.

Maggie turned away from the window, smiling. It was way past her bedtime but she had to know how the night turned out. In the morning she would have them all for breakfast!

Grace was fast asleep when a text came in from Celeste, but she had turned off her phone so Molly would not be disturbed. The text said, "I've been trying to get in touch with you! Where are you? Is your phone not working? Martha's had an accident. She's dead, Grace. Martha's dead. Call me as soon as you get this message. I can't believe you're not answering your phone. Call me!!!"

CHAPTER 40

The heat from the morning sun was warm on the tent and Grace stirred and opened her eyes. Her back was sore from sleeping on the ground, but she smiled when she saw Molly lying with her head on Houston's side. She lay there very still and just took in the moment. This was not exactly how she'd planned things to go, but she had to admit it had worked out well for Molly. This night would be remembered for a long time. She raised up her head and saw Ben staring at her. He winked and nodded toward Molly. Grace grinned and they both crawled out of the tent and went into the house to make coffee and bring juice out to Molly.

Just as soon as Grace walked into the kitchen and started the coffee pot her phone rang and it was Margaret. "Good mornin', angel. How's my camper?"

Grace was surprised that Margaret had already seen the tent. "I'm sore but happy. Molly is still asleep with Houston, Ben's dog."

"Well, I have breakfast made for you and wanted to bring it over so you could serve it when you were ready to eat!"

"You never cease to amaze, Maggie! How nice of you! Come on over and I'll get Molly up."

Grace hung up and shook her head.

"What? What are you shaking your head for?"

"You won't believe this one. My neighbor Margaret has fixed breakfast for us. She's already seen the tent and has the whole thing figured out!"

"Ah. I'll take note of that. A neighbor that stays up at night watching your house."

"Oh, she's not that way! But she does look out for me. So you've met your match!"

They walked outside and Margaret was coming through the gate. Ben ran to meet her to help carry the food to the table. "Hello! I'm Ben Parker! You want to join us, Maggie? It's such a lovely morning." Grace pointed to the tent.

"She's in there, Maggie. You can peek in! You have to see this sight."

Maggie walked over to the tent and looked inside. She laughed when she saw Molly lying over Houston.

She turned and walked back to the table. "What a sweetheart! Grace, I see why you love her. She's beautiful. And what a dog! He's so big! He's nearly as long as Molly, stretched out like that!"

Ben laughed and helped Grace set the table. At Grace's cue, he pursed his lips and whistled, and shortly Houston came bounding out of the tent. Not two seconds later Molly's head popped out of the tent door. "What a cool night. I slept with Houston all night and he never moved!"

"We saw that, honey. Now I want you to meet Miss Maggie. She lives next door and has made us a wonderful breakfast. And oh my gosh, she's made us chocolate muffins! Just for you, I bet, Molly."

They all sat down and enjoyed a tasty breakfast, listening to Molly talk and talk about what a great night she had. Houston was energetic and wanted to play so Molly hurriedly ate and ran off to throw the Frisbee. "How'd things go, Grace? I was dying to know!"

"I guess you can see for yourself that she's had a ball. It went better than I thought but I owe Ben for that. His idea of bringing Houston over here and spending the night in the tent was the perfect way to let Molly relax and get adjusted to all of us. It couldn't have gone better."

"When do you have to take her back?"

"Probably this morning. Sharon wanted to do this slowly for the first few times and I agree with her totally. I want Molly wanting more, instead of wanting to go back to Wilton. She'll look forward to the next time now!"

"Well, I'm headed back to the house. If you need anything just let me know. I'll be home all week, Grace."

Grace walked over and gave her a big hug. "Maggie thanks for the breakfast. I'm glad you got to meet Molly. I'll call you later today and share the details."

The trip back to Wilton was fun. Molly was playing with Houston in the back and Grace and Ben were laughing about how sore they felt from sleeping in a tent. When they reached Wilton, Ben took Houston out and let Molly tell him goodbye. "Hey, girl! I loved last night. Let's do this again real soon, ya hear?"

Molly smiled and hugged Ben. "Thank you, Mr. Ben. I had a great time. 'Bye, Houston!"

Grace walked Molly into the main building and Sharon was there waiting for them. She was anxious to know how things went. Molly hugged Grace and kissed her cheek. "Thanks for the best time I've ever had, Miss Grace. I hope we can do this again soon. Hey Sharon! I slept with a big dog last night!"

Before Sharon could respond, Molly skipped off to tell the other girls about her night. They all squealed when she told them she'd slept with Houston.

"It went better than we'd planned, Sharon. She was a doll. A perfect doll. And Ben had a winner of an idea to bring Houston to my house and set up a large tent. We all slept outside together and had a ball. Molly and Houston hit if off from the word go, and they were inseparable all evening. I think she'll be willing to go for the whole weekend next time. I might even take one of her friends from Wilton with us. That way she'd have someone to play with and not just sit around listening to adults."

"I'm so glad she had a good experience. She deserves to have fun and I know you're so good for her, Grace. Just call when you're ready to do this again. School is starting up before too long in the public school system, so don't wait too long to get this done. You might want to see her every week and then see how she feels about staying with you and going to school where you work."

"I'll get things going. Just wanted to see how this first time went. I think she'll be open to more as the weeks pass. I know time is of the essence because of school, but we have time to get it all in. Thanks for lettin' me have her! It was a joy."

Grace walked back to the truck and got in, wiping a tear from her eye. "She was so cute in that tent. I didn't want to have to take her back. But we'll have more times with her. I'll have to remember that! We're working towards an end, which is me having her forever."

As Ben drove Grace home, she pulled out her cell phone to check her calls, realizing she had forgotten to turn the volume back on. Her face froze when she saw Celeste's text.

She screamed out and Ben slammed on the brakes and pulled over to the side of the road. "What in the world happened, Grace? What's wrong?"

Grace was shaking and trying to dial Celeste back. "It's Martha. She's dead! Celeste said she was killed in an accident. Oh, my gosh."

Ben took the phone and dialed the number. He handed her the phone and put his hand on her shoulder.

"Celeste? It's Grace. Oh my gosh, what happened! I can't believe this! I just can't believe it!"

Silence on the other end. "Gracie, I tried so many times to get you. I've had to deal with this alone. Maryann is out of town and Steve is beside himself trying to calm me down. Where are you?"

"I'm with Ben. We just took Molly back to Wilton. She spent the night with me. Well, with us, in a tent. But talk to me. What happened?"

"She was driving home yesterday and a car crossed the center line and hit her head on. She died instantly, Grace. I've been about to lose my mind. I'm so glad you finally called. Can you come over?"

Grace was shaking and so upset that Ben almost took the phone away from her. "I'll get Ben to take me now to your house. I'll be right there, Celeste."

Ben pulled Grace towards him and held her close and let her cry it out. *What could possibly happen next to this woman? She's had enough to deal with and now one of her best friends gets killed in a car wreck.* He found some Kleenex in the back seat and gave it to Grace, and started the engine.

They pulled back out on the road and Grace told him how to get to Celeste's house. "Oh, Ben. How do I deal with this? I need to be strong for Celeste. She's the one who's been dealing with this on her own for twenty-four hours. God help us."

"Pull yourself together, Grace. I'm here for you. We'll take this one day at a time and get through it. Just don't think too much about anything and take it one moment at a time."

Grace took in a few deep breaths and checked her face in the mirror on the back of the visor. She looked a wreck but it didn't matter anymore. Celeste was inside and she had to get to her and give her some support. *What a nightmare. And Maryann was out of town, of all things. She was going to freak out when she found out.*

When Grace walked through the door, Celeste fell into her arms and they spent the next couple of hours trying to work through the shock of the whole thing. Their best friend was gone. Ben left the girls alone and walked outside, where Steve was working on a lawnmower. He wasn't going anywhere until he knew Grace was okay. And that might take a lifetime, the way things were going.

CHAPTER 41

It was a gray day and the sky was lined with billowy thunderheads that looked like they were going to explode at any moment. It had rained for the last two days and water was standing in the roads and between the gravesites and the chairs that had been put out for the graveside funeral were sinking into the ground as Grace sat down next to Celeste, Steve, and Ken. Martha's family was there, what was left of them. Her mother had passed away earlier that year so her father was sitting next to Martha's only brother, Harry. The wind was blowing and rain had been forecasted for the afternoon, so Grace was hoping against hope it would hold out until the funeral was over. She had no more tears left, but held on to Celeste as the pastor said the last prayers. Martha had been a sister to them both and her death was going to be difficult to deal with. Maryann was still out of town, so they were going to have to face her next week and deal with her grief. The familiar hymns were sung and a poem was read by her brother Harry. He had a wonderful deep voice that somehow calmed the crowd gathered to pay their respects to Martha.

Ben had moved into the background, preferring to stay away from the gravesite. But he was fully prepared to handle anything that came up after the funeral was over. Grace planned on going to Martha's house to help with food and greeting people. So Ben agreed to take her and help in any way he could. He looked forward to this day being over with so Grace could move forward. She had a lot going on in her life that was positive and he was thankful for that. Molly would be a breath of fresh air in the midst of all this sorrow.

There were huge black umbrellas that seemed like a giant black canopy over the gravesite. But it was fortunate that the visitors had decided to bring them because it wasn't a minute after the last prayer was said that huge drops fell from the sky. Thunder was heard in the distance and it caused everyone to scurry to their cars, hoping to miss the downpour. Ben grabbed Grace's arm and held an umbrella the size of Texas over her head. Celeste and Steve were right behind them, trying to get to their car without stepping into the puddles along the road.

"Come on, Gracie. I know you're sick inside, but it's almost over, honey You sure you want to go to Martha's house? Would it be better for you to head home?"

"No, I better go and give Ken some support. There's not much family around to help him, you know. And Celeste just can't do it all by herself."

"Well, I'm here to do what I can. You just tell me what you need me to do. I'm not much good at funerals but I can haul food and move chairs around. Just tell me, Grace."

She reached over for the hundredth time and touched his arm. "It seems all I ever do it thank you for being there for me. I'd like for once to be able to do something nice for you, Ben Parker. I hope that this is the end of sadness in my life and ultimately yours. Molly sure brought a light into our lives, didn't she? I can't wait to see her again."

"I enjoyed it as much as you did! But let's get through today and then we can plan another weekend with our Molly."

Grace warmed at the sound of his voice. The words he spoke just watered her withered spirit. *"Our Molly." Was that not the sweetest thing in the world?* She decided to keep her thoughts to herself and unlocked the door when he pulled up to Martha's home. "Okay, Ben. When we get in there, just help me make sure there are seats for everyone and also plenty of food on the table and something to drink. I have no idea how many will stop by, but my guess is not that many. Martha and Ken travelled so much that they really didn't have too many couple friends. I'm sure his golf buddies will show up."

"Stay focused on what you're doing, Grace, and don't think about anything else. You're doing great, even though I realize inside you're hurting. I'm proud of you."

They entered the house and saw Ken immediately. He was standing alone in the hallway looking at their family photos. They didn't have children, but they had a lot of pictures taken of each other and the places they'd been. Tears were running down his cheeks, but he brushed then away roughly when he saw Grace and Ben walking towards him.

"I know this is a nightmare, Ken. I'm here if you need anything."

"I know, Grace. Thanks. But you know what? I've decided that after this is over today, I'm heading out of town. I don't think I can stay in this house right now. Too many memories. Is that crazy?"

Ben stepped in. "No way, man. Do what it takes to make it through this. It doesn't matter what people say. It's your life."

Ken nodded and walked away, shaking his head.

∽

Celeste was a basket case. All Grace could do was hold her and hand her more Kleenex. It was a disaster that had no end; Maryann was coming home. They decided to all meet at Grace's house so that they could talk and cry and try to deal with the loss of their friend. It was such a shock to all of them and there didn't seem to be an easy way to cope with it.

"Why does this happen, Grace? How could it happen? She was a perfect driver. I've never understood how someone could cross the center line. Were they drunk? Were they on the phone? I . . ."

"Celeste, you have to stop. There is no answer that will bring Martha back. I learned that about Smith's death. I asked millions of questions that floated up into the air and I never got one answered. Not one. We have to deal with it. It was an accident and she's gone. I don't know how we'll get together and have dinner like we used to do, without her. But I know she'd want us to go on living, to be happy, and to keep together. Without a doubt I know that's what she'd want."

"I know you're right. But this sucks, Grace. And poor Ken. He's lost without her. I know he was a blowhard, but he was all talk. Inside he's mush. He adored her."

"I've been in his shoes, remember? It'll be hell for him for a while and then it eases up a little. He's good about keeping busy and he has more friends than Martha did. Golf buddies. They'll keep him busy, I'm sure. Let's get this food put up in the refrigerator and clean up the house a little. I think the people that were coming to see Ken are gone and he acts like he wants to be alone. I'll get Ben to help and let's see if Ken has anything else he needs done before we leave."

As Grace and Celeste walked through every room of the rambling four bedroom house, there were signs of Martha everywhere. She'd decorated the house in warm colors and hung lovely oils from Tuscany in the hallways. It was difficult to see all of her treasured things knowing she'd never enjoy them again. They went in to her bedroom and looked beside her bed. There was a cross hanging across the lamp shade, and a journal on the nightstand. They opened the last page and saw that she'd written a few lines about their cruise trip. Tears streamed down their faces as they came to grips with the fact that this was the last remnant they would have of their friend.

As Grace and Ben pulled out of the driveway a thought occurred to Grace. *Maybe Martha was with Smith in heaven.* That thought made her smile. For she knew that Martha would be running her mouth ninety miles an hour, catching Smith up on everything that had happened since he died. She was lost in her thoughts as she looked out of the window.

Ben glanced at her from time to time her while he was driving her home. *How am I so fortunate to have been given this opportunity to have a relationship with such a wonderful woman?* She's so beautiful and so unaware of it. I need to make the most of the time we have and make some plans for a future with her. This funeral is another reminder, like I need one, that life is short. I may not get this chance again so I'd better do it right the first time.

∽

Grace was off in another world, trying to remember what Smith looked like, thinking of his smile and how much he loved her. How much he did for others. When Ben reached over and grabbed her hand on the seat, for a moment she thought it was Smith. When she turned and saw Ben sitting there, her eyes filled with tears. She couldn't bring herself to say what she'd been thinking. But somehow he read her mind. "It's okay, baby. I know you miss Smith. You'll always love him and that's okay. I can see it in your eyes just now. Let's get you home so you can rest and recover from this nightmare."

Again he'd come through for her, not asking anything back in return. He was a gift, in a way, from Smith to her. That was how much Smith loved her.

CHAPTER 42

Smith started back working at the clinic and it was almost as though he'd never left. The patients took right to him and were drawn to his strength and seemingly effortless ability to remember the names of the patients and insight into their health issues. He was a great help to Dr. Irfan and even assisted in small surgeries. He had no fear of the sight of blood and learned to work on patients with minor issues. Soon Dr. Irfan let him do lab work, as Smith seemed hungry for knowledge. He jokingly said to Smith that he should put 'Dr. Iran Sheikhani and Son' on the door.

Mishael was at the office most days drawing blood, taking vital signs, and getting the patients' wounds cleaned for Dr. Irfan to check. She worked alongside Smith everyday and they made a great team but the feelings she harbored in her heart were growing and becoming more difficult to hide. They often sat outside the clinic in the back where there was a covered porch to shelter them from the heat of the sun, and ate their lunch, laughing and talking about their day. Mishael shared with Smith much of her childhood and wondered what Smith's life was like before he came to Pakistan. She'd been raised in a very conservative family and her father was very strict. If he knew of her feelings towards Smith he would forbid her to work at the clinic.

After the morning rush of patients, Smith signaled to Mishael to meet him outside for coffee. She smiled and waited until her lab work was done and walked outside. "Bita, this is really getting to be a habit with us. We need to be more careful or people will talk. It will ruin chances for me to remain with Dr. Irfan if I am spoken of in that manner."

"I want you to relax. I'm doing nothing out here but talking with you. We aren't holding hands or anything. Not that I don't want to." He smiled at her and got lost in her black eyes.

"I'm happy to sit with you, but I am nervous about my family knowing."

"We work together here at the clinic and they cannot keep you from talking to other people here. I know it's dangerous and I'll be careful. I promise. Just let me enjoy these times with you, because we really have nothing else."

"I know. It is difficult. How are you feeling inside? Any memories coming back? You've not spoken of that for a long time now."

Smith shook his head and frowned, rubbing his black beard. "No, I've not had anything for a while now. I did dream something about a building I was working on, and there were children there I didn't know. I have no clue where it was or if it was real. That's the difficult part of this whole thing. I might be dreaming about things that are real and not even know it. I am hoping against hope that soon something will return."

"I want to know more about you. Where you are from. What you did all these years to get so strong."

Smith laughed. "I'd like to know that, too! Wish I knew where my family is and what I did for a living. I keep reading about America and going through books that Dr. Irfan has. But so far it has triggered nothing. I cannot lose hope, Mishael. It's very important to me that I remember who I am."

Mishael looked into his blue eyes. It was strange to see a man with a black beard, black hair, and blue eyes in Pakistan. That caused more than a little talk in Zhob. She had grown to love his face and his hands. He was so tall and handsome. But she would not allow herself to dwell on what could be; that would be so destructive for her life.

"Maybe you will be coming to supper on Friday as Mahsa is baking some good food for us then. I know Irfan is aware of how I feel about you, and he's very stern with me about it. I respect that, but he also knows how lonely I am. I cannot stay inside four walls and have no relationships, and I'm already so limited to who I can talk to."

Mishael nodded and looked down. She felt trapped in her love for Smith. There was nothing she could do except sit and listen and hold back her feelings. "I understand what you're saying. I am fighting feelings that rise up in me because I know I cannot ever act on them. This is tough for me, Bita. Our choice to get close has caused other problems. I guess we have to decide if we can deal with them or just back away."

"I'm going to enjoy every moment I can have with you, even if it is sitting at the table with Mahsa and Irfan. That's better than nothing. Your smile lights up my day and I live for the times we can sit and talk. I'd go crazy if I didn't have you in my life. But at the same time I don't want harm to come to you, Mishael. Trust me that I'll not do anything to cause more trouble in your life."

"Let's go back inside. I'll probably see you later for lunch."

He touched her hand and walked back into the clinic. His heart was about to burst because he wanted to hug her. How in the world was he going to continue in this direction without kissing her and holding her in his arms? He'd have to find a way to have moments with her where no one could see or ever find out. Her life was at stake and he was highly aware of the dangers. Dr. Irfan had made that very clear.

The day ended with many patients still waiting to be seen. They were sent home to return the next day. Dr. Irfan called Smith into his office and asked him to sit down in a chair beside his desk. The office had meager furnishings as did the rest of the clinic. It was clean and kept up but Dr. Iran could not afford fine furnishings. "Bita, I am amazed at your learning. You have passed far more than I ever thought you would in learning about the patients and treating the illnesses. I feel you have known about this in your past. Your mind is incredible and I don't think we've tapped the fullness of your intelligence yet. I want you to learn more and more, and I'm thinking about giving you some medical journals to study. How do you feel about this, Bita?"

Smith put his arms on the desk and looked at Dr. Irfan. "I owe you my life, Irfan. I'll learn whatever you need me to learn to help you in your work. I'm hungry for more information, I admit. But none of this sounds familiar to me. If you want to show me some medical journals I'll read them at night when I get home from the clinic. It'll give me something to do that is challenging. Should Mishael learn more, too, or do you need her more in the lab?"

Dr. Iran knew where this was going. "No, I think she's fine where she is. I really want you to be working alongside me in more areas and this will help you learn quicker. You need to be careful, Bita. Mishael is walking a dangerous line showing any attention to you in front of patients. It is not acceptable here. Remember that."

Smith put his head in his hands and was silent for a moment. When he looked up at Irfan his eyes were full of sadness. "I'll back away some, Irfan. But I do love her. I might as well say it to you. And I think she loves me. But I know that is death to her so I'll be careful. You don't know how difficult it is for me to have her around and not be able to hug her or hold her hand. I need that relationship so bad but cannot have it with her. Can you see how frustrating it is?"

"I am not blind, Bita. I have seen it coming all along. But you live here and you have to go by the rules here. They are not easy rules but it is all we know."

Smith walked out of the office and headed back to Irfan's home. He felt so alone, so desperate. He had finally found someone he could love and he could not have her. He had to find a way to accept the limitations or he knew Mishael would leave the clinic. He had learned the hard way that a little was better than none. When he reached the house he sat outside on the porch for a while waiting for Irfan to arrive home. He looked up at the sky and watched as the stars came out. Mahsa was inside fixing dinner and there was an aroma drifting out into the night air. He was tired, hungry and lonely. He leaned his head back on the chair and closed his eyes, praying that God would hear open his mind up. He couldn't take it much longer; this not knowing anything about his own life. He was a man with no past and he realized more and more each day that this one fact kept him from having a future. He was stuck in some kind of sick limbo that felt like he was moving in slow motion. He did the same thing every day over and over. Somewhere in his mind he knew he was meant for more than this. But he couldn't for the life of him find out what that was.

He saw Irfan walking down the road and ran to meet him. "We had a good day, Irfan. I am ready to eat and Mahsa has cooked us a good meal."

"Bita, I have become so attached to your being here that I almost dread your memory returning. I know it will come and I pray for it. But I will lose a wonderful man in my life when you go."

"It is a curse and a blessing, Irfan. I, too, will feel sadness and a joy."

∽

High altitude surveillance photos were being studied by the CIA and there were Special Ops forces scattered all over Pakistan. The odds of ever seeing Smith Sanderson alive in Zhob were a zillion to one. Almost as difficult as finding Osama Bin Laden.

CHAPTER 43

According to the best authorities on how to raise children, you should never allow a child to sleep in your bed. Grace couldn't help but laugh to herself as she tucked Molly and her friend Susan into her king size bed. There were so many pillows, stuffed animals, and blankets that you could hardly see the girls. They had spent the day at the park again, and girls had worn themselves out flying kites, racing each other across the lawn, playing with Houston, and staying up late watching movies. Grace decided they could sleep in her bed with her for the first night. She had them for the whole weekend and looking at the two girls piled up in her bed sound asleep, she wondered if she would have enough energy for tomorrow.

It had been a wonderful day; the weather had turned out better than forecasted. It was predicted that it would rain all morning and be cloudy all afternoon. Somehow wires had crossed with the weatherman because it was one of the hottest days of the summer and there was not a cloud to be seen. She stepped out on her porch and looked up at the sky. There were millions of stars out and she took in the warm sultry breeze that was blowing, feeling good inside about her day with Ben and the girls.

Ben never ceased to amaze her in that he was always a step ahead of her. He'd had lunch figured out, he'd brought extra toys for the girls to play with, and had shown the energy of a teenager when he was play-ing with them. She felt very grateful to have him in her life. She'd had no idea things would move in the direction they were moving. She was finding herself thinking of him all throughout the day, possibly because she was not as busy as she normally would be when school was in session. Things would come to an abrupt halt once she got Molly in school. Homework, baths, cooking supper. She had her plate full, but for the first time in a long time she felt happy.

Molly had agreed to stay for the school year and see how things went. She was excited about going to public school but upset because she wouldn't have her friends there. Grace reassured her that she would make new friends, but it remained to be seen how that would all come into play. Grace had all of her records sent to Ross High and got her registered for the fifth grade. They had gone shopping for backpacks, school supplies, clothes, and pajamas. Molly's room was filling up with girlie things and Grace was loving it. They picked out a bedspread and a bulletin board for her to put up notes from her friends and photographs. She wanted the room to feel like home to Molly.

Grace was more than ready to get back to school. She was wondering how Samuel Billings had spent his summer and was hoping his mother was still in good health. There were many things she wanted to change about how the school handled students who couldn't afford food or who had special needs at home. She also wanted to continue the chorus from graduation and do performances during the year. There was so much talent there; it had turned out so well and the response from the community was overwhelming. She walked back inside and climbed in beside Molly, careful not to wake her. What a lovely child she was. She closed her eyes and fell asleep, not hearing a text that came in on her cell phone, which she'd left on the kitchen counter.

❦

Ben was up watching the news, sitting on the sofa with Houston. He'd texted Grace a good night message and was about to call it a night. At 11:00 p.m. his phone rang; he jumped and knocked his tea off the end table trying to answer it.

"Ben? Director Pauley here. Sorry for calling so late. How've you been?"

Ben was shocked to hear his voice, not to mention the late phone call. "Good evening, sir. I'm fine. What's goin' on?" He grabbed a towel and mopped up the tea.

Pauley was careful with his words. "We're doin' a covert operation in Pakistan, and wondered if you wanted to join us. I know you've had enough of Pakistan, but this one might interest you. What do ya think?"

Ben smiled. This guy was good. "What did you have in mind, sir? I mean, I haven't been involved for months now. I have another job. I'm sure you don't need me anymore with all those new guys you moved into position."

Ben knew Pauley was grinning. He knew Pauley well, and he was sure Pauley he wasn't going to be swayed easily. "Well, I have some good men, but you're one of the best and you know it. Just though I'd give you the opportunity, is all. So you miss it at all?"

"I'm not sayin' I don't ever think about it. But it feels good in a way to not have that hanging over my head all the time. The risks involved were huge. I have no risks now. My life is going great and I'm happy. So why would I change anything now?"

"Like I said, I wanted to offer it to you. I get it that you're done. But I was asked to give you the option and I did. You've declined so I've done my job. I hope you have a great night, Ben. I'll keep in touch."

The phone went dead. Ben sat there scratching his beard, wondering what in the world that was all about. Pauley had a way of sneaking into your world, dropping just enough to drive you nuts, and then pulling back. He was certain there was more to this phone call than he let on, and there was only one way he was ever going to find out what it was. That was to go in to Pauley's office and agree to do the job.

Ben liked his life the way it was. He wanted to be around for Grace. Molly was on the scene now and she had worked her way into his heart. Why would he want to go and mess all that up, just to be dropped into Pakistan again? No way. He was done. Pauley knew that but just kept on pushing. He wasn't going to give in, not this time. He got up and turned off the lights, touched Houston on the neck, and headed to bed. Houston jumped on the bed and curled up. Ben pulled the covers over his head and turned out the light. He closed his eyes but his brain would not shut off. *What is Pauley up to? Does he know something that I want to know? They were right a long time ago; once you're in the CIA you can't get out. They won't let you alone. And Pauley knew that phone call would drive me nuts. Damn. He just won't quit.*

CHAPTER 44

Ross High sat back off the road on a grassy hill with a huge parking lot that had been empty all summer long. On this end of the summer morning in August the lot was packed full of cars. School was in session and Grace was at her desk enjoying a quick chat with Brittany. Sitting just outside the door was Anne Meriwether, pretending to be ruffling through the file cabinet, but hoping to catch some news about that handsome ex-CIA agent that she'd heard about. Grace was excited and couldn't wait to tell Brittany about Molly and her first day of school at Ross. Anne had no idea that Grace was fostering a child from Wilton but her ears were wrapped around the corner of the front office, straining to hear every word spoken.

"Brittany! You're gonna love her! She's adorable and I want you guys to be friends."

"Oh my gosh! I'm so excited for you. She's the luckiest girl in the world. I know you'll be a great mom to her and it makes me cry to think she's been there for so long."

"Yes. She doesn't even remember her mother. Her whole life has been at Wilton."

"Who's her teacher?"

"Jim Marshall. I've worked with that man for years and knew him at Brenton before I took the job here at Ross. He's gentle but gets the job done. The kids love him. He'll take the class on field trips and bring in animals; he's very creative and thinks outside the box. Some of the teachers frown on his methods but at the end of the day his students get the highest test scores. How can you argue with that?"

"I wish I could've had a teacher like that. So was Molly nervous about coming today?"

"Yeah, she was. But I told her at anytime during the day she could come to my office and we'd talk it out. That way she doesn't feel trapped or alone. I know it'll take some time but this morning something really neat happened that couldn't have been planned if I'd tried. We were walking into the school early and Samuel Billings was sitting in the hallway waiting on a friend. You know his life was turned around after graduation, don't you? He became popular in one evening. Now all the guys want to hang with him and all the girls love him!"

"I've heard the talk. It's crazy that just that one night could change everything. Kind of scary in a way; they didn't want to be friends with him before. And now he has to scrape them off his arms."

"I know. But he can pick and choose who he wants to be close to. Anyway, he walked up to Molly and squatted down. I mean, he's about six foot four, right? Well, Molly was impressed and smiled and they became fast friends. He told her that if she ever needed anything to let her know and he'd be there in a split second. He said "I've got your back, girl!" I was amazed how quickly she took to him."

"That's so cool. He's a nice guy and he means what he says. He's been on the bad side of the tracks and felt left out."

"Molly was grinning so big! I think she felt special and that's what I wanted her to feel. So we'll find out at lunch how things are going. I'm hoping she'll make some friends in her class; I really don't know how introverted she'll be in this situation. Can't wait for you to see her."

"I'll peek in at lunch and maybe I can catch her. I hope we can be friends. Now I better rush to class but I'll be back at 1:00. Good to see you, Miss Grace. Don't forget the phone call to Mr. Parker. "

"Thanks. I won't. Have a good morning, Brittany!"

Grace pushed her chair back from her desk and propped her feet up for a moment. She was just about to call Ben when she noticed her door was cracked. It wouldn't be beneath Anne Meriwether to be listening in on her phone conversation. It'd happened before. So she jumped up and looked out into the main office. Anne was sitting behind her desk but Grace noticed that the cabinet file drawer was still open. She reached around the corner and slammed the drawer shut, causing Anne to jump. As she looked up Grace just smiled at her and closed her door. The year was starting off with a bang.

Ben's phone rang and rang but there was no answer. She left a message for him and hung up the phone, wondering why he'd be calling her at school. She shrugged her shoulders and pulled her chair up to her desk and stared at the stack of mail and papers on her desk. Three hours later, it was lunch time and Molly was peeking into her office. Grace was so glad to see her and took a much needed break from her paperwork.

"Hey, darling! How was your first morning at Ross?"

Molly rushed over, looking so cute in her skirt and flats and pretty pink sweater. "Oh, Miss Grace! It was so fun! And I love Mr. Marshall! I can't wait to talk to Susan when I get home. She's gonna want to come to Ross, too!"

"Well, don't start anything. I'm lucky Miss Sharon allowed me to take you so quickly. I don't want us to cause a stir at Wilton because you're going to public school now."

"Oh, don't worry. Susan can come and spend the night anytime, like you said. She'll be fine."

"Let's walk over to the lunchroom and I'll eat with you. How's that?"

"Um, I'm supposed to meet Melanie in the lunchroom and . . ."

"Hey, Miss Grace! How are you?" It was no other than the handsome Samuel Billings peeking around the corner of her door.

"I'm fine. How are you, Samuel? How's the first day back going?"

"Well, I've got my first girlfriend of the year, so I'm happy." He looked at Molly and winked.

"I'm headed to the lunchroom, Samuel. Want to walk me over?"

"Yeah, I've got one more class before my lunch but I'll run you there."

Molly rushed over and kissed Grace's cheek and skipped out the door. So much for worrying how she would handle the first day at Ross. Grace got some water out of the fountain and pulled her lunch out of her bag and sat at her desk going over the schedule for the week. She smiled, thinking about how happy Molly had looked when she left with Samuel. This could really change her world. She was just finishing her last bite of sandwich when her phone rang. It was Ben. And he sounded out of breath.

᠙

"Grace? I tried to get in touch with you! Just left Director Pauley's office. Now, don't go crazy. I'm needed for a mission and I guess I've agreed to go."

"Oh no, Ben! Not now . . ."

" Grace, it's nothing, really. I'll be back soon, I'm sure. But something tells me that I need to go on this one, even though I've told Pauley over and over that I was done. You won't be mad, will you? I couldn't leave if you were mad."

Grace felt a rock was in her stomach. She was sinking fast. Ben was leaving and didn't know when he was coming back. It had a familiar ring to it. "I'll . . . I'll be fine, don't worry, Ben. But how long? How long will you be gone?"

"You know I can't say. They don't even know themselves. It sucks, I know. I'm sorry, Grace, but trust me that I feel I need to go."

"I hate the CIA. They just won't leave you alone. I hate them! Ben, we just got started really. And there's Molly. She'll die when she finds out you're gone. What will you do with Houston?"

"Well, that was my next question. Will you and Molly watch him for me while I'm gone?"

"Of course we will. It'll make you feel closer to us. But Ben, why do you have to go. Why?"

"Can't explain it, angel. I just feel like I need to go and believe me I wrestled with it for hours. I have grown to love you so much and I don't want anything to change that. I just want you to think about that while I'm gone. I love you. Can you get that, Gracie?"

Grace had tears streaming down her cheeks, unaware that Mrs. Meriwether was watching from her desk through her office door. "I'll make it, Ben. I know you love me. That's what's killing me. Am I going to lose two men who mean the world to me to that damn CIA? I couldn't take it again, Ben. Do you hear that?"

Ben swallowed a giant lump in his throat and tried to sound reassuring. "Now listen, honey, it won't be that long. I bet I'm back in a week or two. Three tops. But please don't sit and worry. I'll be back one way or the other and we'll pick right back up where we left off. Hug Molly for me and I'll bring my keys to you before school lets out. So I'll see you soon, and we can say goodbye."

Grace put the phone down and her hands were shaking. She saw Anne looking at her and walked over and shut her door. This whole thing had a funny ring to it. She didn't like the feeling she was having in her gut. Somehow she had to find a way to stay calm for Molly, and also for her job. The school year was just starting and she had a full schedule. This was no time for her to be emotional. She sat down and tried to tackle the paperwork and answer phone calls, but underneath the steady voice was outright terror. She knew the risks involved in a mission. She was all too familiar with what *could* happen. And for once she wasn't sure if she could handle another black sedan pulling up in her driveway.

CHAPTER 45

When Ben walked through the doors of Ross High, his instinct told him that he might have pushed his relationship with Grace to a dangerous edge. She had lost her husband over a year ago and he had seen the trauma that his death had caused in her life. She was just now picking up the pieces and going forward, even inviting him in and then Molly. Huge steps for Grace. Now he was asking her to accept his taking another mission, allowing him this freedom without absolutely falling apart.

He had gone over this in his mind for hours before he took the position to lead the team. What was it about this job that got in your blood? Why couldn't he just leave it alone? He wanted more than anything to have Grace in his life permanently and he loved her like he'd never loved before. So what was the point of leaving now? He felt so torn that he sat down in the hallway of the school, which was oddly quiet just before the bell rang to dismiss the kids. He looked around and knew that this was her world. This is what kept her sane and moving forward. He didn't deserve her love if he was going to ask her to step out on a limb with him as Smith had done. He loved his job with the police force and was really getting into working with Houston. There honestly was no reason to go except for this one nagging phone call from Pauley. The mission was concerning the terrorist groups that were forming after the death of their leader, Osama Bin Laden. They were going to infiltrate and find out the direction the terrorists were headed. A dangerous mission, to say the least. He couldn't tell Grace where he was going or when he'd return. It could be one week or five months. Damn, he was good at creating drama in his life. The most beautiful woman in the world was waiting behind that office door and he was headed out to play a game of search and rescue of the worst kind. With weapons of epic proportions.

He got up and walked into the office and turned to the left, where Grace was in her office sitting at her desk. He failed to speak to Mrs. Meriwether, but bumped right into Brittany, who was coming out of "Excuse me! Just headed in to see Grace Sanderson."

Brittany looked up at his face and suddenly put two and two together. "Oh—of course. She's in there. You must be Mr. Parker."

Ben didn't want to seem abrupt but he was desperate to see Grace. "Yes, I am. And I bet you're Brittany. I've heard a lot about you!"

Brittany blushed and waived him into Grace's office with a smile. When he turned to go in, the look on Grace's face said it all. Her face was frozen for a split second into a cry that was so deep, so hurtful, that he could hardly bare to look at her. That told him that she was terrified that he would not come back. He closed the door and rushed to her side, grabbing her and holding her close to his chest. She buried her face there and cried, shaking her head. She just didn't understand why he felt so compelled to go. Things had been going along so perfectly; why did it have to stop now?

"Grace. Look at me. Please don't cry like this. You have every reason to be angry at me and I own that. But I want you to trust me that I'll do everything I can to return home to you and Molly." It sounded weak even to him. She stood there with her hands over her face and then she turned and walked to the file cabinet and grabbed some Kleenex.

"Your promise is empty, Ben. It falls on deaf ears for the simple reason that you have no control as to whether you'll come home or not, or when. I understand that to the core. That's what makes this so tough for me—saying goodbye to you. How can I say goodbye?"

Ben was overtaken with sorrow and torn with the decision he made to leave again. Obviously, the timing was off because she was still raw from Smith's death and the fact that his body had never come back home. What was the best choice here? Why did he feel such a pull to go?

"I'll make it easy on you, sweetheart. Walk out of here and never look back. Know that Molly and I will take good care of Houston no matter what the outcome of this trip is. I'll watch over your home and make sure it's taken care of. Leave me the numbers now of who I need to contact so that you're lawn is taken care of. Tell me the vet you use for Houston. We might as well get down to brass tacks here because you're leaving and I won't be able to contact you 'til God knows when."

Ben knew she was right. There was no easy way. He took his cell out and gave her the numbers she needed and stood there feeling helpless. "I don't know what to say, Grace. I hope you know I love you so much. I am growing so fond of Molly. I can't explain why I feel the need to go on this mission, but maybe we'll find out why very shortly. When I can contact you, I will, immediately. Pray this goes well for us and I need to know I have your blessing. I need to know you'll be here when I get back. Am I asking too much?"

Grace stood there shaking, trying not to show that kind of emotion. Her heart was about to burst and she was about to tell the man she'd decided to let in, goodbye. "I have no words, either Ben. Nothing is going to make this feel okay. Go and do the job you were meant to do, and know I'll be here when you get back. I can't promise you anything else right now. I'm too raw. Too hurt. And too overwhelmed with the feelings I have for you.

Ben kissed her sweetly and held her for a moment and then turned and walked out of the office. He passed Mrs. Meriwether and Brittany, tipped his hat at them, and hurried out the door. When he reached his truck he bent over in the grass and threw up his lunch. The emotions of the moment were tearing his guts out. When he'd made the decision to go, it seemed so clear. Now it wasn't clear at all. As he pulled out of the parking lot he looked back and saw Grace standing at her window. He blew her a kiss and drove off, knowing that might be the last time he ever saw her.

CHAPTER 46

The bell rang and the halls filled up with kids heading to their lockers to get what they needed for the next day. Grace waited at the door for Molly to show up and it wasn't long before she came around the corner with Samuel, laughing and dragging her backpack. When she saw Grace she ran towards her, hugging her and talking about her day. "Miss Grace, I had so much fun today. Mr. Marshall made our history lesson so real! And Samuel was there right at 3:00 to walk me to our car! I love this school!"

Grace forced a smile and hugged Molly. She was so proud of how quickly she was fitting in at Ross and finding her way. Samuel had adopted her as a little sister and was always there watching out for her. It made Grace relax and not worry about what Molly was doing when she was out of sight. "Come on, honey. I have a nice surprise for you! We're picking up Houston after we leave school because Mr. Ben is going out of town for a while. Isn't that great?"

Molly squealed with delight. "Oh, my gosh. Are you serious? That's so cool. How long can we keep him at our house?"

"I'm not sure, Molly. Could be a week, or a month. But he'll love it because you're there."

She said goodbye to Samuel and they both hopped into the car and took off to Ben's house. Pulling up in the driveway and seeing the stained walnut front door, the perfectly groomed yard, the iron fence around the yard, and the tall trees lining the edge of the yard, Grace felt sick inside. Molly jumped out and ran to the door screaming, "Miss Grace! Come on. Let's get Houston! I can't wait to see him!"

"Okay, honey, hold on a second. Let me find the keys in my purse."

Grace opened the door and Houston came bounding out of the back of the house wagging his tail and barking. He was so excited to see Molly. Grace walked through the house smelling Ben's aftershave and the dog food he'd put out for Houston for the morning. She found Houston's leash, grabbed a huge bag of dog food and his feeding bowl, and walked out to Ben's car to put it in the back seat on the floor. She backed Ben's SUV out of the garage and pulled hers in. No point in trying to get Houston in that BMW. When she went back in the house, Molly and Houston were on the sofa snuggling. She couldn't help but laugh. "Look at you two! Five seconds and you're on top of each other! Let's go, angel. Grab the leash and let's put old Houston in the backseat. You can sit right beside him if you want to."

Molly was happy to be able to take Houston home, but she asked a million questions about Ben and when he'd be back. Grace had no answers for Molly or herself. She felt like she was in a bad dream; it seemed impossible that she was facing the same scenario again. How did she get so lucky? Houston and Molly were in the backseat having the time of their lives, and she was lost in her own thoughts.

When they got home Molly jumped out again and headed to the back-yard, where she unlocked the gate and let Houston in. He ran around and jumped up on the patio furniture. He was so familiar with Grace's house that it felt like home. Grace went inside and put Houston's things in the bottom cabinet and heard Margaret hollering across the yard. She opened the back door and went out to meet her, holding back her emotions, which were about to explode.

"Hey, darlin'! How's my girl?"

"Hi, Maggie. Doin' fine. Ben's out of town for a while so I'm keeping Houston for him. You can see it's gonna be a real problem with Molly!"

Margaret looked past Grace and saw Molly throwing the Frisbee to Houston. "Why don't you let me sit here in the yard and you go do what-ever you need to do. I haven't spent much time lately with Molly and this would be a great time for you to have an hour of 'me' time."

Grace started to refuse but stopped herself. She really needed to visit the cemetery. It had been a few weeks and today she really needed that time with Smith. "Sounds like a deal to me, Mag. You sure it's okay? I won't be long."

"You go. She'll be fine with me. I've made brownies and I bought a movie I bet she'd love to see."

"Thanks so much, Mag. You are a lifesaver; you have no idea."

As Grace walked away, Margaret frowned and sat down in the nearest patio chair. *So Ben's out of town for a while. Two guesses as to where he's gone. This girl can't get a break. I've never seen anything like it. He better come home, that's all there is to it. He better come back home.*

❦

Giant thunderhead clouds had moved across the sky and blocked the heat of the sun, and there was a slight breeze that comes up when rain is coming. Grace parked the SUV and walked to the grave site already feeling the stress rolling off her back. She sat on the bench near Smith's marker and quietly took in the silence that lay over the whole cemetery. There wasn't even a bird singing today. Her heart was heavy and she was about to cry again. A feeling of hopelessness was trying to take over what was normally a very optimistic outlook and Grace had nowhere to turn.

"Smith, I've missed you so much. Here I am again, whining about my life without you. I know you had a hand in my getting close to Ben and that drives me nuts sometimes. How did you know we'd get along so well? Was it because you did?" She stood up and turned to look at a man standing beside a grave down the hill. "I don't know how much longer I can take this, Smith. Things aren't working out so well. I lost my best friend, Martha, in a car accident. You can imagine how that made me feel. And now Ben has taken off on another covert operation. I have developed a deep hatred for the CIA. I just don't think I can do this again, Smith."

Grace got up and paced back and forth. It seemed fruitless to continue. *I feel so stupid sitting here talking to this grave. He can't hear me and I'm so frustrated.* She picked up her purse and walked back to the car. Smith seemed so far away now. Unreachable. Maybe this is what her friends meant when they said that eventually she'd stop coming to the cemetery. So now what did she do with all her questions and frustrations? Where should she go now?

Full of sadness, Grace got back in the truck and drove home. She tried to prepare herself for seeing Molly and Margaret. She would have given anything if her phone had rung and it was Ben telling her that he'd changed his mind about going. She wished more than anything that life could have kept on going like it was. Big drops began to fall as she was about to pull up in the driveway. She sat in the truck listening to the rain hitting the roof, drowning out her thoughts. Her chest felt tight, and her heart was as heavy as lead. But there was a little girl inside who was waiting for her, and that one thing saved her from total despair. That and a dog the size of a horse. She took some deep breaths and checked her eyes in the mirror. It wouldn't do for Molly to see tears in her eyes. It wouldn't do for anyone to know that she was broken in half for the second time in her young life. She had nowhere to turn and no one to listen so she got out the car and walked to the door, letting the rain wash way any trace of a tear on her face. The poem Smith wrote was echoing in her head: "*Let the more loving one be me.*"

CHAPTER 47

In the black of night a Pave Hawk lowered itself into a grassy patch of land between low mountains on the edge of Bhakkar. There was no sound as the men slipped off the helicopter and disappeared into the wooded area. The chopper lifted off and was lost in the clouds that covered the sky, and the team began to plan its next move. There was word back in Washington that new terrorist groups were forming in reaction to the death of Bin Laden. Covert was going on all over Pakistan, and Ben's team was heading it all up. Their main mission was to infiltrate the groups and find out any plans they might have of military action against the United States. This would take some time and Ben realized after he met with Pauley the second time that he'd probably not return to the States for months. His stomach went into a knot thinking of how Grace would react, but he shook it off, trying to focus on the work he was there to do. The risks were incredibly high so he couldn't allow himself any room for error. He had to stay focused at all times and trust no one. They separated and were told to report back in five days at the location where they landed. Each man was on his own, acting independent of the group, and totally responsible for his own safety.

It was foggy and damp as Ben walked into Bhakkar, disappearing in the crowd. The rich and the poor were all mixed in together. The streets were dirty on the outskirts of the city but the further he went in, the cleaner and more extravagant the buildings were. This was where he'd be living and he had to fit in like a glove. His men were so good at it that they couldn't recognize each other in a crowd. Their only communication would be a signal on their cell phones. No one would be able to trace any call nor would they connect them to any Americans who happened to live in the area. It was a stark reality to embrace the fact that he might be in the presence of the enemy and not even know it. Nor would they know he was there. A deadly game that Ben was trained to play. Only losing wasn't in his manual. The side of Ben that Grace knew was only a part of him. The other side could be ruthless when need be. Uncompromising and powerful. Frighteningly powerful.

Smith woke to find Irfan standing beside his bed. He sat up sleepy-eyed and yawned. "What's up, Irfan? Is something wrong?"

"No. Quite the contrary. I've decided to take a short trip into Bhakkar. I want you to go with me. Get dressed and Mahsa has fixed us a good breakfast. We will need the food as the drive will be long, and it will be after lunch before we arrive there."

"You think it's safe for me to travel with you?"

"Yes, now I do believe we will be fine. The terrorist groups have moved around and I think this might be a window of time that you can get out with me and see more of Pakistan. It will be a nice trip and I'm looking forward to time with you."

"What about the clinic?"

"Mishael will see the patients and send away those who need more serious care."

Smith smiled thinking of her. "I'll be ready in ten minutes."

Irfan walked into the kitchen and talked with Mahsa. "Fix us something we can take with us in the car, Mahsa. We will need food, I am afraid, before we arrive in Bhakkar. Is there anything you need while I am there?"

"No. I'm fine. You must be careful, Irfan, not to think that the factions are not still around. It may become more difficult to see who the enemy is. Just watch yourself. And Bita."

Irfan nodded, noticing the furrows between her brows. She was worried. He walked over and hugged her, reassuring her that things would be fine.

Smith walked into the dining room and sat down, hungry for breakfast and excited about leaving Zhob for a while. "Irfan, I can't imagine travelling with you across the mountain to Bhakkar. Pretty exciting."

"I knew you would find it interesting and you need to get out some, Bita. I fear for your mind if you have to stay cooped up in the house or clinic for a long period of time."

Smith shrugged, as he knew no different life than he had with Irfan and Mahsa. They ate in silence and both men could feel the tension coming from Mahsa. When they got up to leave, Irfan again reassured her that they would return late that night. Smith hugged her and took the bags from her that held the food they would eat on the road. They headed out and Mahsa locked the door behind them. She thought about asking Mishael to stay with her while Irfan was gone. She got her coat and started out to the clinic, already worrying about her husband and Bita. Nothing could be taken for granted. Not anymore.

The trip to Bhakkar was tedious but Smith never complained. It felt good to be out and see other terrain and he was full of questions for Irfan. He was learning much about the culture and language and blended in very well in a crowd. He had grown to love the people and felt like part of Irfan's family, even though in the back of his mind there was a tug of war going on that had to do with his American background. The unknown drove him insane.

Irfan and Smith spent most of the morning driving and when they arrived, there were throngs of people in the street buying and selling. Smith was a little overwhelmed by the crowds of people and almost panicked because he'd not been exposed to this since the accident. Irfan sensed his tension and tried to calm him down.

"Relax, Bita. This is the time of day that people are out and about. Shopping and driving around in the streets. Don't let it bother you. Just allow yourself to enjoy the sights and sounds of a city. That is something you've not seen in a long time."

"It feels weird, like I've been here before but then foreign at the same time. Where are we headed, Irfan?"

"I came to get some supplies for the clinic and also to visit an old friend who you will like very much. We can stop here at The Village and eat a short lunch, since we did not eat what Mahsa sent with us. Maybe we eat that on our return home."

They pulled up to the restaurant, which looked run down, but later Smith found the food to be delicious. They were seated at the back of the dining room and it began to fill up quickly. Outside, there seemed to be a ruckus, and Irfan stood up to see if he could tell what was going on.

A group of men were outside fighting and one had a gun. Sounds of gunfire shot through the dining room and everyone started screaming. Something inside of Smith snapped and he grabbed Irfan and shoved him under the table. He felt like an animal inside, trapped or cornered. He raised himself up to see if the fight was still going on and it appeared as though the streets were clear again. They sat back down at the table and Irfan looked at Smith. "That may have been a group of terrorists, we just don't know. It is risky for us to remain here so we might eat quickly and then go visit, my friend."

⌒◡

Ben was walking along the road and came upon a restaurant and walked inside. Suddenly he was starved, so he allowed the hostess to seat him and ordered something from the menu he couldn't pronounce. He looked around and spotted an older man and a guy with a dark beard in the back of the restaurant talking. He though he'd heard some gunshots but didn't see any action outside. It felt good to sit and relax without wondering who was watching. He kept his ears open and finished his meal. He watched as the old man and his friend walked to the front of the dining room and paid. They left and Ben finished his meal and stepped back outside, feeling full and ready to find a place to stay.

Dr. Irfan and Smith were already in their car headed to the medical company where Irfan would get supplies for the clinic. Smith remained in the car while the doctor entered the building, watching both directions closely.

For some reason he felt like he was on high alert; it was almost like he was missing something. He ducked down in the seat and waited nervously for Irfan to come out, and then they headed on to his friend's house. When they arrived, it was raining lightly and Smith was glad to get inside the house. Saber Mazari was a kind gentleman who was bent over with arthritis and walked with a cane. When he smiled his whole face was a wad of wrinkles, but his eyes were full of light. He offered them both some warm tea and cookies and they both found a seat in the small dark living room.

"I am so glad to see you, my friend," Irfan said. He and Saber sat and talked for an hour. Smith sat quietly and listened, catching words here and there; just enough to know what they were talking about. Saber reported that he had seen some factions in Bhakkar and was worried about what was going to happen since the death of Bin Laden. Irfan was worried but had wanted to risk making the trip to see his friend. They discussed more politics and Smith dozed off listening to the mumble of words. Soon Irfan was ready to head back home and woke Smith up.

"Bita, time to go. Sorry you were bored, but Saber is good friend to me. I enjoy visiting him so much."

"I've enjoyed being here; just couldn't understand most of what you men were saying. He seems to be a nice man and has such kind eyes. How old is he, anyway?"

"Maybe ninety years old. I don't know for sure. He's seen much in his day and I enjoy to hear his stories. He has excellent memory."

That made Smith wince. "Well he's way ahead of me. I have no memory at all."

They told each other goodbye, and Smith shook Saber's hand and thanked him for the warm tea. Irfan climbed into the car and they drove off, leaving a trail of dust behind them. The roads were dusty and crowded with cars as they drove past the district counsel building. People were still milling about, talking and engaged in business with each other, and Smith watched them with a tinge of sadness, feeling an even stronger urgency to find out what he'd missed during the past year of his life.

It's doing me more harm than good being shut up in that house and able only to go to the clinic and back, he realized. The danger would be there no matter what, and he was about to decide that he needed to get out more in spite of the risk, or his memory would never return. The air was blowing into the car and he felt alive for the first time in a long time. With the same boldness and courage that had helped him through the covert operations he no longer remembered, Smith was determined to find out about his life, and nothing was going to stop him. Not even the threat of death. He sat back in the seat and let his mind wander, but the woman he was thinking about was not his wife who was missing him beyond belief. . It was someone else.

CHAPTER 48

It was close to midnight.

Molly was asleep with Houston. The phone had not rung all night. Grace was about to lose her mind waiting.

In the three weeks that had passed since she'd seen Ben, every single cell in her body was tuned in to the fact that he might not return. She'd done all the right things: covered her job at Ross, taken Molly places she'd never been before, laughed at old movies, eaten with Celeste and Maryann, cried over Martha, and waxed Ben's SUV because she couldn't stand the dirt any longer. But nothing helped her to deal with the days that kept going by without a word from Ben. No one could understand the horror she was going through and she was good at not showing how she felt. Most of the time a smile was pasted on her face and the only time it was off was when she was in her own room and Molly was fast asleep. It was then, and only then, that she'd let herself feel anything. She cried, she screamed in her pillow, and she swore she would never fall in love with anyone again. She had conversations with herself about how stupid it had been to allow Ben in, when he was married to the CIA just like Smith was. He'd quit twice and just couldn't refuse when it came down to it. Even his newfound love for her wasn't enough to keep him home.

Oh, she had a pity party, all right. And sometimes, late at night, she'd call Celeste or Maryann and let her hair down. They were sorry for her but their hands were tied. Nothing they could say or do would make things better. Finally she stopped calling them for fear it would ruin their friendship. So even around her best friends everything appeared okay with Grace Sanderson. But inside she was like a percolating volcano about to explode.

Margaret had an inkling of what was going on, because every time she saw Grace, she could see in her eyes that Grace was angry and scared. She was a sly old lady and nothing much got past her. She had been invited to the Cattleman's Ball by a dear friend of hers, Madeline Carrington. She phoned Madeline and asked if there was any way possible that Grace could go and bring Molly. She explained what Grace had done at Wilton and also how she'd taken Molly in as her own child and was planning on adopting her. Madeline called her "people" and they agreed that a portion of the auction that was a fund-raiser for a local women's abuse center could go to Wilton Children's Home. Margaret was so excited she couldn't wait to call Grace and tell her.

"Hello, darlin'! How's my girl doin'?"

"Oh we're terrific, Mag. How you been?"

"I'm fine, honey. I have some excitin' news, though! You and Molly have been invited to the Cattleman's Ball two weeks from tomorrow at 7:00 p. m. You'll ride with me and we'll dress up! You and I can get Molly a pretty ball gown, and you can dress up in one of your pretty dresses! Won't that be fun, angel?"

Grace put her head in her hands and frowned. *The last thing in the world I feel like doing is going to a ball.* Molly would love it, but I just don't know if I can deal with that right now. How can I tell her no? She's so excited about it.

"That sounds like a lot of fun, Maggie. So what made you think of inviting us to that event? Haven't you always gone with your friend Madeline?"

"Yes! But, honey, she's got it all worked out so that some of the money raised from the auction will be donated to Wilton Children's Home in your honor. Isn't that wonderful?"

Grace was impressed. "That's amazing, Mag. We'll be honored to go with you, and I'll tell Molly in the morning. Thanks so much for the phone call! I'll talk to you in the next day or so and we can get Molly a new dress to wear."

Grace hung up the phone and sat down on her bed. She was losing ground daily. Somehow she had to regroup and focus on something else besides Ben's absence. The dread was building and the thought occurred to her that he might not be home for another month or so. She couldn't keep going like this or she'd snap. Molly needed her to be 'in the moment' and not off in her own world trying to figure out where Ben was. She climbed into bed and looked at her cell phone. There was an old message left from Ben that she'd saved on her phone. She hit "play" and listened to his voice.

Suddenly she burst out crying and threw the phone across the room. She reached for a Kleenex and wiped her eyes, turned out the light, and lay there in the dark for hours before she finally collapsed from exhaustion. She didn't move in the bed until 8:00 in the morning when Houston jumped on her bed and licked her face, and Molly came running and joined them in the bed.

"Hey, Momma. Wake up! It's time for breakfast!"

Grace was in a daze but she wasn't so sleepy she didn't pick up on the word "momma." She didn't want to make a big deal out of it, but she was thrilled to hear that word. Molly had never discussed what she wanted to call Grace. It'd always been "Miss Grace." Grace had never dreamed she would be using the word "momma" so quickly, if at all.

"Okay, you guys! Let's go eat breakfast. Are you hungry, Molly?"

"Yeah! I'm starving. And we know Houston is! I've already let him out in the back yard so he's good. Just needs to eat."

Grace grabbed Molly and hugged her and pulled her under the covers. "Oh, stay here a second and snuggle. This bed feels so good."

Molly squealed with laughter and grabbed Houston and dragged him up on the pillows. "This bed's not big enough for all of us!"

The morning went by fast, and Grace decided to take Molly to the park with Houston. It was a pretty day and the sun was tucked behind a small cloud. Houston was feeling frisky and ran after another dog. Molly chased after him and Grace was behind Molly yelling for Houston. They finally got him by the collar and hooked the leash on his collar. He was getting spoiled living with Grace and Molly and didn't respond as quickly to his commands. Grace decided to be a little more on top of things with him or he'd have to go back through obedience training when Ben got back. If Ben got back…

❧

Molly picked out the prettiest dress in the store; it was light blue and made of taffeta. There was a single bow on the curve of her back that had ties that fell straight down to her ankle. It was sleeveless with a square neckline. She wore a silver chain with one pearl, and a pair of pearl earrings. She was ten and looked at least thirteen. For an hour before they left for the Ball, she spent plenty of time looking at herself in the mirror. Her hair was pulled up in curls with a bit of hair hanging down on either side. She absolutely felt beautiful.

Grace wore a simple light peach dress that was long and flowing. It was strapless and showed off her lovely shoulders and neck. She'd bought a new necklace made of pearls and semiprecious stones. It was perfect for the dress and looked great with some long earrings she'd found in her drawer. After she put on her makeup and pulled her hair up, she checked herself out in the full-length mirror. *I wonder if Ben would think I'm pretty tonight. He told me once he loved me in a dress* . . . She hurried downstairs when she heard a knock, and opened the door to find Margaret waiting with her sweater over her arm. "Grace, it's time. You girls ready? Don't you look lovely!"

"Molly! Maggie is here. You ready to go?"

Molly came bounding down the stairs, nearly tripping over her long dress. "I can't wait to go to the ball! Will we dance, Maggie?"

"I bet you will, darlin'. You're way too pretty not to have a dance."

When they pulled up to the door there was valet parking, so the girls got out and walked into the lovely ballroom. It was full of women in long dresses sipping on wine and eating canapés. Molly was overwhelmed by all the pretty ladies in dresses and heels. Up in the ceiling was a giant silver sparkling ball that was turning around slowly, casting reflections on the walls and floor. The music was playing and some people were already dancing. Grace and Molly found their way to the other side of the room to one of the tables. They sat down and watched all the people dancing, the women's dresses swishing around gracefully on the floor. A young boy came over and asked Molly to dance but she declined and leaned over and held Grace's hand. Grace laughed and pushed her out of the chair. "You didn't come here to just sit by me, baby. Get out there and have some fun! I'll be here waiting on you!"

A few minutes later, a handsome gentleman walked up to Grace and asked her for a dance. She shook her head, but he didn't take no for an answer. He pulled her up and introduced himself. "My name's Josh Henley. I'd like to have this dance with you!"

"I'm Grace Sanderson. I guess I have no choice!"

They danced for two songs and Grace was twirled around the floor like a feather. He was strong and tall and a very good dancer. She was awkward at first but learned to follow his lead, and soon found herself lost in the crowd underneath the disco ball. The next song was a slow dance and Grace tried to walk back to her table. She started looking for Molly and saw that she was still with the young man who had asked her to dance, so she relaxed and let Josh slow dance with her. He smelled good and kept the conversation going so well that she wasn't aware of the time.

After about an hour, Margaret found Grace and Molly at their table and sat down with them. "Aren't you glad you came now?"

Grace grinned. "Yes, this is just what we needed. It's fun to just sit here and watch the women in their pretty dresses. Molly had a great time with Jerrod, that young guy over there. They danced and walked around for at least an hour. I'm amazed at how relaxed she is with this crowd."

Margaret looked at Grace and grinned. "It's good to see you smiling again. I was gettin' worried about you, honey. You need to get out more and not stay holed up in that house every night. I know you work, Grace. And you've got Molly to tend to. But I'm right next door when you need to spend some time with your friends or go to a movie. I mean, you and Ben aren't engaged, are you? You could go out with someone now and again, right?"

"Uh . . . I haven't really thought about that, Mag. I guess I'm more attached to him than I realized. But I did enjoy dancin' with Josh. He's a nice man and a gentleman. That's hard to find these days. He asked for my number and I told him I wasn't ready to give that out yet. He wasn't pushy and that was refreshing."

Margaret took a sip of her wine and smiled. "We'll go right after the auction, Grace. They'll mention Wilton then, and I know you want to hear that. Let me know if you get too tired or if Molly is ready to go home."

Grace sat at the table watching Molly and Jarred dancing again, lost in her own thoughts. Ben seemed so far away tonight, and she hated that feeling. When she was home with Houston and Molly he felt a lot closer to her. Was she dreaming to think he'd make it back? And how long did she wait before she realized he wasn't coming back? She wasn't married to Ben, so maybe the CIA wouldn't send someone to tell her he was dead. Maybe there'd be no black sedan pulling up in her driveway . . . just nothing at all.

The shock of that revelation hit her hard and she felt shaky inside. When the auction was over and they'd mentioned the donation to Wilton, she grabbed Molly's hand and told Margaret they'd better get back home to let Houston out. They walked outside and the fresh night breeze was calming to Grace. She took a deep breath, trying to relax her racing mind, and when the valet brought their car up she got into the driver's seat because Margaret had had a few drinks and was a little tipsy. Molly was getting sleepy and laid her head against the back of the seat.

Grace could see her in the rearview mirror; this was her reason for living right now. Molly. Someone who needed her. She talked to Margaret on the way home so that she wouldn't hear the words echoing in her mind. But after she put Molly to bed and got Houston settled beside her, she went to her room and lay down in the dark. And the words came back to her louder than ever: "I'll be back soon, I promise." Those were the same words Smith had said to her every time he left for a mission. And he never came home.

And now Ben was gone and there'd be no way of her finding out. *Why did I put myself in this position again? How stupid can you get?* She got up and washed her face and brushed her teeth, noticing the lines deepening in her forehead from worry.

She knew one thing for sure. If he ever did come back home, she would make him promise that he'd never go on another mission again. Or she was out of his life forever. This waiting was for the birds.

CHAPTER 49

In the four weeks that Ben had been in Pakistan, he'd run into several factions that were increasing in strength. He'd sat in on a few meetings but had not stayed long enough with one group to pick up any plans that were being made. His cover was excellent and he blended in with the rest of the citizens of Pakistan. All of his men were basically invisible when they had to be; they could sit in a group and listen to what was going on and not even be noticed. It was a real art, and they'd been trained well. He had decided to remain near Bhakkar until he found a group he felt was a serious threat; then he'd remain there until he found out what their plans were in relation to retaliation against America. He could sense a feeling of unrest building in Pakistan and he knew it could lead to something dangerous. His ability to blend in would become increasingly important as the level of unrest grew. The risk of being killed was growing by the day.

The team met once a week at the designated location and discussed the issues they'd experienced while being undercover. They built their plans for the next week based on what had happened the week before. Nothing was pressing; the main issue was knowing whether or not there were factions that were planning retaliation on the United States by whatever means. It was their job to figure out the plan and let their operations go-to man at the Pentagon know. Then that contact would communicate with Director Pauley and any changes that needed to be made would be passed back to Ben. It was a tight effort and there was no room for error. Each man was aware that no matter how casually they were dressed and how easy their manner was, the security level was heightened and the risk level was at the top.

༄

Dr. Irfan enjoyed his trips to Bhakkar so much that he scheduled one every week, taking Smith with him just to get him out in the midst of civilization. He was improving quickly and often mentioned that he felt like his memory was trying to return. This would be the third trip over to see Irfan's friend, Saber, and Smith was really looking forward to it. After he got over the language barrier and Saber also gave in and tried to speak more English, Smith couldn't wait to hear the stories that Saber shared about his life in Pakistan as a professor at a university. It broke the week up and got both men out of the clinic. This particular trip, Irfan suggested that Mahsa and Mishael go along and have lunch with them at the café they had stopped at each previous trip over.

It was a gray day with the clouds hovering over them as they took the back roads to Bhakkar. Smith sat in the back of the car with Mishael, which allowed them time to talk.. He cherished every moment with her and longed for time alone. She felt uncomfortable holding hands, but the desire to be near Smith was overriding the discomfort. Every time she looked at him, he was staring at her with loving eyes. She'd never met a man like Smith. He was so giving, but at the same time she sensed a strength in him that was almost inhuman. She wondered often what he did for a living in America. And why he was in Pakistan. She hoped it was not to do harm to her country, but she'd never admit her doubt to Smith. It was strange to her to care so much about a man she knew nothing about.

They arrived at The Village and Smith got out and took Mishael inside as Irfan and Mahsa followed. The dining room was crowded but the waiter seated them on the right side of the room near a window. Smith took the window seat and Mishael sat across from him, next to Mahsa. They ordered their meals and began talking about one of Irfan's patients who was going to have to be sent to a hospital for surgery. Irfan was talking low and seemed stressed.

"I've done what I can to heal her. She's sicker than I thought and needs surgery immediately. But she cannot pay. I hope they will give treatment to her."

Smith tried to reassure him. "How can they turn her away when she is so ill? Is that the normal way?"

"No, Bita. They may not refuse her treatment. But the cost is high. I worry about her family being able to pay. Many of them are sick, too. They have not enough money to pay for food and go hungry many nights."

Smith listened as Irfan was talking, but his eyes were watching the crowd gathered outside the restaurant window. He knew nothing of what was going on except what Irfan had shared with him. He'd just learned about the dangerous man everyone called Osama Bin Laden and how he was recently killed. He had no idea of the unrest his death had caused, but he felt the energy of the crowd just by watching the behavior of the men standing together.

One man in particular stood out to Smith. He was taller than the rest but dressed the same as the other men around him. He was talking with his hands and gesturing; he seemed to be angry. Suddenly the man turned and looked directly at Smith. He didn't smile or anything—he just stared for a millisecond. Their eyes locked in and then the moment was gone as quickly as it came. Smith felt a chill go over him that made him want to run.

Mishael touched his arm. "Bita, are you all right? You are white as snow."

Smith put his hand on his face and shook his head. He felt weird. What was it about that man's eyes that got him so riled up? "I'm fine, Mishael. Just a weird thing happened, is all."

Irfan sat up and listened intently as Smith continued. "I was watching outside as I was listening to you talk and a man in the crowd suddenly turned and looked square at me. Our eyes locked for a nanosecond and then it was gone. I have no idea who he was or why he looked my way. It was weird. It gave me the strangest feeling."

Irfan studied Bita for a moment and started to say something but thought better of it. "It's probably nothing, Bita. Just a coincidence. That man may have heard a noise and suddenly looked up. Don't think anything about it."

Smith agreed but couldn't shake the feeling he'd had when their eyes locked. They ate their food and left the restaurant, heading on to Saber's home. Mishael could tell that Smith was preoccupied but she tried to get him involved in conversation. He finally let go and tried to enjoy being with her. It was a rare thing for them to be out in public together without having to watch every move they made.

૭๏

They soon arrived at Saber's house and as they walked up to the door, Saber opened it and greeted them all with open arms. He was so excited for their return. "Welcome! I am happy to see you always. Come into my home and make rest for yourselves."

"Thank you, Saber. Greetings from my family to you!" Irfan hugged the old man and took a seat near him in a chair.

Smith and Mishael sat on the sofa with Mahsa, and Saber served them all warm tea. They were full from lunch, but did not want to refuse the cookies he had out for them for fear he would be offended.

"We've been talking about wanting to hear more about your life, Saber. Can you tell us about your work at the university?"

"Of course. Of course. I love to share about work in the university. Many student pass through my door to learn new things about science. They are amazed at the end of the course what they learned about their world. Math is in everything and we use it even when unaware. But even more interesting than my classes and students is endurance of human will to survive. I have experienced firsthand how long truth can remain with a person."

Irfan shook his head and encouraged Saber to continue. "Please share with us what is in your heart, Saber."

"I was captured by terrorists some time past and had no way to escape. They tortured me in physical way until my eyes had blood in them. My teeth some came out. My ears were having ringing sound, and I could not speak words at all. But I remain true to my faith."

Smith came alive listening to Saber speak about his torture. He had seen how Mahsa was bruised when the terrorists kidnapped her because of harboring him. He could not imagine the pain Saber was speaking of. But he believed him. "How did you live through this, Saber? How did you not break?"

Saber shook his head. "It was easy to not give them wrong answer. I spoke only truth to them. I had nothing to hide and it angered the men. They wanted most definitely a story from me about how I accept what they were doing in the name of Islam. But radical Islam is not the Islam we know. The killing and harm to people; the hunger for the power. I simply said no, I do not accept to what you are doing. Then they beat me with poles of steel. They burn my face and put heat to my eyes. I nearly went blind but in my blindness I said no."

Smith and Mishael were frozen listening to Saber speak. They'd never met anyone like him before. Such a strong man to look so frail now, in his nineties.

"How did you get away from them, Saber? How did you escape?" Mishael asked.

"I waited for long time in dark room until I did not hear anyone moving around. I walk along wall to find door and turn knob, not knowing if I find anybody on other side. When I open door, they were already gone and I hurried outside and ran to my home. I was in warehouse not too far from my own house. But no one could hear my screams. My heart was beating loud; I felt my chest would burst open. But I was finally safe inside my home and thanked God for my safety. Many do not go back home. I was lucky."

"What did they want from you?" Smith stood at the back of the sofa and looked at the small man with disbelief.

"They angry at anyone who not accept their control. Their power. They are using the power of radical Islam to take control. I cannot and will not accept that lie."

"How are you not afraid now for your life? They know who you are and that you spoke against them in your classes at the university."

"Smith, you are fine young man. Your eyes not open to the whole truth yet. But you must see that they cannot destroy my spirit only my flesh. So I have nothing to fear from them. They are blind."

Something in the words that Saber spoke sat in Smith's mind and he turned them over and over on the way home. Mishael could tell he was preoccupied and left him alone. He was lost in thought when they left and stayed quiet for a while, because something was trying to surface in his mind. Something he'd learned when he was young. He strained to remember it but it would not come to him. He had learned since he came to live with Irfan that the more he tried to recall something, the farther it moved away from him.

So he finally gave up and reached for Mishael's hand. She turned and smiled at him and for an instant their eyes met and he felt the love again from her. He leaned in quickly and kissed her soft lips and moved back away. Mishael's heart raced and she moved over a little toward the other side of the car. She wanted too much to feel his arms around her, but Irfan would not have it. She didn't want to risk her job or her relationship with Irfan and Mahsa just for one hug or kiss with Smith. But it was painful to be so close and not be able to experience that closeness.

In the front seat, Irfan saw the kiss in his mirror. He wanted to say something to them but held his tongue. It was not his place to continue to tell them what was right. They were grown and it was their choice to decide the path they would walk. Great destruction was on that path, and Irfan wanted to protect Smith; he also knew Mishael's family would not approve. She would become an outcast. He wanted no part in that rejection. But he kept quiet and allowed them the freedom to choose.

The rest of the trip was spent talking about the horror that Saber had experienced and how others must have suffered terribly at the hands of the terrorists. They soon were home and Mahsa began cooking a light supper for all of them. Mishael would have to head home soon because it was getting dark. They set the table and helped Mahsa serve the plates. They all ate in silence, thankful to have visited such a brave man. Smith walked Mishael out the door and they stood in the yard under a tree talking quietly. He hugged her quickly and told her good night, more frustrated than ever at being so close to her but unable to do anything openly. He headed back to his room, tired from the trip and emotionally spent from wanting to remember his past. He sat on the bed, like so many nights before, asking God to help him remember. He laid back and shut his eyes and the face of a man came to him as clear as day. It was the same man who had looked at him in Bhakkar. *Who was that man?*

CHAPTER 50

Smith got up in the middle of the night and walked into the dining room. The house was dead quiet; the only sounds were frogs croaking outside. There was a slight breeze blowing as he walked outside on the porch and sat down in a chair near the edge.. He propped his feet up and sat back in the chair, trying to sort out what was left of his life. His relationship with Mishael was going nowhere. There never would be an answer to the problems they faced, because he was an American and she was a Muslim. He'd been in Pakistan for over a year now and his memory had not returned. He was no closer to discovering who he was and the frustration was building. Somehow he had to make a life for himself. He just didn't know where to begin.

He thought back to the times he'd been to Bhakkar and visited Saber. Both times he remembered seeing a man; the same man who had stared at him through the window in the restaurant. Why did that face haunt him? He sat back and relaxed, trying to allow something to come to him, but it seemed so fruitless. He only knew that he couldn't remain for the rest of his life with Dr. Irfan. It might be time to attempt a trip to Germany to the U.S base there. Dr. Irfan had mentioned there was one of the best medical hospitals at the base and maybe the doctors there could help him recover his memory. The terrorist groups were gearing up and it might not be the most opportune time to attempt a trip to Germany, but when would be a good time?

He was torn between wanting to take that risk and wanting to have Mishael near him. It had occurred to him that he could become a Muslim and slip into the society without any issues. But something inside him told him that was not a good solution. He desperately wanted to find out what his heritage was and was driven to knowing about his past. He couldn't go forward in life until he knew what his past was. He felt frozen in time. He felt alone. And he realized more and more how much he had grown to love Mishael.

෴

Running across the top of his computer was a news flash from the Pentagon. Director Pauley as working on a project at a table across the room. He heard the familiar beeping and walked across the room to see what was going on. The words he read confused him and his heart started racing. The phone rang and he grabbed it, wondering how in the world this could be true.

"Director Pauley. Johnson here. I assume you saw the bulletin coming across your screen. Now I want your men on this immediately. We've never had this kind of thing come up before, but I want you to check into this stat! Our men on the ground have spotted someone who looks like Sanderson. They could be wrong, but they were in the midst of a covert when they saw a man who they felt resembled Smith. They've spent time checking this out and I feel it's time to send your man in to find out. I'm referring to Ben Parker. He'd know if it was Smith and he's already over there."

"I know exactly where Parker is. We communicate constantly about the covert he's involved in. He's in Bhakkar as we speak in the midst of the factions. Are you saying you believe Smith to be in Bhakkar?"

"No. He's in a province called Zhob. To the east of Bhakkar. You'll be receiving papers this morning with the locations he's been spotted. They are pinning down now the exact location of his whereabouts and that will be in the report. Now Pauley, if that is Smith, then something's happened to him. He's experiencing amnesia or something worse or he'd never have remained there. I want you to relay to Parker that Smith may not be himself. That he may not recognize Parker. I am leaving it up to you to get this job done in a manner that is best for Sanderson. He may run if he thinks he's being kidnapped. So it has to be done correctly. I'm sure Parker's the man to do the job. I want constant contact with you,

Pauley. And no mistakes. If he runs, we may lose him forever. And he's one man I don't want to disappear. I want him home."

Pauley was visibly shaken. This news was unheard of. He couldn't imagine Sanderson being alive all this time. He felt like he was moving in quicksand when he left a message for Agent Parker. If this as true and Ben was able to locate Sanderson, it would be the covert operation of the century . . .

∽

Ben was sound asleep when a message came through on his phone. He woke three hours later and go up to get some water. He always checked his phone every time he woke up because the intensity of the operation had increased. There was unrest all over Pakistan and it was getting more dangerous to remain in the country. He was sleepy and felt exhausted after staying up late every night sitting in on meetings held by various factions who were attempting plans to blow up the railroad system in America. It was getting more critical that his men find out some real facts to pass on to the Pentagon in order to gain the greatest protection and minimize damage.

This particular morning it was cloudy outside with the threat of rain. Ben started his coffee pot and sat down at the kitchen table to check his messages. The first two were from his men, reporting what they'd heard during the night. They alternated covering the night hours of the covert because many of the factions met in the middle of the night to discuss and plan actions against the enemy, which was any American within reach in Pakistan and abroad. He clicked through them and came up on a message from Pauley.

He was familiar with Pauley's notes, which were always short and to the point. This one, however, was in all caps. Ben sat up and scrolled down. The hair stood up on his arms as he read the message.

AGENTS IN PAKISTAN HAVE REPORTED TO THE PENTEGON THAT THEY HAVE POSSIBLY SPOTTED AGENT SANDERSON ON THE GROUND.

He stopped reading and put his head in his hands. *What? They think they've spotted Smith? No way! He's dead.* He kept on reading and was shocked to learn that Sanderson, if it really was him, might have amnesia. Or injuries that would've kept him from being able to return to the States. Nothing made sense to Ben as he read and reread the message. His heart was pounding and he got up and paced the floor. *How could this be true? How could he have lived this long over here without being seen? Who took care of him? Oh my gosh, to think he might still be alive is insane.*

For the next five minutes Ben's mind raced. And in the middle of the words that were racing through his mind, Grace popped up and he shoved his clenched fist through the wall of the dining room. *What in the world will happen to my relationship with Grace? I'd have to give her up. There's no way we could continue in the direction we're going if Smith came back home. Grace will freak out. She'll flat freak out. Damn! How do I handle this? I have to answer Pauley now. I don't have time to think this through. Grace! I'm losing you and you don't even know it. It's all gonna hit you right in the face.*

Ben sat back down in the cheap wooden kitchen chair and looked around the room. He was aware he was shaking and feeling many emotions at the same time. His best friend might be alive. And he was going to have to sacrifice the love of his life to bring Smith home. The bad part was that he might not be able to ever tell Smith how much he loved Grace. How he had been ready to marry her before all this came down. With what Smith had apparently been through, and if his memory did return, he'd want Grace to be by his side as he returned to a normal life. Ben was fighting the impulse to run and get his friend, and another to hold on to what he'd found in Grace.

It's not fair! Damn it. It's not fair. I want him to be alive more than anything in the world, but now I have to lose someone to find him. Does it every stop? Does the craziness of this job ever stop?

The phone rang and the sound jarred Ben into a stark reality. "Parker? Director Pauley here. I assume you got my message this morning?"

"Yes sir. Just read it. I . . ."

"I was expecting an immediate call from you. Our communication has to be instant because of the intensity of the threat to every agent on the ground. Now listen up, Parker. They've spotted Smith in Zhob at a doctor's home. The name is Irfan Sheikhani. They've been watching this man for quite some time but never were certain it was Smith. You have to be the one to recognize him and I figure that'll be a no-brainer for you. He was your best friend. You would know him better than anyone. Do you get this, Parker?"

Ben stood at the window looking out at the empty street. Rain was coming down and the damp smell crept into his house. He suddenly felt ill and broke out in a sweat. "I hear you, Pauley. I get it. Now what is this about amnesia? Do they think he might not know who he is? If that's true, he won't know me, either. How's that gonna work?"

"I have no idea how you're gonna handle this, Parker. You're the one who'll have to figure this one out as you go. I'm hopin' that when he sees you something will click. Often it takes a trauma to bring back the memory. Think it through because you'll only have one chance. If he runs, then we may not find him again. We need to try to bring the man home, Parker. We can't leave him here without trying."

Ben sighed and put one foot on the chair, resigning himself to what was ahead. "I'll find him, Pauley. But I can't promise anything after that. I'll keep in touch. If anything changes about his location, let me know."

"One more thing, Parker. You don't sound too happy about us finding your best friend. I'm surprised."

"I'm in shock, sir. I'm blown away by this news. Never thought in a million years that this would be what I'd read on my phone when I got up this morning. I've been goin' to his grave for the last year, for God's sake. His wife . . . how will she handle this? We can't just pop in with him, can we?"

"No way. We'll have to bring Smith to a hospital here and debrief him. We also have to make sure he gets the best medical care. We'll tell her, but we have to be careful. It's gonna be a shock to her. A real shock. Sometimes these things don't turn out too well. The other person has moved on with their life. Found someone else. It can be tough, I'm warnin' you."

Found someone else? Are you kidding? She's in love with me.. "I know it'll be tough but we'll take it one step at a time. Trust me. I'll do my best."

Pauley put phone down and rubbed his face. Something was wrong. Parker didn't sound right. Maybe this was more complicated than he thought. Well, a lot had to take place before he'd have to face any issues with Parker. The main thing was to find Sanderson and try to find out what went wrong. That was going to be a challenge and he knew Ben was the man to do it. But something didn't feel right with Ben. He had been way too distant about the news.

CHAPTER 51

It was Saturday and the sun decided to finally come out from behind heavy clouds and shed its light on the rain soaked ground. Grace woke up again with Houston jumping on her bed and Molly coming through the door right behind him. The bed covers were all strewn around the bed and pillows were everywhere.

"You ready to spend the day with Marcy today?"

"Of course! She's comin' to pick me up at 10:00."

"This is your first time away from me, young lady! I'm not too happy about it." Grace was smiling, and punched her arm.

Molly frowned a little. "Seriously? I'll be back at around 5:00 unless we decide to go to a late movie. Is that okay, Mom?"

"Sure. I have plenty to do, don't worry. Now you better go eat breakfast and I'll let Houston out."

Houston took the cue and jumped down off the bed, ran into the kitchen and stood by the door. Molly laughed and raced to catch him.

Grace lay back on the pillows and let her mind wander off to where Ben might be. Her heart was aching to see him again. To lean against his chest and listen to him talk. Was he ever coming back home? She felt weary of waiting but what choice did she have? And why couldn't he find a way to contact her just once to let her know he was okay? Or when he'd be back? She really didn't understand, in a way, the secrecy of the covert to the point where Ben could not find a way to contact her once. She knew little of the policies because Smith had not seen fit to share them with her. Maybe he couldn't. And Ben was following suit. But she was supposed to be loyal and wait, like a good dog waiting on her master.

Molly broke her spell.

"Mom? Where's the Honey Nut Cheerios? Are we out of it?"

Grace was not used to being called "Mom" yet. But she loved it. "Nope. Look in the upper cabinet. I got it on sale, two for one. Be right there."

She jumped out of bed and washed her face and walked into the kitchen to see the refrigerator door wide open, an open box of cereal on the counter and Molly sitting at the bar eating a giant bowl of cheerios. "What's up with the door open? And where's the milk?"

"Used the last drop on my cereal. Sorry I forgot to shut the door. My bad."

Grace smiled at the remark. Kids were a trip with their words. "Okay, but try to remember to close the refrigerator, will you?"

"Sorry, Mom. I can't wait to see Marcy. We have such a great time. I'm so over school right now and am ready to be off for Christmas. Do you think Mr. Ben will be home by then?"

"Surely he will."

"He better be. I want some presents!"

"That's the spirit."

"I'm just sayin'."

"Yeah, and what happened to the giving end of Christmas?"

"I'll buy him something! That is, if you give me the money!"

Graced smirked and raised an eyebrow. "You just may have to earn that money. I'm just sayin'."

This time Molly laughed out loud. "Stop tryin' to sound cool, Mom. It doesn't work."

"Better get your teeth brushed. They'll be here soon. You need a change of clothes?"

"Nope. Just what I'm wearin'. Besides, I can fit into Marcy's stuff. So it's all cool."

A horn honked in the driveway. Molly squealed and ran to get her purse. She hugged Houston, who had one of her tennis shoes in his mouth, and kissed Grace goodbye. "I'll call, Mom. Have a good day. And don't worry. I'll be fine."

Grace waved goodbye and closed the front door. The house echoed and the silence swept over her.

She ran to dress and brush her teeth and made a spur of the moment decision to visit the cemetery. This would be the first time she had gone early in the morning. It would feel odd to talk to Smith about Ben. But that's what she was going to do. She loved both men but was without either one. It was enough to drive her crazy.

∽

Fifteen hours earlier, Director Pauley had been in contact with Ben in a discussion on the best way to approach the mission of extracting Sanderson from Zhob. In that discussion, Ben informed Pauley that he felt he might need more time in dealing with Sanderson before they pulled out.

The discussion was heated because Pauley wanted Sanderson found and extracted immediately, knowing the intensity level the factions were operating under. He was concerned that neither man would make it to the extraction site just outside of Zhob if too much time elapsed. Ben argued that he wasn't sure what shape Smith might be in, or how he'd be received at the location he was staying. It was a delicate situation that had to be handled carefully, or they would lose the opportunity. Sanderson would run. Both men were rigid, but Pauley knew in his gut that Ben was right. He might meet a lot of resistance on the part of the doctor whose home Sanderson was in, but it was against policy to stop a mission once it began and time was of the essence.

Ben started his journey to Zhob, trying not to draw attention to himself. He had contacted the members of his team and assigned another team member to be leader while he was in Zhob. He informed the men that he would not return to Bhakkar and instructed them to contact Director Pauley for further directions.

He went to the nearest car dealership on a bicycle and picked out a used Honda Accord. It was hot and humid and he was starving. It took a while but he made a deal with the salesman and drove away with the small black car and a title. It felt good to be driving and after an hour he finally paid attention to the hunger pangs in his stomach and stopped to get something to eat. He was nervous and had so many mixed emotions concerning Smith. He could not wait to see his friend, but he feared what he would find when he walked through the door. He wasn't even sure he could get through the door. And what if Smith didn't recognize him at all? There were so many questions that had no answers, and they continually plagued Ben as he drove to Zhob.

Ben's appearance was appropriate for his location, but Smith would probably not recognize him with all the hair on his face and the clothing. He had nothing on him to identify him because of the covert operation he was originally involved in. That would make it difficult for Ben to convince the doctor that he was an American and Smith's best friend.

He arrived in Zhob at dark and found a hotel to stay in. He was exhausted and needed a good night's sleep before he attempted to track down the house of Dr. Sheikhani. He parked his car at the back of the hotel and took a room on the bottom floor, spending a little time going over the directions to the clinic and Dr. Sheikhani's home. Too weary to stay awake any longer, Ben undressed, washed his face, brushed his teeth and climbed into bed. He fell asleep as soon as his head hit the pillow, but in the night he awoke and was riddled with thoughts about how this would play out. He forced himself to go back to sleep because tomorrow would bring its own set of problems. And there was no way he was going to figure out the answers to those problems until he walked through that door.

CHAPTER 52

Morning came too quickly. Ben felt stiff as he rolled over and tried to get out of bed. The mattress was old and had a huge dip in the middle. He got up slowly and stretched, suddenly feeling like he could eat a bear. The stress of yesterday had caused his adrenalin to go haywire and he felt washed out and weary knowing he had a full day ahead of him. He showered and dressed and headed to the first restaurant he could find to get some breakfast. He walked into Khava Café and Grill and took a seat, ordering a full breakfast. He ate slowly, mentally preparing for what he was about to do.

He'd left behind his feelings for Grace and centered himself on how he would approach Smith. All his training as a Special Ops agent was kicking in, and intellectually and physically he was prepared to do the job. Emotionally, he was straining to hold it together, but once he started the mission, nothing would stop him from getting the job done. This was a unique mission because he was about to meet face to face with the man who used to be his team leader, his mentor. But he knew without even seeing Smith that something catastrophic had to have happened for him not to have returned to America. That alone was enough to cause Ben to hesitate. It would be tough to see his friend in any condition other than what he was used to seeing him in.

When he was finished eating, Ben got back in his car and laid the map out so he could study the roads. He drove east for a few miles and turned north on a road that seemed to go on forever. He took two rights and nearly drove into the parking lot of the clinic. He turned left in front of the clinic and went down three streets and turned down an alley. He parked his car and went on foot the other block to what was supposed to be Dr. Sheikhani's street.

Ben's muscles were tense and his nerves were raw. He found the house and studied the outside perimeter. All the blinds were closed, which made it look like no one was home. He surmised that they could be at the clinic, as it was already 9:00 in the morning. Not wanting to remain in the driveway, he decided to bite the bullet and walked to the front door. There was no turning back now.

༄

Ben reached up and knocked on the door. Every single nerve in his body was firing off as he waited for someone to open it. He waited for what seemed like five minutes but was more like two, and someone finally cracked the door open. The man spoke in Urdu, asking him to speak his name.

Ben answered in Urdu. "My name is Ben Parker. I am a friend of the American staying in your home. May I come in?"

Irfan's heart was racing. The thing he had feared the most was happening now. Someone had found out about Bita being in his home. And he couldn't trust that this was an American. From what he could see, the man was Muslim. He could easily be a terrorist. "How do I know you are American? Who are you?"

Ben's voice was shaky when he spoke back to the man at the door. "My name is Agent Benjamin Parker, and I work for the United States government and my partner has been missing for over a year. I believe him to be the man who is living in your home. His name is Smith Sanderson and I am here to take him home. We were best friends. I assure you I am not here to cause trouble. Only to speak to my friend."

For some reason, Irfan knew in his gut that this man was speaking the truth. He could sense the tension in Ben's voice as he opened the door to let him in. "My name is Dr. Irfan Sheikhani. I'll get Bita for you. But I warn you, he will not be the same to you. He has no memory of his past. He has been in my home since citizens found him over a year ago. He was left as dead by your people. I nursed him back to health and he has been here in my home ever since. It has been dangerous for me and my family because of the terrorists groups who are targeting Americans, but I have grown to love Bita as my own son. He is a good man. He will not know you. I give you fair warning, because I do not know how his reaction will be to your coming."

Ben was shaken by Irfan's honesty and by the news that Smith had amnesia. It only confirmed what Pauley had feared. "I appreciate your kindness and trust. I will wait here while you get Smith. I want you to know he was the best agent we had. You may have noticed his mind and ability to remember details—"

Irfan interrupted with a deadpan face. "I'm aware of the covert operations going on in Pakistan. I've been here a long time and understand the position of American in the war on terrorism. That is why the citizens brought him to me. Otherwise, he would already be dead."

Ben stood still and waited. His knees felt weak and his stomach was in a knot. He wanted to see Smith badly but also knew Smith would not know him. It was going to be a difficult conversation. Five seconds later Smith walked through the living room door and stood looking at Ben. Their eyes locked and Ben stood rock still, hoping Smith would say something. Show some sign of recognition. There was nothing but politeness in his manner. No familiarity.

"Irfan has told me you are Agent Parker. That I used to work with you for the government. Please have a seat." Smith was shaking inside. He didn't recognize the man who was supposed to have worked side by side with him. It was a frightening experience.

"That's correct. My name is Ben Parker. And I'm here to take you back to America. I understand you are having problems with your memory. Is that correct?"

"Yes, it is. I can't recall any of my past. It has been difficult for me to move forward in my life as I have no memory of my past at all. I don't even know my name."

"Your name is Smith Sanderson. You lived in Paynesville, Georgia and are married to a woman named Grace Sanderson. She, of course, believes you to be dead. I was sent to inform her of that right after our last covert operation where you were shot down by a terrorist group. Do you remember any of that, Smith?"

Smith sat still with a blank face. *I'm married? To Grace Sanderson.... Paynesville, Georgia. Those names mean nothing to me. Why can't I remember this?* "I feel ignorant, and you'll have to forgive me. But I don't remember being married to anyone. The name Grace Sanderson means nothing to me. Did we have any children?"

"No. But you did a lot of work with Grace for an orphanage and helped many children. You were a highly trained Special Ops agent, Smith. You led teams all over the world and actually trained me. You and I were best friends."

Smith stared past Ben into space. His mind was racing. His heart was about to come out of his chest. All the words that Ben Parker was saying sounded so foreign. Like he was talking about someone else. He felt so strange inside, like he had lost his mind. Gone crazy. Here he'd been hiding out in Irfan's home not knowing anything about his past. And this stranger comes in and tells him that he is a Special Ops agent for the United States government. Nothing made sense. Nothing.

"I don't know what to say, Ben. You don't even look familiar to me. You say I should know you but I see you as a stranger. It's almost too much for me to take in. To hear that I have a wife and worked in an orphanage—it's shocking!. I've been wanting to know about my past for this whole year. I've wanted my memory to return for so long; but what you're tellin' me is not sinking in. It's just layin' on top of my mind heavily. How can I know what you're sayin' is true? And how do I get my memory back? I've made a home here with Irfan. I work in his clinic. I feel like I've lost my mind. Excuse me a minute."

As Smith left the room, Ben was overwhelmed with Smith's reaction. He had known it would be like this if amnesia had really set in. He was not trained in how to bring Smith out of this mental hell. He just knew he had to bring him back to the States, where Smith would receive the best medical care. The problem that could arise would be if Smith refused to come back with him. Ben realized he needed more time to work this out.

When Smith walked back into the room, he'd thrown cold water over his face. He apologized to Ben and sat down, wanting to hear more about his past life. "I'm sorry Ben, please forgive me. I've waited so long to hear what you are sayin' but it's too much for me to take in. I feel weird that I can't remember I have a wife. Grace. Tell me about her."

Ben felt the stab in his chest but ignored it. "Grace is a lovely woman, Smith. She has light brown hair and blue eyes. She smiles all the time and lights up a room. She still works with the kids at Wilton Children's Home, and has since taken a child named Molly to live with her. She had a tough time adjusting to your death and for months went to the cemetery to talk to you. But since your body wasn't there it became increasingly difficult for her to feel peace there. You assigned me the job of watching over her and I've done that for you, Smith.

"Because of the risks involved in our job, you asked me to agree to send a package to Grace if you were killed in action. I sent that to her and also had to walk up to your door and tell her you were not ever coming back home. It was the most difficult assignment I've ever had."

"So she still thinks I'm dead. What has she been doin'? Has she found someone else? What does she do for a living?"

"There's more to tell you about Grace. She's a principal for one of the largest schools in Paynesville. It houses grades 1-12 and she's very active with the children. I've never seen anything like it before, how she handles issues that arise on her job. You would be very proud of her, Smith."

Smith was not used to hearing his name and it still caught him off guard. "So has she found someone else to spend time with? Has she fallen in love with anyone or tried to move forward in her life? I would imagine this has been very difficult for her to handle. Who did she have to turn to? Her parents? Her friends?"

"Her parents died a long time ago. She is an only child. She does have girlfriends who've been there for her from the start. But I have stepped in and taken a big part of her life, Smith. I felt the responsibility since you and I were so close. And you made me promise that I'd watch over her. So that's what I've done." Ben paused but decided not to go on any further about his relationship with Grace.

"So you're here to take me back to the States to a hospital. Is that it? Will I get my memory back? And what if I don't? What kind of life will I have if I cannot remember any part of my past? How can I go to this woman you call Grace and live with her without even knowing her at all? Do you have those answers for me, Ben?"

Ben felt the tension building and tried to calm Smith down. "You have every reason to be upset, Smith. I know this isn't easy for you. A double-edged sword. You wanted to hear about your past and who you are but now that you're hearing it, it's too much. It's overwhelming to you. That's to be expected. I'm sure the doctors have ways of triggering your memory, but all of that is an unknown right now. I can't make you come back. But I feel it's something you need to strongly consider. This will haunt you the rest of your life if you don't try to find your way back home. What do you say, Smith? Will you go back with me tonight, or are you gonna stay here and wonder who you really are for the rest of your life?"

Smith felt panic rising in his chest. This man didn't seem familiar at all, yet he did trust him. But he'd come to know a different world in Pakistan and it was difficult to just walk out and not feel anything. Irfan had saved his life, yet if he remained in Pakistan living with Irfan, it could possibly result in many deaths. He was a man caught between two worlds. And he didn't know which way to go, because neither world seemed right.

"Do I have to make a decision right now? Today?"

"I'm afraid so, Smith. The tension here is building and there's no tellin' what's gonna come down the pike in the next few weeks. I was in Bhakkar recently with a team of Special Ops doing a covert operation. We were mingling among the different factions trying to hear about any plans that were being made for any terrorist activity in America. There is going to be retaliation but we just don't know where or how. I—"

"You're tellin' me you were in Bhakkar all this time? Hold on a minute. I saw you! I remember seeing you outside a window of a restaurant. You were standing in a crowd of people and suddenly you looked directly at me and our eyes locked. Do you remember that?"

Ben stood still with his heart pounding. He did remember looking at someone through a window. "Yes! I do. So that was you in the restaurant? Come to think of it, I think I remember another time in that same restaurant when I saw you and Dr. Sheikhani at a table. Am I crazy or did that happen?"

"We stopped there a couple of times on our way to a friend's home in Bhakkar. You may have seen us during one of those trips."

"Smith, please trust me. You have to go. I can't say enough about this, although I will have to tell you it won't be easy. Grace does not know you're alive. She's already transitioned into a new life and it will come as a great shock to her. And you need to retrieve some of your memory so that you can function or there will always be this void in your life. A big part of your past is a mystery to you that has to be solved. I was hoping that my talking to you would trigger something. But I guess it's not enough to bring it all back."

"I feel nothing when I look into your eyes. You say we were best friends and that we worked side by side. What did we do, Ben? What did I do?"

"You were part of an elite team of men who worked undercover for the CIA in the United States government. You and I led a team together in Afghanistan and that is where you were shot down. You were one of the best, Smith. I've never known anyone like you before or since. But you have to give yourself time because if you went back to Grace now, it would be too difficult for both of you. The relationship would not be there. I think you need to let me take you back and we'll get you the best medical care in the world. You'll have the best doctors in the world to work with you and this amnesia that has a hold on your life. What do you say, Smith? Will you come back with me?"

Irfan had walked into the room and was listening to Ben. He was saddened by the fact that he might never see Smith again. He'd grown to love him like his own son. But at the same time he knew the danger would only increase and it would become impossible for Smith to remain with him in Pakistan.

"I feel you should go, son. It pains me to say this because I've grown to love you. But we must do what is best for your life, Bita. Go with this man and see what happens. You can always return here someday if things don't work out. I'll always welcome you into my home. You have wanted to learn about your past—who you were before, and what your name was. Now you know. Now is your chance."

Suddenly Smith felt extremely nervous and weak. He sat down and put his head in his hands. There was a part of him that just wanted to stay with Irfan. He felt safe there, in an odd sort of way. He had grown to love Mishael and now he wouldn't even be able to tell her goodbye. He knew it was best if he bowed out of her life, but the feelings were so strong. And he knew she loved him, too. The life he had in Pakistan was pretty narrow and limited. The life Ben described was one of power and fullness. How could he not try to find his way back?

Smith stood up and put his hand out to Ben. "I'll take your word that what you say is true. I'll go back to America, even though I have my doubts that this will work, and try to find the answers that have plagued me for so long. I owe you an apology, Ben. You've risked your life for me several times and I owe you. I appreciate your coming here and risking your life again to take me back to the States. You can understand, I'm sure, about my hesitation. I feel excited but afraid. I don't know what's gonna happen and it's the unknown that is keeping my feet from moving."

Ben smiled and looked at Smith right in the eyes. "Smith, I have loved you for a very long time. I'd do anything for you. You saved my life many times during covert and now it's my turn to do that for you. Let's get out of here before some terrorist group gets wind that we're here. It's not gonna be easy gettin' out of here, you know. We're not outta the woods yet. In fact, the danger has just begun. So get your things and let's get goin'. Dr. Sheikhani, thank you for taking such good care of my friend. I'll be grateful to you for the rest of my life for risking your life for a stranger. I can see why Smith doesn't want to leave you."

Irfan walked over and shook Ben's hand. "I feel that it is the best thing for Bita to go with you. If he remains here, he will never get his memory back. And God forbid, if it did return and you were gone, he'd never be able to live with himself for not trying to find his way back to his wife and a good life. I cannot be selfish and ask him to remain."

About that time Mahsa walked out of the kitchen and saw Ben shaking hands with Irfan. "Who is this, Irfan? What is he doing here?"

"Mahsa, this is Agent Ben Parker with the United States government. He is here to take Bita back to America. We must let him go now. It is no longer safe for him to remain with us."

Mahsa started crying and left the room. She went to find Smith and gave him a hug. "I will miss you, Bita. You have been so good for Irfan. And I will tell Mishael you said goodbye. She will be upset but it is best. I know you realize that, too."

Smith shook his head in agreement but grabbed Mahsa and hugged her tightly. "Please tell her I love her and that I wish the best for her life. You have been so kind to me, Mahsa. Your life was in great danger because of my being here. There are no words to thank you for all you and Irfan have done for me. I will never be able to repay you."

"Hush, Bita. Go now and find your way to your life again. Keep in touch and let us know how you are."

"I will do that, Mahsa. I promise."

Smith packed his small bag and grabbed his journal. He looked around the room he had called his own and couldn't believe he was actually leaving for good. He walked back into the living room and stood next to Irfan. He put his hands on Irfan's shoulders and looked him straight in the eyes. "Irfan, you've been like a father to me for over a year now. I've grown to love you and it pains me greatly to leave you and Mahsa. Thank you for saving my life and for teaching me so many things. I will always love you and remember what you have done for me."

Smith hugged Irfan and both men hung on for a moment before letting go. Irfan stepped back and bowed to Smith. "You go, son. Let us know how you are. That is all I ask of you."

Ben grabbed Smith's arm and pulled him toward the door. "Let's get out of here, Smith, before we put them in grave danger. My car is down the street in an alley. If it is still there, we have a chance to get out of here without being seen."

Smith looked back at the house one more time and walked with Ben to the alley, feeling torn. He knew in his gut he was doing the right thing but it was painful to leave his Pakistani family. They both climbed into the rental car, and for the next hour Smith was silent, lost in his thoughts, trying to work through the information Ben had shared with him about his life.

A wife? How could he have a wife and not know her? How could he ever get all this back and function as a human being? They began to talk about Smith's life in Pakistan and his close relationship with Dr. Irfan. Smith shared with Ben how he had developed feelings with Mishael because they had worked so closely in the clinic. He told how he loved her heart and how he enjoyed working on patients with Dr. Irfan.

"I've learned so much from him, Ben. You wouldn't believe how good this man is. It's incredible. Nothing is too much for him and he works long hours to make sure he's seen all the people who are sick or hurt that came to the clinic. He is loved by so many people. I felt honored to be a part of that and so grateful that he took me into his home and life without question. It didn't seem to matter to him that I could not recall my past. In fact, that may have bonded us together even more. I was dependent on him for everything for a long time. When my strength returned he put me to work. Mishael was there to teach me the language and encouraged me to learn more about medicine so that I could be a greater help to Irfan."

Ben listened quietly, straining to keep himself from wanting the old Smith to come back. It was difficult to sit next to him and realize he was a stranger now. Smith had absolutely no feelings whatsoever towards Ben or Grace. It was like they had never known each other, even though they'd experienced life and death situations many times and held other men's lives in their hands. Smith was seemingly oblivious to all of this and just kept talking about his life with Irfan.

"I know it must be difficult for you to leave Irfan and Mahsa. And I had no idea you had developed feelings for Mishael. She sounds like a lovely woman. It's dangerous for her, isn't it, to be seen with an American man?"

"Yes, that is a big issue here. One reason we didn't further our relationship was because she would have been an outcast in her own family and also in Pakistan. It is not acceptable. We couldn't even hold hands in public. All of our contact was at the clinic or at Dr. Irfan's home. She did ride with us one of the trips to Bhakkar. It was a special time but I was tormented that day about my lack of memory. It has haunted me nearly every day since I moved into Dr. Irfan's home."

Ben sat there thinking about what Smith had said. He'd gotten involved with another woman and would probably have married her if it had been approved of by her family. It was hard to put all this together and think about how Grace fit into the picture. It was a pretty complicated mess.

"Just don't think too much about it all right now, Smith. We're headed now to a hotel where we will stay the night. I will contact Director Pauley and let him know that you are with me, and he will arrange a pickup time immediately. This will be a dangerous time, Smith. Terrorist groups are all over the place and if they somehow get wind of a helicopter landing anywhere in Pakistan, we could have serious problems. They could shoot us down right when we are trying to reach the extraction site."

CHAPTER 53

They reached the hotel and pulled into a parking place. Ben went inside and paid for a double room and walked back to the car. They unloaded Smith's small suitcase and went into the room. It was small but clean. Two double beds side by side with pictures of Pakistan buildings over both the beds. The carpet was dark red and the curtains were a heavy velvet fabric. There was a small television in the room, a microwave and a small refrigerator. Ben went downstairs and bought some drinks to put in the refrigerator and got a bucket of ice. He phoned Pauley to let him know that Smith was with him and informed him of the situation concerning Smith's memory. Pauley gave Ben a pickup time of 9:00 tomorrow evening. The extraction sight was the same place where Ben had been dropped off with the Special Ops team. Pauley reassured Ben that doctors would be available to Smith immediately and a debriefing would occur. Nothing was mentioned about the level of risk in getting to the chopper. That was just understood between the two men. They would be lucky to get out alive.

When he returned to the room, Smith was lying on one of the beds with his legs crossed, watching television. "I've not seen much television since I've been here. It all seems so strange, Ben. I'm supposed to know you and you're a total stranger to me. Yet I'm trusting you enough to go with you back to the States. Do you know how messed up my mind is? Can you imagine not havin' a past? All the names you mention mean nothing to me. I wonder why I'm headed back when I cannot fit back into my life. I won't even know my own wife."

Ben walked over to Smith and sat down on the bed. "Hey, man. Relax. There's no way we can figure all this out right now. I know you're goin' crazy tryin' to figure it out but there's no answer right now. I feel weird lookin' at you, because you look like the Smith I knew. That is, except for the dark beard and dark hair. I feel like you should know me. I mean, we were buddies. We did everything together. Now when you look at me, it is with blank eyes. We don't connect like we did for years. It's strange but surely it will all change when you get to the right doctors who can help you get your memory back. I know nothing about amnesia but you aren't the first to experience it. I'm sure these doctors nowadays can do miracles with the mind. So let's trust that things will improve. If not, we'll go to plan B."

∾

After a short nap and a shower, both men were hungry so they decided to drive to a nice restaurant to eat supper. They were near Bhakkar and decided to hit the same restaurant that Smith had been to before. They walked in and sat at a table near the windows. Smith immediately pointed out the spot where Ben had been standing when their eyes locked. They both laughed, thinking of the odds of that happening. Outside there were throngs of people and Ben felt the tension in the air. He wondered if some of his men were out in the crowd listening for anything that might tell them of a plan against America. He'd been so preoccupied that he'd forgotten about the covert operation underway.

"Smith, just to let you know, I was here originally on a covert operation with a team of men to find out if any terrorist acts were being planned against America since the death of Osama Bin Laden. I was called by Director Pauley and he pulled me off that covert and asked me to locate you. I was so shocked that you were alive. All this time I've had to adjust to you bein' gone, and to find out you were alive in Pakistan really messed up my mind."

"I was wonderin' about all that. If you and I were close, then you had to have gone through grieving and moved forward in your life. I want to ask you more about Grace, if you don't mind. Ben, has she found someone else since she thought I was dead? It's hard to believe she'd be still alone after this length of time, if she's as intelligent and attractive as you described her to be."

Perspiration beaded up on Ben's brow as he answered quietly. "I say this with the deepest respect to you, Smith. It would be so much easier if you could recall some of what took place when you and I were doing covert together. You knew at some point that death might be imminent; we both did. That's just part of the risk in being involved with the CIA. You made plans so that if something did happen to you on one of the missions, I would send Grace a package from you with things you had chosen for her to keep. And that's what I did. You also made me promise that I would take care of Grace after your death. I hated to make that promise because I had no idea what that would involve. But I did promise you and I kept to my word."

Smith sat back in his seat and listened carefully to what Ben was saying. All the words were foreign to him, but he knew they were true. He didn't think Ben had any reason to lie. "I had to be the one to drive up in her driveway with one other team member, and walk up to the door and tell her that you weren't coming back home. I did it like I was supposed to, very cold and to the point. But as I was walkin' back to the car I turned back and told Grace that you were my best friend. And that you'd asked me if I would watch out for her. I told her that I'd be around always to make sure she was okay, because I loved you and it was ripping my guts out that you were gone."

A tear came down Smith's face as he listened to Ben. It was not lost on Ben, but he kept right on talking. "So, slowly I began a friendship with Grace. She wanted nothin' to do with me at first, but as time went on, we began to talk and share about our lives and how much you meant to us. We formed a bond that became strong. I found work in Paynesville doing search and rescue and bought a home. Grace and I began dating, and Smith, to be honest, we fell in love with each other. We often joked that you must've known that would happen when you arranged for me to be the one to look after her. You must've known we would hit it off. Anyway, Grace loves you still. She always will. But of course, now I'll have to step back and allow you time to get your memory back and see if you and Grace can make it again. I know it'll be tough, but given time, you may just find your relationship with her is better than before."

Smith had a hard time taking it all in. Grace and Ben had fallen in love. It didn't mean much to him, but at the same time he could see how complicated things were going to get with him back in the picture.

"How do you feel about Grace right now, Ben? Are you still in love with her now?"

Ben was sweating profusely now, and feeling the strain of the conversation. "If I am honest with you, Smith, yes I am. I will always love her. But I understand that you're back in the picture and I want you to know that I love you, too. I don't own Grace. She's your wife. But you understand we both thought you were dead, and you asked me to be in her life."

Smith sat there slowly eating his dinner, thinking things through. Even though he had no memory of the past, his intelligence was intact. He kept his thoughts to himself, but he realized sitting there with Ben that it wasn't so simple to just pop back into his old life. Because he had been presumed dead, everything had changed. He really didn't know if it was the right thing for him to let Grace know he was alive. Yet how could he not? He sure couldn't let her know until his memory returned. But where did that leave Ben? Ben was hung out to dry because Smith had reappeared. What a damn mess it all was. And there was no easy answer.

∽

When they arrived back at the hotel, they went over many things about Smith's life, hoping something would trigger his memory. Ben pulled out his weapons to let Smith see them. Smith handled then like he'd grown up with guns, and that made Ben wonder if his memory just might return. Smith was very agile and moved like a lion. But it was his mind that had made him incredible in covert. He remembered every single thing that he saw. He was a deadly predator when he had to be. For now that was gone in Smith, but it just might come back. So Ben took the time and made the effort to talk about as much of the past as he could, and hoped for some results in the near future. Some memory to come to the forefront of Smith's mind. They finally gave it up at 11:00 and climbed into bed. Both men were mentally exhausted and wanted to be prepared for the next day. Enough had been said for one night.

The next day was spent going over the weapons and how to use them. Ben got in the car and drove Smith to a standing of trees on the edge of Bhakkar. There was no one around for miles and miles. They got their guns out and loaded them with ammunition so Smith could practice shooting. Ben was going to need him when they were running to get to the helicopter. He had to assume that one or more of the factions would find out about the extraction. It was too high a risk to ignore.

Smith picked up the use of the weapons right way; it was obvious to Ben that he was a natural. They shot all the ammunition they'd brought with them and headed back to the hotel to wait out the evening until it got close to time to leave. They ate a quick dinner and went back to the room to load everything and pack the car.

As time approached, Ben and Smith got into the car and headed in the direction of the designated site, their hearts racing with adrenalin. Although Smith had observed the ruthlessness of the terrorists in their treatment of Mahsa, he had no idea what it would be like, what they would do, in an open field if they were there when he and Ben were running to catch a helicopter. They had to park far enough away from the landing site so as to not draw attention to what was about to take place. That meant they had a ways to run in an open field to get to the chopper.

It had turned dark and there were clouds covering the moon, which was to their favor as they crouched down in the woods waiting for the chopper. At 9:00 sharp they heard the sound in the distance and suddenly a black Pave Hawk landed at the extraction site. Ben nodded to Smith and they pulled out their weapons and took off across the open field to the chopper.

Suddenly, out of nowhere, shots were fired; they were coming from all directions. Ben tried to cover Smith as he was running in front, firing his weapon as he ran. They zigzagged across the field trying to dodge the bullets, but they were coming so fast it was impossible to escape unharmed.

Smith tried hard to keep up but was overwhelmed by the shots whizzing by him. Ben kept yelling at Smith to keep running, but things were happening so quickly that it was impossible to think. Ben reached the chopper first and climbed in, turning to see where Smith was. In the dark of night he saw Smith go down and the chopper pilot was yelling that it was time to pull out.

Ben screamed "NO!" and ran towards Smith, with shots whizzing over his head. He bent down and lifted Smith up and slung him over his shoulder and ran the remaining yards to the chopper. It was an impossible feat, but Ben was running on pure adrenalin. He didn't even feel the weight of his friend hanging on his shoulder. He slammed Smith down in the chopper, jumped in, and the chopper lifted off the ground, with bullets popping everywhere. Ben was out of breath and bending over Smith, screaming into his ear.

"Smith, Smith! Don't give up. We'll get you to a hospital fast. Hold on, Smith! Hold on."

Ben held him in his arms and talked to him while they were headed to the American base in Afghanistan. Tears were streaming down his face as he watched his best friend struggle to breathe. The bullet had gone into his chest somewhere; Ben shoved a jacket under his shirt to stop the bleeding.

"Talk to me, Smith. Talk to me!"

Smith whispered into Ben's ear, barely audible in the drone of the helicopter. "I'll never make it home, Ben. It wasn't meant to be. Don't fight it, Ben. It's okay . . ."

"No, Smith. I'm not losing you twice, damn it. Stay with me, man. Don't die on me now. Not after all this."

Smith could barely speak but his last words ripped through the air. "Don't tell Grace you found me, Ben. Let her think I was dead. Don't tell her anything."

Ben was shaking, tears streaming down his face. He didn't want to give up on Smith this time. He had to make it home. "Wait, Smith. Don't do this. Don't worry about anything. Just try to breathe."

"I . . . I'm going, Ben. Look at me now."

Ben wiped his face and looked down at his friend, who was lying in his arms. His face was bloody and there was blood seeping out from under the jacket. Their eyes locked for the last time and Smith whispered slowly so Ben wouldn't miss it. "I . . . love you . . . Ben. . . .I know now who you are. Take care . . . of my Grace. . . .I remember, Ben. I remember . . ."

He was gone.

CHAPTER 54

The Pave Hawk sat down on a piece of land near the U.S. base in Afghanistan. Ben was still holding Smith when medics came and lifted his body out of the helicopter. There was blood everywhere and Ben was so mentally exhausted he couldn't move. A couple of doctors walked up to the chopper and helped Ben get out so they could examine him and be sure he was not injured. Ben slowly climbed out of the chopper and when his feet hit the ground, his knees buckled and he ended up on the ground. Medics came and put him on a stretcher and walked him into the first aid station where he was examined thoroughly before being sent to the officer's mess hall to eat something before going to the barracks.

One of the officers walked up to Ben and sat down while he was eating a small meal. He was an older man with a kind face full of wrinkles. "Heard you had a tough time in Pakistan, son. Just wanted to say I admire what you guys are doing. Covert is not one of the easiest jobs in the world."

Ben looked to his left, forced a smile and shook his hand. "Ben Parker. And no. It's not what I'd want my son to do, if I had one."

"Well, any soldier would say that in a time of war. And the war on terrorism is the toughest because we don't know who our enemy is. Just wanted to say I'm sorry for what happened to your buddy. I know how that feels, believe me."

"This was different. This man was a pro. His mind was off the chart. Then he got amnesia and couldn't remember who he was. He couldn't remember me, or that he had a wife in the States. He and I were best friends. It sucks. It just isn't fair . . ."

"I know, son. War is not fair. Sorry you had to experience this. It's not much payment for all the good you've done in your life. Take care of yourself, son. Maybe take a break from it all."

"I plan to do just that."

The officer walked away and Ben realized he didn't get the guy's name. But he was too tired to care. He just wanted to sleep and forget the whole damn day. But tomorrow was coming soon enough and he'd be heading home to face Grace. He walked to his barracks and without taking off his clothes he fell into bed. His mind was racing with thoughts of Smith, of the run to the chopper, and the last words Smith had spoken. "*I love you Ben. I know who you are now.*" How could he get so close to bringing Smith home and then lose him in the end? It seemed like a bad dream. An impossible dream. To lose his friend twice was more than his exhausted mind could comprehend. And in the end, at his last breath, he remembered he had a wife, and he remembered his best friend. The toughest part of this whole thing was that when he saw Grace he couldn't tell her he'd held Smith in his arms. He couldn't tell her that he tried to bring him back home. It would kill her to know that Smith had been alive all this time and then got killed trying to come back to her and his life.

As he lay there in a bed in the barracks of an American base in Afghanistan, Ben wrestled with how he'd live with that fact for the rest of his life. Because he loved Grace and wanted to be her husband and take care of her for the rest of her life. Was it the right thing to do to withhold this information? Was it best to leave things as they were, with her believing Smith had died from the last covert? What good would come from her finding out about his amnesia and suffering? She'd relive the whole thing all over again.

He closed his eyes and slept soundly but when he awoke it hit him right in the gut again. He had come so close. So damn close.

❦

The trip back to the States was uneventful. Ben was lost in his own thoughts and not fully recovered from the events of the past three months. He was anxious to talk to Pauley and unload all the information he'd found out on the first covert. And he also wanted to share about what he learned of Smith's life in Pakistan. Pauley was a great fan of Smith's and knew he was basically not replaceable. There wasn't another Smith around the corner. To even begin to think about seeing Grace and dealing with that whole situation made Ben break out in a sweat. She was a remarkable woman and had pulled through losing Smith with minimal issues. What Ben didn't know was how he could move back into her life smoothly and not ever mention what had taken place in Pakistan. He wanted to discuss this in depth with Pauley, because they would bury Smith in Arlington Cemetery if nothing was said to Grace. There would be no news broadcast of a soldier coming home to rest. It would be done in a quiet manner and Grace would never find out. But if Pauley saw it differently, and could convince him to open up and share with Grace the whole truth, then his body would be sent to Woodlawn Funeral Home and buried under the grave marker Grace had chosen. After thinking about it for hours, he decided to let it rest until he spoke with Pauley. However the real decision making would be up to him. No one would be able to decide for him that he needed to keep this from Grace. And the important thing Ben had to remember, no matter how tormented he was with this decision, was that Smith would not know either way.

So the promises made to a dying man are sometimes unable to be kept. Especially if the truth will haunt the promise keeper for the rest of his life. Only God knew how Grace would handle such information. But Ben had a funny feeling he was about to find out.

⌒〜⌒

Sitting in Director Pauley's office, Ben felt worn out. The long trip home had done nothing but drain him of whatever energy he had left.

Pauley came through the door looking frustrated but glad to see Ben. Ben stood up and Pauley shook his hand. "Sit down, Parker. Glad you made it home safe. I can see by your face that you're not happy with how things turned out. We're sick about it. Let's go over what happened. Have a seat."

Ben sat down and put his feet up on the corner of the desk. Pauley said nothing. "It was hell from the day I went to see him until we got on the chopper. I gave it my all, Pauley. More than my all. I have nothing left, I tell you. You've finally taken every square inch of me. I'm done."

Ben stood up and walked around the room. He was so tied up in knots he could hardly talk. There Pauley was sitting in his stuffed shirt chair waiting to hear all the details. It made him sick to his stomach. The whole thing was sick. "I went over there on a mission to find out what the terrorists were plotting and we were making some headway. Then you phoned and told me that Smith was spotted by some of your agents. He was followed for months before you let me know. I agree to go see him, to try to convince him to come with me and I discover he has amnesia. He remembers nothing of his past. He doesn't even recognize me."

Pauley looked on with a grave face. He said nothing.

"So just as you requested, I talked him into coming with me. Even though he had no idea what he used to do for a living, I handed him a gun and we worked on shooting for an afternoon so he could get prepared for the extraction. We worked hard and he showed skill he didn't know he had. I could see the old Smith peeking through. But he also had been weakened. I was worried about the risks involved and discussed that with you on the phone. You had nothing to say about it. You just ordered me to bring him back. So when it was time, we squatted in the fields and when the chopper landed we took off. It was going to be a perfect extraction only somehow the factions near Bhakkar found out about it. I've never heard so many shots in my entire life, Pauley. They were coming from every direction. We didn't have a chance in hell to make it across that open field. We were sitting ducks."

He paused and took a sip of water that was sitting on the corner off the desk. Pauley kept his eyes on papers that were in front of him. He looked worried.

"So we took off running like rabbits and I made it to the chopper. I was covering Smith as best I could but he went down. I could see he'd taken a hit and just when the pilot yelled that it was time to get out, I jumped back off the chopper and ran to Smith. Bullets were whizzing by my head. I could've gotten killed! I bent down and lifted him up and put him over my shoulder. I don't even know how I did it, Pauley. He weighs more than I do. I ran as fast as I could, carrying him across the field, and when I got to the chopper I threw him down on the floor and jumped in. The chopper lifted immediately and we disappeared into the clouds. I leaned over and checked Smith out; I could see he was wounded and his face had blood all over it. I grabbed my jacket to help stop the bleeding in his chest. I yelled at him. I screamed for him to hold on. But he couldn't. His last dying breath was to tell me that he knew who I was. His memory had returned. He said not to tell Grace. He said he loved me."

Ben took a breath and wiped his face with both hands. His nerves were shot. Reliving it was killing him. He turned to look directly at Pauley. "I'm supposed to step back into my life with Grace and not tell her I saw Smith. How do you suppose I'm gonna do that, man? That was her husband that she presumed was dead. She'll freak out to know he's been alive this whole time. It sucks. Do you know that? It sucks!"

Pauley could see that Ben was at the end of his rope. He'd been drained physically and emotionally and there was nothing left. "Sit down, Ben. Take it easy. I knew this was gonna be tough on you. But I had no idea you'd be under that kind of fire heading to the chopper. I regret this happened. I really wanted Smith back home. He was a man that we hated to lose. He's one of a kind."

Ben glared at him. "All you think about is the damn organization. You don't care about our lives. It's what we could do for you. I'm done, Pauley. You've seen the last of me. This never should have happened with what's goin' on over there. You knew this covert was high alert. The risk was way too high; we should have aborted it. I knew better. After finally locating Smith and finding out how much he'd suffered, I dragged him to a chopper in the middle of enemy fire and he got killed. Why? I ask you why? Just to get him home so you could put him back to work? Are you nuts, Pauley? Have you stayed in this too long to be able to think rationally?"

Pauley stood up and cleared his throat. "Now, Ben. I know you were close to Smith. But that's no reason to take it out on me. We did what we were told to do. Our orders come down from the Pentagon. I didn't say it would be easy. We both knew the risks were high. I knew the longer you were there, the higher the risk of death. You did the best you could do and no one could expect more."

Ben smiled but it was a sick smile. He wanted to scoop up all the papers on Pauley's desk and shove them on the floor. But instead, he stood up and straightened his shirt and pushed his chair back. "I came in this morning wanting to have a discussion with you about what took place. But I can see it's useless. We are on two different planes about this operation. Smith was my best friend and I'm in love with his wife. I'll sort it out. But don't do anything with his body until you hear from me. At least have the decency to give me the opportunity to talk with Grace if I can. Give me a few days. That's all I ask. A few days. And after this is over, Pauley, you'll never see me again. Do you understand that? I don't care how many missions you have ahead of you, I won't be involved. I'm through with you and the CIA."

Ben got up and walked out of the office. He stepped into the fresh morning air and breathed in a gallon of it. He decided to head home and unpack and then call Grace. She was gonna want to see him and he had to pick up Houston. And then there was Molly. He hoped he was ready for what was ahead. He couldn't plan this next conversation with Grace, it just had to evolve. He only hoped she wouldn't fall apart again. Somehow he had to find a way to say it where she could deal with it. He didn't want to lose her. Not now.

CHAPTER 55

It was a lovely winter day with the leaves in piles all over the lawn. The wind had kicked up and there was a briskness in the air. Grace looked out her office window, wondering how Molly was doing on her math test. Brittany came bouncing in her office and announced she was headed to class. "Anything you need me to do before I go, Miss Grace?"

"Nope. I'm good, Brit. Thanks for askin'. Hope you do well on your test this morning. Molly is in her math class right now taking a test. Let me know how you do."

"Will do. See you after lunch."

Grace got up and grabbed her purse and headed out the door. She was going to eat lunch at home today, just for a change of pace. And it gave her an excuse to check on Houston. She rolled her windows down and let the fresh air into the car, blowing her hair in the back. She felt at peace for once and was excited about Christmas coming this year. She would put up a large tree for Molly and have a ball buying presents for her. It was going to be more fun with a child around. They'd go to midnight service at the Presbyterian Church down the street. Molly had taken up with some girls at the church and was begging Grace to join the church. As she pulled up in the driveway she noticed her car pulled up near the garage. She'd left it at Ben's house with the keys underneath the driver's seat. What in the world was it doing in her driveway?

She parked the car and got out and walked into the house. Ben was sitting on her sofa with Houston, with a nervous smile on his face. "Ben!

Oh, my gosh! You're back! How in the world did you get in the house? And when did you get home?" She ran over to him and hugged him tightly, planting a kiss on his cheek.

"I got in late last night and had to talk to Pauley this morning or I would have called." He grabbed her and hugged her for a long time. It felt so good to have her in his arms. He'd missed her so much. He wished he didn't have to have such a serious talk with her right off the bat.

"I guess I forgot you had a set of keys to my house. How stupid of me! So are you home for good? How did things go, if I may ask? You look so thin and you have dark circles under your eyes! Ben, are you okay?"

Ben looked down and ran his fingers through his hair. His beard was full and his hair had grown out. He imagined that he looked pretty scruffy to her. "No, I'm okay. A little washed out perhaps. This covert lasted longer than planned and I'm pretty worn out, to be honest." He sat down on the sofa and pointed for her to take a seat.

"I'm so glad to see you. Molly is gonna have a fit when she finds out you're finally home. Look at Houston! He's right on your lap, practically. He missed you, Ben. But he was good company to Molly and me."

Grace noticed that Ben seemed preoccupied and more solemn than usual. "Anything wrong, Ben? You're sure you're okay?"

Ben took a deep breath. There was no easy way to begin this conversation, but it had to happen.

"Come here, Grace. Sit beside me. We have to talk. What I'm about to tell you is gonna upset you and surprise you at the same time. I have prayed about it and I feel it's the right thing to do to tell you about my last covert. It's really against policy, but screw it. You matter more to me than policy. I want you to understand first and foremost that I love you. And I would never do anything to hurt you. I've been totally honest with you all along and I don't want anything to change that."

Grace swallowed hard and looked at Ben. "What in the world are you talkin' about, Ben? Did you find someone else? What's happened that has caused you to become so somber? I've never seen you this way before." Her heart was racing because she was scared of what he might say.

"Listen, Grace. What I'm about to say is the truth, so help me God. I was sent over on a covert operation with my team to scout out factions in Pakistan, to secure our safety here in America. All of my team went undercover and we mixed right in with the crowds. It was difficult at times to tell who the enemy was. After about two months I received a phone call from Pauley that . . ."

Grace looked at Ben. "Go ahead, Ben. I'm listening."

"Grace, this is hard to say. I want you to promise to stay calm."

Grace was shaking but she knew this had to be pretty serious for Ben to be acting this way. "Okay, Ben. I promise I'll stay calm. Now talk to me. What's going on?"

"Pauley told me on the phone that some agents had spotted someone that looked like Smith in Pakistan, in a small town called Zhob. He wanted me to cease operations and head to Zhob immediately. I didn't know what to think. Smith was supposed to be dead, by all counts. I couldn't share anything with you before, but I saw Smith get shot down. We left him for dead. Apparently citizens found Smith and took him a long way to a doctor who was sympathetic to the American war on terrorism. His name was Irfan Sheikhani."

Grace was shaking now and very confused. Her heart was about to come out of her chest and she wanted to get up and scream. But she tried to stay calm for Ben, so that he could relay the story to her. Somehow she knew there was much more to be told.

"I was given a map of the area and drove for a while from Bhakkar to Zhob. I found the clinic where Dr. Sheikhani worked and then located the street where he lived. Smith was supposed to be inside the house so I parked my car and walked up to the door and knocked. It took a while for someone to answer, and when he did, he wouldn't open the door all the way. He asked who I was and it took me a while to convince him that I knew Smith. He finally allowed me to enter his home and I told him who I was and who Smith was. He informed me that Smith had amnesia and did not recall any of his past. He had no idea what his name was or anything. I was shocked to hear that Smith was alive and learn about his injuries. The amnesia was going to present a problem because my orders were to bring him home."

Ben stopped and held Grace's hand. "I'm tellin' you this quickly. But it took me a long time to reach a place where Smith would trust me enough to come back to America with me."

Grace almost yelled. "You're tellin' me that Smith is here? That he's back in the States? Oh my gosh, Ben. Where is he?" Her face had turned almost gray with fear.

"No, Grace. He's not here. Let me finish. I finally convinced Smith to come with me. He didn't recognize me at all and no matter what I said to him to jog his memory, nothing worked. But he left Dr. Sheikhani and went with me and we drove for a while and checked into a hotel.

I contacted Pauley and he gave me the time of the extraction and the location. I took out some guns and Smith and I did some target practice out in a stand of trees that bordered the desert near Bhakkar. Smith did well with handling the guns and ammunition. It almost seemed like the old Smith was back. But he still was very confused. I tried to impress upon him the seriousness of the mission. The factions in Bhakkar were everywhere and the tension was high because of the death of Bin Laden. We were at extreme risk at the extraction site.

"At 9:00 that night we headed to the location and squatted down in the trees. When the chopper landed, we ran, me in the front covering for Smith. Suddenly shots came out of nowhere and my biggest fears came true. The factions had gotten wind of our plans to leave and were trying to shoot us down. We were in a wide open field running as fast as we could run. I yelled to Smith to zigzag but everything was going so fast that he couldn't act quickly enough. I made it to the chopper and turned and saw Smith go down. He had been shot. The chopper wanted to leave but I yelled to the pilot and jumped out and ran to Smith."

Ben's voice was loud and he was sweating. Tears were streaming down his face as he looked at Grace. "I tried to save him, Grace! I lifted him up and ran with him over my shoulder all the way to the chopper. I dumped him on the floor and jumped in and we lifted off. It was a miracle we made it back to the chopper. But Smith was hurt bad, Grace. He was hurt real bad. I used my jacket to stop the bleeding. I leaned over him to talk to him and held him in my arms. He whispered to me that he wasn't gonna make it. I begged him to try. But he couldn't. He was nearly gone already. Once more he whispered to me and this is what he said. "'I know who you are now, Ben. I love you. Take care of my Grace. I remember, Ben, I remember.'"

Grace screamed and put her face in her hands. She was in shock to find out that Smith had been alive all that time and no one knew. She felt anger rise up and then deep sorrow. He had lived for over a year with no memory of her. None. So he hadn't been aware of what he was missing. And he didn't know of her pain. That was a blessing for Smith, and she suddenly felt grateful for the amnesia. She looked at Ben with tears streaming down her face. "Did he say anything else? Was that all?"

"That was all, Grace. He was gone."

Ben reached over and held her in his arms. She cried harder than he'd ever heard anyone cry and he had to bite his lip until it bled to keep from losing it. Houston must have known something was wrong because he was licking Grace's hands and whimpering. Ben pulled Grace close to him and they lay back on the sofa, Grace in his arms. He tried to soothe her and whispered into her ear gently. "Grace, I love you. It will be okay from now on. It may take us time to work through all of this, but it's gonna be okay. Smith can be buried at the cemetery and you can finally have closure. Both of us will. It's gonna be okay."

Grace calmed down after a few minutes and sat up. Here was this gentle giant trying so hard to tell her the worst thing any woman could possibly hear in a way that wouldn't just rip her guts out. It was an impossible feat, but he had such a good heart that it softened the blow. She was upset beyond belief but she also knew that nothing would bring Smith back now. Because she'd moved away from her grieving, it didn't devastate her like it would have a year ago. Smith was not coming home, and to know that he had suffered with amnesia for over a year saddened her. It seemed unfair that he didn't make it home and she would never understand why it had to turn out like it did. But as she looked at Ben, the man who tried to save Smith's life twice, she felt nothing but love for him.

"I'm shocked, Ben. I don't know quite what to say. It feels strange to think he was alive all this time in Pakistan but he didn't remember me. Had you not located him and attempted to bring him home, he might have remained there for an undetermined amount of time with his memory still not intact. I've read somewhere that sometimes another trauma brings the memory back. It seems like that's what happened to Smith."

Ben wiped the tears from her eyes and kept her close to him. "I knew this would be traumatic for you; it was for me when it happened. It's gonna take a while for me to get over it. But we have each other, Grace. Don't feel alone in this. We'll help each other get through the next few weeks by remembering the good that Smith did in his life. Now I want you to understand something, Grace. This was my last run. I've resigned for the last time. I made it perfectly clear to Pauley that he'd never see me again. So I'm never going away again. I'm happy doin' search and rescue and love bein' here with you and Molly. I hope after this news you still want me in your life."

Grace looked into Ben's eyes. "Of course I want you in our lives. This was hard for you to tell me and I guess I'm still in shock. That was the last thing I thought you'd tell me, Ben. But in a way, now I know where he is. That's some relief, after all this time. But it seems so sad that he never made it home alive."

"I know it, Grace. Believe me. I wanted to bring him home to you; I tried so hard."

She put her arms around him and kissed his face. "Let's have dinner together tonight with Molly and please bring Houston. We've gotten so used to him around the house that it'll feel strange with him gone." She wiped her eyes and smiled a weak smile. "We've pretty much spoiled him, Ben. So I hope you don't get angry if you have to send him back to obedience training again!"

Ben laughed and stood up. He reached down and pulled Grace up and held her in his arms. "Lady, I've missed you so much, you have no idea. I'm so glad to be home and it feels so good to have you close to me. I'm sorry for all of this, Gracie."

Grace looked up at Ben and felt a peace come over her. "It's good to have you home, Ben. And I know it took a lot for you to tell me about Smith. It just makes me love you more. Do you need to head home and take Houston with you? I was gonna go back to the office, but I think I'll stay home and think about what you've shared with me. I'm still in shock a little bit."

"Grace, I wish I could just stay here. But I know you need time alone. I'll go home and do some work and come back in time for dinner. What can I bring?"

"Just you, Ben. Molly will be so glad you're home. But she may give you some trouble about taking Houston home. She slept with that dog every single night!"

Ben smiled and scratched Houston's head. "He's a special dog, all right. We'll be back in a couple of hours, Grace." He walked over and hugged her again and kissed her softly on the lips. "That feels like heaven to me."

❦

Sitting alone in her living room, Grace took in the realization of all that Ben had shared with her and it hit her like a wave coming in from the ocean. She sat there riding it out until it left as quickly as it came. And after a few times of feeling that wave, she realized that it couldn't hurt her anymore. She had grieved for Smith for so long that she was ready for closure. She said a prayer to God that Smith would be at peace and no longer in pain. And she prayed that one day she would see him again.

She spent the afternoon listening to music and cleaning the house. She sat outside on the porch watching cars go by, letting the words that Ben said to her soothe the pain in her heart. She would have a new life now, setting aside what was behind and going towards what was in front of her. Ben had shown that he was willing to risk his life a second time to bring Smith home to her. She would never forget that as long as she lived.

When it was nearly 3:00 she drove to the school and picked up Molly. She was waiting for her at her office. "Hey, Mom! Why aren't you in your office? Where have you been?"

"I have a surprise for you when you get home. So let's go, kiddo! Did you have a good day at school?"

"I made an A on my math test! Aren't you proud of me?"

"I have no words!"

They walked to the car and Grace got in, turning on Molly's favorite music.

"So what's the surprise? Did you buy me something new?"

"No. That's not it."

"Did I get a letter in the mail?"

"No."

"Um . . . Mom? Is Mr. Ben back home? I know he's not!"

Grace smiled but tears were running down her cheeks. She hoped Molly couldn't see. "You little mess! Yes! Ben's home! He's taken Houston to the house for a few hours but will come back tonight for supper. We have to go home and cook a great meal for Ben!"

"Oh, Mom! I'm so excited. He's finally back. I love Mr. Ben."

"I love him, too, honey."

CHAPTER 56

On a cold day in December the body of Smith Sanderson was lowered into the ground at Woodlawn Cemetery. Grace and Ben were the only people there and they held hands together at the gravesite. Grace said a prayer and they turned and walked away, knowing Smith was at peace at last.

Grace pulled her coat up around her and climbed into the car. She was quiet for a few minutes, lost in her own thoughts. Ben reached over, without saying a word, and took her hand. They drove to Ross High, where Molly was waiting; this was going to be a special day. Ben had promised Molly that they would look for a Christmas tree when she got out of school. This would be Molly's first Christmas with Grace, and it was going to be the best Christmas she'd ever had.

When they reached the Christmas tree lot, Ben got out and helped Molly look for the perfect tree. Grace waited at the car, taking pictures when she could get them to stand still. Finally, after forty-five minutes of checking out every tree on the lot, Molly found the one she wanted. It was a tall tree with hundreds of branches. She was so excited she couldn't stand it. Ben paid for the tree and hauled it to the SUV and got the owner of the lot to help him tie the tree on top. Grace made sure she got a photo of the car with the tree on top and Molly standing near. They drove home singing Christmas carols and pulled up to the house honking the horn. Margaret came out waving and helped them get the tree off the roof of the car. Ben put it in a stand and carried it into the house and stood it up in the corner of the living room. Grace had made hot chocolate and they all sat around the tree talking and laughing. It was one of the best nights in the world.

As Christmas approached, packages found their way underneath the tall tree. Grace let Molly buy small gifts for her friends at Wilton, and the foundation paid for gifts for all the children at the orphanage. Molly got to hand out the gifts to all the children and it really made the meaning of Christmas clear to everyone. Margaret came over one evening and had the four of them stand near the tree, and she took a photo which Grace then used for a Christmas card to send out to all her friends. It was a picture of Ben, Grace, Molly and Houston, who had a red bow tied around his neck. The tree was full of hundreds of lights and covered in ornaments. Grace had strung red garland around the tree, and gold ribbon draped the boughs. It was the prettiest tree Molly had ever seen.

Ben had done his own shopping. After what he'd experienced on his last covert operation, he fell deeper in love with Grace. There was a bond between them that was unspoken but this bond would carry them through a lifetime of love. Ben had looked everywhere for a special gift for Grace, and finally there was a small wrapped gift under the tree from him to Grace. It was going to be the best Christmas ever because this Christmas Grace would adopt Molly as her daughter and Ben would give Grace the small gift underneath the tree.

It was an engagement ring that meant forever love.

And tucked inside the box was a poem that had new meaning to both Grace and Ben.

If in this journey we are
taking together
the love that is shared
between us
is not the same . . .

If in our time together
as little as it may be,
the giving is done in a lesser
way by one . . .

If our hearts are knit together
Yet one of us

Presumed Dead

is afraid to feel
the pain of being so close
but so far away,

Let the more loving one be me.

EPILOGUE

Grace and Ben were married on an afternoon in the spring when the flowers were in full bloom and the trees had a fresh green robe of color. A pastor from the local Presbyterian church conducted the wedding as Grace's friends looked on. Ben asked some of his buddies from the search and rescue department to come and Houston was by his side. Molly was the flower girl and she was the happiest she'd ever been. Margaret kept Molly and Houston while Grace and Ben went on a honeymoon.

Two years later, there was a baby born to Grace and Ben. A little boy. And after a few seconds of deliberation, they called him Smith. In his youth he showed intelligence beyond his years and grew to be as tall as Ben. He had a mind that could remember details and was an excellent athlete. When he graduated from college he came in one afternoon and said he wanted to be a Navy Seal or work for the CIA in the Special Ops services. He knew nothing about his father's background nor did Ben ever encourage Smith in any direction. It must have been in the blood.

Molly graduated with honors and was a high school teacher for ten years, moving into position of Principal of a high school in Sloan, Georgia, where she lived with her husband. She had five children and brought them all home to see Grace and Ben during every holiday.

Houston died at seventeen years old, but not without siring a litter of puppies, one of which remained with Grace and Ben for many years. The days passed by, one on top of the other. And in a drawer in her dresser, way in the back underneath some fresh linens, was a box that held the cross that had belonged to Smith. Every time she touched it Smith's last words echoed in her mind. *Take care of my Grace.* He remembered her at the end. That was all that mattered.

Other books written by Nancy Veldman:

Coming Home
The Journey
Withered Leaves
Dream Catcher
The Fisherman

<u>Novels</u>
The Box of Words
Edgar Graham
The Physician
Presumed Dead

Author's Note

Nancy Veldman is an author, pianist, and watercolor artist. In the last 15 years she has released 9 piano CDs, authored five spiritual books, published four novels, and sold over 5,000 watercolors. She is founder of The Nancy Veldman Ministries, a foundation that helps people in need and was given the Key to the City of Memphis for her humanitarian efforts for mankind. Nancy has owned Magnolia House, a gift shop located in Grand Boulevard in Sandestin for eighteen years and encourages women to step out and reach their dreams. Visit her Website at magnoliahouse.com and her YouTube video. Be inspired.

Made in the USA
Charleston, SC
24 March 2014